MW00723777

THE
HIVEBORN

THE HIVEBORN

PAUL COLLINS

A BOHEMIAN INK BOOK
ANDOVER, KANSAS

THE HIVEBORN

Cover painting by Howard Levy

This book is printed on acid-free paper.

Bohemian Ink Publishing
PO Box 627
Andover, KS 67002

www.Bohemian-Ink.com

First printing 2006

ISBN-13: 978-0-9726051-8-2
ISBN-10: 0-9726051-8-5
LCCN: 2006928984

Printed in the United States of America

ACKNOWLEDGMENTS

With thanks to my brain-stormer, Randal Flynn, and Avatar Polymorph, my tech support.

Special thanks too go to Josiah James for his belief in The Earthborn Wars, to Meredith Costain for putting up with my constant queries, and to Reverend Dr Jim Connelly for the prayer.

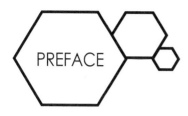

PREFACE

The story so far ...

Fourteen-year-old ensign Welkin Quinn has his life mapped out on board the terraforming skyworld, *Colony.* But his destiny takes a steep dive when *Colony* aborts a mission to colonize Tau Ceti III, and returns to the near mythical homeworld, Old Earth.

The elders of *Colony*—tyrants, long-ensconced—face two threats to their eminence: the rebels aboard *Colony* that have been relegated to the lower decks and the human survivors of Old Earth, the Earthborn. For a long time an urban myth has been propagated that the lower deckers have mutated into cannibalistic monstrosities. When Welkin discovers that the subterranean denizens are as human as himself, and in fact more humane than *Colony*'s hierarchy, his worldview is shaken. The elders learn of Welkin's enlightenment, and he is discarded on the planet's surface, which is now ravaged by warring tribes.

Luckily for Welkin, he is captured by Sarah, whose gang is intent on returning Earth to some semblance of order. Threatened by cannibalistic ferals and Bruick's blood-loving jabbers, Welkin promptly realizes that he has no choice but to accept Sarah's "family." Sarah knows that his technological knowledge will be a great asset for her small group. Welkin, who possesses superior strength due to be being raised in 1.5g on *Colony*, soon proves his worth against the family's enemies.

One of the things Welkin learns is that the Age Plague that had swept through *Colony* 90 years out from Old Earth has also run rife on the planet. Sarah seems to be one of the few Earthborn to have survived the progeria. She's all of 18. To Welkin, his captor is very much like *Colony*'s elders—one of the Chosen. This sense of awe allows him to partially relinquish his Skyborn doctrines and turn his back on *Colony*.

Sarah must now fight on two fronts. Bruick has done a deal with *Colony*. The Skyborn leave his fortified stockade alone and provide him with Lurisdicton, a longevity drug—which will draw thousands to his cause; he will provide *Colony* with information not only on Sarah's burgeoning family, but all the Earthborn families in Victoria.

When an attempt is made to assassinate Sarah, she realizes that she must take the battle to Bruick. Eventually, she and a small contingency of her family begin making the trek to his fortress. Along the way, her group is ambushed by *Colony* troopers and Bruick's jabbers.

After a fierce battle, Sarah's family triumphs. In defeating Bruick's jabbers, Sarah and Welkin lose some of the friends who have been dearest to them. The threat of the jabbers has been overcome, but the more ominous threat of *Colony* remains ...

Two years later ...

The Earthborn factions have proven to be more resilient than *Colony*'s elders could have imagined. Sarah's dream has been realized; the family has successfully established a settlement with a stable agrarian lifestyle in the Dandenongs. Entire communities are flocking to be a part of the newly established society. Despite having a water mill for grinding corn and wheat, a pond system brimming with fish, and corrals of livestock, Sarah's continuing problem is how to feed so many mouths.

Not all of the newcomers assimilate into Sarah's family. Tolk arrives one day with his followers and immediately begins to cause dissension in the community. Warning Sarah and her family of the imminent threat of one who is simply called the Prophet, Tolk spreads disharmony among the people with hopes of deposing Sarah and taking command.

More pressing matters come to hand when a Skyborn named Arton is rescued from a crash site. His delirious ramblings reveal that *Colony* has created a Doomsday weapon for a mission called "Cleansweep"—a new chapter in *Colony*'s campaign of genocide.

Welkin decides the only way to combat this new threat is to get aboard *Colony*. A suicide mission, Welkin intends to go alone, but is ultimately joined by Sarah, her sister Gillian, and his best friend Harry. After fighting off a cave clan ambush, the four of them enter the storm water drains at Dights Falls, intending to use the underground caverns to gain entry into *Colony*. While in the caves, they save a Skyborn called Ferrik who is being ritually butchered by those who dwell in the dark passages. Ferrik throws in his lot with his rescuers, explaining that he can take them safely through *Colony*'s security matrix before the code is changed.

The newly formed group of five eventually breaches *Colony*'s defenses. In the lower decks, Harry and Welkin meet with old comrades, comrades who have formed a formidable fighting unit of lower deckers. With this newfound support, the group infiltrates the upper decks, ascending in their search for the secret laboratories where the elders are testing the Cleansweep experiment.

Taking a molecular biochemist as a hostage, Welkin and Harry pass through several security checkpoints that require neural ID, retinal detection and authorization codes. They reach their destination; the hostage escapes and triggers the alarm. Suddenly the area is in lock-down.

The fighting unit of lower deckers comes to their aid. The lower deckers steamroll through the immediate opposition and incinerate the laboratories where the killer virus is being tested on hapless Earthborn. There is no time to celebrate, however. They discover that *Crusader*, another homeworld, is approaching Earth. It will arrive in three days.

A hasty conference takes place. It's agreed that Sarah will lead her family and the lower deckers who wish to join it as far away as possible before *Crusader* lands. Welkin and a select team will stay and see if the newcomers are for or against the Earthborn.

Welkin's team smuggles aboard the shuttle that carries the elders of *Colony* to meet with the diplomats of the orbiting *Crusader*. The shuttle docks. Using their knowledge of *Colony*, they easily navigate the maintenance shafts of *Crusader*. They discover that the newcomers support the elders' plan to see Earth cleansed of its current inhabitants. This, though, proves to be the least of their worries. Upon further investigation, they realize that no one on board *Crusader* is wearing class insignia. Welkin observes that they operate as "working bees, each with the same single focus."

Desperate to know more, Welkin decides to jack into *Crusader*'s neural network. Though his brain has downloaded a wealth of knowledge, Welkin cannot assimilate it and is left disoriented. *Crusader* troopers storm aboard *Colony*. As Welkin and his team watch, the crusaders stun their victims, produce a probe, and inject a tiny parasitic bug (like a nerve ganglion) into an eardrum of the fallen colonists. The victims recover within seconds and, drone-like, join the ranks of the crusaders.

Colony is in chaos. Its troopers are fighting a losing battle against the crusaders. No matter how many they kill, the crusaders' ranks are being swelled by victims of the parasitic bugs. Also, many colonists are no longer sure who is on their side and who has been taken over.

Comprehension of the neural download washes over Welkin: One hundred years before, on the fringes of Orion's Belt, *Crusader* had discovered an Earth-like planet. They met what appeared to be an agrarian society. However, the beings were the puppets of a hive race, an ancient entity with a million minds and bodies. The Hivemind, as Welkin interprets in English, now has one sole purpose: to absorb the inhabitants of Earth into the cosmic community of Oneness ...

Against overwhelming odds, but assisted by the current chaos, Welkin's team commandeers two space shuttles. They barely escape the ensuing firestorm.

In the absence of Sarah and Gillian, Tolk has overthrown the family and revealed that his true identity is the Prophet. Those who remain live in fear of him. When Sarah and Gillian return, they refuse to submit to the demands of Tolk. To set an example, Tolk gives orders that Sarah, the blasphemer, is to be "cleansed by the purity of fire."

As the pyre is being lit Welkin and Ferrik arrive in the stolen shuttles. Tolk's people flee but the assembled family gives chase. The fire is quickly extinguished and Sarah is saved.

Though Cleansweep and Tolk have been vanquished, the lives of Sarah's family remain in jeopardy. The threat of *Colony* has been consumed by *Crusader* and reborn in a far more devastating form: the ancient and implacable Hivemind.

The Earthborn Wars continue ...

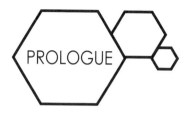

PROLOGUE

It was a garishly lit room. One wall was a solid bank of holographic schematics. They showed the Planet Earth as seen from various orbits, including a number of geosynchronous positions.

A number of men and women moved about the monitoring center, conversing little and in monotone. Occasionally they touched each other gently, hand to forehead, or brushed a kiss upon an ear. They possessed an air of self-contained efficiency and spoke only when necessary. There was no chitchat here. No individual personality traits. Just the order and precision of automata and a profound kind of peacefulness, the kind sometimes felt in very old churches or cathedrals, but even there somehow lofty and more than human.

"We have a lock," said one of the women. The main schematic's colors solidified, revealing the shape of New Zealand. In a series of rapid steps the schematic zoomed in on the eastern coastline of the north island. The Coramandel Peninsula was jagged with fiords and the dense scrub came to the edge of the sea, which churned against the rocks in a line of white foam that glared painfully in the sunlight.

The image shifted slightly and moved in further till a long-abandoned seaside town could be seen at the left hand side of the schematic. The camera swung onto three individuals, two mature women and a six-year-old. A section on the right hand side turned green.

"The rebels are in there somewhere. They have dug themselves in beneath that mountain," said a lieutenant.

The captain pinched his nose in thought. "We need plans of their position."

"We have established it was once a mining town called Waihi. There is also a dormant geothermal power plant. But few records of those days exist. A unit has infiltrated the base and the surrogate is well-placed."

"Then we will be thorough. Proceed with all diligence."

"Certainly, sir."

The captain stared stonily at the schematic. Once this pocket of resistance had been assimilated, the Earthborn would know peace ...

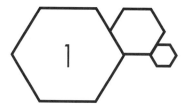

1

Welkin Quinn moved quietly. He stopped often to listen but as usual there were no noises. Everything here—even the silence—had a deep muffled quality, as if holding its breath.

He reached up and adjusted the lamp fixed to his miner's helmet, making it brighter. The dark eerie silences of the mine were starting to spook him. They always did on these nightly patrols but someone had to keep an eye on the sentries, keep them on their toes. There was the rub. As Sarah, the family's chief, pointed out, you couldn't keep even a crack military unit at high alert for extended periods. Senses dulled, muscles tensed for action wearied, and the adrenaline stopped pumping. People became complacent. Why, just last week, he had caught two lookouts *asleep*. He had frosted them well and truly. It would be a long time before either of them slipped up again. He hadn't reported them. He figured everybody should get to make one mistake in their lives. The only thing wrong with that was that the family— now facing its most formidable enemy—would never get to make a second.

He brushed aside these annoying thoughts. As somebody once said, they had people, not angels, to work with. He took a deep breath and grabbed the metal rung of a ladder that led up through the ceiling of the mine tunnel he had been traversing. After his experiences on *Colony*, he had developed a mild acrophobia but he shrugged away the sense of vertigo and gritted his teeth, climbing steadily. Within moments he was inside a narrow shaft that telescoped up for almost 300 feet.

By the time he reached the top, his arms and legs ached and his breath was coming faster, but he was glad to see that he wasn't completely puffed. He was getting used to all this exercise. The Martha Mine they now called home had 15 levels and over 110 miles of tunnels. Cave-ins over the years had closed many of them, but there still were enough shafts to test even the fittest Earthborn. And nearby was the Deep Well, where nanodiamond turbines still spun. The turbines here were only just beginning to wear out after more than a century. They were powered by heat diffused up from the magma tens of miles below. Compression-expansion clappers geared into the turbines which operated in vacuum-sealed chambers using magnetic levitation to avoid friction. Unfortunately the turbines' power was still largely inaccessible without a working knowledge of micro-electronic systems, at scales of one thousandth of a millimeter and below. Some of the Earthborn had begun to search out old texts and use the Elder-modified *Colony* shuttles' equipment in an attempt to decipher them. There were problems, however, due to the vastly different types of computing tech. Meanwhile, much of the Deep Well was off limits, the very air sparking with discharging electrical potentials in many places, wreaking instant electrocution upon the unwary.

Welkin climbed from the top of the shaft and gulped fresh air. Above him, the Seven Sisters of the Pleiades punctured the smog-laden atmosphere. Myriad other stars littered the southern sky but most were invisible now to the naked eye. A lone satellite moved slowly, its light a hard point. Welkin shivered in the chill wind. Around him were the grey-black Andesite slopes and forested peaks of a small mountain range. The waste volcanic rock from the old mining town had long since vanished beneath rotted vegetation and shifting soil. Two or three diamondoid heat vents stuck out of the forest, curious angled structures higher than trees that glittered under the starlight, hot air wavering the dim night sky immediately above them.

"Tell me you've come to relieve me," said a voice nearby.

Welkin peered at the large youth hugging himself and stamping his feet. The Kiwi accent wasn't as bad as he had been led to believe. They pronounced some vowels differently, especially the "E" which sounded more like the "i" of "it" than the "e in bed." Lesley became Lisley, sex became six and vice versa. The other thing the Australians noticed was the appendage of "but" and "eh" at the end of some sentences. Nonetheless, it was decipherable. More so than the trouble he had had with the Australian dialect when he had first been rescued by Sarah. Everything was abbreviated and ran into a long continuous line of babble.

Welkin snapped back to the present. "No such luck, Zinn. But I come bearing a gift. Hot soup. Where's your mug?"

Zinn, a solidly built youth with an eye patch and a big grin, snatched up a tin mug and held it out. Welkin took a thermos from his knapsack and filled the mug with steaming thick ham and pea soup. Less than 18 months earlier this would have been a celebratory dinner. But now, what with subterranean vat and hydroponics farming, it was almost standard fare. Zinn held the cup tightly in his hands and started sipping, swearing softly every time it burned his tongue.

"What's the report?" asked Welkin, peering around. Four miles away to the west the sea glittered. Slightly farther away but to the north, he could see the lights of a small seaside town, Timora. In the harbor, heading back to the town, were several fishing boats, visible by their cluster of lamps. No doubt they would be bringing back rich catches of barracuda, hoki, red cod, and schnapper.

Zinn continued to sip his soup as he answered. "All clear, Welkin," he said. "Only movements I've seen are the fishing boats, eh. No airborne activity, but." He waved his hand at the horizon. Somewhere over there, just over 1300 miles away, was the coast of Australia. The land of their new enemy, the Hiveborn. The family had come to this place, this gouged and rugged east coast of New Zealand, nearly a year ago. At first they had entertained hopes of immediately siphoning the power of the geothermal sink, but progress had been slow. A year in which they had frantically fortified the adjacent old gold and silver mine, discovered by Ferrik and Arton on one of their reconnaissance missions, a year in which they had trained and armed themselves, then waited for the expected attack to come. Only it hadn't come. It was what Sarah called a Phony War; it was the hardest war to fight because after a while you started to fight yourself, as Welkin had discovered with his sleeping sentries and a host of other infractions. Luckily for the family, the Kiwis hadn't seen their arrival as an invasion, and many of the smaller, roaming communities had actually joined them.

"Only thing moving up there are the satellites," said Zinn morosely. "Hey, there's another one." He pointed and Welkin followed the outstretched hand, spotting another pinpoint of hard unwavering light sailing across the sky, oblivious to the other more distant sparks of light that made up the Milky Way. This satellite had fine hard filaments extending from its surface, barely visible—ancient nanotech solar arrays. "You think they're watching us from them things?" Zinn asked, gazing at the satellite with a grim expression.

"We have to assume the worst," said Welkin.

"Seems to me that's all we been doing," Zinn said with some asperity. "No offence, Welkin, but nothing's happened all these months, eh. Maybe the Hiveborn don't *care* about us. Maybe all this hiding and watching and sneaking around is a waste of time … " Welkin's face went blank and Zinn quickly added, "I don't mean nothing by that," he said. "Just … you know … that's how most people feel."

Welkin nodded. He knew that was how most people felt. He felt it himself. Except he knew it wasn't true. He had jacked into the Hiveborn computer net via his own neural jack and had downloaded terabytes of data, data still stored in the rod logic nanofibers that were spread through the fluid of his brain case. There the memories waited to be accessed, perhaps by accident, the way a smell or a song could suddenly retrieve a long forgotten memory of childhood. Even though he could not directly audit the alien data there was an odd kind of "leakage", as if a door had been shut tight, locking away all the information, but allowing some of it to seep out through the cracks like daylight. Without knowing how, he knew that the Hiveborn had not given up on them, had not forgotten them. With the same terrible conviction, he knew they were ensconcing themselves on Earth, doing just what the family was doing: fortifying, building, preparing. He saw glimpses of vast engineering projects planned for the future— a bridge on nanodiamond towers all the way to Tasmania, a Panama canal that could widen to 50 miles in width and open currents from the Atlantic to the Pacific, like a giant thermostat … All re-hashed plans from Earth's past, mixed in the detritus of ideas from dozens of cannibalized societies and ways of thinking … Preparations, plans. All for a day that would soon come.

"It's all right, Zinn," Welkin said, clapping a hand on the big youth's shoulder. "I hear the talk. What are they calling me now? Worrywart Welkin?"

Zinn stifled a guffaw. "At least it's better than Wacky Welkin."

Both laughed quietly in the darkness. Welkin packed away the thermos and moved back to the shaft. "Eyes open, Zinn," he said.

"Eyes open, Welkin. Thanks for the soup, eh."

Welkin swung his legs over the open shaft and descended.

"There's nothing wrong with the lookout system," said Welkin. There was a trace of impatience in his voice. Gathered before him were the family's Committee members. Sarah, her younger sister Gillian, Budge, Denton and Con represented the Earthborn, while the Skyborn were represented by Welkin's sister, Lucida, Elab, Efi, Ferrik, Theo, Arton and Harry.

Welkin pointed at a map pinned to the wall showing the local terrain and the main entrances to the mine. Beside it was another chart, this time giving a 3-dimensional "cutaway" view of the extensive mine, known colloquially as Martha. The mine's full depth was nearly a mile and there was a large network of interlinked tunnels, some extending for two or three miles and opening out on the other side of the range. On the terrain map various red markers denoted lookout positions. Next to the mine was the Deep Well, half-wrecked, extending to areas now uncooled, where human beings could not venture without being broiled alive.

"Nobody's saying there is," said Theo. He had been leader of the Doves on board *Colony* before joining up with Welkin and the Earthborn. Due to the Earthborns' wasting disease, he and a few of the Skyborn were among the oldest in the family. The Skyborn had been novelties among the Earthborn, mainly for their receding hair and lined faces, anomalies on a planet where most died by the age of 21.

Theo stretched his arms to loosen his tired muscles. "But the fact remains that by the time they see something, it will be too late to mount any kind of serious defense."

Welkin raked a hand through his thick blond hair and sighed. He too was tired; the nightly patrols were playing havoc with his bio-rhythms. He would have given it up long ago, except that he felt his presence amongst the guards maintained the sense of urgency. At least, that was the argument Sarah used to convince him of its importance.

"I'm not arguing with you, Theo, I'm just saying we shouldn't give up one system till we find another, and maybe not even then."

Sarah—who had been leader of the family for as long as anyone could remember—rapped the table for attention. Her high cheekbones, skin taut across them, gave her a fierce not-to-be-messed-with appearance. "What's on the grapevine?"

The "grapevine" was a network of spies scattered around Victoria and New South Wales, particularly clustered near the big cities and towns. Welkin, Theo and Harry had set it up, flying in under cover of dark, using a system of rewards and radios to encourage the flow of information. The spies passed along useful Intel but none of them knew a great deal about the family, where it was located, or why it wanted information on the newcomers. Most of them were just ordinary Earthborn, trying to survive.

"The Hiveborn have secured Melbourne," said Welkin grimly. "*Colony* is now out of bounds. Far as we can tell, there isn't a single uninfected human in the city. And now they're moving into the smaller satellite communities, setting up townships and farms."

"Which attracts even more flies into the web," said Theo.

Welkin nodded. "A snowball effect. Create an oasis of civilization and security and every lost soul and scratch farmer for two hundred miles will flock there. And become infected."

"I've made some calculations," said Theo quietly. "They're pretty rough and ready, but even working conservatively, the Hiveborn could infect every single human being on the planet within five years. And they could do it a lot quicker if they wanted to."

Silence greeted his figures.

"We need to become proactive," said Welkin. "Even if they don't come for us directly—and they will—it won't be long before the infection reaches our door."

"We've heard all that," said Denton. He was the youngest of the Committee, and felt he should have more of a voice. "It's better to sit tight."

Voices buzzed in argument but Sarah quieted them. "Let's table that for tomorrow's monthly policy meeting," she said. "Right now we have some news." Everybody looked at her. Welkin resumed his seat beside Gillian, his partner, and now looked at Sarah with surprise. He was usually one of the first to hear of any developments.

"I haven't mentioned this till now because I thought we all needed encouraging news." She paused for dramatic effect and Elab, sitting at the back, and Harry beside him, made rude noises. Sarah grinned. "Okay, okay. Keep your shirts on. Timora's mayor and city council have finally agreed to open up trade relations with us and to allow full social intercourse. In fact, we've got the run of the town."

Welkin stared. "How in Space did you manage that?" he asked.

"My natural charm. I'm surprised you had to ask," said Sarah. Crow's-feet appeared around her eyes as she smiled. After a moment she added, "We're also entering into a mutual defense pact and in any emergency we've agreed to allow their citizens into Martha."

The room became noisy again. "Hold it down!" Theo shouted and the noise dropped off.

Sarah nodded a "thank you" to Theo. "Understand this. It's going to be a long term business partnership and both sides are going to benefit."

"That's a lot of people to fit in," said Elab. "There must be nearly two thousand people in Timora."

"Two thousand two hundred. And counting," Sarah acknowledged. "Look, domiciling them is a short term policy that will only be activated in an emergency and there's plenty of room in the deeper mines. And if it comes to that, we might need all the fighters we can get."

"They're farmers and traders. What makes you think they can fight?" Harry asked.

"First off, they're *here*. They're still alive. Secondly, that's where you come in."

"Me?" said Harry, blinking in surprise.

"You. One of your new duties—and part of the agreement—is to start training a Timoran militia. We'll work out how to arm them as things develop. Theo says the new workshop has produced six laserlites this week and more than three times that number of old-style ballistic rifles and dozens of crossbows. And that's just a start. Who knows, perhaps we can get the gravity amplifying cannons up and running. *That* would be too good to be true." She suddenly stood up and stared at them. "But we're not the ragtag band of survivalists we were even one year ago. We've come a long way, in part thanks to Welkin's raid on *Colony* last year, especially the two working shuttles."

"And two occasionally working shuttle pilots," Welkin said, glancing at Arton and Ferrik. That elicited a laugh.

Sarah smiled at the pair in the front row. "And two working shuttle pilots," she agreed. "Even if they are a bit gung-ho at times." More laughs during which Arton flushed and looked down.

Early the next day Welkin, Gillian, Sarah and Theo stood waiting outside what was loosely termed the "front door" of Martha. A guard post nearby was also manned as were numerous lookouts on the ridges that rose sharply on either side of the narrow valley, at the head of which the mine entrance was situated. There were also guards stationed in crow's nests in the massive pine trees that filled the valley. None of them could be seen, but that was by design.

They did not have long to wait, and they heard it before they saw it. A noisy clanking rumble that was outside all of their experience. Welkin and Sarah shared their mild consternation by frowning at one another. Then a strange contraption drove out of the forest, following the rough path used by those accessing the valley. It was a machine on four wheels and it puffed out great clouds of gray smoke from an exhaust, this being the source of the noise.

"My God," said Sarah in wonder. "It's a car. An internal combustion engine of some sort."

Welkin stared at it. "That's a car?"

"Not a flash one, but yeah, it's a car. You've never seen one actually working?"

"I've seen pictures. And vids."

"And none of them looked like that," Theo pointed out. "It must be right out of the twentieth century!"

As the cannibalized vehicle approached they all quickly stepped back out of the way. Although it had a driver and was not on automatic pilot—assuming it had such a feature—it gave the impression of having a mind of its own, rather like a wild horse only recently broken in. Welkin tried hard to appear nonchalant, but he could feel his heart thumping with excitement.

The hybrid shuddered to a stop. The engine coughed and spluttered, then died. Two men climbed from the front seat of the enclosed cabin. There was a chemical smell in the air. The family members sniffed, trying to identify it.

"Methanol," said the driver. He was a tall gaunt figure with a ragged mop of hair and a lopsided grin. "We get it as a by-product from some of our manufacturing processes. But we're looking into harnessing methane gas direct. Some ways off but we'll get there."

Sarah stepped forward and put out her hand to shake. "Welcome to Martha, Mayor. This is Welkin, our Chief of Defense. And this is my sister, Gillian, and partner, Theo."

"Pleased to meet you all," said the mayor, shaking hands all round. "Seems like all one big happy family, eh? And call me Pat. We don't stand on ceremony here."

Those who hadn't already met the mayor were surprised at his age. He had obviously outlasted the wasting disease. He must have been at least thirty, and apart from graying hair and a little flabbiness, seemed alert and fit.

"We'd better get going," Pat said. "My crew's dying to meet you fellas."

The mayor ushered them into the rear section of the car. It was a bit of a squeeze and definitely "unceremonious" but Welkin for one liked the Timoran mayor's informal approach. When they were all securely in and the door jammed shut Pat climbed behind the wheel and started the engine. It roared as the mayor pushed down on the accelerator and blew out a cloud of clogging smoke which drifted back and almost smothered the rear of the vehicle.

Pat put it into gear and again nailed the accelerator. The car leapt forward in an alarming manner and the passengers clutched the doors and seats, wondering what they had gotten themselves into. The wheels had solid tires made of a spongy but solid composite from a more recent period of history, one prior to disaster.

The mayor gestured at the other man, a Fijian with an afro the size of a crow's nest. "Like you to meet Severo. He's going to be your guide today. Anything you need to know, anything you want, just ask Severo."

The islander turned and gave them a toothy smile. "The car's ace, eh?" he said.

The family members adopted their automatic grins. They assumed "ace" meant tops.

Pat brought the car around in a skidding turn, its inside wheels threatening to leave the ground, and aimed for the narrow gap between two trees where the grassy "road" entered the rainforest. The passengers eyed this gap with some concern. It didn't seem wide enough for the vehicle to fit between. At the last second Welkin actually shut his eyes and held his breath. Then they were miraculously through, unscathed, but not unshaken.

Welkin decided this was a dangerous way to travel and resolved to stick to cruisers and shuttles. Or his own two feet.

"She'll do nought to thirty in fifteen seconds flat!" Pat boasted, turning round and gazing at them. Welkin nodded back, smiling, pretending to be impressed by this information. Suddenly he gripped the edge of his seat.

"Look out!" he yelled. Pat whipped around. The car had left the road and was hurtling towards a towering fern. He wrenched the wheel over and the car scraped past the bole of the fern and juddered back to the road.

Pat threw them a quick grin. "No worries," he said. Severo seemed unperturbed by the whole event, sitting quietly with his arms folded across his ample chest, his full lips parted in a full time grin. He was obviously used to Pat's driving, or perhaps he had—by necessity—become fatalistic.

The car raced across bracken and through the forest, shaking and rattling, its engine laboring and belching smoke. Somehow they made it out the other side in one piece. Welkin sent up a silent prayer, then realized he was clutching Gillian's hand rather tightly. Or she was clutching his.

The road to Timora was little more than a bush trail in places. In others, it didn't exist except in Pat's imagination. He drove across areas of flat rock, grassy paddocks, and alongside a winding river where sheep cropped the grass short and gave it a park-like feel. Although they had been here for some months, the Skyborn among them still pointed excitedly at the sight of a real sheep. Once they even saw a deer as it flitted across their path. That had been a talking point for days, boosted by the fact that those who hadn't seen it said those who did were lying to big-note themselves.

Along the way, Pat pointed out places of historic interest, both those before the international crisis that sent the terraforming ships rocketing out into the universe, and those of more recent significance.

"Judging from what you've told me of life in Australia," Pat mused at one point, "it's patently obvious that here in Aotearoa we got off lightly. We seem to have avoided the worst of the degeneracy you've talked about and I figure we probably bounced back the fastest. And for that I thank our isolation from the rest of the world. And no offence intended, but that's why it's taken us a long time to make up our minds about you. We've gotten along just fine up till now on our own. Things are reasonably peaceful though there's brigands inland and pirates out to sea, but all in all we've done okay. But times change as they say. The younger folk want more, want their horizons bigger ... Don't know where it'll all end. But you're all welcome and we're looking forward to a period of mutual prosperity. I'm going to put that in my speech today. A fine phrase, don't you think? Mutual prosperity. Has a good ring to it."

"You seem to have maintained a higher level of technology as well," said Sarah, indicating the car.

"We have, though we didn't know we had, if you see what I mean," said Pat. "We've kept up some of the main roads, too, and we've got telephone links to most of the North Island. We've also got radio, but we're careful with that. Always been afraid we'd get overrun with refugees. Few broadcasts we got from Australia and other places on the short wave sounded pretty damn awful, so we stopped talking. May sound mean but we had our own kin to take care of and we had our grandchildren to think about."

"We must've scored a lucky shot when you answered our calls," Sarah said.

Pat turned briefly and glancing at Severo, nodded. "Severo here was lurking, as he calls it. Just listening to world news so to speak. There was hell to pay when he told everyone he'd been speaking to someone in Melbourne. That he'd given away our coordinates."

Severo laughed heartily. "Lost my job, eh. But I like this one better, boss."

Pat snorted. "Lucky the rest of 'em didn't string him up. But they're slowly coming around to our way of thinking."

"What about power?" Theo asked.

"Oh, we got a powerhouse up and running nearly seventy years ago. Hydroelectric. Had to cannibalize parts from other power stations and it's been tough keeping it going, making replacement parts, you name it. Mind you, fully accessing the Deep Well could really get us going. We're hoping you can help us out."

"Shouldn't be a problem, at least for hydro," said Sarah. "The Skyborn among our group can do most of that stuff. They're the ones who set us up in the Dandenongs back home. You told me at our last meeting that you also had medical facilities. Can we see them today?"

"Whatever you want," Pat said, shooting down an incline and performing a screeching turn at the bottom. Welkin was beginning to feel queasy. Fighting Hiveborn seemed less risky than this.

Eventually they arrived at the town's outskirts. The streets here were composed of brick laid down like cobblestones or parquet flooring and obviously scavenged from older buildings, though in the center of town the bricks were all new and bright terracotta. Timora clearly had its own brickworks. There were also lampposts strung with copper wire and fixed with lights. Some paving was made of cannibalized nanodiamond, some rails of sections of hard and fused carbon nanotubes, all still unscratched and unweathered. A few ancient nanosolar-powered camping lights were also placed here and there, their glowglobes incongruously more useful in this new age.

Seeing the direction of their gaze, Pat said, "Light bulbs are difficult. There's a tight hippy community some miles north, and by gee they're cluey. It's all plain as day how to make 'em, but you just try it. Finicky work. Trial and error, but we seem to have done it."

Sarah was impressed. All her life it had been a struggle to stay alive, much less have time to create electricity and light bulbs. She felt as though she had stepped back in time four hundred years—way before the final war.

Along the roads they passed large numbers of people, all gaily dressed. They waved and smiled though Welkin noted that there were a few scowls in the crowds. Can't please everybody, he thought to himself. Understandable, too. Most Timorans knew the Aussies had fled some potent enemy. What was to stop that enemy from following them over the Tasman? Not much.

"Is it a holiday today?" Gillian asked.

"That it is, miss," said Pat. "The first new moon after the seven stars of Matariki have risen is the start of the Maori New Year. That's the seven sisters to you and me. Folk come in from all around, even from the South Island. We figured we might as well coincide introducing you while everyone was here. Take advantage of the good public spirit abounding in heart and mind."

Sarah nodded. "It's important to keep these customs alive. It's our heritage. So much has been lost since the last war."

"You're right there," Pat said. "There's not a pure blood Maori alive—fact is most are more of everything else than Maori. But every one of 'em could tell you that the Maori god Tane threw a star into the sky where it split into seven pieces. And that's how they got their name Matariki."

Sarah looked around, a trace of sadness building on her weathered face. She remembered how she had grown up in the ruins of Melbourne, fighting for her life, losing friends and loved ones, scrabbling for the barest existence. It seemed unfair that here—a mere 1300 miles away—people were living in a semblance of harmony and reasonable prosperity. And they had time to remember their past. Yet it also filled her with hope. This is how it should be, she thought. This is how it begins anew. Small towns embedded in farming communities—the first level of production, and indispensable in supporting any kind of light industry and the road back to civilization. No matter that you found robots used as scarecrows, their plastic and composite shells broken by gaping holes.

She clutched Theo's hand tightly, her green eyes bright. He nodded quietly. He understood. His own throat was tight with unspoken emotion. Growing up on *Colony* was literally as well as figuratively light years from Sarah's childhood, yet the oppressive control of the elders had not prepared him for this kind of *laissez faire* freedom. He supposed that this was what you called a rural democracy. He understood they had even had regular elections. Pat—the head of the community—could be voted out. Theo shook his head. Democracy was still a tough concept for him, despite having lived in the family for nearly a year now.

The ceremonies lasted several hours and were exhausting, but fun. There was much food and drink and many rambling speeches. A hundred members of the family arrived an hour after Welkin and the others, traveling by foot, and joined in the festivities. Soon it was impossible to tell them apart:

Earthborn, Skyborn and Kiwis all mixed together in a harmonious if somewhat lumpy whole.

Minstrels finally set the pace and everyone began dancing. There was so much food that the family didn't know where to begin. A lot of it was indigenous to New Zealand, and therefore totally unknown to the Australians. Welkin and Gillian were intrigued with the way the Maoris cooked their food in the ground.

"Sure," said Severo. "We call it a hangi, eh. Heat the rocks and place 'em in the pit. Wrap corn husks and palm leaves around the meat and fish and surround it with thistle. Takes hours to heat the rocks, but. Chuck in some La'i roots and veggies like kumara—that's sweet potato—and away you go. Over in Rotorua they use geothermal steam but we ain't got none here, eh."

Gillian peered into the pit that was now releasing a steady flow of steam. Her elfin face wrinkled at what she saw. "Wouldn't the food taste ... smoky?"

Severo laughed. "Even pakehas get used to it, fella."

Severo proved to be an affable and knowledgeable guide, and an untiring one. No matter how many questions they asked, he seemed happy to supply the answer and was only too willing to show them about.

The Maori haka was the most exciting event of the afternoon. It involved much sticking out of tongues, slapping thighs, stomping the ground and bending of the knees. The dancers screamed out their words in Maori: "*Ka mate! Ka mate!*" they chanted.

"What's that mean?" Welkin asked. The faces the dancers were pulling and their intonation looked and sounded quite fierce.

"It is death! It is death!" said Severo. "But don't worry, eh."

"*Ka ora! Ka ora!*" the Maoris continued.

"That means, 'It is life! It is life!'," Severo added. "The haka is simply meant to instill fear in the enemy. It worked well when the Europeans first invaded Aotearoa—that's the Maoris' original name for the North Island."

"What does it stand for?" asked Sarah.

"The land of the long white cloud," Severo said. "Anyway, these days the haka's only performed at ceremonies."

After the feast, Sarah asked if they could visit the medical center. Theo and Gillian remained behind to participate in the Timorans' answer to the haka, a lively dance that involved lots of skipping and forced smiles, but Welkin went along with Sarah. "Line dancing" made him wonder if the Earthborn had truly lost their minds. Not in all his studies on board *Colony* had he ever seen anything so patently stupid as people all lined up together, dancing to someone calling out corny lyrics. Still, dancing itself was foreign to all Skyborn. It was something their ancestors did. It was a "liberating" expression of mood or something. Whatever it was, it didn't sit right with him. Theo obviously disagreed—either that or he was more adventurous than Welkin. And he seemed only too ready to draw Sarah into his way of thinking.

The medical building was a large brick bungalow several blocks from the city center. Inside, it was bright and airy and though few doctors and nurses were on duty today (several were on standby), the center had an impressive air of purposeful order.

Severo took Welkin and Sarah to see the Head of the center, a Dr Daniel Ratahe, a pot-bellied jovial youth whose hairline had retreated some distance. He was a Maori, one of the original people of New Zealand. He greeted them enthusiastically by giving each a huge hug and a "*hongi*", a nose-to-nose rub, and immediately took them on a tour of his facility.

"It was my great-grandfather who started it all," Daniel said. "He was a member of the expedition which located the buried university library at Rotorua. Miraculously, nearly all the books were intact, as were the compact recording cubes and other storage media. A combination of the right level of humidity and temperature and being completely sealed off from vermin. We discovered that the last librarian there—a woman named Elsa Churchill—deliberately had the library hermetically sealed for future generations. A woman of great vision and optimism, if you ask me. Imagine. The world was falling apart around her and she gave her life—literally!—to save at least one repository of knowledge. We've even traced her descendants and they are one of Timora's leading and most respected families. Did Severo tell you we're building a statue of her in memoriam? It will be erected in the town square. Without her, the whole of North Island would still be in darkness, and I don't just mean no lighting." He laughed at his own joke. "Anyway, one of the first caches deciphered was the medical database and library. My great-grandfather—Harold Ratahe—had been working as a kind of country doctor, using methods little better than those from the Dark Ages, the original Dark Ages that is. Well, that cache was a goldmine to him. He started reading and learning, and soon he was teaching what he'd learnt and people came from all over Aotearoa to his medical school. We got rudimentary power back on and since then we've not looked back. One day we will get the computing systems in order. There's talk of an engineering school, too."

"It's all very impressive," Sarah said. "I wish the rest of the world was like this."

"Well, maybe it can be now. What we never had before was any method of rapid travel. I must confess that ever since your arrival at Martha I have had a dream. May I tell you?" He didn't wait for their permission but rushed on. "I want to set up medical schools all over the world. Everywhere. What do you think of that? I could achieve that now that we have access to your space shuttles. Astonishing things, these shuttles. The power of ancient wisdom. To be dragged forward by a miniature black hole—while we still use candles made from animal fat, in the hinterlands."

Before Welkin could point out that the Earthborn was probably nearing the end of his natural life, Sarah said, "I think that's a wonderful dream. And we will do whatever we can to help."

The doctor gripped Sarah's arm. "You mean that? You think my dream is important?"

Sarah covered his hand with her own. "I think it's very important. The only thing I would add to it is that we make it a school in general, teaching not only medicine but engineering, as you said, and everything else, too. A school to rebuild civilization."

"Oh, my," said Daniel, his eyes distant. "I think you're the first person I've ever met who had dreams even bigger than my own."

"Perhaps you would start with us," Sarah suggested. "Would you permit a team of doctors to train our medicos in herbal lore? Our Skyborn team can reciprocate in other areas. The shuttle computers for example have pretty extensive memories. And perhaps one day the neural jacks some Skyborn still have can be available to some of us, if we can use *Colony* again."

"I would be delighted," said the doctor. "Consider it done. I will start organizing it at once. Severo, you finish showing them around. I must get on to this right away."

And with that he hurried off, bellowing orders even before he was in sight of any of his colleagues and workers. Sarah smiled and turned to Severo.

"Dr Ratahe said it was his great-grandfather who discovered the medical cache. Is it coincidental that his great-grandson is the head of this center?"

"Dunno, really," said Severo. "Timora—like much of Aotearoa—works on a system of what you might call guilds, eh. Skills are handed down within families."

"Are they exclusive?"

"Nah. We've been very careful to avoid those kind of restrictive practices. The guilds train apprentices all the time, but. If Dr Ratahe's son didn't want to be a doctor—and heaven help him if he didn't, he'd never hear the end of it from his father!—then he could be traded to another guild without any fuss. The only restrictions are on absolute numbers within each trade, but that only applies to the township itself. Newly graduated journeymen and women are constantly taking their skills to other communities. So far no one has been turned down because of quota limits. We're still primarily a farming community, but I'm stoked, eh, that all children go to school now—a law that came in some twenty-six years ago."

They were standing near a window, bathed in hot sunlight. Welkin stood slightly to one side, watching Severo and Sarah converse. He started to say something and Severo half turned towards him. In doing so, Welkin saw something flicker briefly in Severo's ear. *Hiveborn*! His heart missed a beat.

Severo completed the turn and saw the startled look on Welkin's face. For a second they stared at one another, then Severo shoved past Sarah and ran off. Sarah blinked back her confusion.

Welkin raced after Severo, shouting back at Sarah, "He's Hiveborn!"

Welkin sprinted down the corridor and burst through the doors at the end. He blinked in the sunlight and stared about, spotting Severo 200 yards away. He gave chase, his sturdy Skyborn legs rapidly closing the distance between them.

Severo pelted down a street, ducked into a narrow lane between houses, then raced across a square full of people attending the festivities. He bowled over several, eliciting yells of derision. Welkin had a slightly harder time getting through the crowd who were disposed to be angry at this antisocial behavior. A couple of men tried to block his path, but he had learnt a trick or two in his travels and left the men sprawled on the ground gasping for breath.

At one point Welkin lost sight of Severo. He jumped up on a stall loaded with fish and oysters, drawing more angry rebukes from the stallholder and the passers-by. Then he saw Severo ducking into a butcher's shop.

Welkin sprang after him and burst into the premises. The butcher raised a meat cleaver in a threatening fashion. "What's all this about?" he demanded. "Enough of your rough-housing. On your way!"

Welkin stared mutely at the butcher and the several customers waiting to be served.

"Is there a back door?" he finally said, breathing hard. One of the customers nodded towards the back, but the butcher scowled and made to come round the bench and grab him. Welkin ducked beneath his outstretched hand and ran through to the back.

He crashed through the door shoulder first. Stumbling, he then righted himself, before something struck him from behind and he went down.

When Welkin came to, he was in a room with several men and women. They were peering at him with disapproval.

"Welkin? Are you all right?" It was Sarah's concerned voice.

He groaned and sat up, holding his head. "I think a brick wall fell on me."

Daniel bustled up and examined the wound. "You'll live to fight another day," he said, still jovial despite the other scowling faces around them. One of the disapproving faces was Pat's, the mayor.

"You've caused a lot of damage, fella," Pat said. "And I don't mean just to property. Of all the days to pick for your high jinks! Just when we were trying to mend fences and get my people used to yours."

Daniel laughed out loud, startling everybody.

Pat began, "Now Daniel … "

"Don't 'now Daniel' me, Pat. Last I heard everyone's innocent till somebody can prove otherwise. And even then, the guilty are entitled to give their version of events. Or has that changed recently? Are we still in the Dark Ages? Maybe we should just lynch the guy, as a face-saving gesture, of course."

Pat's resolve crumbled. It was hard to be angry with the doctor. "Oh, very well. Tell us what happened, Mister Welkin."

"It's just Welkin. And I'm afraid I failed. He got away." He gingerly touched his bloodied scalp. That would be another scar for his head.

Sarah stepped in front of him. "No, he didn't," she said. "After he knocked you out, I took *him* out. He's in the next room. I left Theo and Gillian to keep an eye on him, despite demands to the contrary."

"Severo's a respected citizen of Timora," Pat blustered. "You can't go chasing him around town and knocking him out. I won't have anarchy!"

"I'm sorry about that," said Welkin, peering about. "Where are we? Is this place safe?"

"Safe?" asked Pat, confused. "Of course it's safe. It's our local jail. And you're in it. And we're on the third floor, just in case you're thinking of escaping."

Welkin relaxed slightly. "He's one of them," he said. "He's Hiveborn."

Pat stared at him in perplexity. "Hiveborn?" he blustered. "You mean he's one of those things you people have been talking about? An alien?"

"They're parasites," Welkin said.

"I don't care if they're para-chutes," said Pat. "That's the most ridiculous thing I've ever heard. I've known Severo all my life. He's all right—a Timoran, born and bred." He paused for breath. "He's part Samoan, of course. But that's way back in his ancestry." He squared his shoulders. "Anyway, Severo's certainly not one of your Hiveborn."

"You're right," said Welkin. He rubbed his lantern-jaw, wondering how to describe the aliens. "He's not exactly a Hiveborn. Severo's not an alien but an alien creature has colonized him and is in control of him. The Severo you know is gone. His memories are there. Even his personality is probably unchanged. The Hiveborn use their hosts as they find them. But they subjugate their emotional will. Like a virus takes over a computer. And they add another set of memories. Shared memories of the Hivemind."

Murmurs broke out in the room but Pat was getting angry. "Rubbish." He turned to Sarah. "What's all this about? We invited you into our homes, we—"

"Pat, shut up and listen." This was Daniel. He turned to Welkin. "Can you prove what you're saying?"

Welkin nodded. "I think so. An extremity of the parasite is visible though most of it is hidden inside the surrogate."

"Well, let's take a look then. I must admit to being curious."

The doctor guided Welkin and Sarah into the next room, leaving it up to Pat and the others as to whether they would follow or not. After an exchange of grumbles they did.

Severo was lying on a table, his head propped up on pillows. Theo and Gillian stood back from the bed when they entered.

Welkin acknowledged that Severo was being guarded by Theo and Gillian, but he said, "Why isn't he restrained?"

"Because," said Pat from the doorway behind, "we're not in the habit of restraining our citizens without due cause, though I expect it's different with you people."

Welkin moved to the prone body and turned Severo's head on its side, exposing his ear. Inside, the tiny filaments or cilia could be seen. Daniel's professional curiosity piqued, he leaned close to examine them. Though they looked like hair at a casual glance, under closer scrutiny it was obvious they weren't. Nor did they behave like hair. They moved. Tiny ripples passed through them, independent of air currents in the room. Indeed, their movement resembled that of sea anemones. Welkin felt dizzy. Memories flowed through him, knowledge of machines that fed into the Hivemind, ones that were for birth and ones that were inside the hairs, biological … he was reminded of rod-logic nanocomputers, so small they could fit inside individual cells and still hold vast amounts of data … a cubic centimeter like a million human brains' worth of memory, if you could write the software … Welkin jerked back to reality as someone spoke.

"Well, I'll be," said the doctor. Pat came up behind him, blocking Theo's and Gillian's view of the prisoner.

"What are you saying, Doc? Is there something wrong with Severo?"

"That," said Daniel, pointing at the writhing cilia, "should not be there. It is not part of our anatomy."

"Then he *has* been taken over by some alien?" Pat's face was going paler by the second.

"Can't say, Pat, but I will say this." He turned and faced the others. "I believe these people."

The mayor's shoulders slumped in defeat. "What do we do? It seems so preposterous."

Daniel scratched his thinning hair. "First thing we do is get Severo to my hospital. I will make a thorough examination of him."

"You need to keep him sedated," Sarah said. At Pat's indignant look she added, "He *is* sedated, isn't he?" She took a step toward Severo but it was too late.

Severo suddenly leapt off the table. Before anyone could stop him he had reached the window and was diving through it. A gasp went through the room and everyone crowded to the window and stared down.

Severo lay crumpled on the road three stories below, a blossom of blood unfurling beneath him.

Daniel led the concerted rush for the stairs and moments later they were gathered around the body. Not too close—it wasn't a pretty sight.

"He went into the pavement head first. Crushed his skull in," Daniel said needlessly. He grabbed a stick and pushed aside a section of skull, exposing the sodden mass of the brain but also a pulpy greenish mass that leaked a bright red viscous fluid that must be its blood. It was clearly dead, like the host. "That," said the doctor, "is not human."

"That's definitely Hiveborn," said Welkin and he looked grimly around at those gathered there in the street. "They're here. They're among us."

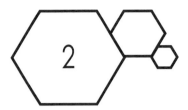

2

The smell was gut-wrenching. Daniel had removed most of the skull, exposing the nearly shapeless mass of Severo's brain. He had separated the alien ganglion, placing it on the autopsy table several inches away. He could not remove it entirely as dozens of tiny filaments had spliced into various parts of the brain and he wanted to study them *in situ*. For more than an hour he had carefully and slowly dissected the parasite, probing its interior and looking for significant structures with a portable electron microscope from one of the shuttles, *Procyon*. A black and white holoscreen projected 3D black and white images from the microscope, of an outlandish world of blobs and blocks and rods.

Crowding up behind him, covering their noses and trying to breathe solely through their mouths, were Welkin and Sarah, Pat, and a number of other official and medical personnel. Daniel was assisted by a second doctor and two nurses.

"Jesus," said someone in the pack. "What a stench."

"Quiet back there," Daniel ordered. He finished tracing a major nerve pathway back to what appeared to be the creature's frontal lobe, though the comparison with human brain physiology was obviously suspect.

He put down his scalpel and wiped his brow. "I would like a nice cup of tea," he said to no one in particular. The mayor went to the door and motioned an aide to fetch one. The boy left, reluctant to miss what was happening in the room.

"Well, Daniel?" Pat asked.

"Why don't we sit down in the lecture theater?"

A few moments later they were all seated. Daniel stood at the podium as if delivering his weekly lecture. He looked at Welkin. "You were quite right,

Welkin. This thing is not from this planet. It's as alien as it gets. The cells don't have proper cell walls. Parts look more like mechanical nanosystems, parts like prion-affected neural systems. What was once called Mad Cow's Disease. From what I can tell, it was indeed controlling our friend Severo. And it's linked heavily to his cortex, so it needs a developed, complex thinking brain as a host. A bird or a rat wouldn't be enough."

There was a kind of collective gasp—not of disbelief, but of horror.

"Can it communicate?" Sarah asked.

"It can talk. We heard it talk. It used Severo's larynx. Orchestrated the nerve impulses. Yes, it can communicate."

"No," said Sarah, "what I want to know is, can it communicate by other means?"

"Ah, I see. You are worried that it has told its friends it was discovered. I'm not sure. If you mean some kind of telepathy, I doubt it. How would such a thing work? What organ would power it and what would that organ look like under the knife? No, I doubt it. There are strange structures there but nothing like radio, nothing that doesn't make a kind of sense. But it's very hard to say. It's as though some element is missing beyond symbiote and host, as though their evolution left them vulnerable in some regard. A living organism would be much more helpful."

Welkin said, "I think they share some state of mind, or memories. On their own skyship, *Crusader*, they used language. They used the language of their hosts, which happened to be English. But the way they stormed aboard *Colony*, and seemed to know everything by group intelligence … it smacked of common behavior. At least from one source."

"I'd agree with that," Theo put in. "As Welkin says, maybe not between themselves, but something was definitely telling them what to do."

Welkin clicked his fingers. "Where was he running to? What is near that butcher's shop?"

Pat looked over at him. "Severo lives near there."

"You need to search his place."

Pat returned to the door and called over an islander by the name of Omas. "Get some of your people over there. You take charge."

Omas nodded and headed for the foyer door. Welkin called out, "Be on full alert. There might be more of those things … " Omas clutched an assault rifle to his chest, swallowed, and went out.

Daniel gazed at Welkin and Sarah. "So what happens now?"

"We must get back, warn our people," Sarah said. "In a weird way I'm glad it's started. Everyone's been getting way too complacent."

"You still want a medical team?"

"Well, yes, but it doesn't seem a priority right now," said Sarah.

"Maybe it is more important than you think," Daniel replied, his face unreadable. "I will come with you. I'll finish my autopsy back at the mine, if that's all right."

The mayor looked relieved. "You're taking that alien thing with you?"

"I believe so."

"Fine by me. Keep us up to speed on this stuff, Daniel." He shook his head. "Damnable business. Damnable. Severo was a good man."

Three hours later, Welkin and the others, accompanied by Daniel and a coffin covered in a shroud, arrived back at Martha. The coffin attracted many odd looks but no explanation was given. Sarah reminded the others that the policy meeting was scheduled for later that evening. She invited the doctor to attend and cautioned all of them to say nothing of events in Timora that day.

At eight o'clock that night, roughly two dozen people—the High Council of Martha—were gathered in the main conference room, about 1200 feet underground. There was 500 feet of basalt directly above them. Daniel sat at the back of the room and several people looked over at him curiously, but neither Sarah nor the others introduced him. Aside from those who had been in Timora that day (though Welkin was not yet present), there was Harry, Elab, Clifford, Ferrik, Arton, and Efi. In one corner, taking notes, was Angela—the same Angela who had worked for Tolk, the notorious and Machiavellian Prophet. Several of the others looked at her askance and she seemed uncomfortable under their gaze.

"Listen up, everyone," Sarah called the meeting to order.

One of the newer council members, a short hard-faced woman named Hester, put up her hand. Sarah nodded to her. She got to her feet slowly and looked around. Sarah watched her carefully. Hester was forceful and blunt and had a way of getting the younger people on her side that worried Sarah. Hester's views were usually too far to the right to make Sarah—and many of the Committee—comfortable.

"Nothing has changed in a month," said Hester. "Yet the agenda for this meeting remains the same. What to do about the Hiveborn. The fact, and one that is as tired as the question, remains that we should do nothing. There is no evidence that they will target us any more vigorously than other communities. Indeed, Timora—only an hour's walk from here—is a far more inviting target than we are, buried as we are inside our mountain stronghold. I say again, do nothing. Aggravate nothing."

She sat down. Sarah did not breathe a sigh of relief. She knew that Hester had barely got started. The others did not see this. Theo jumped to his feet, hot under the collar.

"Are you deaf as well as blind?" he demanded. "Did you not hear my forecast yesterday? Five years and it's all over. And that's a *very* conservative estimate."

Hester did not even look at him. She said wearily, "There he goes again. Estimating this, estimating that." There were several sniggers in the room and Theo's temper flared, but he held it in check.

Patrick O'Shannessey had no such control. He was one of Sarah's most ardent followers, him and his sister Mira. He stood towering over Hester. "And who d-ye think *you* are?" he bellowed.

Theo waved Patrick down. Luckily Mira had some control over her brother. She pulled him back down into his seat. Nonetheless, his blazing eyes did not leave Hester.

Theo mentally cursed Patrick. They didn't need a screaming match. He said patiently, "An infected host—a zombie—can infect his entire family in one night. Each of those can then infect a new family the second night. And so on and so on. With an average family of five members that's a little over seventy-eight thousand people in a week. You do the numbers."

"Numbers, numbers, numbers," said Hester in a sardonic voice, staring straight back at Patrick. She turned frosty eyes back to Theo. "Fairytales to frighten the young. Do they have seventy-eight thousand parasites to dispose of in a week? Every week? What is there, a factory line for parasites?" More sniggers. "Besides, who's even *seen* a parasite?"

Sarah smiled. She had been waiting for this. Theo lost it. "What in Space do you mean? You think we're making this stuff up?"

"Are you?"

"You know what you are? You're crazy. Or—"

"Here it comes," said Hester, smiling broadly. "Or I'm one of them, right? Do you want to look in my ears, Mr Skyborn? Perhaps you should bring a doctor to these meetings and he can check we're all still human." Open laughter now. But it stopped abruptly when Daniel stood up.

"I'm a doctor. I know what the heathen creatures look like." He crossed to Hester who was momentarily too startled to put up a verbal defense. He grabbed her head, turned it and looked in both ears with a small device that contained its own light source.

Hester struggled and finally pulled away from him. 'What is this?' she demanded.

Patrick clapped like a maniac.

Daniel stepped back. "She's not infected," he said. "At least not yet." He looked meaningfully at the others seated around Hester. They pulled back as though he might at any minute search their ears.

Despite the failure to find anything, the doctor's mere presence and his deadly serious manner sent a chill through the room. Sarah was pleased. Daniel resumed his seat.

Theo stood again, more collected now. "I'm glad that the self-appointed leader of the opposition is not being controlled by an alien parasite." His words added to the sobering effect of Daniel's little performance. "But it highlights our vulnerability—"

The door opened and Welkin came in carrying a box and some papers. He and Sarah exchanged glances and he sat down. "Sorry I'm late," he said. Hester returned angrily to her seat.

Theo continued. "The Hiveborn will not be stopped. Most especially they will not be stopped by wishful thinking and clever phrases." He looked at Hester and now the sniggers were on his side. "We know from the grapevine that they have taken Melbourne and Sydney and are moving into the suburbs. But the movement is not random. They are setting up networks, beachheads, building warehouses to store weapons as well as what we suspect are tens of thousands of parasites ... They are conducting a military operation and if we are to assume that the expansion we can *see* is all that is going on then we deserve whatever doom awaits us. Does anyone here really believe they are not using the orbiting satellites to study and map all human communities? Does anyone really believe that a race so ancient, so vast in its experience of warfare, would not take the war to its most formidable foe earlier rather than later? That we have survived so far is a miracle. Mark my words. We must take the war to the Hiveborn. We cannot stick our heads in the sand and hope they will pass us by. If we do, we will just get our asses shot off." More laughter, but of an uneasy kind.

Hester stood. "'That we have survived so far is a miracle'. You said that, Theo. 'Earlier rather than later'. Your words also. If they are so militaristic, if we are so formidable, why have they not attacked? Why haven't they destroyed our shuttles? Where are they? Where are their spies? What are they waiting for?" She gazed around at all the faces. "We have done nothing to anger them, and they have left us alone. Isn't that a lesson worth listening to? If you shove a stick in a hornet's nest you will stir up trouble. Again I say, do nothing. Wait and watch." She sat down.

"Every day they establish themselves more firmly on this planet," said Theo. "Every day they extend their networks, possess more hapless human beings, strengthen their own numbers at our ultimate expense. Every day we wait is a day that weakens us. Perhaps they're so sure of themselves, so confident, with so many conquered worlds behind them, that they can't consider the possibility of hurrying—or losing. We must not wait."

Hester spoke up again. "Even if your bogeyman does exist," she said, "there remains another danger. If they capture just one of our people and— *possess* them, as you put it—then we are all in danger, for they will then know our whereabouts, our strengths and our weaknesses, as well as all access points to Martha."

Sarah cleared her throat. "It seems to me we need better Intel. We sit here in our hole in the ground and we are operating on conjecture."

"Gathering intelligence is dangerous," said Hester. "It'll lead them back to us."

"Doing anything is dangerous, Hester. You know that. The omission of an act may be just as perilous as its commission. But is all intelligence dangerous in the way that you mean? For I take it that you are again voicing your concern that one of our number could be taken over by aliens and made to betray us?" Hester grudgingly nodded, not quite sure where Sarah was going with this. "Then if there was a way to find out what the Hiveborn are doing without that risk—?"

She didn't wait for an answer. Instead she nodded to Ferrik who was sitting at the back. He took a deep breath and came up to the front. Sarah gave up her position to him.

"Hiya," he said. "I know everybody here except the doctor. Pleased to meet you, sir. My name is Ferrik. I'm a shuttle pilot. Formerly of *Colony*."

Daniel smiled at him. "I am Doctor Daniel Ratahe. From Timora."

"Can we get on with it?" said Hester, bored with the formalities.

"Arton and I have been working with Theo and Elab on a plan." He looked around at them. "You're all aware of the network of satellites in orbit around the Earth. What some of you may not know is that Arton and I, while working with *Colony*, were responsible for inserting some of them into their orbits."

The level of curiosity in the room had risen palpably. "Well, we wondered if there was some way to co-opt the satellite surveillance system. Those satellites are designed to map the earth throughout the electromagnetic spectrum and to study a number of variables such as river systems, forest growth, agricultural land use, road systems, shipping, you name it. They were also programmed with military objectives.

"We want to infect these satellites with a virus—a worm to be exact—so that we can get all the same information the Hiveborn are getting, see what they're interested in looking at, and intercept their communications. We could then use them as an early warning system in case of attack. We also believe we may be able to create a surveillance 'blind spot' where Martha exists—making us more or less invisible."

"Have you got this worm ready? Who designed it?" asked Efi.

"Hetti—Theo's computer genius—designed it and it's ready to go. All we need is a green light."

"Won't the Hiveborn find it?" someone asked.

Ferrik shrugged. "As far as we can tell the Hiveborn are not innovators. They use whatever technology they come across, though I'm quite sure they have stuff we haven't seen yet, stolen from other races in the Galaxy. But right now they're using Skyborn satellites run with Skyborn-designed operating systems. Designed in fact by Hetti. Now I don't understand all the computer stuff, but Hetti says that the 'worm' will hide inside the satellite's software, in the background, yet continue monitoring Hiveborn activity. This it will beam down in discrete hi-speed bursts when the pulses can't be detected."

There was a buzz of excited conversation. Sarah let it go on for some time, despite the expression on Hester's face. Ferrik sat down and chatted quietly with Theo and Elab. All the while Welkin watched the proceedings, saying nothing. He had the air of a man waiting for something.

Finally Sarah called them to order again. "It seems we need to vote. Should we adopt Ferrik's plan and infiltrate the satellite system or do as Hester has suggested and avoid drawing attention to ourselves?"

Hester said, "I'm not stupid, you know. Voting for Ferrik's plan is like becoming a little bit pregnant. Once we do this we will become committed to the larger plan. I vote against it."

Sarah called for recess and coffee was served as people discussed the proposals. Hester worked the room, drawing people aside and talking to them in intense whispers. It was clear her words were having a sobering effect. Sarah frowned, shooting a quick look at Welkin who was still sitting back, apparently unconcerned.

Harry sat down next to him. "It's not looking good," he said.

"Isn't it?"

Harry gazed at him. "Okay, what's going on?"

"What do you mean?"

"Oh, come off it, Welkin. I've known you too long. You can't even bluff at poker. You've got something up your sleeve."

Welkin raised an eyebrow. "Have I?"

"Fine. Be like that. But the vote is swinging against us." He got up and returned to his seat and Sarah once again called order to the room.

She was about to start the voting when Hester stood up. "I've already polled the room. We don't need a secret ballot. A show of hands will do." She faced the room. "All in favor of rejecting Ferrik's plan, raise your hand."

About 60 per cent of the room did so.

"Thank you," said Sarah. "But no vote can be ratified unless it's taken by secret ballot. You know that, Hester."

"Sure. Just trying to save some time." She sat down, looking smug.

Harry and Theo and Ferrik, sitting near the back, were looking anxious. They knew the vote would be close, but hadn't thought it would actually go against them.

"Are there any other submissions before we put it to the vote?" asked Sarah. Hester frowned and swiveled in her seat.

Welkin cursed mentally. He had hoped the vote would have swung their way without having to show his trump card. He stood up and went to the front of the room carrying his box. Daniel rose too and joined him. Hester's frown deepened.

"I have one," said Welkin. "While there is much of merit in what Hester has said here tonight it is no longer relevant. Ferrik's plan is the only viable route. Indeed, even it is not enough. Therefore I would like to propose that, in addition to co-opting the satellites, an expedition be launched to mainland Australia to obtain a live parasite for medical examination with a view to finding some way to destroy the rest of them."

There was a loud silence—then the room erupted in voices, foremost amongst them Patrick's and Mira's. Hester was on her feet in an instant vainly trying to be heard. Sarah let them squabble, then called for quiet.

"This is outrageous," Hester said. "New submissions cannot be called once voting has commenced. Those are the rules."

"Then why didn't you object when I allowed Welkin to submit?" asked Sarah.

"Be that as it may, the situation hasn't changed. The vote is still to sit tight."

"I'm sorry," said Welkin, "but that's not the case." He opened the box and lifted out an autopsy bowl containing a worm-like organ.

"This is an alien parasite. It was removed from a man called Severo in Timora earlier today. He was our guide. When discovered, he made a run for it. When captured, he jumped out of a third floor window and dove head first to the ground, killing both himself and the parasite."

"And ruining our chances of studying it properly at the same time," said Daniel above the clamor. "There were a dozen witnesses."

Everybody crowded up and peered at the dead alien. There was no doubt that it was not of terrestrial origin. The color, the shape, the cilia and filaments, the red thick ooze, more like jelly than blood, even the smell of decay—all were queasily different. Alien.

"The Hiveborn planted a spy in Timora," Welkin said. "Does anybody here think that was accidental? A coincidence?" No one said anything. "They know we're here and they're watching us. The war with the Hiveborn has come to us. It's now time to defend ourselves. We need Ferrik's plan. And we need a live parasite." He paused and looked around at the now stricken faces. "We have to go back to Melbourne."

The vote passed without a hitch. This time, only Hester and her coterie dissented.

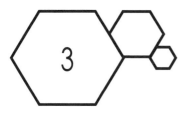

3

Paranoia resulted.

It did not take long for the rumor to spread that an alien parasite had been found in Timora in control of a host, and one in a key position. From that, it was soon clear that anyone anywhere could be infected. To deal with this Sarah instituted the age-old buddy system: no one travels alone or remains alone. Scarves, hoods, balaclavas and earmuffs were banned. She realized the solution was in some ways worse than the cure: it accelerated the feeling of paranoia but they could not take the chance that Martha had been compromised.

Checkpoints were also introduced as was a total communications blackout. Hatch, who had helped Welkin and Theo develop a jamming system on board *Colony*, set up a similar system blanketing the whole of Martha. An investigation back in Timora had revealed a sophisticated comm. unit in Severo's house. It was clear he had been trying to get there when Sarah knocked him out. If so, it meant the parasites could not communicate other than by normal physical means.

Sarah put the comm. room under guard and Welkin issued all lookouts with devices designed to pick up stray broadcasts.

It changed the atmosphere inside Martha. They were now, in a sense, under siege. Sarah observed that the aliens, by their very nature, were already winning the war, and not a shot had been fired.

"And make no mistake," she said one evening to Welkin and the others in their close cohort. "This is a war. There has never been a divide so vast and so unbridgeable. Not the old wars between capitalism and communism, between Christianity and Islam ... All those squabbles fade by comparison with this. This is a war for the survival of the human race. If we lose it, we go out. Forever."

Gillian sighed. "Then we better win it soon," she said. "The number of fights we've had to quash this week alone has trebled. Nobody trusts anybody. People are building doors and locking them at night."

"How stupid," said Welkin. "That's exactly the kind of behavior that will help zombies create more zombies."

Sarah spread her hands helplessly. "What are we going to do, Welkin? They have a right to be scared. 'Struth, *I'm* scared. I keep trying to peer into my own ears. Would I *know* if one of those things had taken me over? Did Severo know?"

"He knew when he ran."

"And before that?"

Welkin shrugged. "I can't say."

Gillian shivered. "Can we change the subject? I'm already spooked enough, thank you."

"How is Operation Acquisition going?" Sarah asked Welkin.

"We're getting there," he said.

Actually, both groups were having problems. Operation Acquisition consisted of Welkin, Gillian, Arton (since they needed a shuttle pilot), and Hatch, a member of Theo's team from *Colony*.

The first problem was how to approach Melbourne. Landing in country Victoria was an obvious possibility, but the chances of stumbling on an infected community or—worse—a single infected individual, was remote. And this wasn't a waiting game for the Earthborn. The clock was ticking. If the Hiveborn had a spy—or spies—watching them, then they had to assume there was some kind of countdown. They needed to get in, grab several infected hosts (along with their still living parasites) and get the hell out of there.

Then there were other problems: actually infiltrating a Hiveborn community raised all kinds of issues and was a situation where ignorance could get them killed—or worse. Then the actual acquisition of individuals, rendering them unconscious without harming them or the parasites ... the technical and social problems were endless.

It was little consolation to Welkin to know that Ferrik's team was having its own problems. Operation Eavesdrop consisted of Ferrik—as pilot—along with Harry, Elab, Lucida, Theo and Hetti—Theo's computer genius.

The challenges they faced were different from Welkin's but still difficult. They must achieve orbit, maneuver to a number of satellites—some in polar orbits, some in geosynchronous orbit—insert the virus, and get back to Earth, all without being detected. In theory, they could just infect one satellite with the digital worm. Since it was part of an informational interdependent network of satellites it would quickly infect the others. But they needed to make this work the first time. No mistakes were permissible.

Ferrik decided they had to provide the Hiveborn with what he called an Occam's Razor. This was a method of scientific thinking. It basically said go to the simplest explanation first.

"So we need something obvious for what we're doing, in case they spot us, or find our tracks, right?" asked Harry.

"You got it."

"Okay," Harry said. "They've been doing this a long time, encountering heaps of opposition along the way. So why don't we make it look like we're trying to destroy some."

"Works for me," said Elab. "Satellites are the 'high ground'. Any military operation would look to use them against the Hiveborn in an all-out attempt to stop them once and for all."

Theo, who was also present, looked thoughtful at this but said nothing. Ferrik nodded. "So we make it look like we're sabotaging some satellites above Hiveborn-held cities."

Hetti clapped her hands. "Perfect," she said. "The Hiveborn find the bombs, remove them, and—believing they've solved the problem—leave the worm intact. In any case, it's been designed to camouflage itself and hide. And you know what? I can make it so that *removing* the bombs is what activates the worm."

Ferrik smiled around at them. "Let's do it."

Theo wished them luck and sauntered out, his beetling brow creased in thought.

Two days later, in a private meeting, Sarah stared at Theo. Arton and some of the Skyborn had suggested another war option. "You're serious?" she asked.

Theo nodded. "You said it yourself, Sarah. This is a war to the finish. There won't be any second chances for us."

"But destroy Melbourne? The whole city?" Sarah's normally firm shoulders sagged.

"They're not human any more."

"You don't know that," Sarah said. She got up and paced. "There may be a way to separate the parasites from their hosts without killing the person."

"And you don't know that," said Theo, gently. "How long do we wait? With some of the antimatter we got from *Colony*, I believe we can build an antihydrogen bomb big enough to level Melbourne and its surroundings, totally wipe out the main Hiveborn settlement in one go, without any casualties on our side."

"It still might not get them all. Or it might destroy the whole continent. You tinker with technology others made tens of decades ago."

"I don't think it would do any of that. But it would destroy most of them as well as the *Colony* wreck and their adjacent *Crusader* skyship on the ground, plus any of the *Crusader's* antimatter-powered shuttles. They might set off a chain reaction if they go up, cause more intense damage. If nothing else, it would set them all back months, years even. And with luck, if they have a queen bee or whatever, we might even get her. That might end whatever communication set-up they have, and if they don't have a backup, like a queen in waiting ... "

Sarah chewed her lower lip. "I don't know, Theo."

"We would have the upper hand. Look, right now, we're running scared. Desperate missions to take over the satellites, to acquire living parasites. These are a rearguard action. Firing at the enemy whilst in retreat. We need to take the fight to them in a way that brooks no opposition." He paused for a moment then went on. "I don't like this either, Sarah. But do we have the right not to do it? If the fate of the human race is in the balance as we both believe it is, do we have the right not to throw everything at them that we possibly can? Can we afford the luxury of ethical qualms? Of merciful considerations?"

Sarah stopped pacing and stood for a moment, swaying slightly. "Jesus. *I don't know.*"

He took her in his arms and held her. She rested her head on his chest. "Why does this have to be up to me?" she asked in a small voice. "We won our fight with *Colony*. With everything else. I'm tired of fighting. I just want to—"

"You just want to settle down and raise a family." He tugged her towards the bed. "We could get started on that, you know."

She laughed, but sobered almost immediately. "Okay. Here is how it will happen. You assemble a team. You build the bomb. You devise a delivery strategy. Then you wait. Nothing happens without my say-so and we keep the whole thing under wraps. If this were to get out and they had a spy amongst us, then they wouldn't hesitate to bomb us first."

"Makes you wonder why they haven't," Theo mused.

"They don't aim to kill anyone," Sarah said. "They kill us and they don't multiply. They want us alive and intact. They won't be able to comprehend what we're doing when we seemingly kill our own people."

Theo stroked her graying hair. "Now that that's sorted out, how about doing something for *our* descendants?" She laughed again but let him pull her to the bed.

Two weeks later the two teams departed. Welkin and Ferrik shook hands, not sure if they would see each other again. Harry clapped Welkin on the back and insisted they were both too ornery to die. Welkin said he hoped so.

Sarah and Theo were probably the most upset. It's always more difficult to stay behind, thought Sarah, than to go into danger. Too much time for thought. The others had persuaded her to stay behind. They needed someone back at base to coordinate both operations.

She hugged and kissed them all. The other members of the Committee were also there. The missions had been kept a secret, though it was general knowledge that some plan was being put into effect. Hopefully, nothing could be communicated through Hatch's jamming signal.

It was night when the modified *Colony* shuttles lifted off. The saucer-shaped pods with their front forks leapt forward quickly, dragged by a tiny black hole, pushed forward by gravity manipulators in the forks. Laser "torches" shoved air out of their path, reducing friction. Sarah and Theo watched them till they were two white, pulsing globes shooting away at high speed, quietly fading into the horizon.

Nearby, someone else watched; in their ear, a sea of tiny cilia writhed.

4

Ferrik's shuttle *Capella* raced for the other side of the planet, staying low and below the radar. He felt information flow through his neural jack. One of the few Skyborn left with such a useful device, his fingers slid over the optical-dendrimer polymer cable. They had mapped the movements of the ex-Skyborn satellites enough times to chart all the blind spots, the unseen air corridors where they could go for broke. Yet they still had to stop several times and find concealment on the ground, waiting for the satellite positions to change, thus opening up new safe—and *unseen*—corridors. The only reason it worked was that there were not enough satellites to provide continuous blanket coverage of the earth's surface. On top of that, the shuttles were equipped with standard stealth anti-sensor equipment. Luckily gravity wave detectors, which might find their shuttle's black hole, needed to be positioned in space in grids a million miles wide, and there was nothing like that around.

"If they spot us … " Harry said, gazing up through the forward screen at the night-time sky.

"They don't have orbital missile platforms, Harry," Ferrik said. "No linear accelerators to throw rocks at us. Hopefully no beam weapons or gravity cannon. They must be using their power and manufacturing for something else, something more important … If they spotted us they would still have to come and get us. And we're armed, remember."

"How long till we reach the next corridor?"

The navigator was a beautiful black woman named Veeda. She looked up. "Three minutes. We need to check our speed. We don't want to get there too soon."

Ferrik busied himself with a holographic panel near the plasma computing banks for a few moments, bringing the shuttle's velocity down to under a 1000 miles per hour. On a large forward viewscreen they had an aerial map of the terrain they were flying over. Overlaid on this were colored rectangles and curved sections. The blue ones denoted safe corridors, blind spots. They did not always intersect but shifted slightly every few minutes. They were heading towards a long thin blue rectangle (the shuttle's course was represented by a pulsing blip) which did not quite make contact with the rhomboid blue section they were flying through. Indeed, there was a thin red line still visible between the two. That red line showed air space that was currently being monitored. As they watched the two blue shapes moved closer.

"Half a mile from linkup," said Veeda. "Eight seconds and counting."

As she counted in the background and the shuttle blip raced towards the red line, the two blue sections suddenly kissed. The red line vanished and the shuttle shot into the long thin rectangle. Moments later, the rhomboid behind them started to fragment as more than one satellite's surveillance "window" made inroads into it.

Harry slapped Ferrik on the shoulder. "Nice flying," he said.

In this fashion they made it to the other side of the world, undetected. They found a spot in southern India and set down in a jungle clearing to wait for night.

Harry wanted to explore a nearby ruin. He took a gun and, at the last minute, Elab accompanied him. Ferrik wanted to go too, but he was voted down. In a pinch, both Harry and Elab could probably pilot the shuttle, but they certainly could not carry out the mission. It would be all they could do just to get the craft home again.

Harry and Elab climbed down from the loading bay hatch having scanned the jungle from the shuttle first. There didn't seem to be anything dangerous in the vicinity and they made rapid progress through the ferns and knee-high grass to the ruin, which turned out to be a Christian church. By the state of decay, they figured it must be from before the great catastrophe, before their ancestors launched themselves into space.

There was little in the way of furniture remaining and all the windows had been destroyed. Over the centuries most durable nanotech items would have been cannibalized. Anything wooden had been burnt for firewood or building huts long ago. What interested Harry more than missing furniture however was the graffiti on the walls. It had been gouged in with some kind of pointed implement, probably a compass. There were comments like "Where is God?" though few were in English.

"Hey, look at this," Elab called out. Harry went over to see what he had found. It was an old bible, covered in cement dust and with some kind of lichen growing on the cover. Elab had found it beneath a fall of debris from the ceiling. Harry told him to take it back with them. Sarah had been building a library for years and would love anything they could add to it.

"How long do you think this place has been empty?" Elab asked.

"Hundred years, at least."

"Man, it gives me the creeps." The church, though ramshackle and gutted, still had a cool silent quality that made them speak in whispers. Frescoes on the walls, though faded with time and neglect, showed biblical scenes. In one a star glowed in the Heavens and three men on camels seemed to be making for it. The star had been made from an exotic material and seemed to be constantly fluorescing, even in the daytime.

"Bit like us," said Elab, "aiming for a bright light in the sky."

"Well, they found theirs."

"How do you know?" asked Elab.

"I read books." Harry's communicator beeped. He flipped it on.

Ferrik's face stared out at him. "Something's coming your way," said Ferrik. "Better get back here."

They burst out of the church into sunlight and headed for the shuttle. There was a noise off to their right in the undergrowth and they broke into a run. Elab dropped the bible but kept going. Harry skidded to a stop, stooped to retrieve the book and as his hand came up holding it he found himself staring into a nightmarish face.

It was a tiger.

Harry froze. He did not even dare to swallow. The tiger was less than six feet away, staring back at him. It was huge, its pelt a bright splash of color, and its face seemed even bigger, especially the jaw and the teeth that glistened with saliva. He could smell its breath from where he stood.

He knew there was no time to go for his laserlite. This thing was the end product of millions of years of evolution: it was a killing machine, as deadly as a shark, as fast as a striking snake. If he moved, he would be dead before he knew it.

Or would he?

Why was he still alive? The great cat eyed him and suddenly it started to pace back and forth in front of him, never taking its eyes off him. He decided he had to risk straightening up. If he stayed in this posture for another moment, he felt his back and legs would give way and he would topple forwards. The sudden movement might startle the great beast.

He didn't want to startle it.

He moved very slowly. He pulled the book a little closer, then eased ever so slowly into an upright position. The tiger didn't even blink but kept pacing.

Feeling giddy with the achievement, Harry took a slow cautious step backwards. Still the cat did not pounce. He took another.

This time the cat stopped and looked at him. It yowled. Harry just knew it was about to attack. But then it turned and walked away.

Harry spun around and took off. He hit the shuttle saucer in a flying leap and swarmed up the outside ladder. Elab was leaning out of the hatch and grabbed his outstretched hand and hauled him inside. They fell on top of one another.

"I thought you were behind me. Where were you?" Elab demanded, still trying to get over his fright.

"You saw it?"

"Saw it? Why do you think I took off like that?"

"You dropped the book. I stopped to pick it up," said Harry.

Elab scratched his head. "You stopped to pick it up? A useless old book that the tiger wouldn't have touched and we could have gone back for later?"

Harry looked at him sheepishly. "I guess when you put it like that … "

"You're an idiot," Elab said. "Speaking of which, how come it didn't eat you?"

Harry told him what had happened then had to repeat it for the rest of the crew. Ferrik blamed himself. As captain of the shuttle he was technically in command of this mission. It was his job to forestall trouble—not encourage it.

"Okay," he said. "No more jaunts. We stick to the job at hand." Later that day, while they remained grounded waiting for nightfall, Harry found a letter tucked into the back of the bible. It was from a little girl. Her Christian name was Ruth and she was nine years old. The letter was part letter, part diary entry, and part prayer. Harry felt embarrassed reading it. Ruth had lost her parents. She could not find them and prayed to God to be reunited with them. She spoke of the chaos in the city and how nothing worked any more. She hoped her little brother wasn't scared. She was all alone in the church and had not seen anyone for many days though she had heard shooting in the distance two days earlier. The entry ended with these words, "Someone is coming. Could it be Mama? Perhaps it is someone who will look after me ... "

Harry had tears in his eyes when he finished. He felt a strange connection with this child who had been dead for over a 100 years which he could not explain. Even the incident with the tiger seemed somehow related.

He put the book away and joined the others for supper.

Two hours later, a dark moonless night fell swiftly on the jungle. Even then they waited. Most of them slept, waking briefly to check the time or because their nerves kept rousing them from uneasy dreams. Each one of them knew they were going into danger. They also knew that they could not be captured alive. Daniel had issued them with pills that they were supposed to pop in their mouths in the event they were captured. The pills would not dissolve and could even be safely swallowed, but if bitten into, then death would follow in seconds.

None of them liked to think of that eventuality, but all knew that the plans of Martha must not be compromised.

Harry and Elab were talking desultorily, having both slept for a few hours. "You think you could do it?" Harry asked. Elab did not need him to explain the question. It was on all their minds, more so as the launch time ticked closer.

Elab shrugged. "Dunno. What about you?"

"I'm hoping, if it comes to it, it'll seem like the better choice."

"I'm with you on that," Elab said with feeling. "You ever wonder what it would be like? Being 'possessed' by one of those things? Would you still have your memories? *Colony* had pills, treatments to wipe your memories, but I doubt they'll work on the parasites. That would be just as bad as death anyway. No memories and most of you would be gone."

Harry swallowed. "I think I just had a dream about being taken over. Come to think of it, it was more like a nightmare."

"Yeah. I get the willies just thinking about it."

"Well, don't drop your suicide pill," Harry said. "It's a lot smaller than a book."

"Oh, that's real funny," said Elab. "Old Butterfingers Harry is giving *me* advice."

"Butterfingers? Who calls me Butterfingers?"

Ferrik came in at that point. "Just about everybody, I think," he said. "You guys ready? It's time."

"I think I want a diaper," said Harry.

"Me, too," said Elab.

Ferrik looked at them and rolled his eyes. "Is this what heroes are made of these days?"

"Hey, no heroes here," said Harry.

"Fine," said Ferrik. "Diapers are being dispensed up front. You better hurry. I already put on two of 'em."

Elab and Harry chuckled.

"Okay," said Ferrik. "Here we go."

The *Capella* lifted off vertically. The moonless night made them invisible to the naked eye and, as planned, the entire bulk of the planet was between them and the Hiveborn beachhead at Melbourne. They were also in satellite shadow.

With luck they would make it to orbit undetected.

The ascent went smoothly. Veeda at the navigator's console monitored sensors. "Nothing's picking us up so far," she said.

"At least not by conventional means," said Harry.

Lucida appeared from aft where she had been organizing their cargo of bombs. "I heard that," she said. "When did you become such a pessimist?"

"Me? A pessimist?" said Harry, staring at her in surprise.

"You call that optimism?"

"Yeah. I like to consider all options."

"I think you got your nouns mixed up."

"Or your brains," said Elab.

Harry kicked Elab in the shin. "Ouch. That hurt. You want to disable me just as we go into battle? A fine friend you are."

"Approaching orbit," said Veeda. "No signals. Looks like a clean extraction."

"Let's hope so," said Ferrik, "otherwise we'll be having some company mighty fast."

Moments later they were in space.

Ferrik guided the ship into the trajectory required to pick up the first polar-orbiting satellite. Because their speed was slower than the satellite's, all they had to do was wait for it to come along. Ferrik added another holographic viewscreen showing the Earth below—or "above"—them. Since there was no moon the world below them was barely illuminated. There were lights of course though nothing like what once was seen from space before the big catastrophe. Still, it was reassuring to see pockets of humanity scattered everywhere across the globe, although some of the lights were probably hardly more than bonfires around which gathered a dozen or so people. On a thermal viewer there were volcanoes, bushfires, lightning and some heat sources from coal heating, electricity—in places—and semi-functioning ancient devices. Remnants of a once great world. Harry felt sorry for those—like Ruth—who had lived through it.

"Satellite approaching," said Veeda.

"You got a visual?"

"No, not—hang on, yes I do. There she is."

A tiny dot of light appeared moving across the star field. "We're slightly off," said Ferrik, glancing at his readouts. He got a fix on the satellite and simply ordered the ship to match vectors, which it did with an efficiency that was impressive.

"Let's grapple her in," said Ferrik. He and Harry and Elab went aft to the repair bay, designed specifically to receive objects from space. They remained in an observation room and set in motion a huge space arm, articulated with various multi-jointed robotic grapples which moved smoothly, more like an insect's mandibles than anything. A large holographic viewscreen in the side of the observation room showed the satellite drifting less than 20 feet away.

Ferrik verbally directed the automated arm out towards it and it snagged the satellite first time. Elab opened the bay doors and the satellite was brought inside. The bay doors closed and air was pumped back in. The three donned ancient dendrimer polymer-enhanced pressure suits and their diamondoid screen helmets. Ferrik insisted it was a safety precaution only.

Lucida then appeared, bringing the first bomb. Hetti joined them and together they opened up the satellite and hard-wired the bomb in place. Hetti programmed it, adding several layers of activation into the satellite's operating system through a portable plasma computer interface. At the same time she loaded the viral worm.

The whole thing took less than ten minutes.

"Good job," said Ferrik. "Now let's get this one back in its orbit and find lucky number two."

They evacuated the bay, pumped out the air, and deposited the satellite back into space. Then Ferrik went forward and brought them into alignment with the second targeted satellite.

This one went even more smoothly than the first. The only hitch occurred when they were closing the bay doors after returning the satellite to its orbit.

The doors refused to close properly. They couldn't spend time fixing them. They had to get to the other satellite and refit it inside of the next 30 minutes, otherwise they would have to wait another 90 minutes for it to return.

"We can do the next refit in suits. I'll make sure the bay is pointed away from the suit. Cosmic radiation will be negligible for that brief amount of time. Come on."

They all kept their suits on. Veeda located the third satellite exactly where they expected it to be and Ferrik brought the ship alongside. His maneuvering was getting a practiced feel.

Before he went back to the repair bay Veeda stopped him. "Can I help this time?"

She had been stuck in the control room the whole time and was obviously bored.

Ferrik shrugged. "Why not? Get suited up."

The job went slower this time. The pressure suits, barely noticeable when there was air around them, puffed up under the pressure differential and made movements slower and more awkward. However, the dendrimer polymer material was semi-intelligent and amplified strength and sweat barely popped out on their brows as they lugged the bomb over to the satellite. Though it had no weight in the zero gravity field of space it still had significant mass. At least the pressure suits helped by adding to their muscular abilities.

Once again Lucida and Hetti hard-wired the bomb in place and downloaded the software, including the virus. They had just returned the satellite to space when there was a strange thud. Ferrik realized it was conducted sound coming up from the decking through the soles of his magnetized boots. The others had noticed it too.

Ferrik looked around. "Anybody know what that was?"

"Beats me," said Harry.

"Hey, look at that," said Elab, pointing. There was a tiny hole in the starboard side of the bay. They crowded around and peered into it. A small object, probably a meteor, had ripped through the thin skin of the bay. Judging by the angle of the hole it had gone straight up and out through the open bay doors.

"Elab, get a seal on that," said Ferrik, then stopped. Elab was staring at something, his face ashen. Ferrik turned. They were all staring. Lucida's helmet was full of blood.

"Space! Quick. Get her inside," yelled Ferrik.

Veeda put a hand on his arm. "It's too late, Ferrik," she said. "Look."

She was right. The meteor, probably the size of a pea, had gone in through one side of her diamondoid helmet, despite its strength, and out the other. There were tiny droplets of brain matter floating in the air along with a frozen spray of blood, so fine it was easy to miss.

They did what they could for her. Although they could not spare the time they held a brief service. Welkin would have wanted this much, at least. Harry read from the bible Elab had found in the church. They did not commit her remains to space. There wasn't time, and besides, Lucida had said on many occasions that she didn't want to ever go back into space.

The prayer read, everyone took their stations for the next and riskiest part of the whole mission. They were quiet and demoralized, but more than one person's life was at stake.

The next two satellites were in geosynchronous orbit some 22,000 miles above the earth. One was visible from Melbourne and stayed there, except for some slippage from side to side. These satellites were on a different system than the pole-to-pole satellites and Hetti felt they needed to seed at least two of them with the virus.

Ferrik and the others knew that as soon as they swept around the earth's curvature to the other side they would be in full view of whatever space or ground based radar systems or telescopes that the Hiveborn operated, not to mention their commandeered skyship, *Crusader*. Ferrik was hoping to use the sun to partly hide their approach. With this in mind he computed a complex orbit that took them out wide from the planet and brought them in to the first target satellite with the sun at their back. Added to this he hoped that the modified Skyborn shuttles could be mistaken for those of the *Crusader* or any Hiveborn shuttles. There was some chance that they could buy precious minutes through simple mistaken identity, though their gravity warp shuttles had different flight vectors from *Crusader's* antimatter drive shuttles.

He would keep his fingers crossed.

Whether it was the fingers or something else, they made it to the first Pacific satellite without mishap. Ferrik brought the *Capella* alongside and they quickly hauled it in and started the refit. They ran into a slight problem in that the operating system was more advanced than the polar-orbiting satellites. Hetti had to perform a quick upgrade on the virus. She did this in record time and they lobbed the satellite back into its original orbit.

And still they seemed to be in the clear.

"I don't like this," said Harry in a whisper.

"You'd rather they came at us guns blazing?" Elab asked him, also in a whisper.

"I wish I was home in my bed, deep underground, maybe with a cute girlfriend." His eyes strayed briefly to Veeda, who was facing the other way. Elab raised an eyebrow.

"Why are you guys whispering?" Veeda asked without turning her head.

Harry flushed. "Nothing," he said. "Nothing at all. We were just—I was … "

"You got a lock yet, Veeda?" Ferrik asked.

"Just getting it. There. It's on your holoscreen."

Ferrik looked around briefly at them. "Okay. This time we're going to get noticed. We're going for the satellite closest to Melbourne. Anyone with enhanced vision will be able to see us. Stay alert."

The *Capella* pulled away from the satellite and rapidly built up velocity. Ferrik didn't bother trying to hide this time. Speed was what they needed now. Speed and a lot of luck. Harry stared at the forward viewscreens, wondering how Welkin was doing and why he hadn't come on this mission. Maybe he'd felt there was less chance of direct contact with zombies this way. The thought of them—of what the parasites did inside their brains— still made him queasy. In fact, it was making him feel ill now. He wondered if there were any sick bags handy.

"No signal acquisition," said Veeda. "We're still invisible, except to the curious natives."

"What about radio transmission? Harry?"

Harry shoved in an ear piece, listened for a beat, checking a broad range of frequencies. In reality the plasma and quantum computers did that better than a human could. "All clear. No unusual traffic. But then we might not pick up a coded directional signal."

"We're coming up on our target. Order straps to lock in. This is going to be a bit rough." Ferrik didn't have time to do this by the book, but plugged in his neural jack for extra input. He used his speed to climb to a higher orbit, saw that he was dropping back towards the satellite, whizzed past it, then used a burst of speed to bring it up on the shiny lump of metal and foil. He killed his speed only a few feet from the satellite.

"Fancy flying, Ferrik," said Veeda, admiringly. Harry frowned. It hadn't occurred to him that Veeda might like Ferrik. He would have to revise his future marriage plans. A shame. She seemed like a really nice girl.

"Let's move it. Just Elab and Hetti. Veeda, you and Harry monitor sensors. Yell if you see anything." Ferrik and the others hurried aft. The process of pulling in the satellite and refitting it was almost second nature now and they had it down to an art. A fast art.

But it wasn't fast enough.

"We got something," Harry said over the intercom. "Company maybe."

"Maybe?" said Ferrik from the bay. "Either we have or we haven't. Where is it?"

"That's just it. It's on the moon."

In the bay, Ferrik, through his neural jack, received the data Harry had received. It showed that there had been a radio burst about 90 seconds earlier followed almost immediately by what was clearly the visual signature of some type of shuttle craft taking off from the moon's surface.

"Jam all earth-side traffic, Harry. Broadband. The lot. Maybe Earth doesn't know."

"Already jammed. How are you guys going?"

"Fair. We should be long gone by the time they get here."

They went through the process of refitting the satellite, once again assisted by the pressure suits. Everyone was getting jumpy and making clumsy mistakes. Elab dropped a spanner and had to dive after it, nearly ripping his suit on the control console.

"Everyone take a deep breath," Ferrik ordered. Panic sweat was stinging his eyes and now he desperately wanted to wipe his brow. The suit, which had seemed quite comfortable before, was suddenly claustrophobic and hostile.

Hetti downloaded the virus and hit the same problem as before except this time the patch she had worked up for the Pacific satellite didn't work.

"Damn it," she said. "My patch has contaminated the system. It's gone into diagnostic mode. I can't download the virus till it finishes."

Ferrik groaned. "How long?"

"Let me check." She ran some kind of subsidiary program, then looked grim. "Fifteen minutes."

"You're joking."

"You wish," she said.

"We can't do it," Ferrik said. "We'll have to abandon it."

"It won't work," Hetti said. "By the time the diagnostic is finished, it will have removed the download at the Pacific satellite. The geosynchronous satellites will still be fully functioning eyes in the sky and they will nail us on the ground."

"But if its own defense mechanism hunts down and destroys the virus, then what's the point?"

"The point is," said Hetti, "that if you stop arguing with me, then somewhere in the next thirteen and a half minutes I can construct a program that will render the guidance software and the virus invisible to the diagnostic scan. Okay?"

Ferrik had to make a decision. Fifteen minutes should still be plenty of time for them to get away, but they were risking their lives. On the other hand, that was why they had come here. To get the mission done. For the first time in his life, Ferrik realized that he was dispensable, that there was in fact something as arcane as a "greater good." It was a lonely kind of feeling.

"Do it."

The time ticked by. Ferrik crossed to the console and peered at the holoscreen. He had difficulty matching it to the computing maps within the ship's memory systems. He called to Harry via the neural jack's comm. connection. "I think my jack is on the fritz," he said, unplugging it. It was a problem that had occurred occasionally over recent months. "Check time of arrival on that shuttle, Harry."

"I already checked it."

"And?"

"Ten minutes."

"But that's not possible. It'd take this shuttle an hour to get to the moon and that's at higher gravities."

"As you say, boss," said Harry.

Ferrik reined in his emotions. "Why didn't you say something?"

"You're on an open comm. link down there, and I don't have access to your neural jack. I heard what you and Hetti said. I figured we were here to do the job."

A silence, then, "You ready to be a hero?"

"I don't know. Heroes always seem to get dead, fast. Personally, I'd rather be a live chicken than a dead hero."

"Guess you signed up on the wrong mission."

"Funny you should say that."

"If they get here before we're done we'll be sitting ducks."

"Yeah, our gooses will be cooked."

"Keep me posted, Harry."

"You got it."

A few minutes later: "Ferrik?"

"Yes, Harry."

"There's a heap of radio activity up there. It looks like ... it *looks* as if there's a bunch of miniature satellites in moon orbit. A lot of the activity is coming from the far side and being bounced around by the satellite network. Possibly with laser communications."

"What's that about?"

"It's got me beat."

"Anything getting through to Earth?"

"No, but I think that may be the cause of all the excitement."

"You decipher any of it?"

"One of the lasers is leaking information in our direction here and there, it must be malfunctioning, but it's too compressed. I'd need Hetti's help."

"Okay. Just record it for now."

In the repair bay, Hetti performed miracles. Two minutes before the diagnostic finished and three minutes before the Hiveborn shuttle was due to arrive she had a program. The diagnostic finished on time. They downloaded the new data, sealed up the satellite, and got it back into space. Then Ferrik returned to the control room in record time.

He had the engines fired up before Elab and Hetti had strapped themselves in.

"Here we go. Let's get the Space out of here." He accelerated away from the Melbourne satellite and it quickly disappeared astern. "I'd love to know what's going on up there." He gestured at the moon. "They must have kept a shuttle on the surface, maybe in one of the craters, just to monitor orbital activity around Earth. Cunning bastards."

"That's why our activities on the other side went unnoticed," said Veeda.

"Yeah," Harry agreed, nervously eyeing the screen showing the quadrant of space in which the moon sat. The Hiveborn shuttle was a metallic glint in the middle of it. "Moonless night."

"That was just dumb luck," said Ferrik.

"Maybe," said Elab. "But the elders always said luck comes to those who deserve it."

"I don't remember them saying that," said Harry.

"What do you remember them saying?"

"Oh, you're the smartest kid in the class, Harry. One day you'll be Chief Elder."

"Yeah, right." Conversation petered out. They could all see that the Hiveborn ship was veering off its original trajectory in order to intercept them.

"Here they come," said Ferrik.

The Hiveborn ship came in guns blazing. Ferrik dodged the first attack easily. Indeed, there was a clumsiness to the maneuvering that gave him momentary hope. But only momentary. Whoever was piloting the other ship learnt quickly, as did the gunner.

Ferrik ordered them all into pressure suits, helmets and all.

"You got any ideas?" Harry asked Ferrik. He and Elab were operating the weapons systems, but a lack of training made their own attempts as poor as the Hiveborn's initial inaccuracy.

"I'm going to dive down into the atmosphere. To follow us they'll have to come in at the same speed. We'll both be in radio blackout. But I've got to set us up for re-entry first."

The Hiveborn ship swept past. A low-level pulse hit the left front guidance fork, leaving it a smoking ruin. A streak of hot, blue swearing erupted from Harry's mouth.

"Seems they guessed what I was planning. The black hole's still under some control."

"We can't re-enter?"

"Not at speed."

Moments later the battle was over. The Hiveborn gunner crippled the Earth shuttle's other guidance fork, leaving the black hole sitting still in front of the saucer. Ferrik had to shut them down before they went critical and lost the singularity completely. If the safety system came on line, the gravity drive would implode into m-brane hyperspace—basic string cosmology, according to the textbooks—and vanish from their world, taking them along with it. At least the Hiveborn would go with them if it came to that, thought Ferrik.

Right now they were dead in the water.

"Guess this is where they blast us into cosmic dust," said Harry. He turned to Veeda. "If we'd survived this would you have gone out with me?"

Veeda looked startled then managed a smile. "I would have loved to."

Harry's heart lurched. "Just my luck."

They waited for the final blast that would send them into the final darkness. But it didn't come. Instead there was a beep from Veeda's console.

She frowned. "Incoming message."

"Patch it through on ship-wide audio," said Ferrik.

The speaker crackled for a second then cleared. "This is the captain of the *Luna*. Shut down your weapons systems and prepare to be boarded."

They all looked at each other. Harry reached over and took Veeda's hand in his. She clutched it tightly. "Is this the part where we start popping pills?" he asked, a catch in his voice.

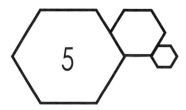

5

Welkin's shuttle, the *Procyon*, flew low, its forks holding its black hole before it, lasers burning away atmospheric friction, largely outside of the visible spectrum—only a slight bluish tinge revealed the lasers' actions. Arton was in the pilot's seat and followed much the same process as Ferrik had followed: the holoscreen at the front showed safe corridors in blue and danger areas in red. But the fact was that their journey was far shorter, only a 1000 miles or so.

They still had not solved the problem of how to approach Melbourne close enough to carry out their mission nor how they were going to make a snatch, as Hatch had started calling it. Also along for the ride were Gillian, Daniel, a medical assistant named Karl, and a female cruiser pilot called Joy.

They were cruising along at approximately 100 feet. Below them the sea disappeared behind them at frightening speed, its surface a choppy gunmetal gray under what was becoming an increasingly overcast sky.

"Rain ahead," said Arton.

"Good," Welkin said. "Anything that makes us hard to see suits me."

"It'll get a bit bumpy."

As the storm closed in Arton took them up to 200 feet. They had a clear corridor ahead, at least as far as landfall in about half an hour.

As visibility dropped off outside, conversation inside also languished. Gillian sat down next to Welkin and put her arm around him.

"We keep doing this," she said softly so that only he could hear.

"Doing what?"

"Going into danger. You think we could find another lifestyle sometime?"

He smiled. "Listen to you," he said. "Miss Gung-ho herself. Wasn't it you who rushed off to the camp all by yourself?"

"That was a previous life. I've mellowed since then."

"That I have to see."

"I think I'm tired," Gillian said, resting her head on his shoulder. "And the bad guys just keep getting bigger. Every time we knock one of them down another one pops up, only he's even deadlier than the one before. I'm over it."

"Amen to that."

"If we come through this, I want to have a family."

He gazed down at her, startled. Her eyes were closed, so she didn't see the smile start on his face, but she heard it in his voice. "Really?"

"Uh-huh."

They landed near the old family farm in the Dandenongs, the site of their battle with the prophet Tolk, and their last home before moving to Martha.

They spent that first rainy night inside the shuttle and for a long time they watched the rain clouds part and flash into vapor on the viewscreens. The monotonous drone of pattering rain seemed detached from the storm they were watching, as though it were a soundtrack playing independently of the storm. One by one they drifted off to sleep only to awaken before dawn while it was still dark. Their webbing restraints automatically detached themselves.

They had four cruisers on board. Each was wired with explosives in case of discovery. An hour before it was due to get light, Welkin, Gillian, Hatch and Joy all set off to cover different sections of the approach to Melbourne and surrounding areas. They would take photographs and gather whatever information they could.

"Under no circumstance are you to make contact with anybody. I don't care if you see your long lost sister wandering along a country road. You stay away. We need information and we need it to come back. You keep radio silence unless it's an emergency."

"And if we get caught?" asked Hatch.

"BANG," shouted Gillian, making Joy flinch.

Welkin shrugged. "Don't get caught."

"I can't believe I volunteered for this," Hatch grumbled as he mounted a cruiser. "I'll be seeing you all."

He gunned the gyros and shot out of the cruiser bay door. He barely cleared some trees and was soon lost to sight.

"Maybe we should have given him a bit more training," Gillian said.

Joy seemed nervous and reluctant to leave. "You don't think they'll spot us?"

"The satellites aren't programmed to pick up anything as small as a cruiser and it's unlikely the Hiveborn will see a one-person vehicle as a threat."

"But you don't know that for sure, do you?"

Gillian placed a hand on Joy's arm. "Yes, he does. Just don't ask him how he knows. He gets all Zen-Buddhist when you do."

Joy managed a laugh. "Okay. Eyes open."

"You too, Joy." She revved up, took a deep breath, and sailed out of the bay, handling the cruiser with a great deal more skill than Hatch.

Alone now, Welkin and Gillian hugged briefly. "You be careful," she told him.

"*You* be careful."

"Okay, we'll both be careful."

Welkin watched her go, his heart in his throat. If something happened to her he didn't think he would be able to carry on. Or rather he didn't think he would want to carry on.

He mounted the cruiser and signaled Arton who had remained up in the control cabin with Daniel. "Everyone's away," he said. "Just me left."

"Good hunting," Arton said and Welkin heard the doctor echo this sentiment in the background.

He guided the cruiser out through the bay doors which started to close behind him. Immediately he veered away south, the same direction Joy had taken, though he would change course shortly and quest through the south-west quadrant. None of them knew how close they could approach Melbourne on one-person cruisers. This was part of the process. He just hoped they all survived.

Dawn light crept up the sky in the east and ragged clouds glowed red and pink. Welkin flew at treetop level, disturbing colonies of yellow-crested cockatoos and long-beaked magpies. Birds did not bother him though. He was more afraid of running into a swarm of fruit bats returning from their nightly feed. Fruit bats often flew in great clouds numbering thousands of individuals. To fly into such a cloud on a cruiser was suicide, even with computer assist.

Welkin soon found what he was looking for: a narrow river overhung with trees. He followed this for some time, skimming only a few feet above the water. It slowed his progress but made him almost impossible to detect, either from the air or by any ground-based radar short of the ancient Jindalee over-the-horizon systems, whose ruined towers dotted Northern Australia. He was, however, seen on at least one occasion by a group of men and women bathing in the river. They were too startled to do more than freeze as he shot into view from a bend in the river and raced over their heads. He had a fleeting glimpse of gaping mouths and staring eyes and then he was gone.

Some hours later he knew he was within a few miles of the outskirts of Melbourne. This is where it became dangerous. He must gain height to obtain useful photographs. No one knew for sure what changes the Hiveborn had made to the city or the surrounding terrain. Information fed back through the grapevine was patchy and fragmented and did not always add up into a coherent picture. They knew that a lot of the inner city had been rebuilt and an entire warehouse and administration district had been constructed along the Yarra River where the old Flinders Street train station had once stood. Stretching out from there, like a spider web, was a network of new roads and power conduits. At least, this is what they thought they knew.

Welkin came to the edge of some hills and gazed down at the plain below on which—in the distance—Melbourne was built. All that he could see from here were ancient ruins and tree-covered mounds that had once been buildings. A few rusted metal skeletons and nanodiamond spires still reared into the sky, festooned with climbing plants and the nests of seagulls and pigeons.

He hovered at tree level, scanning in all directions. He saw no movement either on the ground or in the air.

"Well, here we go," he murmured to himself and gunned the accelerator, climbing rapidly to cloud level, about 5000 feet at the moment. The thick woolly cumulus clouds were drifting slowly east, away from their thermal source. He floated with them, switching from cloud to cloud as necessary. He also switched on the digital camera as soon as he gained sufficient height, putting it on automatic. He heard the soft click as it took its first photo.

Welkin systematically quartered the area, hanging just below the clouds and slightly inside. Not enough to obscure the pictures but possibly enough to give him some cover. He also shot off some video footage when he saw a line of trucks heading out of the city.

He had been doing this for an hour when he saw the two cruisers coming for him fast. His radar had not detected them, they were jamming it with puffs of some sort of sparkling, computer-controlled chaff that flew around them for a time before running out of power. Like 20th century dog-fighters the cruiser pilots were using the sun to conceal their attack run. And it almost worked. The only thing that gave them away was that Welkin happened to see their shadows on the ground below.

His hours of training, in both mock dog-fights and the real thing, paid off. Thinking was doing and in the same moment that he saw the shadows he had nailed the accelerator and veered into the cloud, the automatic controls compensating. For a moment, eerily, the clouds seemed like red jelly and he shuddered. A laserlite pulse seared through the space he had occupied a second earlier.

The cloud offered only limited cover. They could still track him by radar though they probably wouldn't risk firing more pulses. The radar wasn't accurate enough for that. In any case he wasn't hanging around to find out. He had all the pictures and video he needed. He edged the speed up till the cruiser was fairly screaming through the air. In seconds he shot out of the cloud heading back east. Three miles away thick forest carpeted the earth. If he could reach the safety of the trees he knew the Hiveborn would be no match for him, no matter what arcane technology they may have brought back with them from the stars.

But his attackers had anticipated his move and one of them was waiting for him. That was nearly his end but Welkin had lightning reflexes and he had learned through hard experience that the best offence was often the most unexpected. So he flew straight at the Hiveborn, not veering an inch.

The Hiveborn clearly did not know what was going on. Welkin was not behaving as he should. Was this a suicide attempt?

The Hiveborn's automatics started to swerve the cruisers aside but not fast enough. Welkin's cruiser almost brushed the pilot's head, the shock rendering her unconscious. She slumped against her controls and the cruiser started to descend in a slow spiral, landing automatically. Welkin doubted he had seriously injured the zombie, but it was one less attacker.

He did not know where the other was and did not wait to find out. He raced across the intervening space and dived in amongst the trees, rocketing above tree and shrub-shrouded roads no longer used by wheeled traffic. Now he was glad for the automatic safeties despite the constant jiggling and weaving.

He did not see his attacker until the man dropped down out of the trees above him and tried ramming him, much as Welkin had tried ramming his colleague. Luck saved Welkin. Then they were tearing along side by side, both machines trying frantically to avoid trees and each other. The zombie reached over and tried to shove Welkin out of his seat. Welkin reared back and punched him. The blow must have rattled the zombie and he pulled a little distance away. They were still screaming along above the road, every now and then weaving past trees and other obstacles. The zombie reached for his radio and Welkin whipped out his laserlite. He did not have the heart to shoot the man so he fired at the cruiser's control panel, blasting it to ruin, then put another shot into its engine. It sputtered and smoke vented as it tried to self-repair, panels sliding over each other as it sealed off damaged circuitry architecture. The Hiveborn cruiser fell behind.

Welkin was the first to return to the shuttle and he spent an anxious two hours before he spotted another cruiser skimming the treetops. It was Gillian. She had a scorch mark across one cheek but otherwise was okay. Welkin sat down, suddenly aware that his legs were weak and he was breathing hard.

Hatch did not return until nightfall. He had been cornered by a gang of cruisers and had led them a merry chase north into rural Victoria. He had holed up at some falls and waited for dark. Both he and Gillian had their cameras' data in CRCs, as well as several hours of video. All in all it was a good day's work.

Except that Joy never came back.

It was only later, some time in the middle of the night, that Arton realized there was a recorded message in the databank. It seemed Joy had broken radio silence for a hi-speed burst and the computer had mistaken it for a normal data entry.

"The control room was never empty for more than five minutes," Arton kept saying. "I should have heard it come in."

"It's not your fault," said Welkin. "There was nothing you could have done."

The message was decompressed and they listened to the sounds of laserlite fire and Joy's harsh breathing. She sounded like someone in intense pain. " … cornered … too many … Damn them, damn them to hell! But listen— I found a way in … " Static, then: " … pulling the plug … goodbye … " There was a series of beeps.

"Oh God," said Gillian. "That's the countdown—"

There was a muffled explosion and the recording went silent. Gillian blinked back tears. Welkin put an arm around her.

Hatch stared at the control panel. "She blew herself up," he said in wonder. "But she was so scared of death … "

Nobody slept well that night. Outside the wind howled and at some point rain hammered the shuttle. The sound of it was oddly comforting and eventually most of them drifted off into a disturbed and restless sleep. The next day they were red-eyed and weary.

After breakfast, they got down to reviewing the data.

Hatch's photographs proved the most interesting in the end. He had distant shots of Melbourne airspace and it seemed full of cruisers. Antimatter-powered shuttles took off and landed twice during the time he was watching. At least one went straight up, apparently into space. He also videoed a fleet of hover-trucks, energized by plutonium powerpaks, snaking north out of the city. Each truck was flanked by two zombies on cruisers—also, of course, with powerpaks—and several more cruisers circled several hundred feet up, keeping lookout.

"Whatever the cargo is, they think it's valuable," said Gillian.

"My guess is they're full of parasites," said Welkin.

Hatch nodded. "I figure the zombie bastards find a town or village, invite all the locals in, and bam! Bunch of new recruits. Talk about conscription!"

Daniel frowned. "How quickly does assimilation occur?" he asked.

Welkin thought back to the time on *Colony* when he, Theo and Ferrik had witnessed Hiveborn recruits "infecting" crew personnel: the alien body sliding into the ear canal; the eyes becoming aware, yet somehow remaining vacant; the rigid limbs growing lithe; and the all-powerful mind of the Hive taking possession. "Under thirty seconds," he said.

The doctor stared at him. "Are you serious?"

Welkin nodded. "They're fully functional within a minute. And they know things without being told. You know what it was like? It was like inserting a data-filled CRC into your computer. Suddenly it knows things it didn't know before."

"So they have some way of communicating directly with the parasites wherever the parasites are stored and in whatever storage medium they are held."

"The red jelly," said Welkin. "They're kept in vats of red jelly."

"The jelly is a nutrient which they can absorb directly. As we've speculated … perhaps they've developed a chemical method of communication. Insects already do that on Earth. They could then program the parasites with all current knowledge whilst they're still in their 'womb' so to speak. That way as soon as they're planted inside a hapless host, they're up to speed instantly." He shook his head in wonder. "Very impressive."

Hatch hefted his laserlite. "Well, I've got something else that'll impress the little bastards."

"Anybody see how we could make a close approach to Melbourne?"

Gillian and Hatch shook their heads but Gillian looked thoughtful. "Joy did."

"That doesn't help us much," said Welkin.

"Could try cleaning up the message," said Hatch. "Lot of static there. Maybe something inside the static."

"Good idea. You and Arton get on that right away. Gillian and I will keep going over the photographs."

They spent the next few hours at it. Daniel and his medical colleague Karl, made pots of coffee and sandwiches. Karl was a biochemist. Recently, he had also trained as an anesthetist in case they needed to render their "acquisitions" unconscious. All this was new to him and he seemed in awe of these people who so nonchalantly risked their lives and put themselves in danger. His own life had been rather sheltered, he realized.

They found nothing that was useful.

The city was well guarded, both on the ground and in the air. Hopefully Ferrik's mission was going well. If the virus had been uploaded successfully, it would mean that their shuttle would become invisible to satellite surveillance, quite apart from the other benefits of viral infection.

That afternoon they regrouped. Hatch and Arton had been unsuccessful in cleaning up the recorded message from Joy. They'd identified one word— "medium"—which hadn't been heard before but there was no context to it.

"Okay," said Welkin, "as I see it we don't have much choice. I say we hit the convoy of trucks. We can track them from a fairly safe altitude and see if they split up at all, then go for the smallest group."

"I thought we wanted parasites inside living hosts?" said Hatch.

"We do, ideally. But whatever happens, we need live parasites. It may be that we can capture some of the guards and truck drivers. Karl, you need to rig some kind of spray gun for the anesthetic. Everybody is to carry a net. We know the zombies will kill themselves rather then be captured and we have to prevent that at all costs." He looked around at them. "Any questions?"

Hatch put up his hand. "Can I un-volunteer?"

"Sure you can," said Welkin. "Soon as we get back to Martha."

"That sucks."

They found the convoy 200 miles north of Melbourne. Though the hover-trucks could make good time over cleared roads or empty fields, there was a shortage of these outside of the metropolitan area, which itself had only been "tidied up"—as Gillian put it—in recent months. Indeed, except for the Kiwis, they were all amazed at the changes they had been able to see of the central city area. The Hiveborn might be the most lethal plague ever to hit Earth, but they were a damned neat one.

They watched the convoy as often as they could from a height of some 40,000 feet, ever mindful of the continuously shifting blue corridors and patches on the satellite monitor. They did not know for sure if Ferrik's team had been successful or not. They could find out but only by bouncing a coded signal off the nearest satellite. If they were wrong, the satellite would immediately know who and where they were and would spare no time in alerting the Hiveborn.

On the second day, the convoy split into two. Five trucks continued north and four headed west. Welkin ordered everybody to battle stations.

Three hours later they struck. Like his own earlier attackers, but without smartchaff, they lifted from the treetops and then came out of the sun, moving with lethal speed. They destroyed two trucks and several cruisers before any resistance was offered. Welkin and Gillian and Hatch shot from the rear bay on armed cruisers and engaged the high-flying sentries while Arton took the shuttle in, neutralizing the remaining flankers.

They grounded near the two remaining trucks which had been only lightly damaged. Arton and Karl rushed out with anesthetic sprays and nets. They were halfway to the nearest truck when it exploded. The force of the blast knocked them backwards off their feet. Shrapnel ripped off one of Karl's fingers and gave Arton a gaping scalp wound that sluiced blood down his face. They were just picking themselves up, when the other truck exploded. They hit the ground again.

Moments later, Welkin, Gillian and Hatch set down close by and came running over. Gillian tended to Karl's hand wound while the others gingerly approached the smoking wreckage. Luckily the powerpaks were designed from old-time materials and had not been dispersed along with their toxic, radioactive plutonium cores. They found no body parts, but there were thousands of barbecued parasites scattered across the ground in a large radius.

"They were booby-trapped," said Welkin. "The trucks were booby-trapped."

"But why? It doesn't make any sense," Arton said, while Gillian wrapped a bandage around his head. "They didn't know we were coming."

Welkin waited for Gillian to tie off the bandage. "Yes, they did," he said. "They knew."

"Huh?"

Hatch nodded in agreement. "Yeah. *Huh?*"

"Look, these things have been out there for millions of years. I know that. It's all in here." He tapped his skull. "Think about it. They must have encountered every kind of resistance and retaliation imaginable. And they're prepared for it. Booby-traps. Backups. Backups within backups. Triple quadruple redundancy. And endless bloody patience."

"You don't paint a very promising future," said Arton. He held up his face so Gillian could wipe the blood from it.

Hatch scratched his head. "What chance have we got against that?" he wanted to know.

Welkin actually smiled. "Every strength has its weakness," he said cryptically.

"Meaning?"

"Meaning that maybe—just maybe—human beings are kind of unique in the Galaxy. Maybe they've never run into anything quite like us."

Gillian and Karl had joined them. Gillian said, "Is that one of your download intuitions?"

"Yes, it is. And I'm getting another one right now."

"What?" Arton demanded.

"That this place is about to become hotter than a hornet's nest."

They searched the sky. "Let's get out of here," said Gillian. The cruisers were guided back on board and the *Procyon* took off at high speed. Welkin was glad that *Colony*'s shuttles were so vastly superior, courtesy of the elders' modifications when they had arrived on Earth. Sticking to tree height it went north, heading for the open desert of the continent's interior. It soared across fields and forests, tearing away leaves and canopies; it followed rivers, dove into gorges, all the time carefully staying within the blue safety zone.

They spent the night near Darwin in a dry river canyon, the high sheer walls of which afforded them near perfect protection from alien eyes in the sky.

But as they sat down to dinner, it was a listless demoralized group who faced each other across the table. For some time, they ate in silence.

After dinner Arton returned to the control room to monitor sensors and go over the data gathered earlier by the scouts. He was becoming slightly obsessive with this and Welkin worried that the mission failure might be affecting him badly.

"So what do we do now?" asked Daniel. He at least was still cheerily optimistic. He had collected some dead parasites at the explosion site—choosing ones that were not entirely carbonized—and he and Karl had been dissecting and running tests on them.

Welkin held up his hands, helpless. "Our main mission is a wash-out. Going anywhere near Melbourne—or Sydney for that matter—would just be a suicide mission and that's not our job here. We have to acquire living humans hosting living parasites. The only way I can see of doing it is to infiltrate a small town or community. We can make out we're traders and we want to set up some kind of exchange system."

"But we could be walking into a trap. An entire town could be infected and we would not easily know this," said Daniel.

"That's right. And I guess peering into people's ears might be taken the wrong way, even if they're not zombies."

The doctor chuckled at the idea. "Well, we have the anesthetic spray. Perhaps the best we can do is simply waylay people at random and hope we strike lucky. If not, we apologize profusely and get out of there."

Welkin smiled. "I like your approach, doctor. That's much the way I'd figured it. I think we lie low here for another day, let things settle down, then head into New South Wales, check out coastal towns north of Sydney."

"Let's not forget," said Gillian, "that we're still dealing with dangerous people. Even if they're not zombies, there's plenty of folk out there who shoot first and eat later."

Daniel and Karl stared at her. Karl said, swallowing, "You don't mean—"

"That's just what I mean. Somebody says they'd love to have you over for dinner, my advice is get out of there fast."

The meeting broke up, but a moment later there was a yell from the control room. Welkin and Gillian exchanged startled looks then raced forward. They found Arton poring over maps of Melbourne. He had a big grin on his face.

"Are you all right?" Gillian asked. "How's the head?"

"I'm fine."

Welkin looked at him and said a little grumpily, "You ever hear of the boy who cried wolf?"

"You ever hear of the boy who cried water?" Arton asked straight back.

Daniel and Karl had joined them by now and everybody looked at Arton as if he was beginning to crack under the strain.

"Look, I think I know what Joy was trying to tell us. She did find a way to approach Melbourne. You see, I suddenly remembered that Joy had been in the group of people I was training to pilot shuttles. You know Sarah's idea that we've got to pass on our knowledge, duplicate our skills? Well, Joy wanted to fly shuttles. That's why she learned to fly a cruiser first."

"So?" Welkin asked.

"Well, she understood the flight characteristics of shuttles. Look at the map here. I worked out where she had to be when she sent the message. The pulse was also picked up by each of your cruisers. They don't have the means to record that kind of thing but it still registers in the data log. By triangulating the signal I realized she was over Port Phillip Bay, down near the peninsula, heading north—the change in signal strength told me that. So she was heading *into* the bay."

"Again, so?"

"And she said the word 'medium'." He looked around at them, as if expecting them to get it. When they didn't, he groaned. "Water is a medium."

"Water?" Hatch said.

"Yes, water. Water is—in aerodynamic terms—a fluid medium exactly like air. It has the same characteristics. Bernoulli's Theorem—which explains how airplanes generate wing lift—was originally developed with water pressure in mind. Our shuttles however fall *into* a modified gravity well, cleared of friction effects by lasers. Though it's more of a power drain, they can deal with denser mediums. Anyway, the long and short of it is, we can get right up close and personal to Melbourne by traveling under water!"

They stared at him.

Hatch said, quite casually, "Is he certifiable?"

"Definitely," said Gillian. She reached out and placed the back of her hand on Arton's forehead, then looked at the others gravely. "He has a fever."

"Probably a brain fever."

"Don't you need a brain for that?"

"Will you all shut up and listen?" Arton suddenly shouted in exasperation. "Ouch. It hurts when I scream. Look, this is what Joy was trying to tell us. Don't you see? The *Procyon* can travel under water."

"It's a shuttle, Arton, not a bloody submarine," said Hatch, not unkindly.

"Wait a minute," said Welkin. "Let him talk."

"So-called *space* shuttles are hermetically sealed craft with self-contained propulsive systems." Their faces were still blank, except Welkin's. "They're airtight."

"Oh," said Gillian. "Like submarines."

"So they don't leak?" said Hatch.

"And what Joy knew from studying our shuttles' gravity warp drives was that our shuttles don't care whether they're flying through vacuum, air or water. It's all the same to them, other than in terms of ultimate velocities and vectoring and the energy cost of reducing frictional resistance. Our shuttle's lasers will boil the water a bit, that's all." He tapped the map which featured Melbourne and, just south of it, close to the city center, the huge expanse of Port Phillip Bay. "We can submerge somewhere off the south coast of Australia, even as far away as Tasmania—or further if you like—and we can travel under water, into Port Phillip Bay, and right up to the docks and the storm drains. A bit slower, perhaps, to avoid leaving a giant wake of vapor." He suddenly grinned. "It's like having our own tunnel right into town."

The others exchanged looks. A slow smile spread around the room.

The noises from outside were eerie. For some reason, all sounds within the shuttle were magnified, echoing. They had been submerged for nearly eight hours moving on a steady course northwards, leaving a trail of superheated and shock-dead sharks and other marine creatures in their wake. In a few more minutes they would pass between the headlands and enter the bay. If anything was going to happen it would be in the next stage of the journey.

Even their own voices seemed muffled by the weight of water above them and they tended to talk in whispers.

"Entering the bay now," said Arton. They had turned down the cabin lights so that as few telltale signs as possible leaked out the portholes. Because of this Arton's face reflected the lights of the control board in front of him. Data from his computer screen could be seen written across his eyeballs, reversed, and mysteriously hieroglyphic.

No one said anything for long moments. Then a deep rumble became audible. Arton killed the shuttle's speed so that it coasted along at just a few knots.

"A ship," said Arton, looking up at the ceiling. "A big one. Let's hope they aren't using sonar."

The rumble grew and became a distinct *chugga-chugga-chugga*. Then just as quickly it faded. "I'm going to send up a micro-buoy."

He hit a switch. There was a soft whooshing sound. Moments later data started to feedback. "I've up-linked to the satellite."

Welkin thought back. After leaving their hidey-hole near Darwin they had headed across the Indian Ocean, swinging round in a great curve till they were aimed at Antarctica. Along the way he had decided to risk sending the coded signal to the nearest satellite. It was a risk, but he had known that he would need good hard data if they were to pull off this mission.

They'd been rewarded with Ferrik's pre-recorded voice: "You are now tuned to Station Peek-a-Boo. You have a green light."

So Ferrik's team had been successful. The satellites were now infected with the worm. That meant Welkin's shuttle was invisible to those monitoring the satellite feeds. It also meant they could download data and actually study Melbourne in real time from space. The zoom capabilities were sufficient to read the label on a can of baked beans—if they knew the right target—if they could use enough of the thousand or so satellite fiber cameras without alerting the Hiveborn.

Arton now called up a view of Port Phillip Bay. His own computer overlaid a ghostly blip where the shuttle would have been if it were on the surface. From this they could see that there was very little shipping in the bay. The boat that had passed them recently was already crossing the Tasman, heading for Tasmania. No doubt it contained thousands of warm pulsing parasites just itching to get their tentacles into some earthly eardrums. Welkin was tempted to go after the ship but after a brief discussion he dismissed the idea. None of them had any experience with ships or even sea travel. Too many things could go wrong.

"Better the devil we know than one we don't," he said finally.

They kept going, moving in closer and closer to the city end of the bay. As they drew nearer they called up satellite real time viewing and zoomed in on the city center and docklands. What was once Southbank, opposite Flinders Street train station, was now a vast complex of warehouses, administrative buildings and dormitories, all linked by cleared roads and a passenger transit system. It seemed almost impossible that so much had been done in so little time. It somehow shamed the Earthborn that these aliens had landed and accomplished so much. But Welkin pointed out that the aliens had the benefit of vast experience and more advanced technology, not to mention an inhuman ability to organize, cooperate and work. Welkin doubted that there was one idle conversation in the whole city, nor a curse or an argument. Everything was harmonious.

As they closed in towards the shore Welkin remarked, "Well, it's time to bring a little disharmony to paradise."

Reaching a point some 200 yards offshore they allowed the shuttle to sink gently to the bottom and sit there while they studied the real time feed from the satellites as they cruised overhead, sweeping vast chunks of the terrain as they did so. Although the polar-orbiting satellites gave clearer, more detailed views of Melbourne, and offered varied angles, each optimum viewing period was no more than 12 minutes' long for each pass. By then, the angle was too steep. They achieved the best results by combing the different shots. One thing that became instantly clear was that the Hiveborn did not utilize water transport. Other than the ship that passed overhead as they entered the bay there was not one other surface craft in sight, either on the bay or in the river.

"I think we can move upriver," said Arton. "There are bound to be storm drains emptying into it."

Welkin nodded. "We suit up and go in through the drains and pop up wherever we need to, grab some zombies, and hightail back here. I like it."

"With luck," said Gillian, "we could do all this by nightfall."

Welkin shook his head. "I want to wait till dark before we go in. It may not help us much but I've got a feeling the Hiveborn are more dormant at night. Something to do with their world of origin … "

They spent the rest of the day planning and getting whatever sleep they could. It was agreed that everyone except Arton would go. They needed the doctor and Karl to supervise the proper acquisition and anesthetization of zombies, and they needed as many guns to cover them as possible. Welkin was beginning to think they should have brought more backup, but it was too late now.

Arton moved the shuttle into position. Using his local scanners, he located the entrances to three storm drains clustered together beneath the water line. There was no way to tell which of these would offer the best passage into the city. Some might be collapsed and impassable; others blocked further along and made habitable for cavers.

An hour before they were due to start, they all convened in the cargo bay. Daniel and Karl had their equipment stored there—knapsacks containing medkits and a sealed medical container to preserve live specimens—and the pressure suits they would wear underwater were also stored in lockers nearby. Welkin and Gillian showed the two medical men how to use these.

Arton was unhappy he was being left behind, but Welkin pointed out they needed to keep their best pilot for what would probably be an emergency takeoff.

At the appointed time, they suited up, checked each other out, and took up their loads. Arton, looking glum, cycled them through the airlock. Welkin had reconfigured the suits' programming so they could walk along the bottom without buoyancy problems.

Outside the airlock they found the bottom covered in debris. They were able to make their way across this with little difficulty. Welkin had worried that the river bottom might be a dangerous sludge of mud and silt that would ensnare them, wasting their time and possibly placing them at risk.

Visibility was so bad Welkin was forced to use infrared lamps. He didn't dare use ordinary light since it could be seen from the nearest bank.

"Go to infrared everybody." A digital overlay appeared on the inside of his own faceplate. Suddenly the bottom of the river leapt out in detail and there, dead ahead, were the three dark drain mouths.

He had no idea which one to choose but as he stood before the eight-foot diameter drain he felt a continuous surge of water from the left hand mouth and nothing from the other two. He led them into the active drain, figuring that it must be reasonably clear of debris to produce such a surge. Walking against the current wasn't easy but with the assistance of the suit's artificial muscles it was doable and would certainly aid a quick getaway.

However, there *were* obstructions. The base of the drain was silted up and impeded their walking. There were also a great many broken crates, pieces of furniture, and general detritus that had nowhere else to go, discards from the rebuilding program above, clogging the base of the pipe.

Despite this they managed to penetrate into the system for several hundred yards. At some point they emerged from the water and after this they were able to retract their nanodiamond faceplates and wade through the flow that was now hip deep.

It was tiring and the water was cold, despite the suits. Nor were they able to travel in a straight line. The drains branched and branched again and many were blocked off. The water surge had found its own torturous dog-leg journey to the river.

After more than an hour of this, Welkin called a halt at the base of a metal ladder. The rungs were rusted and deformed and encrusted with slime and garbage.

"I'm going to see if I can get the cover open and take a look around." He started climbing. Gillian watched with apprehension.

The ladder led into a narrow tube in the ceiling of the tunnel and continued on up for another 20 feet where it stopped beneath a metal cover bearing a holostamp with the words "RIVERSIDE INFRASTRUCTURE INC." Welkin stood still and listened for any sounds that might indicate there were people above. For all he knew this access tube opened into a Hiveborn dormitory. He must be very careful.

When he heard nothing for several long minutes, he placed his shoulder under the cover and shoved. Nothing happened, except the holostamp text changed to a flashing, floating "SEAL DAMAGED." He tried again, straining till every muscle in his back complained and sweat had broken out on his forehead.

Finally he gave up and climbed back down.

At the bottom he paused to get his breath back. "This may not be as easy as I'd hoped," he said. He led the way along the drain and they tried the next access tube. This time Hatch climbed up but he could not budge the cover here. Either it was rusted shut or there was something heavy and immovable resting on it. The next five were all the same.

But the sixth was different. Welkin was at the top again and was about to give up when he felt a slight give in the cover. This time the holostamp concerned changed to "SEAL ACTIVE" with a rotating hand giving the thumbs up. However, he still couldn't move it. He hissed down the ladder for Hatch to join him.

Hatch scrambled up and joined Welkin at the top. It was a tight squeeze. Hatch was big and nearly filled the tube by himself. Somehow, however, they managed to both get their shoulders under the cover and heave.

Nothing.

"Once more," said Welkin. They put their backs into it again and suddenly the cover plate listed up and over, landing with an almighty clang.

The two men froze, listening for sounds of alarm. They heard nothing.

Welkin took a deep breath and looked at the chamber above. It was some kind of warehouse. There were endless pallets stacked with crates and plastic bags. The writing stamped on their sides was bizarre. It reminded him of Sumerian pictograms, only the "pictures" were of nothing he had ever seen.

He whispered to Hatch. "I'm going up to have a look around. Get everyone on the ladder."

He crawled out and moved to the nearest pallet, listening for sounds of habitation. Again he heard nothing. He decided the only way to thoroughly check the huge space was to gain some elevation. On the wall nearest him was a ladder leading up to a catwalk. Moving boldly, as if he had every right to be here, he climbed it and stood on the catwalk.

The place was an endless series of stacked pallets. Only in the far corner was there a complex of offices and rooms. There was no sign of anybody.

Welkin climbed back down and ran to the cover plate. He called everybody up out of the access tube and replaced the seal. Then they hurried across to the offices which they found to be empty as well.

There was a back storage room. Welkin went in first and somebody jumped on him. He yelled, twisted round, and drove forward with his body, slamming his attacker into the wall. There was a violent *ooomph*! as the impact winded the man.

But it didn't stop him. Ignoring the pain, the man came straight back at Welkin. Then Hatch waded in. Together they held him down though the man was amazingly strong; it was all they could do together to keep him immobilized. When he realized he couldn't escape, he started screaming for help. Daniel rushed up and inserted a metal prod in the man's ear. There was a spark and a sizzling and the man went limp.

"Space!" said Welkin. "If they're all like that then we've got our job cut out for us."

Daniel produced some medical instruments and started to remove the parasite from the man's ear.

"Wait a minute," said Welkin. "We need it intact."

"Too late," said Daniel sheepishly. "I seem to have … er … administered too much juice. I'm afraid it's dead."

The doctor continued working. The long internal filaments slid out easily, their linkages into the brain apparently dissolved by the electric shock. He placed the parasite in a sealed jar and started to cover the corpse when the man moved.

The doctor jumped back in shock. Welkin came over. "He's still alive?"

"Apparently."

"I thought killing the parasite would kill the host."

"Me too. Seems we were wrong."

The man groaned but did not awaken. Daniel washed out the ear cavity with sterilized water and patched it up. The man's eardrum was permanently perforated and he would have diminished hearing for the rest of his life.

A short time later the man's eyes flickered and they managed to get some water into him. He revived a little after that, enough to tell them that his name was Jacobs. Then he lapsed back into sleep.

They decided they couldn't stay where they were. It was possible someone might have heard the man's screams for help or that someone would come looking for him.

Welkin and Gillian decided to scout around.

They left Hatch on guard, his laserlite at the ready, and crept out the back door. It was dark even though the moon was up, partly obscured by high flying clouds. Some distance away there was a road and more buildings, some of them lit up. Silent vehicles were moving on the road but there was no foot traffic.

Welkin signaled Gillian to cover him, and he darted through a patch of darkness to the side of a three-story building that stretched away for 200 yards. He then beckoned Gillian to join him, in turn covering for her.

From here they could make their way under cover of shadows to a point overlooking the road and could actually see some way in either direction.

To the east the road ran down past the remains of the old railway station which the Hiveborn had partly rebuilt. In the other direction, it disappeared into a complex of what looked like warehouses and possibly dormitories. Not far from their position, a bridge crossed the Yarra River and several hover-trucks were passing over it, heading south.

They decided that crossing the road was out. "It's too exposed," said Welkin. "And for all we know there could be lookout positions we can't see from here." Gillian agreed. In the end they went back and checked out the long building. They found it was an infection factory. At one end were holding cells, presumably for uninfected humans. A narrow chute led from this at the end of which was a contraption that clearly held the human still while a parasite—taken from a row of small vats nearby—was introduced into the victim's ear.

The vats were empty which made them think the conversion factory wasn't yet up and running. They decided to take advantage of this.

Everybody moved in. Hatch, exploring the factory, found a section on the second floor that was more easily defended and they carried Jacobs up there and made him as comfortable as possible. He woke an hour later.

"Who the hell are you lot?" he wanted to know. Daniel had given him a pain-killer while he slept and at first he didn't seem to realize what had happened to him.

As they started to explain his face went through a terrible transformation, as if memory were flooding back. "Ohmigod, ohmigod," he kept saying. He gestured for them to stop at one point. "I remember," he said. "I remember. It's like a dream but I remember." He cupped his hand over his infected ear and winced. "There's a roaring in my ear."

"A small price to pay for your life," Daniel said.

Jacobs nodded desultorily.

"What can you tell us—?" Welkin began.

Jacobs' eyes widened with sudden realization. "You have to get away from here. Now. Quickly!"

"You need to calm down," said the doctor solicitously.

"No, you don't understand. *They know you're here.*"

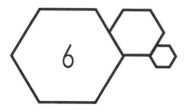

6

Sarah returned to her office, feeling disgruntled. She knew what the problem was. She wanted to be off with Welkin and Harry. She felt guilty sending out her best scouts, family members like Patrick and Mira, and fervently wished she could be with them. She wanted to be out there, in the thick of things.

Instead, here she was, about to sit down at a desk, a desk covered with *papers*. Most of her life she had barely had enough paper to scribble her name on. Now that she had both paper and even some rewritable electropaper, she seemed to be drowning in it. The day they had found the crates of writing materials in the stores they had taken from *Colony* she had been overjoyed. Now she wasn't so sure. She gazed at the plaque on her desk which she was ironically using as a paperweight. Someone had carved her name on it, and underneath they had etched: Commander-in-Chief.

She sighed. It had been her job—they had voted her into it soon after their arrival at Martha—to fortify their new stronghold, make it impregnable. They had taken to calling her *Mayor*, like they were founding a city (and maybe they were). Some young upstart even called her *ma'am*. Once. Now everybody called her Commander-in-Chief. And she had a new job. To orchestrate the war against the Hiveborn. To defend the human race. And to remain alive. No more gallivanting off and risking her life. No more field actions. No exceptions.

Noblesse oblige …

They had even talked about getting her to swear an Oath of Office but she had managed to squelch that one, at least for now. Funny how people liked the old rituals. Liked ceremony. They would probably want her to wear a robe and a funny hat. Well, to hell with that. Wearing funny hats should be a firing squad offence.

"Okay," she murmured to herself. "My days of being a guerilla fighter and a one-woman demolition team are over. Accept it. And get down to work and stop procrastinating."

She called Denton and Efi via the intercom. "Let's get started," she told them. A few minutes later they trooped in and sat down.

"I need to implement the decisions of the policy meeting," she said.

"You're setting up a War Cabinet?" Denton asked.

"Yep, and you two are in it. Denton, we need that War Room. I suggest you co-opt as many people as you need. Number one priority is continuous telemetry from the satellites—assuming Ferrik's team succeeds—and total real time communications with all squad commanders. Enlist Skyborn specialists and liaise with the Timorans for raw materials, but get it up and running. I thought we'd have more time but events seem to have gotten ahead of us. Efi, you're going to help me put together the personnel. Theo will be my second and we'll work down from there." She took a deep breath. "And I want Angela in it."

Denton and Efi looked up. "*Den ksero*," Efi said. "Is that wise?"

Denton agreed. "There's still a lot of bad blood about Tolk and what he tried to do."

"Then it's time we buried it," said Sarah. "I need the best I can get and I don't know if you've noticed, but Angela has an uncanny grasp of tactics and strategy."

"All we're saying," said Denton, "is that it won't be popular."

"Good. Maybe they'll vote me out of office and I can go back to a field command."

"*Aye!*" Efi smiled, shaking her head. "You're incorrigible."

"You'll help me sell it then?" There was a hint of pleading in her voice.

"I'll help you sell it. Then they can lynch us both at the same time."

"Better than being barbecued at the same time." They both smiled. When the prophet Tolk had been temporarily in control of the family he had sentenced both Sarah and Efi to be burnt alive at the stake. Only Welkin's timely intervention had saved them.

"Have you told her?" Efi asked.

"No. I'm going to do that right now," said Sarah. "You two get on with things. Efi, in terms of the personnel, just put together the 'most likely' list and we'll go through it together."

"Theo's looking for you," Denton said.

"Uh … tell him I'll catch up with him later." She didn't want to see Theo right now. She knew he would have a bunch of hard questions and even harder demands for her.

She left Denton and Efi to it and went looking for Angela. She didn't know how the woman would take the idea of being part of the War Cabinet. Angela was probably one of the most lethal women that Sarah had ever encountered, but she also had brains and a wary patience that Sarah admired. Too often she herself had rushed headlong into a danger she should have studied first from a distance. She wanted … no, she *needed* Angela's unusual mix of talents.

She found her in a small office in what was loosely called the administrative tunnel, though some had taken to calling the different parts of the mine *warrens*. Sarah thought that fitted. They had been driven underground by the arrival of the Hiveborn and they would operate as an underground movement … at least till it was time to hit back in force.

That made her think automatically of Theo and she tried to push that thought away again. Angela looked up as she came in. She was transcribing notes from yesterday's policy meeting, adding them to a data log.

Sarah sat down and looked at her. Angela was dark-skinned and very attractive, though her sheer leanness and whipcord muscles gave her a hardness that reminded people inevitably of a lioness. Except she had a great mane of black hair …

"Something wrong?" Angela asked, utterly forthright. Another trait Sarah liked though she detected something else too: a prickliness, as if she had done something wrong and was being accused of it. Given her inevitable treatment by some members of the family—despite Sarah's general amnesty for her and some others of Tolk's brigade—Sarah didn't find it too surprising. But perhaps she could change that.

"No. Well, yes there is. I don't think you're doing much of a job here," Sarah said.

Angela bristled, but stifled it just as quickly. "If you don't think I'm up for this, then reassign me. I'll do whatever I'm asked to do." She paused. "If you feel you need to demote me, that's okay too." Her jaw was working but she kept a cap on her emotions.

"I am going to reassign you," Sarah told her. "I don't know if it's a demotion. I want you to join my War Cabinet as Tactical Officer."

Angela stared at Sarah. She was so shocked she was speechless. Then she did something she hadn't done since she was five years old. She burst into tears.

Sarah gave her a handkerchief and she blew her nose. "You want *me* in the Cabinet?"

"Yeah. Think you can handle it?"

"But I thought—"

"You thought wrong. I need your skills." She stood up. "Think it over."

Sarah headed for the door. Before she got there Angela called out, "I've thought it over."

"Good. First meeting is tonight, twenty hundred hours."

"Sarah—?"

"Don't worry. You'll be fine."

Angela smiled and dabbed at her eyes. "Eight o'clock then."

Sarah went out, feeling good.

The feeling did not last long. Angela's appointment had somehow gotten out. When Sarah arrived to chair the first meeting of the War Cabinet—it was nominally her decision who was in and who wasn't—she found she had a mini revolt on her hands. The revolt was led by Hester who she had reluctantly appointed to the position of Logistics Commander. It suited her abilities and it was politically necessary. Somewhere along the line, the family had grown large enough—and diverse enough—to generate internal political divisions, sometimes quite heated ones. The various camps had to be accommodated. Harmony and cooperation had to be maintained at all cost.

Sarah sighed. She supposed this was the price of democracy, but it gave her a headache all the same.

"Settle down," she called. Someone had placed a hammer on her bench and she banged it loudly. The room quieted. "Hester?"

"Is it true that you have appointed one of the persons who recently supported the homicidal maniac known as the Prophet to this War Cabinet?"

"A number of appointments have been made, Hester, including yours. None have been confirmed yet."

Hester stared back at Sarah. "Am I to take that as a threat?"

Theo was there. He spoke up. "Take it any damn way you please. Let's get on with the confirmations so we can actually do our jobs, or have you all forgotten there is a war on?"

"I have forgotten nothing," said Hester coldly. "Nor will I forget. All right, proceed with the confirmations." She sat down. Efi organized the voting-in of each of Sarah's appointments. A few questions were thrown at each candidate, more for the sake of form than for any substantive reason. If democracy was new to them, they were also new to it. Indeed, they probably felt more comfortable with the form of democracy required in conditions of war than that more suited to a free and peaceful society. Most of those in the room had never known peace, only survival.

Hester's confirmation went without a hitch though both Theo and Sarah had uncharitable reservations with the woman. She might be good at her job but she was abrasive, critical, and had the interpersonal skills of a great white shark.

Problems arose when it came time for Angela's confirmation. The former Tolk supporter sat at the back of the room, looking straight ahead, her hands calmly folded in her lap. She appeared not to react to any of the acerbic comments launched against her and only once smiled—and that was when Hester described her as lacking in any kind of social charm. Hester also said that Angela did not treat her with the proper respect. Despite the circumstances of the meeting, that almost got a round of applause. Sarah mused that if Hester continued in this vein she would end up winning Sarah's argument for her.

But it couldn't last. Others had problems with the appointment and things quickly came to a head. A vote of confidence was requested.

Theo stood up. "That's out of order," he said. "There can be no vote of confidence against a commander-in-chief under war conditions. They're accorded emergency powers and must exercise them as they see fit."

"Nevertheless," said Hester, raising her voice to be heard, "a commander-in-chief who does not have the confidence of her people is little more than a tyrant. Not unlike the late lamented Prophet himself." And here she shot a look at Angela. Sarah almost smiled. She had to hand it to the old cow. She was a street fighter of the old school. Sarah almost liked her at that point. She wondered what she was like in a corner.

Sarah stood up. "Actually, I agree with Hester. Since you've seen fit to question my authority on this matter I see no alternative. I hereby resign."

And she walked out of the room.

An intense silence fell, then the room erupted in uproar. Theo found Sarah in the mess hall half an hour later. He dropped into a chair beside her. She was on her third cup of coffee.

"You won," he said.

"So?"

"They put their tails between their legs and howled. They also reversed their confirmation on Hester. She's out of the Cabinet."

"Put her back in."

"What? I thought you'd be pleased."

"Look, I'd like nothing better than to get rid of her but there's two reasons I can't. Maybe three. One, I picked her. Just like I picked Angela. I need them to back *all* my decisions, not just the ones that'll keep me happy. Two, she's more dangerous out of the Cabinet than in. She represents the views of a significant section of the family and they need to feel they are involved in this fight. I don't have to tell you that the idea of the Hiveborn is still a little hazy in the minds of most of them."

"And the third?"

Sarah laughed. "I kind of admire her. She's tough. No holds barred."

Theo shook his head. "Okay. I'll run back and slap their wrists and tell them to toe the line. Their commander-in-chief's line."

"I'll be along shortly."

"I get it. Let them sweat."

"Right."

After that, she had no more trouble with them. Even Hester seemed to make an effort to fit in and get on with the job. More pleasing to Sarah, however, was that everyone very quickly came to see the obvious merits of having Angela in the Cabinet. She was efficient, painstaking, and she never let her own ego get in the way. She did what was best for the family and not what was best for her. She soon became as indispensable to Sarah as Theo and more so, as problems began to arise between her and Theo.

Their problems arose from Theo's proposed bomb plan. And it did not help that they were lovers, that they were living together and planned to marry. Somehow this made it more difficult.

They had the same conversation over and over.

"As far as I'm concerned," said Sarah, "it's something to be used as a last resort, when all else has failed."

Theo looked away, exasperated. They were in their private quarters preparing for bed. "I understand your reluctance, but this is no ordinary situation, Sarah. We can't afford to be wrong. We can't afford to make one mistake. Because we're not the only ones who'll have to pay. Our kids will pay. Their kids will pay. The human race will never stop paying."

"That's not fair."

"I'm sorry but this isn't about fairness. The antimatter bomb is a tactical *gift*, a way to launch a pre-emptive strike against the Hiveborn while they're still weak and before they've managed to infect half the globe."

Sarah did not look at him. She saw the wisdom of what he was saying, and sometimes she agreed with him, but she was very reluctant to order the deaths of thousands and thousands of innocent human hosts.

Theo understood that. "There's no reason to suppose that the hosts can survive the death or forcible removal of the parasites. If there were … "

Sarah placed a finger on his lips, shushing him gently. "We have to wait and see, Theo. We have to wait and see what Welkin discovers in Melbourne."

"What if that's too late?"

Sarah took his hands in hers. "I need your support in this, Theo. I can't do it alone. I'm so damned tired of always doing it alone and I just can't anymore … "

He nodded, giving in to her. Command was a lonely place, and they had both been there for a long time.

That night a different bomb went off.

Blaring alarms jerked them from deep sleep. They stumbled out of bed and threw on whatever clothes were handy, grabbing weapons at the same time. They were out in the corridor running less than 70 seconds after waking up.

Sarah called Denton but couldn't get through. She located Efi on the second try, but Efi knew as little as she did. It was Angela who brought her up to speed.

"The hydroponics farm in tunnel West One is gone. Looks like there's been some casualties. Lights are out down here, power's off too."

"Sabotage?" Sarah asked as she raced along an access corridor linking two mine tunnels.

"For sure. There's bits of shrapnel everywhere and it's a mess, Sarah. People are screaming. Look, I've got to attend to some of the casualties."

Sarah found a communications station and broadcast a general appeal for all medical personnel to get to the West One tunnel immediately, along with medkits.

Sarah and Theo arrived there ten minutes later. It was a big mine and although there were rail carts linking some of the tunnels, this was not one of them. The scene that greeted them was horrendous. The hydroponics bays were completely destroyed. Hoses were ruptured. Several had not been turned off and were gushing forth their nutrient fluids, creating a thick black sludge that made walking precarious.

"I'll see to that," said Theo, hurrying off to find the main valves.

Smoke stung Sarah's eyes. She stopped and surveyed the damage. Portable lamps had been set up in several places. Medical teams—already trained for field conditions—were tending to the wounded. She saw several bodies lined up in a row, covered in sheets and jackets. She looked away. Nothing she could do there.

Right now she needed to quickly assess the cause and origin of the explosion, preferably before too many more people arrived on the scene and trampled the evidence into the ground. She grabbed a boy who was running past.

"You busy?" she demanded.

"Nah."

"'Struth, what a mess. Look, get some of your mates. You stop people coming in. No sightseers, okay? Just crucial personnel. Medical people, Cabinet members. Nobody else, got it?"

"Got it." The boy ran off, puffed up with importance. The Commander-in-Chief had co-opted *him*, had given *him* direct orders!

Sarah found a flashlight and played it over the wreckage, most of which was still smoldering. It was the work of only a few moments to locate ground zero for the blast. The bomb had been placed near the vats of nutrients and the power adapter that utilized leakage from the nearby old-time geothermal sink. The destroyed adapter had linked to the flicker lights used to accelerate the plants' growth and run the pumps.

Whoever did this knew exactly what they were doing. Theo came up beside her. He was drenched and didn't smell too good, but the hoses had stopped gushing.

"It's a mess," he said.

Sarah suddenly had a bad feeling. "Oh, crap," she said and got to a comm. station. She sent out a broadband alert warning people not to congregate in groups. Everybody needed to attend their pre-assigned battle stations and disperse.

Then, minutes later, a second bomb went off. This time it destroyed part of the main power grid and several tunnels went dark. But thanks to Sarah's warning, no one was hurt this time. Sarah ordered repair crews to the independent power stations and linespeople to restore conduit and adapters to the geothermal Deep Well. Since the grid had parallel linkages most of Martha was still functioning.

"Thank God Denton suggested we do it that way," Sarah said. "Otherwise right now the whole place would be pitch black."

"Not nice for us Skyborn softies," Theo said with a light laugh. On *Colony* in the final battle to stop the elders using a lethal virus against the Earthborn, Welkin, Sarah and Gillian had used the Skyborn's fear of the dark against them and turned out all the lights.

Sarah and Theo pitched in and helped with the repair and clean-up jobs and in transporting people to the infirmary. They lost six people that night and had twice that number wounded. The hydroponic farms and animal vat birthing centers were priorities for the family and many people were employed on them on rotating shifts. Martha had to become self-sufficient as quickly as possible. Which meant that the freezers that had been built in the deepest levels and stocked with game shot by the hunters were also possible targets.

Sarah called a meeting of the War Cabinet that night. Damage reports were read out by various key personnel.

At the end of it Sarah thanked those reporting, then dismissed them before turning to the War Cabinet itself. "What we have feared most has taken place. There are infiltrators amongst us, saboteurs. We have to assume they are Hiveborn though it's not impossible that the Hiveborn have enlisted the help of ordinary humans for work of this kind. Against them, we can do little, except be better prepared and extend the guard. I'm afraid we will also have to institute some kind of ID system. Much as I hate that, we have to know who comes and goes around sensitive areas. People have to be checked and double-checked. If they have no purpose in restricted sections, then they must be held for questioning."

There was an uneasy murmur in the room.

"Listen up! Tonight has shown how vulnerable we are." She paused. "In addition to these measures, I feel we must start a systematic check of everyone in Martha and flush out any zombies. This check will need to be repeated on a regular basis but at random intervals. No one can be exempt. Not me and not anyone in this room. If we don't do this, then I fear the Hiveborn will have already won. Fear will spread through this stronghold like a wild fire and what morale we have left will be in tatters."

They didn't like it but they went along with her measures. Oddly enough, one of Sarah's most vigorous supporters was Hester.

Afterwards, Sarah confided to Theo, "It worries me when Hester's on my side."

Theo laughed. "Yeah. I know what you mean."

They instituted the parasite checks the next day. It was an involved and—initially—clumsy procedure since the checkers also had to be checked, as did those who checked the checkers of the checkers. The system would quickly have fallen apart if Denton hadn't taken charge. He put in place a tag system. The tag was a paint that could only be viewed under ultraviolet light and of which there was only a small supply. Denton put it under lock and key and gave one key to Sarah and kept the other himself.

As people were cleared, they were dabbed with the paint, issued weapons and scanners that could detect the paint, as well as anesthetic sprays for neutralizing any "contaminated" personnel they found.

None was found.

A gloomy War Cabinet met two nights later. Sarah concluded that her fear that the Hiveborn might be using uncontaminated spies seemed to be the case. If so, it made the task of protecting vital areas of Martha far more difficult.

"I'm afraid we're going to have to start vetting people. If they don't have a significant history with the family, they need to be relieved of their posts, at least for now. We also need to pick a kind of anti-spy committee. They need to consider when Hiveborn could have gotten to members of Martha and to isolate all those affected. Then we'll get the medical teams onto examining them in detail. We'll just have to try to clear them as quickly as possible and return them to active duty."

Theo nodded. "It seems to me that the most likely point of infection had to have been after the Hiveborn attacked *Colony* and before the last of us evacuated the ship. Which includes me."

"I'm afraid I agree," said Sarah.

Efi shook her head. "Look, that's the obvious infection route and if we were talking about an ordinary virus I would agree, but we're not. This is a highly intelligent species. We've assumed all along that they've done this before, probably thousands of times. And they've learnt—otherwise they wouldn't still be around."

Theo frowned. "What's your point?"

"My point is this. The parasites are too damned clever to leave open obvious solutions like the one you're proposing."

"What's the alternative?" Hester asked.

"Two that I can think of right away. One, they may just have hitched a lift. Hidden out, inside clothing, in one of the shuttles, anywhere. They could then transfer themselves to anyone they chose, preferably somebody who had no connection with *Colony* and the Hiveborn. Two, they may have infected someone at that point and then transferred later."

"Wait a minute, wouldn't that person know? Wouldn't they remember?"

"Would they? *We* can wipe memory, why couldn't they?"

It was a frightening thought. Any one of them could have been a "traitor" and might not be conscious of it. "But there would be some evidence of that kind of transfer," said Sarah.

Efi nodded. "Yes, there would. One eardrum would be perforated. They'd be hard of hearing on that side."

Theo frowned, leaning close to her. "WHAT? WHAT DID YOU SAY?"

Everybody stared at him for a second then burst out laughing. Efi grabbed him by his jacket and waved her fist in his face, laughing as hard as the rest. The tension drained out of the room. Fear was replaced by rueful smiles.

"Okay, Efi," said Sarah, "it's your idea, you run with it. Write a program to check everybody for evidence that they may have been host to a parasite." She waited a moment, then: "And check my bloke here first. *Before* he comes to bed tonight."

The room dissolved into gales of laughter. Theo laughed hardest of all.

That night Efi was attacked.

She was in her apartment. That was a fancy name for a room gouged out of the side of a tunnel and lined with anything she could scavenge: diamondoid sheaths, cardboard, wooden lids from crates and the like. She had even plastered one wall. The plaster was a new "discovery" and as yet the mix was not very effective but it created a reasonably smooth though very grainy texture that was quite pleasing to the eye. And Welkin had told her that in Timora they had paint. She couldn't wait to get her hands on some to make the place seem more like a home.

She had just finished bathing, "bivouac" style: bucket of warm water, a small bar of soap, and tiny cup for rinsing. She came back into the main room with a towel wrapped around her and somebody jumped her from behind. They were immensely strong and quickly got an arm under her chin and started choking the life out of her.

Efi couldn't breathe. She was gasping for air and already felt lightheaded. A few more moments and she knew she would lose consciousness, never again to regain it.

A few feet away from her was her table and on it, her medical kit, all laid out: bandages, pill bottles and hypodermics. If she could just get to the table … some of the hypodermics were kept permanently charged in case of emergencies. The electric lamp was also there.

But how to get to the table?

During all this her attacker never made a sound. His attempt to kill her was very methodical, very calm, almost impersonal. But time was running out for her. Her vision was swimming and she could not suck in the tiniest gasp of air. Then she realized she didn't need to get to the table if she could bring the table to her.

She suddenly arched her back, reaching out with one foot. Before her attacker realized what she was doing she had hooked her foot up and under the table's cross board and jerked the whole thing towards her. The lamp crashed to the floor, plunging the room into darkness.

And in the darkness there were violent sounds of struggle and several hoarse grunts.

"Death occurred at oh four twenty," a voice intoned. There was no emotion in it. The speaker was Steve Dogherty, a doctor brought into Martha as part of Daniel's team. He stepped back from an autopsy table, revealing a pair of pale naked legs.

Sarah and Theo stood nearby. Sarah had tears in her eyes. "What went wrong?" she asked.

Steve shrugged. "The creature self-destructed in some way I don't understand."

Someone stepped forward from the shadows. It was Efi. She had a blanket wrapped around her shoulders and she looked pale. "I didn't know, Sarah, honestly I didn't," she said.

An orderly took one end of the wheeled autopsy table and started to push it out of the room. Lying on it, pale and still in death, was Denton.

"This is going to wreak havoc," Sarah said. "When it gets out nobody is going to trust their own brother."

"I don't think it can get any worse," Efi said, trying to console her.

But she was wrong. Just then the lights went out. Everywhere.

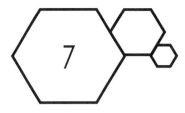

7

A spray of stars. Velvety blackness. The Hiveborn spacecraft eased forward, making contact with the smaller craft. A docking tube moved forward like an octopus tentacle, its clamps locking onto the *Capella* and spreading like glue. Inside, the captain of the *Luna* drew his weapon. Moments later he and most of his crew boarded the ship.

They entered stealthily, but—not fearing death—they did not take particular precautions. There was little the humans could do. In fact, the scene that greeted the captain confirmed his conviction that humans were unstable creatures.

The control room was littered with bodies and blood. Clearly some of them had been casualties of the Hiveborn attack but some just as clearly had killed themselves so as not to be captured. Curious.

The captain checked the cargo and found what he expected: bomb-making equipment. The humans' attempt to destroy the satellites' usefulness for Hiveborn bases on earth had been predictable. It had been attempted many times before. Only once had it been successful. That was the first—and last—time. Indeed, in the vast and illustrious history of the Hiveborn, there were only ever initial successes. There were never repeats.

The captain had the craft's mysterious engine design uploaded into a data-ring for later assimilation, then ordered it destroyed while he downloaded the logs of the shuttle and had an explosive device rigged and set. He turned to order his men back aboard their craft but died before he was able to give the order. He was the unlucky victim of an "initial success" … a *first* …

His crew died at almost the same instant.

Ferrik, Harry and Elab and the others picked themselves up. They were covered in blood as the captain had seen but had mistakenly believed was their own. The blood belonged to Lucida. Ferrik thought she would have approved.

They collected the Hiveborns' handguns. By the look of them they were far more advanced than the laserlites used by the family.

Then they boarded the Hiveborn craft.

Ferrik led the attack on the control room. The shuttle had internal gravity, similar to the pseudo gravity in the modified *Colony* shuttles. Definitely more advanced than their own drives. Luckily, however, they had no gravity cannons … He was sure the craft was capable of great things, despite not having a black hole to suck it forward. Talk about alien technology …

There was no talking. Before the Hiveborn had boarded, the family had quickly laid their plans and they knew exactly what each of them had to do.

Ferrik and Harry made their way forward from the docking bay, after closing it and initiating separation from their old ship. They knew that an explosive device had been rigged. Its detonation would be the signal to take the Hiveborn ship.

Elab, Veeda and Hetti had headed aft to check the cargo bay and staterooms, in case there were any stray Hiveborn. Ferrik and Harry stationed themselves in the companionway outside the control room and waited.

They did not hear the explosion, but the gravity shock wave rocked the ship ever so slightly. On this cue they burst into the control room. They did not offer mercy. Too much was at stake. They opened fire and took out the two zombies sitting at the comm. tower and the navigator panels. They were dead before they hit the deck.

Ferrik ordered Harry to lock himself in the control room and wait for his return. Harry stopped him.

"Sorry, Ferrik. I have my orders from Welkin and Sarah. Pilots are not to be risked where others are available. You stay here and lock yourself in."

"Harry—?"

"I can't fly this thing back to Earth, you can. End of discussion." The door slid shut in Ferrik's face and Harry was gone. Ferrik smiled ruefully.

Harry moved to the end of the main companionway, then crab-crawled aft to the cargo bay. He had no desire to have his head shot off, either by a gung-ho Hiveborn or a nervous Hetti. When he reached the bay he poked his head around the corner. A laserlite flashed and hit a spot two feet above where he crouched.

"It's me!"

"Harry!" Hetti gasped. "I'm so sorry."

"Don't be. You were following orders. If I'd been dumb enough to walk in on you I would have deserved what I got. Report."

"We have three of them holed up in cargo bay two. We can get in but they can't get out."

"Let me have a look."

There weren't three Hiveborn. At least not live ones. Realizing they were trapped and would be questioned they had elected to take their own lives. One of them had calmly pulled out her gun and shot the other two in the head, both of whom had just as calmly stood there and accepted their fate. She had then turned the gun on herself.

"That's a shame. We might have beaten Welkin to an acquisition. Hey. One of them just moved."

"No way," said Elab. "Oh Space. You're right."

"Quick," said Harry. "Get a medkit. I'm going in."

"Harry, that's not a good idea," said Veeda. "What if—"

"What if we can get a live one," Harry finished. He got the door open and stepped in, his gun aimed at the man who had moved. As he went closer he could see that the man's hands were empty and nowhere near the dropped weapon. Still, he took no chances. He fired a low level charge into the floor plating inches from the man's hand. He responded only sluggishly. Then he opened his eyes.

"Who are you, the Lone Ranger?" the man asked.

Harry bit back his surprise. "Who's the Lone Ranger?"

"Damned if I know. It's just a saying. You know, like it's raining cats and dogs. You ever *see* it rain cats and dogs?"

"Not me," said Harry. He moved a little closer, still keeping the man at gunpoint. "Who are you?"

"Me? My friends call me Goose. Say, you got anything for the mother of all headaches? I feel like somebody dropped a brick outhouse on my skull."

Harry almost laughed then saw that the side of the man's head was burnt. Not badly but it looked painful. He collected all the weapons and beckoned Hetti in with the medkit. She gave Goose a shot of morphine and he dropped into sleep.

While he slept Hetti checked the parasite lodged in his ear canal. It was quite dead. The radiation from the weapon had fried its nano-mechanichemical neural circuits, not to mention its entire nervous system. Hetti set about applying some dermiblend to heal the man's facial burns. Elab checked the other two. They were quite dead. He dragged them closer to the airlock. They would be jettisoned later.

"Find out what you can about him," said Harry. "Elab?"

"I'm going to check the weapons systems. The more we know about those babies, the better."

"Good. I'm going forward. Veeda? Ferrik will need you, too."

"I'll be up shortly," said Veeda.

Before he went Harry had Elab shackle Goose's legs and wrists, just in case.

Ferrik was in paradise. As soon as Harry came in he rushed over to him. "You've got to see this, Harry. This ship … it's … it's un-frigging-believable! I don't just mean its speed capabilities—they're fantastic too—but its astrogation computers, sensors, weapons, everything. This ship makes ours look like a museum piece. Wait till we get it back home. If the tech-heads can reverse-engineer it, we're going to have the most formidable space navy anybody has ever seen."

He then proceeded to take Harry on a tour of the control room. Within 20 minutes Harry was thoroughly impressed. Veeda came in as the tour finished.

"It's even got some kind of force field," said Ferrik. "It can take a direct hit in the billion electron volt range and come back for more. I don't understand what makes it work, no wonder they're so cocky, it's similar to our gravity control systems, but—"

"Ferrik, we need to get out of here."

Ferrik stared at Harry then came back to reality. "Piece of cake. The ship will strap us in … launch … probably ten seconds or less … I think … "

They grabbed seats and the ship's alien computer buckled them up. Overconfidence again, they were too used to total and swift victory.

"Wait a minute," said Veeda. "You planning on heading home?"

"That was the idea."

"I think you should hear what Goose has to say first."

Ferrik stared at her. "Goose?"

"Oh, Space," said Harry. "I totally forgot." He quickly brought Ferrik up to speed on what had happened in the cargo bay. Ferrik told Harry to run sensor scans of the entire solar system, (Harry stared at him like he was crazy but soon realized he *could* run scans of the whole system) and went aft with Veeda.

They found Hetti trying to make Goose comfortable. She had somehow gotten him into a bunk in one of the staterooms. She'd had the presence of mind to shackle him to the bunk and make sure he could not reach anything that might be used as a weapon. No one really knew what the state of mind of an ex-zombie was like. Maybe they still had some kind of residual loyalty to their recent overlord.

Goose proved to be a hardy individual. He greeted Ferrik when he came in. "Captain, I presume," he said, his voice nevertheless weak. "Hetti here says you're headin' back to Earth."

"That's right," Ferrik said. "Our mission is done here. We're happy to take you back and see that you get the best medical care as well, then—"

"You can't," said Goose.

"What do you mean, I can't? Is there something wrong with this ship?"

"No. It works fine. I was the pilot."

Ferrik stared at him. "You remember stuff, don't you?"

"I can read their symbols. And I remember everything," said Goose, swallowing. "That's why you can't go back to Earth."

"Where should I go?" Ferrik had decided to humor the man. Clearly he was still suffering some kind of post-traumatic stress.

"The moon," Goose said. "You have to go to the moon."

" I can't do that. I have orders."

"Listen to me. These are ancient Hiveborn shuttles, but on the agrarian world, *Crusader* discovered that the Hiveborn mothership itself had been destroyed in the invasion of that planet. You remember the skyship that led the bastards here from that poor world? That world which had fallen only a few decades before? Well, *Crusader* wasn't alone, there were *two* of them. *Crusader* and *Victory*. Two skyships from Earth. Both taken by the Hiveborn. Both used for the journey to Earth, along with the Hiveborn shuttles." Ferrik stared. Goose nodded. "That's right. *Victory* took a long looping orbit and came in behind the moon, staying well out of sight of Earth. It's standard operating procedure with the Hiveborn. That other skyship is on the moon. On the far side."

"So what?"

"It's not just parked there for rec leave."

A chill came over Ferrik. He sat down. "Go on."

"The skyship has been dismantled and used to build an underground installation the size and like of which you can't imagine."

"What's there?"

"I don't know."

"If you don't know, then why in blazes do you want us to go there?"

Goose looked like a man who had seen the devil up close. He had the most amazing blue eyes that seemed to bore right into everyone. "All I can tell you is, that's the most closely guarded place in the solar system. You ever hear of the Legend of Fort Knox? Well, that's the newcomers' Fort Knox. Only it's more than that. It's like their Holy City as well, all rolled up in one."

"What are they hiding there?"

Goose shook his head. "I don't know. But it's the most important secret they have."

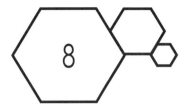

8

The ground shook as though a great beast was waking from hibernation. Tables rattled, spilling their loads. In the complete dark it felt like they were being buried alive. Screams pierced the air alongside strident alarms.

"Everyone just hold still for a second!" Sarah yelled. She felt her way around her office until she found a drawer. It had been jarred open by the force of the blast. She found the flashlight and shone it around the room.

Efi, Theo and Steve were anchored to various bits of furniture. Efi's face was drawn. "Maybe it can get worse," she said.

"A whole lot worse," Sarah agreed. Another rumbling sound made her pause. "Are we being attacked from outside or within? Theo?"

Theo let go of the filing cabinet he had been holding on to. "That first explosion came from down here. The other wasn't that far away. I'd say we have another infiltrator. Possibly more than one."

Sarah nodded. "That's how I read it." She thought for a moment. This was bad. It was one thing to defend yourself against alien attack, even aliens using the bodies of human strangers. But aliens using the bodies of your friends posed a grave psychological problem. How could you kill your brother or sister? Your child, or parent? It made her think immediately of Gillian.

"Sarah?" Theo said.

Sarah realized she had been deep in thought. She swung the flashlight back up and Theo shielded his face against its light.

"Sorry," Sarah said, flicking the light to one side. "You'd better get out there and see what's happening. If the antimatter generators get hit, it's goodbye Martha." She was about to suggest he get the emergency powerpak lighting on, when the pilot lights glimmered. They looked as though they might go out again, but held firm.

"Right," Theo said. "Efi. You up to it?"

Efi nodded. "Sarah? They wouldn't kill everyone, would they? They need surrogates, and won't have them if they kill off whole settlements."

"Don't think me an alarmist, Efi," Sarah said. "But history's full of conquerors who let whole populations live so long as they surrendered unconditionally. It could be we're proving an itch that's too hard to scratch."

"We'll give as much as we get," Theo said at the door. "Efi?"

Steve said, "I'll come too. There's bound to be injured people out there."

Sarah tossed Theo a collar mike. "Keep in touch. I'll be upstairs."

They headed out. Sarah quickly gathered together some items she might need, stuffed them into a backpack, and exited at a run.

She needed to get to the War Room, the only place from which the family's efforts could be effectively coordinated.

But getting there was easier said than done. There had been several cave-ins, though none too severe, but enough to slow her passage and, in one instance, force her to dig out rock, enough to widen the tiny gap that was all that remained of the tunnel. When she scrambled down the other side she found a hand sticking out from the debris. She recognized a wide silver band on a finger. It belonged to Hester. She scrabbled to clear the rest of the body, but stopped, knowing her efforts were futile. She checked for a pulse, found none, and hurried on. What really frightened her right then was her seeming immunity to so much death.

Along the way she came across small groups, each equipped with flashlight and laser weapons, all heading to their battle stations or already there. She chatted briefly to them, remained positive and encouraging, and moved on.

Full emergency lighting came on a short time later, making her journey easier. She was passing a series of power rooms, where large heat exchanges tapped into geothermal vents, as the lights flickered on then off then steadied again. As they did so, she thought she saw movement in one of the rooms.

She immediately dropped down and rolled through the open doorway, as noiseless as a mouse. Why wasn't there a defense crew here? Were they dead? Or worse?

Given the nature of the enemy, she decided to assume it was *worse*.

In here, even the emergency lights were off. She waited a moment to let her eyes adjust then did a slow sneak towards the nearest of the heat exchanges.

There was a small scuffling noise, like someone was hunched down, changing position, doing something …

She moved in on the sound, her right index finger hooked around the trigger of the laserlite. She didn't feel scared, she didn't feel angry, she just felt that old sense of rightness, like she was doing what she was born to do: hunt the enemy.

So it was business as usual.

There was an electrical hiss, then several clicking sounds, like something flipping switches or pushing buttons. Then silence.

If that's a detonator, thought Sarah, then I'd say it's just been primed. *We have countdown.*

It was still too dark to see much but she thought she heard the sound of someone moving her way. She wished she had some night-vision goggles. She stared straight ahead, tried to pick them up in her peripheral vision, forcing herself not to turn her head towards the approaching noises.

There. She saw it. A hunching shadow moving against the larger darkness.

The laserlite was already on low beam. She kept the shadow in her side vision, aimed, and just as the shadow started to pass her, fired.

There was a grunt followed by the sound of a body hitting the floor.

Sarah flipped on her light, saw a dark-haired girl sprawled there and quickly concentrated a low beam shot into her left ear—the one that seemed to have a twitching darkness at its center.

Sure that the bug was dead she turned her attention to the girl and actually breathed a sigh of relief when she saw it wasn't anyone she knew. After checking her pulse and making sure she was okay, Sarah retraced the girl's steps as best she could, coming quickly to one of the large heat exchangers. She played her flashlight over its surface and into every nook and cranny she could find. And came up empty.

Then in a sudden insight she scrambled up the side of the exchanger and peered over its top edge. And there it was. A compact explosive device showing a tiny countdown window.

It was set to blow in 56 seconds.

Sarah climbed all the way over, sat straddling the device, her weapon laid aside. *Okay. I can do this*, she muttered to herself. *I've done the classes on how to defuse bombs.* She had in fact made everybody take the classes. It was no surprise that the Hiveborn would try to infiltrate them and then sabotage them. It was standard operating procedure.

Right. Find the power source. Even if there's nothing that looks like one, it'll be warm to the touch, like a transformer. Okay. That's got to be it. Funny shape, though. What if it isn't—?

Forty-two seconds.

Assume it is. You don't have time to be wrong. So, if that's the power source then there has to be some way for it to send an electrical signal to the detonator. Wires. Lines of solder. Unless the power source is inside the detonator. Jesus. Then it could be radio-controlled. Would they use radio to send a signal five inches? Why not? Harder to stop. Is that the detonator? Could be. It has some residual warmth too.

Damn. Definitely no wires.

Twenty-eight seconds.

She shoved her collar mike close to the bomb. It produced a tiny howl of static. *It is a radio link. Damn. Damn. Damn.*

We didn't cover this in class. So that means you have to think. Fast.

I know.

She took two quick deep breaths, felt a measure of calm return. Pulling the detonator out would probably set off the bomb. So somehow she had to stop the radio signal reaching the detonator. *Right. Well, assuming that's the radio then I need to stop it somehow. But how?*

Fifteen seconds.

She felt out the shape she'd thought was the power source with her fingers. It wasn't a plug-in module. *No luck there. Okay. Nothing for it then. It's do or die time.*

Snatching up her laserlite, she set it to full, took aim at the radio housing, clenched her eyes tightly shut, and pressed the trigger.

She heard the vaporizing hiss, held her breath for a moment then breathed out and took a look. The radio was gone. Molecular history. And the countdown clock had stopped at three seconds.

Not bad.

Sarah checked the other two heat exchangers then got out of there and headed towards the War Room. On her way she broadcast on a general channel. Too bad if the enemy picked it up as well. She quickly related how anybody could disarm one of the bombs then broke into a run. She had a feeling things were about to get a whole lot worse.

Theo headed straight for the Deep Well. If the zombies were on a suicide mission, that was where they would plan their swan song.

Although the pilot lights were operating, it was still dark in the maze of tunnels that criss-crossed Martha. Luckily the family had tidied the place up, so no debris cluttered the ground. They'd been moving for nearly quarter of an hour when they received Sarah's broadcast about the bomb disposal techniques. Theo grimaced. He didn't even want to think how she'd picked up that little gem of knowledge.

Then he saw two family members striding purposefully along the tunnel ahead of them.

"Hold on," Theo said to the others, shining his flashlight at the two figures. "Who's there?" he called out.

The couple continued walking as if they hadn't heard him. Theo called louder, training his flashlight on the path up ahead so they couldn't miss its bouncing light.

They stopped then, and turned. One of them shielded their eyes and called back. "Hey, Theo. What gives? Will you turn off that confounded light?"

"Oh, it's you, Patrick," Theo said. "When you didn't stop I had you pinned for zombies."

Patrick laughed. "Oh aye. Zombies we be now?"

"Who's that with him?" Efi murmured to Theo.

"Who you got there with you, Patrick? Is it Mira?"

Patrick's laughter stopped. It suddenly sounded odd to Theo anyway, false, or hollow. It unaccountably made him shiver. Patrick grabbed his companion's arm and they spun about, fleeing down the tunnel.

Theo was slow to react. "What the heck's got into you—"

Efi brought her laserlite up and perfunctorily pumped its stock into her shoulder. She squeezed off a shot. Patrick stumbled against his companion. As they went down in a heap, the giant man spun in midair and fired a pistol. The crack it made in the confines of the tunnel was deafening compared to the second *hiss* of Efi's laserlite.

Patrick jerked backwards. His companion scrambled for the pistol but Efi's marksmanship was deadly. She flopped over the already dead Patrick.

Theo ran over to them, his mind still reeling with what had just happened. *Patrick?* he thought. How—? He wasn't Committee, but he was damn near it. He was certainly Sub-Committee.

Steve knelt down beside the bodies. "Dead," he confirmed. "The other one's his sister, Mira." Without looking for a response from either Theo or Efi, he shone a pencil light into their ears. "Converts," he said simply. He aimed his laserlite into their ears, having switched it to low beam, and methodically fried the alien parasites.

To Steve these two were just hosts to alien parasites. To Theo and Efi they were much more.

Theo patched through to Sarah, updated her on what had just happened. "Looks like Patrick was converted. Mira, too." He listened to Sarah's worried response. "I know they had clearance down on this level. Sure. We confirmed they'd been taken over."

"That's bad news," Sarah said, sounding breathless. She had to fight down her despair. "We can't trust anyone. Look, from now on, we'll need to make random checks. If anyone complains, pull rank. You're Committee. Any of the old family will bow to that. If anyone baulks at it, you'll know how to play it."

Theo nodded. "Okay. We'd better push on. If they sabotage the Deep Well, we'll be blown to smithereens." He listened to Sarah for a moment. She was still some distance from the War Room but had received Intel indicating there had been at least five explosions. Chances were that Patrick and Mira had only been responsible for two at the most. That left at least a couple of saboteurs on the loose. Possibly more.

"Have you checked them for explosives?" Sarah said. "If they haven't got anything on them they might've already planted them."

"I hadn't thought of that," Theo admitted. "That's your Earthborn experience for you." He turned to Efi and Steve. "Better check them for explosives. And be careful. They might be rigged." At Efi's querying look, he added, "That's booby-trapped to you."

Sarah smiled, imagining Efi's contorted face. At any moment she expected Efi to sprout some Greek, like she usually did when she was flustered or frustrated. Instead all she heard was an almighty explosion.

"Theo?" She stopped dead, straining to hear against a backdrop of noises both near and far. "Theo?" Sarah shook the mouth mike frantically. But it was dead. Not even static was coming through now.

Sarah stood for a moment, absolutely still, trying to digest this. She felt like a huge fist had grabbed hold of her heart and was squeezing it. *Theo's dead.* She wanted to scream, shout, do something, but it was like she'd had a massive Novocaine shot to her whole body. Total numbness. *He's dead and we never got a chance to patch things up.*

Slowly, very slowly, her mind started to work again. Feeling came back into her limbs. She turned, started back down towards the Deep Well, moving like an automaton. Then she stopped. If Patrick and Mira had been booby-trapped, there was nothing she could do for Theo and his team. But she still had a job to do.

She bit her tongue, sending a tiny shock wave of pain through her jaw, then spat the blood out and turned back towards the War Room. Okay. She'd do her job, her *noblesse* bloody *oblige*, and take care of the living, not the dead.

9

Ferrik was torn by indecision. What Goose had just told them had far-reaching consequences. If correct, the war between Earthborn and Hiveborn could last indefinitely. And there would be no doubt as to the outcome. On the other hand, he was in command of a shuttle that could divulge many Hiveborn secrets. With that sort of Intel, the odds would be slightly less uneven.

"Do I want to jeopardize everything I have just on your say so?" Ferrik wondered aloud.

"Your decision," said Goose. "But if I were you, I'd make up my mind quick smart. These shuttles have recognition codes. Since you won't have keyed in your authority tag, the Hiveborn will know the shuttle's in alien hands. They've got self-destruct mechanisms, too."

Ferrik's eyes widened in alarm.

Goose smirked. "I've already hacked in and disengaged it. But they'll still know you're here."

Ferrik grunted in annoyance. "Thanks. Let's do it," he said.

"We can't!" Veeda said. She stood between Ferrik and Goose, figuring Goose's hypnotic eyes might be swaying Ferrik's decision. She pointed at Goose without looking at him. "We don't know where his loyalties lie."

Hetti joined Veeda. "She's right, Ferrik." She chanced a look but turned back to Ferrik almost immediately. "Sarah gave us the green light against half the Committee's wishes. Don't botch it up, Ferrik."

Ferrik turned to Harry and Elab. "What do you guys reckon? Go for the moon or head back before they come looking for us?"

Harry had already made up his mind. "One's the easy option and one's the hard option. I hate the easy option. I say we go in there and teach those alien bugs a lesson they'll never forget."

Elab nodded. "Look, what Hetti said is right. In principle. But you're the commander *in the field*—and that means you have to make field decisions based on Intel not available to headquarters. You know as well as I that you are within your rights to proceed as you see fit. Besides, we're not here to win the battle, we're here to win the *war*." He shot a sheepish look at Hetti and Veeda. "Sorry, but that's how I see it."

Before Hetti and Veeda could intervene Ferrik said, "He's right, and you both know it. This might be the one and only chance to hit them where it hurts."

Goose spoke up and everyone wheeled around in shock, as though they had forgotten he was there. "Down on Earth all you guys are doing, and can ever hope to do, is kill one another." He held up his hand as Hetti opened her mouth to say something. "May I quote the manual? Under the heading 'Explosive and irretrievable situations': 'Hit the enemy when and where they least expect it'. I think that applies to this situation."

"And they'll not be expecting us to take the fight to them," Harry said. "And if I may quote from an Earthborn manual: 'Whatever your enemy covets you should covet more'."

"Firstly, I don't remember any damn manual," Hetti said. "And secondly, I think you made that quote up."

"But it's a pretty good one, hey?" Harry said.

"This is no joking matter," Veeda said.

"No it's not," Ferrik said. "But if the Hiveborn consider the moon base to be their most important secret, then it means that it's the single most important thing for the family to investigate and, if possible, sabotage."

"*If* Goose is telling the truth," Hetti pointed out. Veeda seconded that.

Ferrik shrugged apologetically to Hetti and Veeda. "I'll take responsibility. Whatever we do, we can't let Lucida's death be in vain. I say we make 'em pay for that. Welkin will appreciate it."

Hetti and Veeda hesitated a moment then stood aside as Ferrik left for the bridge. Elab and Harry followed.

Once seated, Ferrik had cause to wonder if he should have brought Goose with him. If he had been the captain of this vessel, it would make piloting it so much easier.

Harry joined him. "If you're thinking of getting Goose up here, I wouldn't. Right now the girls are threatening mutiny. Putting all our lives in his hands any more than you already have will tip them."

Ferrik motioned to a co-pilot's seat. "You're right. We're intelligent guys. If we can't handle a super-tech shuttle with instructions written in a foreign language, then what good are we?"

"Automatic or manual? Automatic's easier, especially when we have the moon's coordinates."

For answer Ferrik reached forward and shifted an icon within a semi-solid schematic. It felt like punching his hand into dense mud. The warp engines whined and as Ferrik maneuvered the craft around within the schematic, the shuttle responded to the icon's new position.

"Child's play," Harry said. "I'd still have gone for the automatic pilot option."

Ferrik snorted. "That's why I'm the pilot and you're the co-pilot."

Elab had taken up position at what he figured was the comm. seat for tactical command. He started testing the various controls while they were still in empty space. No point waiting till they were in the middle of an engagement.

Harry was also learning. He took an educated guess and punched some buttons. The thrusters kicked in pushing Harry and Elab back into their seats. "I think I've keyed in about 1g. Any more and Goose mightn't make it." He looked aft. "I sure hope the gals strapped themselves in."

A distant shriek of voices indicated otherwise.

They entered a low moon orbit an hour later. Worried that automated sequences might have already been activated, Ferrik took them in as swiftly as he dared. Soon they were just yards above the lunar surface. They skimmed across the airless desolate terrain until they touched the edge of the darkened side. Ferrik sent Harry back to get coordinates, or anything else that might prove helpful, from Goose.

Despite the almost fail-safe features that the shuttle boasted, Ferrik misjudged shadows and depth and distance. The planetoid landscape of the moon was disorienting for the Skyborn, despite his training on board *Colony*. As Skyborn often said on Earth, "It's one thing to train in the sims, it's a completely new story out there in the real world."

Harry returned some time later.

Ferrik swung in his seat, sparing a brief glance before turning back to the viewscreen. "You've been missing some spectacular scenery. What'd Goose have to say?"

Harry eased himself into his seat. "He said you can't miss it. There's a homing sequencer on the head up panel." He reached forward and tapped a tab. A flat screen popped up. It displayed a basic map of the moon's terrain. On it, a tiny dot that represented the shuttle was about to miss the Hiveborn installation.

"Veer left and we hit it?" Ferrik said. He opened a port viewscreen. Sure enough the terrain was lit by an eerie glow.

"We'd better land somewhere fast," Harry said.

Ferrik shook his head. "Following Goose's thoughts, do the unexpected. They won't think for one second that we'd just fly in there as though we'd been invited."

Harry made a doubtful face. "Then again, by now they must think we're suicidal. And that's *exactly* what a suicide pilot would do."

As Ferrik veered toward the moon base Elab said dryly, "But then who can say *how* an alien thinks?"

Ferrik dropped them down into a space run. A convoy of space to land vessels were powering along the run and Ferrik simply followed them in. They hovered for a while when the convoy eased to a halt. Some of the vessels landed on the red terrain while others, like Ferrik's shuttle, hovered, kicking up lazy plumes of grit.

"Now I know how a minnow feels when it's about to be swallowed by a shark," Harry said, pointing.

A huge circular hatch in the ground—at least 200 feet across—sphinctered open and the convoy edged forward, each descending vertically into this dark maw. The camouflaged hatch slid shut after Ferrik dropped the shuttle beneath it.

Hetti and Veeda entered the bridge, bringing Goose along at Ferrik's request. They might need his guidance here. All three took seats at the back and gazed nervously via the schematic at a vast underground installation. The ship was on a huge elevator platform that was dropping down into the ground for at least 350 yards. They passed huge pipes, conduits and catwalks. Clouds of steam rose from vents in the wall, adding to the eeriness. They caught glimpses down long tunnels into vast workshops and saw row upon row of gigantic tanks hooked to frosted pipes.

The platform ground to a halt. The vessels about them maneuvered to a landing dock.

"Looks like we're the biggest, so last in line," Ferrik said.

"Never thought I'd be pleased about being last," Harry said.

"Oh, I don't know, I've always thought of you last," said Elab from the tactical comm. seat.

"You're a really funny guy, you know that?" said Harry. Elab smirked at him.

They waited silently while the vessels disgorged figures that filed away into various entrances.

"See?" said Goose. "They're not paid to think. As long as you don't attract too much attention, and you emulate their way of walking, no one's going to bother you."

"What now?" Harry said.

"There's only one bay big enough for this baby," Goose said, pointing to an accommodating area. "I can take us over there, unless you'd prefer to steer," he added.

Ferrik got up. "You sure that ear bug's gone?" he asked Hetti.

She went to give a serious reply then snorted. "I'm an expert on viruses. Not bugs."

Goose took Ferrik's position. He was much more efficient at maneuvering the shuttle. Ferrik was embarrassed that they hadn't trusted Goose from the start. Still, he reasoned, if they'd been wrong, he could have self-destructed the shuttle, killing them all. Too, now that he had navigated them into the installation, how were they going to get out?

The shuttle landed on the parking apron. Goose ordered the door to open and a ramp slid out and down. "She's all yours, Captain," he said to Ferrik.

"Great, thanks," Ferrik said. "Okay, this is how I see it. Harry, you team with Hetti and Veeda. That way each team has a pilot in case things go wrong. Your job will be to follow Goose and me at a discreet distance. Our primary objective is to check out what's so secret about this base."

"What am I doing?" asked Elab.

"I want you to stay here and guard the ship—at all costs," said Ferrik. Elab didn't look happy with this but after his little "in the field" speech he didn't feel he could object.

"Why are we following you?" Hetti asked Ferrik. "I mean, why aren't we going with you?"

Goose answered that one. "You'll rarely see Hiveborn clumping together. They don't chitchat, so don't gossip when you're out there. They don't skip, jump for joy, laugh and they don't stare at one another and smile. Maybe it's their weakness, maybe they can only assimilate bits and pieces of other species and cultures—with no evolutionary pressure to think smarter than their victims, it could make sense. They walk like automata, and that's what their surrogates are. Mindless machines, really, that the Hiveborn use to get around and subjugate other species. Remember these things and you'll be fine."

"They sound like a riot," Harry said.

"It's no fun for the surrogates, I can tell you that," Goose said. "My mind's been turned to mush ever since I was taken over."

"So what happens if we discover the secret of this base? What then?" asked Veeda.

"Whether we find out or not is irrelevant," Ferrik said. "We've got enough electromagnetic pulse bombs and shaped explosives to cause at least a little concern. Plant them at the right locations, and we'll reap serious damage. It'll be a bonus if we find out what they have here."

"What happens if we get separated?" Hetti wanted to know.

"We meet back here within three hours. And if anyone fails to rendezvous, the others are to use whatever means it takes to get out of here." He looked at the cavernous space above them. The gateway to outside was almost hidden by distance. "They probably open that whenever a convoy comes in. You wait till it's halfway open, then make a play for it. If you do it any earlier, they might close it on you."

"I don't want to spoil your scenario, Ferrik," Goose said, "but if things go wrong they won't be opening the portal. That's a cert."

Ferrik noted the look of unease cross everyone's face. "Then we'd better make sure everything goes all right. Let's go."

They left a clearly unhappy Elab in charge and stepped outside, looking cautiously about. Goose's knowledge of the hangar only extended as far as the exit. "From here on in, we're walking blind. I was never given clearance to go beyond the hangar," explained Goose.

"You mean they don't trust their own people?" Ferrik asked.

"I've thought about that," Goose admitted. "Seems to me that the Hiveborn have a hierarchical society, just like us. Maybe a lot of the surrogates are manipulated by worker drones who have a specific purpose. I was a pilot, and not needed outside of this area."

"I guess that makes sense," Ferrik said. "But what happens when we step through this door? Won't they know we're not supposed to be somewhere other than the hangar?"

Goose smiled crookedly. "That's where their little supremacy hype falls flat on its face. There's no individual thinking as such—especially the workers. They're single-minded about what they're doing. And because no one exchanges pleasantries, no one's going to even notice us. That's my theory, anyway."

"Theory?" Ferrik asked.

"That's all it is," Goose said, snorting. "My mind's been dormant for two years. I was just a passive observer, watching things go by. I picked up stuff but it wasn't analyzed, just stored away I guess. Maybe things will start making sense now. Then again, maybe they won't."

"Great," Ferrik said. He stiffened then, as a group of zombies walked past. They had a military precision about them, like toy soldiers, Ferrik thought, toys pumped up with energy juice and set to defend a designated area.

The rank and file passed, and Ferrik and Goose reached the portal. Ferrik checked that Harry and the others had similarly been left alone by the zombies, and then he pressed his hand against the activator. The portal hissed and slid open.

They stepped through, urging the others to slow down in case they caught up. Ferrik closed the door behind him, and they walked slowly down a corridor. All the signs were in the Hiveborns' language, but some icons seemed universal. A hand with a slash running through it meant no admittance. At least Ferrik hoped it did.

Goose concurred and they checked that Harry had seen them enter the room before hurrying in.

"Looks like they don't lock doors around here," Ferrik said quietly.

"I doubt that anyone's ever been so brash as to enter their inner sanctum," Goose said. "But you can bet anything you like, they won't make the same mistake twice."

"With luck the bugs won't be around to make any mistakes in the future," Ferrik said.

They walked along a darkened corridor. From up ahead a sound like a vacuum bot grew in volume. Ferrik grabbed Goose and they back-tracked fast. They hurried past the door they had entered just in case they bumped into Harry's party. And ran straight into a zombie.

The Hiveborn might have kept walking, oblivious to their presence, except Ferrik and Goose were almost running. It was something the Hiveborn didn't do unless there was a definite reason.

"You're in a restricted area," the Hiveborn said mechanically.

"No kidding," Ferrik said. He lashed out with a solid left hook. The zombie's head spun around, taking the rest of his body with it. He did a 360-degree turn and collapsed.

"Ouch," said Goose.

"Ditto that," said Ferrik, shaking his numb hand.

Harry and the others crept through the door. He indicated the fallen Hiveborn without speaking.

Ferrik shrugged. "Give me a hand with him, will you?"

Goose and Ferrik grabbed a leg each and pulled the Hiveborn into what appeared to be a storage room.

"He's too big for you," Goose said. Before Ferrik could say anything, Goose tugged the man's uniform off him. It was a simple wrap that fell over a human's body and melded tight when two pieces of fabric touched. He then pulled his laser gun and pointed at the Hiveborn.

"We don't just kill people like that," Ferrik said, deflecting Goose's aim.

Goose frowned. He knelt and stared into the zombie's ear. Sure enough the Hiveborn's filaments that it used to control the surrogate were quivering in agitation. They looked like miniature squid legs in spasm. "The moment this thing wakes up we're goners," he said. He snatched an electroboard that the Hiveborn had been holding, and stood up.

Ferrik pulled out his own laser gun and set it on stun. He pumped off a shot and the surrogate's body twitched. "That should keep him out for a few hours."

"Or not," Goose said.

Ferrik pushed past him. He had killed many people during his time on Earth. It didn't get any easier as the toll mounted. And he had no intention of adding more guilt to his conscience.

Ferrik and Goose walked along in silence for a while. Overhead parallel pipes followed the corridor around and all met at a crystallized junction mounted in the ceiling. Ferrik stopped beneath it.

"Whatever's going on in there must be important," Ferrik said.

"All roads lead to Rome. Wasn't that a saying?" Goose said.

Ferrik shook his head. "Never heard of it. Anyway, let's see if we can somehow find whatever goes on beyond that juncture box."

Up ahead stood two zombies. They were standing at casual attention. At the sight of Ferrik and Goose they moved perfunctorily to intercept them.

"Let me handle this," Goose said. He stood a little straighter, glazed over his eyes and tucked the electroboard beneath his arm.

"All yours," Ferrik said, waving his hand behind him, warning Harry of trouble. They were already in sight of course, and could only slow down their pace, hoping nothing untoward would eventuate.

"We probably have a leaking valve," Goose said. He looked briefly at his electroboard then pointed past the checkpoint.

The zombies stood to one side deferentially as though Goose were a senior official.

Noting this, Goose turned to Harry's team. "It's through here. Don't delay." Goose swept by without breaking step. Ferrik followed meekly as though he were a simple drone.

Ferrik and Goose waited for Harry and the others to follow them through, then walked between two gigantic tanks. Each must have held a million gallons of fluid.

"I've never seen silos as big as these," Ferrik said.

Goose followed his gaze. "They're not carrying wheat, I'll bet. Better keep moving. If this is their top security location, they probably have heat and motion monitors scanning us right now."

They kept moving. Every now and then Goose would stop to inspect a valve's sensors, just in case anyone had been put on alert to check their movements.

They didn't wander for too long. Already it seemed to Ferrik that their time must surely be running out. So far they had seen several teams of workers, and all had basically walked past them as though doing so was routine.

Perhaps it was the detachment the zombies displayed that chilled Ferrik. Whatever it was, it motivated him to be decisive. "Start planting your explosives. Spread out around the base of these silos. We'll at least rupture them from the bottom."

"You're assuming that whatever's in them is going to flow out from down below," Goose said.

Ferrik nodded. "That's a reasonable assumption," he said.

"It might be a gaseous substance in there," Goose said, tapping one of the monstrous bins. It was full of something.

"If it's a gas we might all go up. But our lives are nothing compared with the damage we'll cause these things," Ferrik pointed out.

Harry came over. "I just saw two zombies staring at us. They didn't stop, but they were clearly communicating with someone."

Then Hetti hissed, "They've turned back. Here they come."

Ferrik swung out of view, leaving the others to confront the zombies.

"I'm Thompson," said one of the zombies. "Who are you and what are you doing here? This is a restricted area."

Goose stepped forward. "Don't you know who I am?" he demanded.

The zombie seemed unfazed. "I know you are of higher rank than myself and my partner. But again, I must ask who you are. It is a directive."

Goose held his board out, hoping for divine intervention. It came in the form of Ferrik, who put Thompson's partner into a sleeper hold. The man struggled momentarily then collapsed. Thompson drew a weapon but Harry and Goose quickly wrestled him to the ground.

The zombie was strong. Lower gravity meant one side of the equation was easier but body mass retained momentum. He heaved Goose off him, then elbowed Harry in the face. Harry reeled back and the zombie scrabbled for his weapon. Hetti beat him to it. She squeezed off a shot at point blank range. The man yelped and fell back.

"Is he dead?" Hetti asked, stunned. This would be her first kill.

Goose rolled him over and nodded. "Don't worry, Hetti. It was him or us." He turned to Ferrik. "What about yours?"

Ferrik slapped Thompson's face. For a moment Ferrik looked worried, but the man stirred. Ferrik pulled his laser gun.

"You're stunning him, right?" Veeda said.

"I am," Ferrik admitted, "but not for the reason you're thinking." He aimed the nozzle at the side of the zombie's face and gave him a medium stun charge.

Thompson's face jerked to one side. Ferrik tugged his head around and inspected the man's ear. "The bug's dead," Ferrik said. "Just like when you got zapped on board the shuttle, Goose."

Goose felt his charred skin. "Yeah, only mine wasn't a stun, it was on lethal." He self-consciously felt his scarred face.

Ferrik looked up. "Okay, Harry, Hetti, Veeda." He tossed them his knapsack of explosives and electromagnetic pulse grenades. "Get moving with these. Use the lot—yours too. I don't think we're going to be needing them. Goose, give me a hand with this guy. If we can wake him, we might get some sense out of him."

While the others scattered around the complex and set their explosives, Ferrik and Goose dragged the official to a culvert where pumps seemed to feed into the tanks.

The zombie woke slowly. Ferrik slapped his face and the man's eyes opened.

"What happened to me?" he said. His eyes widened when he saw where he was. "What are you doing with me?"

"Steady," Goose said. "I was a surrogate too. I think we might've discovered a way of killing the parasitic bugs. Leaves a helluva scar, though."

Thompson groaned. "That's the last of my worries."

"We're from Earth," Ferrik said. "We can't wait around. Do you know what this place is? We've counted six huge silos. Do you know what's in them?"

"Six?" Thompson croaked. "You're kidding yourselves. The bugs have more like six hundred of them down here."

"But what are they for?" Ferrik repeated.

"Parasites," Thompson said. "Every tank contains over three million growing parasites. The tanks are the feeding bays that nurture them."

Ferrik sat back, clearly stunned at the news. The whole damn moon base was a vast alien *nursery* ...

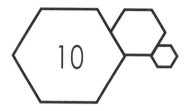

10

A cold chill ran down Welkin's spine. "What do you mean?"

Jacobs tried to sit up. The doctor gently pushed him back down. "Before you—freed me—an order went out to find you. Someone spotted you. They know you're in the city."

"Do they know *where* in the city?" Hatch asked.

Jacobs shook his head. "Just this quadrant."

"Then it's not too bad."

"It's worse than bad. You don't understand their mentality. They won't just send in a couple of patrols. They'll *inundate* the entire area, after sealing it off. There won't be any way in or out bigger than a rat hole."

"In that case we'd better get a move on." Welkin eyed Jacobs, then looked at the doctor.

Jacobs interpreted the look. "I can travel."

"You sure?" asked Gillian.

"I'll damn well hop on one leg if I have to."

The others smiled. Jacobs was all right. They were ready to go within minutes. "Okay," said Welkin. "What's the shortest way to the boundary line?"

"North, towards Richmond."

"Won't they be expecting that?"

Jacobs snorted. "They'll be expecting *everything*."

Gillian blinked. "Sorry I asked."

"We're out of here," said Welkin.

Hatch took point and led them through the maze of office corridors and workrooms. The Hiveborn had an obsession with linking everything together, building walkways, catwalks, smashing through walls and joining adjacent buildings. They weren't completely there yet, but they were on their way. The net effect was to create the feel of a rabbit warren. Or a hive.

Hatch used these links as much as possible, thus keeping them indoors and out of sight of unseen watchers. If they ran into someone—*when* they ran into someone—they'd just have to deal with it as best they could.

As they moved, Welkin hung back and talked to Jacobs who was being helped by Gillian and a crewman by the name of Marquez. "I want to know what possession is like."

Jacobs shrugged then winced as pain jolted through him. "Like I said, it reminds me of sleepwalking, but being awake while you're doin' it. Only you ain't the boss. You ain't even thinking your own thoughts."

"But you remember everything that happened to you?"

"Yeah, like a vid camera that's been left running. It's got no say in which direction it's pointed or what it films." He hesitated. "It's not—unpleasant, you know. Fact is, I guess it's not anything. And there is an odd sort of purpose."

"What do you mean?" Gillian asked. She didn't like this talk of possession not being a horrible nightmare experience. It worried her, as if she thought some people might like it.

Jacobs frowned. "It's like a kind of mild pressure. It fills you, fills everything. But it's their purpose. It's what drives them."

"Drives them to do what?"

"Take over. Absorb. Move on. It's what they do. It's *all* they do. They see it as a way to bring harmony to the universe."

Welkin stared. "You mean they're on some kind of universal *peace* mission?"

Jacobs nodded, then laughed, though it was a little hollow. "I guess that's it. Bunch of reformists, huh? Hands across the Galaxy!"

"A hell of a way to solve disputes," muttered Gillian.

"But effective," said Jacobs.

"Too ruddy effective, if you ask me," Gillian said. "Sarah's read about communism, and that's what all this sounds like to me. Sarah said rarely did a communist country advance technology."

Welkin filed all this away then went forward to join Hatch. They had come to a section where the linking passages ended and they would have to cross an open street to reach the buildings on the other side. Welkin didn't like it.

"It's your call," said Hatch.

Welkin pressed his face to the window, scanning the street below—they were on the second floor—first one way then the other. It was a wide empty street. Empty of cover. Getting the slow-moving Jacobs across there without being spotted would be a nightmare, worse if they were spotted.

He looked at the street again then suddenly, on impulse, looked up.

Welkin and Gillian stood looking down at the membrane that spanned the street, rooftop to rooftop. Covering the streets was all part of the Hiveborn's obsession with enclosing everything, linking everything, recreating some claustrophobic warren of their birthplace maybe. Jacobs said he'd seen glimpses—mental snapshots, if you like—of cities on other worlds, roofed over like this, then sprayed with rough grainy compound that made the cities resemble nothing more than gigantic ant heaps, like those once found in a place called Africa. There was even, he insisted, some kind of aesthetic appeal connected with the ochre earthy compound.

Hatch's face soured. "Next thing you'll be telling us is the bugs've got *art*."

Jacobs looked at him oddly for a second. "Maybe they do. I never thought of it like that, but you might've hit on a good point."

"Looks pretty flimsy to me," said Gillian.

"It's not," said Jacobs. "Tough as hide. Tougher."

"And you know that how?"

"Blessed if I know."

"He's right," said Welkin. "It's stronger than reinforced glass."

"It better be."

Welkin went first. As he inched out onto the membrane, which was alarmingly thin, he fervently hoped that his "download intuition"—as Gillian called it—was accurate. Otherwise, he was about to rediscover the law of gravity, and without any help from a falling apple.

He made it halfway across and stopped. Below, through the membrane, he could see the street. It was fuzzy and his depth perception was affected by the material, like looking down into a pond. So far so good. He waved for the others to follow and one by one they edged cautiously out onto the membrane which had no obvious signs of support, other than where it welded itself seamlessly to the edge of each opposing rooftop.

The others were still only midway when Gillian hissed a warning.

Everyone froze, except Welkin, who was already on the other rooftop. He ducked down then peeked a look at the street below. A six-person patrol had just jogged into the street, checking doors and peering in through windows with heat-seeking video darts. One of them held some kind of flared device which he waved back and forth in front of himself, as if sweeping the street with some invisible ray. It looked like an ancient bluetooth hacking rifle to pick up their molecular broadcasting devices. Luckily their equipment was military-grade and internally shielded against this sort of prying eye. Welkin watched the detector rifle being deliberately swept back and forth—it was both very directional and limited in scope.

Welkin had his laserlite out. He didn't know if it could shoot through the membrane or even if that would be a good idea. Maybe a hot beam would start a chain reaction and the entire membrane would turn instantly to ash.

The patrol moved down the street, reached the spot directly beneath where the fugitives suspended 70 feet in the air above them. Welkin held his breath. If even one of them looked up …

He caught Gillian's worried eye, tried to smile at her, but she wasn't buying that.

The patrol seemed to take an eternity, almost as if they sensed something. They continued to double-check nearby doors and shop fronts. The video darts circled around. After a long time they suddenly moved on down the street, but it was fully ten minutes before they were completely out of sight. Welkin sagged with relief, then signaled the others to start moving again.

A short time later they were traversing rooftops jammed with power conduits, piping, ventilation tubes and mysterious housings whose smooth sides and height prevented them from peering inside the opening. They could see out at intervals around the upper edges. Hatch thought they looked like smokestacks, but the Hiveborn didn't burn fossil fuels—or anything else for that matter.

"I think they're high volume air intakes," said Jacobs, uncertainly. "They mix it with something else. Like carburetors. I'm not sure what."

"Maybe it's part of the process that makes the red jelly," said Gillian.

Daniel concurred. "The red jelly acts like a complex amniotic fluid. It wouldn't surprise me at all if it enabled a complex gas exchange."

Using the rooftops they put several "city blocks" behind them, getting closer and closer to what Jacobs said was the boundary with the next quadrant. Fortunately, this quadrant also contained the sprawling Yarra River and so would still offer them a way back to the shuttle, albeit a long one fraught with its own dangers.

But if they thought crossing the boundary would be easy, they were sorely mistaken. When they came within sight of it, they discovered that it was more heavily patrolled than anything else they'd encountered since arriving in Melbourne, and it wasn't just at street level. The rooftops—still some four blocks away—were clearly swarming with zombies.

"Well, that sort of quashes that idea," Welkin said, trying to hide his disappointment.

Gillian shrugged. "Maybe it's for the best. If they're building up their forces there maybe they're depleting them elsewhere. I say we double back and go out the way we came in."

Welkin had to agree, though in the interests of both safety and information gathering; they took a different route back—one that should bring them closer to their original entry point from the storm water drains. They were within two blocks of this spot when they were attacked.

It seemed to come from nowhere. There was no shouting, no warning sounds, just a hail of pulse beams vaporizing chunks from the wall above their heads, pinning them down.

Hatch and Gillian returned fire as best they could, while Welkin scrambled back several yards and shinnied up the side of a ventilation unit. From here he was able to get a look at the attackers. As he expected, it was a standard six-man patrol. Only they weren't looking for surrogates—this was real ammunition they were packing.

He was about to shinny back down, when he had an idea and glanced back the way they had just come. Behind them was a maze of rooftop obstructions and one long corridor that led through the center of it.

He got back to the others, explained his idea, then led the way, making sure that the patrol could see they were retreating. As he had hoped, they followed. Hatch and Gillian let out convincing death screams when pulse beams struck nearby, suggesting that their force was being significantly depleted.

When they reached the corridor, they raced down it. Midway they stopped and, with help from each other, scrambled up and over the sides, positioning themselves along the top. Then everyone except Welkin and Gillian, who were the best shots with the laserlites, armed themselves with the anesthetic guns and waited.

It was almost too easy.

The patrol came jogging down the corridor, bunched up except for one man who lagged about five yards behind, limping slightly. Welkin nodded to the others across the other side. Everyone readied themselves.

When the patrol was immediately below them, they sprang down amongst them, firing the anesthetic guns non-stop. Welkin and Gillian took out the video darts and did their best to make sure none of the zombies returned any lethal fire, but on the whole their job was easy. The patrol was completely taken by surprise.

Except for the laggard.

When he saw what was happening, he reacted curiously. Instead of firing he charged into the melee then keeled over.

It was all over within seconds.

Welkin and Gillian dropped over the walls as Daniel administered stronger anesthetic doses directly by injection. When he came to the laggard, Welkin put a hand on his arm.

"There's something odd about this one."

Gillian brought her laserlite to bear on the sprawled figure. "You want me to shoot him, just to make sure?"

"Hey, don't shoot!" The laggard was suddenly wide awake and scrambling backwards on his hands. He hit the wall, still with Gillian's laserlite in his face. "Don't shoot," he said again.

"Gillian," said Welkin. Reluctantly, she lowered her weapon but still kept it at the ready.

"Who are you?" Welkin asked.

"Roddy."

"Check his ear, Doc."

Daniel peered into Roddy's ear while the young man squawked. "It's not there," the youth said. "It's gone."

The doctor straightened, a look of surprise on his face. "He's telling the truth. It's gone. But it *was* there."

Welkin stared at the youth. "You had a bug in your ear and now it's gone?"

Roddy nodded.

Gillian snorted. "What? It just packed its bags and went on vacation?"

Roddy gave her an aggrieved look. "They don't take vacations."

"So where is it?"

"Here." He reached into his backpack and pulled out a glass jar containing a parasite. Everybody stared at it, amazed.

Daniel took it from him, peering through the glass closely. "It's alive?"

"Dead as," Roddy said, reverting to idiom.

"How did you get rid of it?"

Roddy shrugged. "Dunno. Woke up one morning and it'd fallen out of my ear. Didn't even try to get away. It was kind of slow, like it was sick or something. Then it stopped moving."

Welkin gave Daniel a questioning look. "I'll have to examine it, but this could be extremely important, Welkin. If it got sick, I want to know what with. Maybe it caught something from this lad or maybe it's allergic to him or maybe it's just down with their equivalent of a head cold. There's no way I can tell till we get back to the lab."

"Then let's do that." Welkin turned to Roddy. "One thing, though. How long have you been carrying on this masquerade, pretending to be one of them?"

"About a month now. Been waitin' for a chance to get out of the city, but ... " He fell quiet, almost as if he were embarrassed.

"But what?"

"Well, I kind of like it here." The others stared at him incredulously.

"You *like* it?" Gillian was almost offended.

"Well, I never had three regular meals before or medicine or clean clothes. And I never got to see the sun, did I? I like being up here instead of ... " He shuddered slightly. "Instead of *down there*." Down there referred to the subterranean sections of Melbourne where most of its inhabitants lived out their lives or at least spent the bulk of them.

He had been a caver. Gillian was oddly sympathetic but she still had to push further. "But at least down there you're in control of yourself. You're not a—a *puppet*."

"Yeah," the boy sneered. "I was me own boss, all right. In charge. In charge of being scared and hungry all the time, in charge of seein' me family killed. Oh, yeah. I had a great time."

Gillian had lost too many of her own family to repudiate what the kid was saying. It was during the brief silence that followed that Gillian, sensing something wrong, wheeled around.

"Everybody will lower their weapons!"

They turned to find Marquez holding a laserlite and pointing it at them, his finger on the trigger tab. His face was expressionless. "Marquez?" said Daniel, puzzled. "What are you doing?" He took a step towards Marquez and the laserlite swung his way. Welkin restrained the doctor.

"See his ear? There's a tiny tendril still poking out. He's been taken."

"Jeez," said Hatch.

"Your weapons," barked Marquez. Now!" Welkin placed his laserlite on the ground. The others followed suit.

Marquez bent down, retrieved a satellite communications device from one of the comatose patrollers, and straightened. He put the device to his ear but never made the call.

Three quick pulses hit him in rapid succession, so fast they could have been fired by a machine. One took out the device, the second vaporized his laserlite, and the third hit him in the leg just above the knee. He went down without a cry. Seconds later the others were on him and Daniel had him anesthetized and was tending to his wound.

This done the others turned to find Roddy holding the laserlite, grinning.

"That was pretty amazing shooting," said Welkin, not quite certain what Roddy was going to do with the laserlite next.

"Yeah, I'm a dead shot all right. I can shoot out a toad's eye at one-fifty yards."

Welkin whistled. "Tell me something, Roddy, how come you took the time to hit the comm. and gun and only shot him in the leg? Why didn't you just kill him outright?"

The boy looked uncomfortable. "I figured he was a friend of yours."

"He was. Is. But that still doesn't explain … "

"I ain't never killed a person before." The answer was sulky and muttered, as if Roddy was somehow ashamed of this lapse.

Welkin laughed. "Well, that makes you all the more welcome with us."

"You mean I can come with you? Out of the city?"

"Yep. As long as you put that toad shooter down."

Roddy looked down, only then realizing he was still holding the laserlite. He hurriedly dropped it and laughed embarrassedly. Welkin helped him to his feet and turned to Hatch. "When we get back I want Roddy here to establish a sharpshooter unit, okay?"

Hatch was still awed by the shooting. "You're not half wrong, boss."

Roddy proved even more useful. He knew the rooftops like the back of his hand and was also privy to the most recent dispositions of the other patrols. When asked how, he produced one of the bluetooth detector rifles the patrol in the street had been using. It turned out you could extend its range but that was more useful for them, trying to avoid the multitude, than for the zombies, trying to find a small shielded group amongst many.

Welkin immediately had Roddy boot it up and extend its field, sweeping the rooftops between them and the entry point. It was all clear.

"Okay. We're going to have to do this in relays," he said. He asked Roddy if there was anywhere some of them could hide while the others carried the bodies the two blocks to the warehouse roof. He didn't query their need to take the bodies with them, just showed them to a hidey-hole buried deep in the rooftop maze and adjacent to one of the mysterious housings. These, it turned out, affected the scanners in general, creating tiny blind spots on the examined landscape.

"I don't like this," Welkin confided to Gillian as they were about to set out with the first three comatose bodies. They had collapsible stretchers which had been extended. "It's too easy."

"You're too paranoid," she said.

He stared at her, his mouth dropping open. "Me? I'm paranoid?"

She looked back at him innocently. "If the shoe fits ... "

Welkin grunted but otherwise let it go. Gillian was known for her downside assessments of operations. Indeed, if there was a silver cloud she could be counted on to find the dark lining.

With Roddy leading the way and operating the bluetooth radio rifle they set out. Roddy bore a laserlite, held at the ready. He had taped the detector to it, making it resemble a toy. Gillian brought up the rear. The others carried the unconscious men and women.

The entire operation took less than 30 minutes. Then they were back for the last lot. In less than an hour they were on the rooftop of the building adjacent to the warehouse wherein the entry to the storm water drain and their scuba gear could be found.

"Whew," said Gillian. "Glad that part's over."

"Me too," said Welkin, but his attention was taken by something poking out of the backpack of one of the unconscious men. He pulled it out and stared at it. It was some kind of communication device, that much was clear, but exactly what kind he couldn't tell. It had a small screen, a couple of jack points, and a protrusion with a recessed center at one end that had a strangely familiar shape.

"Roddy, what's this?"

Roddy looked at it. "Oh, that's a unifier."

"Unifier?"

"Yeah. When they want to upload or download information to the Hivemind, or just network with each other, that's how they do it. If they have to sacrifice some of themselves temporarily for mass thinking, they use the human brain to take the burden. That part there that sticks out a bit, that fits over your lughole. Then a hookup slides out and makes contact with the bug in your lughole." He described it like he was describing the way a radio worked: matter-of-factly.

Welkin's eyes went wide. He experimented with the jacks, found that one of them came out on an extendable cable. Gillian reached out and grabbed his wrist.

"No. It's too risky."

He smiled at her, a gentle, slightly sad, smile. "Everything we do now is a risk."

She gazed back into his steely eyes and slowly removed her hand. "Last time you—"

"That was last time."

"What are you two talking about?" asked Daniel.

Hatch answered, a sour note in his voice. "When he got on board *Crusader* he hacked into their comm. system. Downloaded lots of stuff. And nearly fried his brain."

Daniel turned to Welkin. "It's not my place to tell you what you should do, but we can't afford any more dead weight right now. And we especially can't afford to lose our leader at a time like this. No offence meant."

"None taken, Doc. But we must know what's going on. We could be walking into a trap, going into that warehouse. Or maybe they've already found the shuttle and right now there's a little welcoming committee waiting for us on board. This mission is larger than any one of us. It's larger even than the family."

The doctor sighed. "You're right, of course. Do what you must."

Before anyone else could voice their opinion, he jacked in. He felt a cold dizzying moment, then an almost unbearable sense of *connectedness*, as if the absolute isolation of each individual human being—indeed, the isolation of *being* human—had suddenly and graphically been brought home to him. He almost gasped. He was feeling something humans never got to feel: it was like belonging to the universe, a universe of voices ...

He savagely yanked the jack from his neck, rubbing the spot where the connection had taken place, though in truth it had happened deep down inside his soul. He felt a terrible almost crushing moment of loneliness as the bliss of belonging started to fade, like a dream, leaving a yearning sadness with its passing.

"That was quick," said Gillian, making light of the whole thing.

"Yeah," said Hatch. "And you didn't faint or puke up this time."

"How long was it?"

"You don't know? Fifteen seconds maybe."

"That's all? It felt like an hour. Or a day."

"So what's the situation?"

He frowned, sifting through all the data that had been newly downloaded into his cerebellum. Several pieces of data floated together and stuck. He stood up suddenly. "They're planning an attack on Martha. We've got to warn them."

"Do that," said Hatch, "and these buggers'll be down on us like seagulls at a sardine catch."

Welkin looked from Hatch to Gillian. They had achieved their mission: captured the parasites. They were a treasure trove for the scientists and doctors back at base and might spell the difference between winning and losing this war. And more than anything else in this world, Welkin wanted the thing Gillian had spoken of late one night.

A one-on-one family. A future.

But then so did the people at Martha.

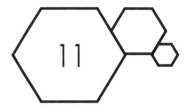

11

Sarah reached the War Room without any more encounters with infiltrators and saboteurs. There she found Angela and two others trying to assess the damage and get a general picture of what had happened so far. Sarah was immediately impressed with how Angela had picked up the ball in her absence and run with it. That's what the chain of command was all about.

"Right, bring me up to speed," said Sarah as she sat down at her main console.

Angela quickly briefed her. Six detonations in all, four fairly minor and self-contained, but two with potentially deadly long term consequences: half of Martha's water supply had been obliterated along with the pumping station that kept the cistern full and two batteries of heat exchangers had been knocked out, reducing their power reserves by nearly sixty per cent. Backups were being brought online and repairs were already underway.

The battle situation was different and far from clear.

Sarah raised an eyebrow. "We're dealing with a handful of saboteurs at most, surely?"

"I don't know," said Angela, looking pensive. "I doubt that we are anymore. Maybe that's how it started but I think they're planting more than bombs."

Sarah scowled. "Parasites? They're converting people?"

"That's my guess. It doesn't make sense otherwise. Duty stations have dropped entirely out of the network. Entire squads have vanished. Unless there's one mother of a hole somewhere and the bastards are just strolling in, then that's got to be it. That's my thinking, anyhow."

Sarah nodded. "I guess that's what they do best. Why use bombs when a few parasites can accomplish the same thing. What I don't understand is, how'd they get the things inside in the first place? We've been screening everyone and everything that comes in and out of Martha for weeks now."

"I reckon they brought in just one."

Sarah stared at her as the implications registered. "They *bred* it? In here?"

"Why not? The things probably reproduce by splitting or something. One of the tech guys told me that's what amoebas do."

"Any guess what the reproduction cycle is?"

Angela pondered the question. "Not long, that's for sure. Even if it takes three days for a complete cycle and you gave 'em a month, that's over five hundred of the little beasties."

Sarah groaned. "Let's hope that's a worst case assessment."

"We need Theo to organize his squads as quickly as possible. I think this is just a cover for an all-out attack."

"Me too," said Sarah, wincing at the mention of Theo's name. She would have to tell Angela that Theo was dead, but the thought of putting it into words, making it concrete and real, was too much for her. But Angela must have read something of this in her face.

"What's wrong?"

"It's Theo … " she managed then gulped.

"I know," said Angela. "But it's only a scratch after all. Guys are such babies sometimes."

Sarah blinked, staring. "He was just scratched?"

"Okay, he got third degree burns on his backside. So he doesn't sit down for a week … " She suddenly stopped. Sarah had burst into tears and the truth suddenly dawned on Angela. She threw her arms around the older girl and hugged her.

"I'm so sorry, Sarah. I thought you knew." She wiped her own eyes. "You thought he was—?"

Sarah nodded, sniffling, then she started to laugh, wiping away tears and snot with the sleeve of her jacket. Angela joined in the laughter.

"I'm glad he's not dead," said Sarah. "'Cause now I can kill him for putting me through this!"

They held each other a moment longer than got down to business again. "I want you to deploy surface troops," said Sarah. "Round them up."

"I've already mustered them at their battle exits. They're ready and waiting."

"Good work. Okay, send them out."

Angela spoke into a mike, issuing the order, then turned back. "They'll be sitting ducks up there," she said, "if the newcomers decide it's a whole lot easier to just flatten the entire mountain."

"From everything we know about them, they're not inherently violent. They want to assimilate us. They want us to join them. They wipe us out and they lose a bunch of valuable recruits. At least, I hope that's what they're thinking."

An urgent call came in. There was gunfire in the background. "The situation here is pretty grim," came a man's exhausted voice. "This is Upper Level B-12. They've got us backed up to the elevator. I've ordered a pull out. No way we can defend this pos—"

The radio went dead.

Sarah swiveled in her chair, illuminated the wall schematic showing the layout of the tunnels. She color-coded Level B-12 and it leapt out in bright red.

"Damn," said Angela under her breath. "I forgot about that. Here, I've got other reports. Let me code them in." Sarah gave up her chair and Angela quickly and efficiently punched in the sit-reports for the different levels—or at least those that had reported in so far. When she had finished a clear pattern leapt out at them.

The upper levels were being systematically taken over.

"Guess you're right about the attack," said Angela. "They wouldn't bother with this kind of strategy if they weren't meaning to come in, loaded for bear."

Wilson moved quietly, sticking to shadows, watching where he placed his feet. There was a lot of rubble about and smoke had started to fill the air. *Something's burning*, came the thought, but it wasn't his thought. It was the opinion of the thing that controlled him. Wilson—the real Wilson—existed in some dreamy place far removed from the events taking place around him. He was dimly aware of them, like listening to a news broadcast whilst half asleep, but felt no urgency about them.

For the first time in his life, he did not feel fear. *Any* fear.

The effect of this, even in his dreamy state, was intoxicating. But at the same time another sentiment rubbed at him, insistent, annoying, like a pebble caught in his shoe. It was the idea of wrongness. Of violation.

But even that sensation of mild outrage was too dreamily distant to worry about. Instead, he calmly watched the "movie" unfolding around him, piqued by only the mildest curiosity as to what would happen next.

The smoke had thickened and he could hear the crackle of flames now. Suddenly a woman blundered towards him, coughing. She stumbled and Wilson reached out and caught her, helping her to stay upright.

"Thanks," said the woman. "Who's that?"

"Wilson. C Brigade."

"What are you doing up here?" The woman was still wheezing but managed to peer at him in what might have been a suspicious way.

"All units were ordered to B Level, pronto."

"Where's the rest of your squad?"

"Lost 'em in the fighting. I've been wandering round for the last thirty minutes. I'm not familiar with this level. Anyway, I just found my squad leader. He's dead. On the floor there behind you."

The woman turned. At the last second she realized her mistake. Wilson, a large heavy man, tripped her, using his weight to push her over then falling onto her back, effectively pinning her to the floor. He reached behind into his backpack, removed one of the People and, despite the woman's writhing and screaming, managed to introduce it into her left ear. For a moment her screams for help turned to shrieks, then she stiffened and went silent.

He climbed off her and stood panting, waiting.

Moments later she stood up, dusted herself off, and turned to Wilson. "Where are the pods?"

He told her where she could collect them. The real Wilson listened in. He knew that each pod contained a dozen of the People.

Just then a laserlite pulse speared out of the smoky darkness and caught Wilson in the chest. As he crumpled and died the real Wilson woke long enough to emit a silent cry of exultation. The woman died a split second later.

Theo stood over the body of Wilson and the woman, scowling. If this was how they were forced to win, then he wasn't completely sure he wanted to.

"Identify them and tag them," he snapped at his orderly, moving away down the tunnel with his squad. Strictly speaking, he wasn't on Operation Clean-up anymore. Sarah had ordered him to the surface to oversee what she believed would be the imminent attack by the Hiveborn. It was a risky move. They might win the surface battle only to discover that they had lost Martha to the parasites' slow and steady assimilation program.

But orders were orders, even from one's partner.

Suddenly, sirens blared. Followed by the heavy chimes that meant they had just gone to DefCon One. The attack had started.

Theo quickly rallied his squad. Together they raced down the tunnel they were in, hit a steep ramp, and pelted up it, reaching Level One and the main entrance five minutes later. Here, there was a traffic jam as several other squads had responded in the same way.

Theo stood on a crate and shouted for quiet, then sent the squads through with a semblance of order. Once outside, the troops deployed as they had been trained. There were many pale faces amongst the raw recruits.

In the War Room, Sarah, Angela and Efi listened to scouts who had returned with eyewitness field reports; listened to new reports as they came in and checked the monitors showing the hazy dispositions of surface defenders versus alien attackers.

So far so good.

According to the initial reports, the aliens had landed some distance from the mine entrance and were massing for a full frontal attack. As far as Sarah could see from the restored video feed, and from what she could glean from the most recent squad reports, that's exactly what the attackers were doing. The fact that the aliens outnumbered the surface defenders by five to one not only gave them the clear advantage in any face-to-face conflict, it must inevitably cloud their judgment.

And Sarah was counting on that.

The one advantage the surface troops had—and it was one that Sarah fervently hoped would reduce the number of casualties—was that they held the high ground. The aliens would have to attack upwards, charging up a slope of about 12°. Not steep, but enough to effectively reduce the odds somewhat. And right now Sarah would take everything she could get.

On the surface, Theo surveyed his forces. Their dispositions were about as good as could be expected. Better, in fact, than he had hoped for. Most of them were fighters, having survived childhood and still breathing; but they were new to discipline, new sometimes to the very concept of being a team player.

He wondered if they would obey him at the most crucial moment. Well, he would see. Soon, events would take over. The rush and fervor of battle would close over the men and women before him now and many would succumb to the old instincts of one-on-one battle. Formations would break, squads would disintegrate, people would die needlessly.

Theo expected it, had tried to strategize with it in mind. And any minute now his battle plans would be put to the test.

A runner slammed to a stop beside him. "Sir, all outliers are in. Backdoors are sealed. Message from the War Room is: 'How green is my valley?'." The youth frowned, not understanding the final part of the message. In actual fact, Theo had already received the message through his comm. link, but they had long ago decided not to wholly rely on the communications system, but to trust the old-fashioned sort: runners bearing messages. It was too easy to sabotage or jam a comm. system. If it happened at a critical moment, all could be lost.

"Thanks. Get a drink. Rest. I'll need you soon." The youth nodded, loping off to the canteen area. Theo watched him go. The boy was about 14. That was old amongst the Earthborn, few of whom expected to reach the ripe old age of 21. Or at least that's how it used to be. Their medicos were already making great inroads on progeria, the genetic condition that predisposed the Earthborn to a kind of early old age.

Theo put his thoughts back to the coming battle, scanning the enemy through binoculars. It wouldn't be long now.

When the attack came, Sarah and Angela were reviewing the schematic of the tunnels, one of which presented a three-dimensional view, including the surface valley above, that could be rotated and viewed from any angle. The computer was even sophisticated enough to transpose the various verbal and electronic reports into a color-coded visual which showed the "enemy" surging forward across the valley and up the slope towards the defenders.

"How long?" Angela murmured, almost to herself. Sarah took it as a question. "Thirty minutes, Theo reckons."

Angela glanced at a digital clock on the console. It was counting down from T-minus 40 minutes. "That's cutting it close," she said.

Sarah followed her gaze, shrugged. "That can be manually reset at any time. It operates like a reverse dead man's switch. If we're dead, it goes off as planned. If we're alive, we can reset it."

Sarah and Angela watched the "enemy" on the video feed charge up the slope. They were sustaining heavy losses from the withering fire from the defenders deployed above them. Sarah frowned, keyed in a message to Theo, suggesting that they try not to inflict too many casualties on the aliens.

"Crazy way to fight," said Angela, though it wasn't a criticism.

"We just need them to give up. And anyway, I've got a feeling that killing large numbers of them wouldn't change their minds, except maybe to use some kind of tactical weapon to smear this whole mountain. We can't afford to make this attack so expensive that they resort to that. And don't forget, those are human beings out there, both Earthborn and Skyborn."

"The Hiveborn probably win most battles because they know their enemy can't possibly like killing their own people."

Sarah chewed at her lower lip. "If only we could reproduce the anesthetic weapons. That way we could convert our people back."

"They won't ever give the luxury of time for that," Angela said.

Sarah glanced at the wall clock. She grabbed a mike and barked a request. "Jennings, I needed that confirmation five minutes ago!"

A static-filled burst of sound came back at her. "Hold on, Sarah! Almost done."

Despite the severity of their situation, Sarah smiled at the remark. To Angela she said, "You think that's a treasonable statement?"

"Definitely. A first-class hanging offence."

They turned back to survey the battle, the sound of pulse rifles and laser guns muted, along with the screams of the defenders. Eerily, the attackers made no sound when they were hit. They either ignored it and kept on coming or else they dropped silently to the ground and lay there.

Topside, Theo had his hands full. Discipline was breaking down and he had to use all his tact, authority and plain old bad language to browbeat his squad commanders into responding and riding hard on their fighters. The lines had to stay intact.

But only for another ten minutes.

Theo turned to his periscope man, pushed him aside, and peered through the ancient device designed to prevent commanders from losing their heads by sticking them up where they could get shot off. It was a simple practical piece of technology that needed no power. And Theo preferred seeing things with his own eyes. Anything on a vid screen always had a faint sense of unreality for him.

The enemy had originally formed up in three long ranks, throwing only the first two into battle, and keeping the third in reserve. Theo didn't like that though he had expected no less. Fortunately, the possessed humans were not great fighters: their reaction time was noticeably slower than the free humans and their instinct for where to strike was dulled. But they made up for this in total fearlessness and a tendency to keep fighting even when mortally wounded. They were like the Berserkers of a bygone age, undaunted by pain or the thought of death.

Five minutes later they came close to overrunning Theo's command post. Somehow, a small detachment of zombies had worked its way up the ravine behind the command post, a path Theo had assessed as impassable, and hurled itself upon the field headquarters.

The first Theo knew about it was when the periscope man beside him suddenly slumped, a bright red flower blossoming in his chest and cauterizing immediately. Theo caught him, lowered him to the ground, and came up firing.

Seconds later, he was in hand-to-hand combat with the alien equivalent of a death commando. And the man was good. Too good. Theo wondered if the control had been lessened to allow the man some free will. Then the man grinned at him and he realized the awful truth.

"You're not possessed!" he blurted out, deflecting a fatal blow with a vibro-blade.

"Not me, mate," grunted his attacker. "But you will be soon. That or dead!" And with that he lunged, straight onto Theo's concealed blade. Blood erupted from the man's mouth, foamy with oxygen: a lung hit. The man was about to drown in his own life fluid.

"Medic!" Theo called after disarming the man. He wanted this one alive. Meanwhile, he got off two shots, firing into the melee of bodies, nodding with satisfaction as two more attackers dropped in their tracks. Then a woman broke through, slashing at him, opening up a deep cut on his cheek. Theo stepped back, falling over the prone man. In an instant the woman was straddling him, plunging her blade down again and again, going for his face, his eyes, his throat. Theo deflected the strikes, but only just. It was like fighting a wildcat and his Skyborn upbringing prevented him from going for a killing strike. He felt the knife cut his neck and blood spurted.

Suddenly the girl flinched then collapsed on top of him. Theo peered up into the youthful face of Jennings. He was holding a metal canteen, having just used it as a battering club. The next moment he was telling Theo to stop crying like a baby, and that all his "nick" deserved was a quick dressing, which he promptly produced.

Careful not to stretch his neck just yet, Theo pushed off the girl, noting that his first attacker was dead. "Thanks, Jennings. And for your information, it hurts like hell. Now tie the girl up, and get her back inside. I want her interrogated."

Jennings got to work.

Theo looked around. The battle for the headquarters was over. The commandos were either dead or captured. He turned his attention back to the main battle, saw that the lines still held. But, the defenders were taking heavy casualties from zombies that refused to die, even when blasted at point-blank range. Obviously, the parasites had some way of enhancing human biology and bypassing tissue and organ damage—at least in the short term.

He gazed down the hill, saw that the third and final rank of Hiveborn were racing up the slope. That was the sign.

Theo grabbed a mike and relayed the order to all his squad commanders to withdraw inside Martha. As he watched, those at the rear started to fall back. They then stopped and provided cover for the forward troops to pull back. And so it went in a kind of clumsy leapfrog.

Theo ordered the field HQ to be abandoned and he and his command staff headed for the nearest entrance, their retreat covered by a special squad of sharpshooters.

Minutes later he was racing through the tunnels, heading for the War Room. Like everybody else, he kept to the tunnels marked with glowing green lamps. He had been running for less than four minutes when a series of muffled detonations sounded on all sides and a whirlwind of dust and litter engulfed him.

Sarah stared at the schematic of Martha. A series of bright gold lights flared briefly at various points, even as the dull rumble of explosions came to her ears and, moments later, shook the War Room.

When the lights had died down an entirely new pattern of tunnels had been revealed—a deadly maze designed to confuse the enemy and allow the defenders to fight a more lethal guerilla-style war. Some of the tunnels led to dead ends where vents would douse the attackers with sleeping gas. Others would just send them in endless spiraling circles. But even these tunnels had sniper holes, trapdoors, hidden panels.

And Sarah had other ideas. She gazed into the video screen, noting that the alien ships— including their troop carriers—seemed unguarded …

"Theo's on his way in," Angela said suddenly.

"Good. Tell him to use the south entrance. Change of plan."

Angela relayed the message then straightened up, eyeing the schematic which was still "evolving." On the surface, the Hiveborn had grouped outside the various mine entrances. As Angela watched they started pouring inside.

Meanwhile, another squad was roaming amongst the bodies, evidently searching for something. When they found what they were looking for they performed some kind of procedure. Angela frowned.

"What are they up to out there?"

Sarah leaned over, took a look, and grimaced. "They're rescuing parasites."

Angela stared. "You mean they're saving the bugs and just leaving the people to die?"

Sarah nodded. "Listen, let the medic bods know about this. I don't know when—or if—we'll get access to the surface again, but there have got to be survivors up there."

"Then we should also assume that any of our people who are in reasonable working condition will be possessed using the spare bugs."

"I reckon so. That's why nobody knows too much. Especially the pattern of the maze. Speaking of which, it's time to switch over the guide lights."

Angela punched a button. All the green lamps that had lined the safe un-booby-trapped tunnels flickered and went out while others, in adjacent tunnels, came on. If the enemy assumed these lights indicated the path to take then they would be sorely—and sometimes fatally—disappointed.

Moments later Theo burst in, sweaty, disheveled, and bleeding. Sarah stifled her reaction, and her natural instinct to throw her arms around him; instead, she pulled out a medkit from under the bench and threw it to him. He grinned, knowing how much it hurt her not to come rushing across the room.

While Theo tended to his injuries, helped by Efi who was chief medic, Sarah and Angela analyzed the data coming in from more than two dozen sources, including eyewitness accounts using spy holes to see into the maze of tunnels. The Hiveborn were flooding the upper level. Many, so far, were trapped in tunnels that went nowhere or just returned them to their starting position, though some of these circular links were so subtle that many Hiveborn were starting on their third or fourth trip around the same circuit.

Yet it was only a matter of time before contact was made, though if Sarah had her way it would be delayed for as long as possible. Already, squad leaders were reporting numerous casualties amongst the Hiveborn resulting from sniping, gas attack, trapdoors, and other strategies.

But Sarah made sure she never forgot just how alien the attackers were. Loss of an entire battalion (or two) might deter a human commander but could have quite the opposite effect on an alien mentality.

Theo came up behind her and slipped an arm around her waist. She relaxed into his embrace but never took her eyes off the holos in front of her. Theo also studied them.

"How are the backdoors?" he asked suddenly.

Sarah stiffened slightly. "They're fine," she said, almost reluctantly. "No activity in the area."

"That may not last for much longer. They're not stupid. They'll know most mines are interlinked."

Sarah nodded, then turned to him. "What do you want to do, Theo?"

He leant forward and kissed her lightly on the cheek. "You know what I think we *should* do."

"My objections haven't changed."

"I understand that, but we can't afford to lose the option. If they find the backdoor, then that's it. It's time to make a decision."

Sarah looked across at Angela. "What do you think?"

Angela looked startled, still not used to being consulted on such high level issues. "I think the bomb should be deployed but not used."

"Not used?"

Angela shrugged. "It's of no use here unless you're thinking of having a self-destruct option and personally I'm not too crazy about that. So let's deploy the sucker. We don't have to use it. But if we need to, at least it'll be in position and ready."

Sarah looked at Theo. "You happy with that?"

Theo stared back a moment then nodded. "Makes sense. At least we can hit back at them, if all else fails."

"What makes you think it'll make any difference? It might even just bomb us all back into the Stone Age."

"Better the Stone Age than some alien nirvana."

Sarah moved over to her console, tapped in a code, and looked up at Theo. "Okay. Backdoor is primed and ready. Go do it."

Theo hesitated a moment then went across and embraced Sarah, kissing her properly this time. She kissed him back, clinging to him for a long moment. Angela was careful to keep her eyes on the holos.

"Make sure you come back," said Sarah. "Don't be some goddamned hero, okay?"

"I promise. No hero stuff."

Sarah's eyes glistened. "So get out of here, before I change my mind."

Theo kissed her again then hurried from the room. After he'd gone Sarah sat down and took a deep breath. She felt a hand squeezing her shoulder and looked up to see Angela behind her. "I'm sure he'll be okay," she said.

Sarah nodded. "I just hope we're all okay."

"It's the right decision."

"Is it? Is bombing an entire community ever the right decision?"

Angela had no answer to that.

Theo raced down to the lower levels of Martha to what was nominally called the Bomb Room. Here a large silvery canister sat on a trolley. His personal squad was waiting for him, having been alerted by Sarah's code.

"We're in play," Theo said as he raced in. "Let's get moving."

They wheeled the trolley out, clamped it onto a set of miniature railway tracks, then scooted it along, sprinting alongside. Several minutes later the tracks led them into what was clearly a hangar, complete with waiting aircraft, a three-seater HOTOL, or horizontal take-off and landing spaceplane, an ancient chassis married with some molecular cross-bar holochipping courtesy of the Skyborn.

Without pausing they rolled the trolley off the tracks and up the HOTOL's sloping rear ramp. As Theo raced forward to the cockpit the others clamped the bomb in place while the co-pilot and navigator followed Theo.

Theo jumped into the pilot's seat, let the plane strap them in, and lit the HOTOL's ionjet scramtorch. A muffled roar vibrated through the polyflex hull of the ship. The rear ramp swung up and locked in place. Theo crossed his fingers and said a quick prayer. He wasn't a pilot, and had only grabbed quick lessons when time allowed.

Ahead of the shuttle, for perhaps a mile, was a long tunnel that dipped low for a short space before tilting up at a steep angle. The tunnel itself was an old mine but had recently been expanded.

"Give me some juice," said Theo, "and let's get this baby out of here."

He felt the ancient luxury spaceplane become airborne and saw the cabin elongate, changing its polyflex neoceramic shape. He slowly eased on the throttle command and the ship sailed down the tunnel, picking up speed.

The walls on either side, barely ten feet away, blurred past. Despite the automatics, the effect was both alarming and nauseating. They would be small, sleek and dispensable, but would they be hidden?

Theo forced himself to stare straight ahead. If he got too close to the walls, proximity alarms would sound. Automatics couldn't deal with rock falls from explosions blocking the shaft. He was still praying as the forward thrust pushed him back into his seat.

Luckily for him, this mission didn't require fancy flying automatics. It just required a steely determination to do what was necessary.

Sarah watched the spaceplane's progress on a special holo dedicated for that purpose. At the end of the mile long tunnel she watched as the bay doors ground slowly open and without pausing the three-person spaceplane shot out into a valley on the other side of the mountain. The tracking camera followed the HOTOL long enough for Sarah to see that it did not immediately go for height but instead raced along the valley barely a 100 feet above the floor. The valley itself snaked along through the mountains for nearly eight miles before opening onto the sea. From there, Theo would keep the craft low, skimming the wave crests all the way to Australia.

As she watched, a sudden dark feeling swooped on her, sending a chill through her limbs. It was a premonition—that she would never see Theo again. She swallowed quickly, pushing the thought aside. Right now she needed to focus.

"They're away," Angela called out unnecessarily. "Just got their call sign."

"Thanks." Sarah knew her voice sounded funny, but she ignored Angela's look and started issuing orders again, coordinating field maneuvers, calling up holo projections from the computer.

Before long, hand-to-hand combat had recommenced in the upper levels and reports started coming in of casualties. Two entire squads were wiped out in an ambush where the Hiveborn successfully penetrated part of the access tunnel system that honeycombed the maze section. Sarah ordered that section to be detonated. That way no one could use it.

Angela suddenly spoke up. "Two more bombs have just been found on the lower levels. They've been deactivated."

Sarah grimaced. "Cannons ahead, cannons behind," she muttered to herself. "What's that?"

"An old war. Keep the bomb disposal teams at it. We still running checkpoints and random searches?"

"As best we can. It's pretty crazy down there."

"That I can believe." Sarah thought for a moment. "We must have a bunch of parasite prisoners by now, the comatose kind. Get them down to the labs. It'll give the brain boys more to play with. Tell 'em to try anything they can think of. EM pulses, ultrasound, microwaves, subsonics, the works. They're no use to us as fighters, anyway, so they might as well be doing something."

Angela grinned and got on the radio, snapping out orders. She respected the think tanks but couldn't stop herself from feeling they were otherwise pretty useless. Some of them couldn't find their own quarters without help.

While Angela got on with this, Sarah stared once more at the holo showing the alien vessels. Reaching a decision, she thumbed on the mike. "Get me Mawson." A tinny voice acknowledged the order and Sarah killed the connection.

The dark premonition was back and she didn't like the feel of it one little bit.

Theo's assessment that he would not need all his flying skills for this mission proved quickly false. As Sarah had seen from her holo deck, Theo took his spaceplane into the meandering valley, keeping her low and hopefully invisible to whatever kind of technology the aliens used to scan for enemy vessels. If nothing else, they'd be a hard target to hit amongst the boulders and craggy peaks, though the plane was really intended for sub-orbital cross-continent flights. On top of that the HOTOL had been set on black camouflage. Finding it by sight on such a dark night would have been next to impossible.

He never knew if the aliens got lucky or if they were just a whole lot smarter than him. As the spaceplane shot from the valley end and dived over a 500 foot drop to sea level an intense beam of high energy radiation pulsed out at them from a nearby peak. If they had risen for height instead of diving down they would have been vaporized. As it was, the outside edge of the coherent beam clipped their tail, cooking a number of redundant circuits and causing one of the gyro stabilizers to malfunction.

The plane slowly flipped over, corkscrewing down towards the sea. Theo damped the opposite stabilizer and brought her under control manually by using the positioning jets.

"Nice recovery," said Miles, his pale faced co-pilot as they belly skimmed the waves, sending an impact shudder through the entire ship.

"Where are they?"

"Ten o'clock, a thousand yards."

"Damn." The aliens had the high ground. He pulled hard at the controls, but the spaceplane banked around and down. Another beam sliced through their previous position. The sea reared up like a monster.

Theo's navigator, Renko, gripped the arms of his chair. "Theo?"

"We're ditching!"

The spaceplane hit the water hard. The cabin shuddered with the impact, sending anything not strapped in crashing around the interior. It kept going, down and down and down. At low speed and 300 feet it wallowed. After a few moments, he checked the controls.

Theo sat frozen at the controls. "I don't believe it," he said. "The damn thing swims."

Miles took a deep breath, still coming to terms with the fact that they had survived the plunge. "We're capable of switching to hydrojet—in case of crash-landings at sea. Makes sense it's also a submersible."

Renko made a clucking sound. "If we make it back in one piece, I wanna transfer outta this insane asylum."

"I'll double that," said Miles.

"Me three," said Theo.

Mawson came on the line. Sarah picked up. "Mawson."

"Yes, ma'am."

Sarah winced slightly at the "ma'am" but let it go. "You remember what we talked about the other day?"

"I was wondering when you might call."

"I think it's time."

"Send me all the dispositions and any other relevant Intel. I'll brief my crew. You wanna sit in the hot chair on this?"

"No. You send up your specialist. She can run the show from here."

"Will do." The line went dead. Sarah eyed the enemy ships. If they could take the ships, or at least sabotage them, it would delay any follow up tactic by the Hiveborn. And that meant, if all else failed, that they could evacuate Martha, get everybody to the fallback shelter on North Island and from there—who knew? They could go anywhere in the world.

The problem was, that might not be far enough.

Angela tapped her on the arm. Sarah looked up. "I've got Ferrik on the line."

Sarah blinked, then scrambled for the other console. She slammed her palm on the audio pad. "Ferrik? Where are you? Is everything all right?"

The line was poor, full of static and breakups, but still reasonably clear. Quantum dot encryption circuits enabled the normal delay for Earth-Moon signals to be bypassed by bizarre quantum linking effects. " ... trying to get through to you ... all jammed ... Mission was successful. Repeat, mission was successful. We also scored a new ship so don't ... shoot first, all right?"

"That's great news. We won't. Now get back here. We need you, but stay high and wait to hear from us."

"Soon as I can. But there's more." A burst of static drowned out the next words. All Sarah caught was the word "Welkin." Sudden anxiety drained her.

"Say again, Ferrik?"

"Am sending you a data burst. Update of situation on the moon." Did he say the moon? "Welkin's mission failed. He and his team ... danger of being captured. Am going to attempt rescue. Any orders?"

Sarah thought swiftly. If Welkin's mission had failed then they were out of options. It meant that very soon the Hiveborn would have complete access to Welkin's intimate knowledge of Martha's plans. She had no doubt that, given the chance, Welkin would commit suicide before letting himself fall into enemy hands but he might not have a choice. Whatever else happened that had to be prevented. She swallowed, feeling a constricting sensation in her throat.

"Proceed with rescue. But Ferrik, if rescue fails, it's imperative that Welkin and Gillian do not fall into enemy hands. Do you copy?"

There was a long pause, then, "Copy that."

The line went dead and Ferrik's face disappeared. Sarah sat back and started to shake.

Theo headed north. It was possible the attacking ship was able to scan their position underwater in which case he did not want to give away their intended destination. He just hoped they couldn't pick up any residual radiation from the bomb. Theo knew it was well shielded but no one really knew the limits of the aliens' technology.

That's when the first explosion occurred. The entire shuttle bucked like a wild horse. Theo would have fallen out of his seat if he hadn't been buckled in. "Dammit, what was that?"

Renko ran some scans. "Some kind of passive bomb. There're more on the way. I think they must be dropping them in on top of us."

"So they know where we are?"

"Looks like it."

"Do we know where they are?"

"Give me a minute."

"We may not have a minute!" Another explosion rocked the spaceplane but this one was further away. "At least they're not precision drops," Theo muttered to himself. "Renko?"

"They're following us, right above, and a little forward. I guess they're trying to predict our course."

Theo started zigzagging immediately. More depth charges exploded but none came as near as the first one. Theo glanced at Miles. "We got surface to air missiles, right?"

"Right."

"How many?"

"One."

"One?" Theo almost spat the word.

Miles shrugged. "We re-jigged this contraption in a hurry. It was a civilian spaceplane. One missile. That's our total complement. You got a problem with that, write out a complaint in triplicate and submit it to the appropriate department."

"We got an appropriate department?"

"Nope."

"That's what I thought. Thanks for your advice."

"Always tryin' to oblige, Captain."

"How accurate are those missiles?"

"They'll home in on almost anything."

"Fine. Get a heat signature for that ship and key it in."

"Will do, but there's one problem."

Theo stifled a groan. "And what would that be, Miles?"

"The blast generates a secondary EM pulse that will shut down all electromagnetic systems. That includes ours. We're inside the pulse radius."

"Which would effectively sink us. What's the radius?"

"Well, we're underwater, so I can only give you my best guess."

"Your best guess?"

"Yes, sir."

"And what would your best guess be?"

"At least a half mile of water."

"That much?"

"Affirmative, sir."

"And the pressure limit of our hull is?"

"Dunno, sir, but it's probably around five hundred yards of depth."

"How did I know you were going to say that?"

"Clairvoyance?"

"Okay, set it up. I'm going to drop down as far as I can go, then we run for it as the missile heads up. Hopefully, we'll put enough horizontal distance between us to make it."

"Aye, aye, Captain."

Sarah palmed the audio off. Ferrik had just called back.

"It's bad, isn't it?" said Angela, studying Sarah's face.

Sarah nodded. "Ferrik says he can't get Welkin out and he can't—neutralize him. He thinks we have one hour at most. Then the bugs will know everything we know."

Angela stared, aghast.

"What are you going to do?"

"What else can I do?"

She pushed the audio pad again.

"Fire!"

Miles punched the launch button. There was a *whoosh* and the spaceplane rocked slightly. Theo nailed the throttle and the craft surged forward, pinning them all to their seats.

"Renko, how we doing?"

"Total vector, three hundred yards."

"Time to impact?"

"Five seconds. Right on target."

"Renko?"

"Four hundred yards."

"Come on," said Theo, trying to shove the throttle past the stops. "Four hundred and fifty yards," said Renko.

"Gotcha!"

"Brace for impact," said Theo. He held his breath, hoping against hope that the EM pulse would not reach them here. Then he realized the time had already come and gone. Traveling at the speed of light the pulse would have hit them an infinitesimal moment after the detonation of the missile.

So that only left the …

The shock wave hit. The spaceplane banked and adjusted its shape, attempting to keep a streamlined form more suited for water even as deep-throated metallic groans ran along the length of the ship, as if it were banging along between the hulls of two bigger ships. A console blew out, spewing sparks over Renko and giving him a severe flash burn.

Then everything went quiet. Theo righted the ship. After a moment he turned it southwards.

"Everybody okay?"

"Sort of," said Renko.

"Get to the medkit. Give yourself some spraygel and painkillers."

Renko nodded and moved his hand unsteadily.

A series of *beeps* sounded. Miles checked his control board. "Coded message coming in."

"Decode it."

Miles did so then looked up, oddly sober.

"Well?" Theo glanced across at his co-pilot, realized he was ashen-faced. He turned back, nodded quietly to himself. "Let me have it."

"We're to proceed with our mission. Deploy bomb. Detonation for T-minus fifty-five minutes—from now." He swallowed. "They want us to nuke Melbourne."

Theo nodded again, feeling as if everything had gone still. "I know." But Miles didn't hear the words. Theo was talking to himself. All Miles knew for sure was that he had never seen such a grim expression on Theo's face.

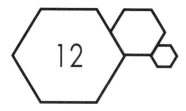

12

Welkin made a decision.

"Clifford and I will go," he said. Gillian opened her mouth to protest, but Welkin glared at her. She closed her mouth, said nothing, but Welkin could read her concern. "We've got to get a message out. If we do a burst, they'll find us all, like Hatch said. So this is the only way. If everything's okay, I'll send Clifford back. If he's not here inside of forty minutes, assume you're on your own—and that the enemy might know everything we know."

"That's a mighty big risk you're taking," said Hatch.

"We've got our blues," Welkin replied, referring to their suicide pills. "Besides, the risk was taken the moment we set out to penetrate Melbourne."

"You mightn't get a chance to use the pills," Hatch said. "Remember they're toting live ammunition, too. Let me come," he said suddenly, hefting his pulse rifle.

"They need you here," Welkin said. Hatch looked away sourly. Welkin shot Clifford a look. "You ready?"

"Hell, no, but let's get going before I change my mind."

Welkin grinned. Suddenly Gillian was in his arms, kissing him in a very emphatic way. Clifford raised his eyebrows. "Say, can I have one of those?"

"Uh-uh," she said, laughing. She seemed more alive than ever, with the aura of potential death around. At least Welkin knew she wasn't in danger from any of the transmittable diseases that used to haunt the Earthborn—like most of the family she had had the benefit of a quick chip test with a drop of blood. Some things couldn't be reversed yet, but Skyborn technology had eradicated some of their previous worries.

Welkin disentangled himself from her, squeezed her hand, and picked up his laserlite. Roddy's bluetooth scanner was now taped to it. "Forty minutes," he said.

Gillian scowled. "We had to go and stow our gear in a blind spot, didn't we?"

Welkin shrugged. "No help for that now. Come on, Clifford. Let's go."

They moved out, taking the stairs down to the street level, moving cautiously. In the last half an hour the bluetooth "rifle" had revealed a great deal of movement in the neighborhood. More than usual, Roddy had said. Welkin had no doubt that most of the squads they were picking up were search parties. The zombies didn't try to conceal their electronic signals from the directional scanner that was looking for them. But once again, the advantage lay with the fugitives. Every moving blip that showed up on the scanner had to be an enemy. Whereas those that showed up on the Hiveborn devices could be friend or foe. It meant that the Hiveborn were reduced to finding them by the old-fashioned traditional method: looking in every nook and cranny.

When they reached street level they kept going down, finding the stairs to the basement. It was full of dust and debris and rat droppings. Obviously, the Hiveborn general cleanup hadn't reached everywhere yet.

As they searched the area there appeared to be no obvious exit.

"Look around. Somebody must've burrowed over to the buildings on the other side at some point."

Suddenly over their heads they heard the sound of heavy footsteps. Welkin frowned, aiming the scanner directly up. Damn, the thing didn't have a vertical dimension. You had to actually point it. He had just been fanning it back and forth in front of him.

Dust drifted down from the ceiling.

"We gotta hide somewhere," hissed Clifford.

"No. They're too thorough for that. We need a way out of here *now*." He motioned Clifford back to the shadowy far side of the basement where he'd been looking for some kind of egress: maintenance hatch, hand-dug tunnel, underpass, anything.

According to the scanner the squad above had fanned out, and was methodically checking the first floor. It was only a matter of time before one of them found the steps leading down into the basement; if some enterprising Hiveborn thought to point his or her scanner *down* at the floor, Welkin and Clifford would be busted.

They needed to get out of there.

"Hey, come take a look at this," came Clifford's urgent whisper. Welkin hurried over, peering at the wall where Clifford was pointing. As far as he could see there was nothing there. "Stand back," urged Clifford.

Welkin did so, scanning the wall again. This time he saw it. As old as the brickwork was, there was a slightly newer patch in the shape of a doorway. It was hard to see but once you got the pattern of it, it stood out like a flashing neon light.

"If we vaporize it, it'll lead them right after us," said Welkin, frowning in the dark. Suddenly, he looked down at his feet. They were standing on old, rotten floorboards. He jounced up and down a few times, feeling the sway of the joists. Then they heard the door to the basement steps creak open.

"Jeez, somebody's coming."

"Prise them up!" Welkin whispered urgently, indicating the floorboards. Clifford dropped to his knees, pulling something like a crowbar out of his backpack. In a flash he had two floorboards up, just enough space to squeeze through—for someone rake-thin.

They flung their backpacks into the dark hole. Clifford squeezed and wriggled through, grunting as bits of his flesh caught on splintery wood. In a blink, he was through. Welkin cast a look back. He noticed a flashlight beam playing across the bottom part of the stairs. Then he too wriggled through the gap, dropping into soft powdery earth that had an old, dank smell. As he rolled aside, fetching up against a concrete abutment, Clifford reached through and carefully fitted the floorboards back into place.

They held their breath.

Creaking footsteps slowly crisscrossed the floor above them as they huddled in the dry darkness beneath the floorboards. Tiny shafts of light flashed through chinks in the boards, momentarily illuminating the crawlspace. In one such flash Welkin saw Clifford—or rather received a "snapshot" image of him—frozen in a kind of crouch, head turned slightly up in a posture of strained listening, not daring to move, probably—like Welkin—not daring to breathe.

Then the footsteps came closer. Someone stood directly overhead. Dust fell into Welkin's eyes, got up his nose. He felt a sudden and explosive sneeze coming on.

Just as he clutched his face to stifle the sound the footsteps died away and so did the urge to sneeze. Welkin was left feeling weak and shaky, as though he'd just run a marathon. As the footsteps receded up the stairs he breathed again. Next to him in the dark, so did Clifford.

"That was close," whispered Clifford.

"Too close. Let's see if there's a way out of here." Still feeling shaky from the close encounter, Welkin squirmed around, flicking on his flashlight and playing it ahead of him. At the furthest stretch of the beam, which illuminated a long low colonnaded space, he could just make out a brick wall. "Well, it goes in the right direction, under the street."

"Lead on, boss," said Clifford.

Welkin belly-crawled towards the wall, moving between old plasteel foundation posts. The crawlspace was thick with cobwebs and the accumulated dust was so thin and dry that the tiniest movement sent it whirling into their eyes, ears, noses and mouths. Welkin several times had the urge to sneeze again but managed to suppress it.

When they were halfway across, below what was presumably the middle of the road above, Welkin felt something under his hand. He brushed away dust and uncovered a bottle. He aimed the flashlight at it to read the faded inscription on the side.

"What does it say?" Clifford asked.

"Co-ca-co-la," Welkin said, sounding out the syllables.

"What's cocacola?"

"Some kind of drink?"

"Clever. Guess that's why they bottled it, huh?"

Welkin grinned, dropped the bottle, and crawled on. At the base of the brick wall, he stopped and panned the beam of the flashlight around. He was in what looked like a cul-de-sac with no obvious way out except for the way they had come in. Aiming the beam upwards however revealed something entirely different.

"What do you reckon that is?" Welkin asked Clifford as his partner crawled up beside him.

The flashlight beam revealed a narrow circular tube that went up at a sharp angle. It was large enough to crawl into but looked too smooth to gain much purchase.

"No idea," said Clifford, "unless it was for some kind of delivery. You know, like in the old days when people had coal delivered to their houses."

Welkin chuckled. "You've been watching too many old vids. People haven't had coal delivered since the mid twentieth century. But you might be right. Think you can get up it?"

"I'll give it a try."

Clifford squirmed into the entrance, twisted on to his back, settled his pack on his stomach, and reached up for fingerholds. He obviously found some because, quite suddenly, his legs disappeared into the tube.

For one panicky moment, Welkin thought something had grabbed him. "You okay?"

"Fine. This is easy. The tube comes in sections, each about a yard long. Where they meet there's a nice deep gap. Come on."

With that, Clifford started up the tube. By the time Welkin had stood, twisted round, and pulled himself into the first section Clifford was already 15 feet above him. "You got monkey ancestors, have you?"

"If that's a slur on my family tree, I'll make you take it back," echoed Clifford's reply.

"You and what army of primates?"

A moment later Clifford's voice drifted down the tube again. "I'm at the top. It comes out on a fairly steep lane." Welkin made it the rest of the way and wriggled out of the opening with Clifford's assistance. Looking around, he realized they were in one of the narrow streets that intersected the center of Melbourne. In fact, this was the eastern and upper end of what had once been Flinders Lane and about 30 feet higher in elevation than the street they'd originally been trying to cross unseen. The warehouse itself was directly behind them.

Without waiting, Welkin ducked into a nearby doorway. Clifford followed. Welkin used the scanner to check the vicinity.

"All clear," he whispered, then added: "Up *and* down."

Two minutes later they were standing on the floor of the warehouse where they'd entered the city from the storm drains. Unfortunately, the spot where they'd hidden the scuba gear was directly beneath one of the towers Roddy had warned them about, creating a virtual dead zone on the scanner.

"An entire army could be hiding in there," said Welkin, giving the scanner an impatient shake.

"So we do this the old-fashioned way."

"Guess so. And as the leader of this expedition I order you to go point."

Clifford grinned. "So you'll be bringing up the rear?"

"Yeah."

"Great. Point and rear. The two most dangerous positions in any scouting operation. How come we didn't bring a third person?"

"What, so you could skive off and go in the middle? You a wuss?"

"Paid up member."

"Well, your dues just ran out. Get going."

Clifford threw Welkin a mock salute and started crawling between the stacked pallets and bales of foodstuffs. Welkin let him get about ten yards ahead then followed, pistol clutched in his hand. As they neared the spot, Welkin could see Clifford slow to a baby's crawl, inching forward past a pallet, scoping the way ahead. After a long moment of this he edged back and signaled Welkin to join him. Maintaining strict silence, Welkin closed the gap and crawled alongside.

Clifford put his mouth to Welkin's ear. "Coast seems clear. The pallet where we hid the stuff is about twenty-five feet the other side of this one." He gestured at the pallet they were hiding behind.

Welkin then whispered in Clifford's ear. "Doesn't mean it's safe. You cover me."

Clifford nodded. He rolled up his trouser leg, revealing a holster. Loosening the handgun there he then covered it. Hefting his laserlite into position, he checked the charge, and gave Welkin a thumbs-up.

Welkin took a deep breath, got to his feet, and circled back around the pallet, crab-crawling to keep low. The target pallet came into sight. He stopped, checking that the area was clear.

He darted forward, staying low. Crossing the intervening space in a blur of movement he slammed heavily into the pallet, almost knocking the wind out of himself. But he was more worried about becoming a target for some sniper.

As soon as he made contact with the pallet he froze, quieting his breath, breathing through his mouth. He let his eyes do the scanning. Left, right, up, down. All the time, listening. He'd learnt many lessons from Sarah in their years together. One of them was always to listen. Another was to smell.

Of all the senses, the eyes were most easily deceived.

That's when he heard it. And knew.

It was a trap.

Everything seemed to slow down and happen at once. He spun round, signaling to Clifford. He saw his friend pull back into hiding, then half a dozen nearby pallets seemed to explode as their covers were thrown back and a dozen Hiveborn leapt out, pulse rifles zeroing.

"Drop your weapon!" barked one of them.

For a second, Welkin was tempted to shoot it out. He had no hope of winning but getting shot would be easier than swallowing a pill. But then he still had an ace up his sleeve. Clifford.

Shrugging, he dropped the laserlite, and straightened up. The Hiveborn squad leader approached cautiously, frisking Welkin quickly and expertly.

The commander signaled his men to spread out, and it was clear they were looking for Clifford. Welkin just hoped he'd had enough time to get away. But the moment also presented Welkin with an opportunity. Right now all eyes were on the men spearing off into the corridors between the pallets. Welkin backed up slightly, hands behind his back, feeling for something. He found it. A piece of thick wire. He quickly bent it back and forth and snapped it off, sliding it up his sleeve just as one of the Hiveborn grabbed him and dragged him away.

Outside in the street another small group joined them. They herded Clifford in next to Welkin near the center of the squad.

"So much for you escaping and rescuing me later," said Welkin sourly.

"Was that the plan? I thought it was we both get captured, tortured, then heroically commit hari-kari."

"No, that's the plan I was hoping to avoid."

"You should tell me these things," said Clifford.

"I will next time."

"That's what I like to hear."

"What?"

"That there'll be a next time."

Welkin grunted good-naturedly, flicking his eyes over their captors. There were about eight of them, all heavily armed. Curiously, they did not bother shackling them. Welkin wondered why, then experienced a prickling sensation down his spine. They wouldn't need to be shackled if they were about to be converted …

Without even meaning to, his tongue probed the tooth near the back of his mouth, the false one that contained the cyanide capsule. To activate it he had to nudge it aside with his tongue then bite down on it. Apparently, death would be almost instantaneous and painless. He wondered how they knew it was painless, or was that just wishful thinking?

Whatever happened, they must not be possessed. The knowledge they carried in their heads was far too valuable. Better they were dead.

The commander, who still hadn't spoken to Welkin, led the way to what Welkin assumed was a conversion station, though surely by now most inhabitants of the city had either been possessed or gone deep underground.

They were led inside and to his horror Welkin saw a large vat of red jelly. He felt a sick empty feeling in his stomach and applied a tiny amount of pressure to the false tooth.

Peering into the vat, the commander then stepped back. "Your lucky day," he said to Welkin in a conversational tone. Welkin looked at him in surprise, removing his tongue from the tooth. It was always a shock when a known Hiveborn behaved in a very human fashion. But it made a weird kind of sense, too. The parasite had to use not just the body, but also the mind and psychology of the host creature. In this they were the ultimate parasites, not just leeching nutrients from the host, but an entire social fabric as well. They integrated over time. "Seems we're out of units."

"Tough."

The commander shrugged. "Plenty more at headquarters," he said jovially, and gestured for his men to lead the captives outside. Welkin exchanged a look with Clifford who nodded back, almost imperceptibly. If they were going to do anything it needed to be soon.

They marched down the lane and into the city proper, crossing what had once been Swanston Walk. Welkin suddenly realized they were heading for the old Melbourne Town Hall building and with this he knew it was time to act. They were moving up a narrow alleyway that cut between two crumbling facades. Once out of the alley they would be lost.

Twenty feet ahead Welkin saw an obstruction barring their path. Hopefully it would force the soldiers into a narrow file. He stumbled against Clifford, tapping out a code on his wrist. Their eyes locked for a second. And just as the front part of the guard converged and made their way around the obstacle Welkin slipped the wire from his sleeve and drove it with lightning speed into the left ear of the Commander. As he'd hoped, the officer went into instant analeptic shock. Welkin didn't wait but took out the next nearest guard in the same way. Meanwhile, behind him, Clifford retrieved his handgun from its ankle holster. He quickly struck down a guard. Welkin only saw this from the corner of his eye and marveled that Clifford had managed to keep the gun hidden.

The Hiveborn snapped out of their guard mode and into attack mode. Pulse weapons came up, taking aim. Welkin threw himself on another guard, managed to pierce the parasite with his wire, then used the guard's body to take the brunt of the first shot. By then Clifford was opening up, fanning the guards who were knotted together and presented, in numerical terms, an easier target. Not that the guards gave a damn about shooting other guards who were in their line of fire. Hosts, it seemed, were pretty dispensable when it came right down to it.

There were only two guards left now. As Welkin manhandled his shield victim, he stepped back and fell over the body of the Commander. In that instant he was a sitting duck. One of the remaining guards whipped up his pulse weapon, finger squeezing on the trigger at point-blank range. At the last second, a body rammed Welkin from the side, knocking him over. There was a flash of the pulse rifle and two quick answering flashes.

By the time Welkin scrambled to his feet it was all over. Everyone was down. Including Clifford who had saved his life.

Welkin knelt beside him. He had a pretty bad chest wound, though it had self-cauterized. He grinned feebly up at Welkin. "Told Gillian—I'd save— your worthless arse." He was having trouble breathing.

Welkin swallowed. "Can you walk?"

"Just you watch me."

Welkin scooped up a pulse rifle then helped Clifford to his feet. Stumbling, and moving with painful slowness, they got out of the alleyway and into what had once long ago been a department store. Now it was some kind of storage facility. Welkin knew that with Clifford in this state they needed to stay off the streets, maybe wait until dark.

He found a hidey-hole from where they could also take peeks at the street below. It wasn't long before the bodies were discovered and removed. Not all the humans nor all the parasites were dead. Welkin presumed that those without serious injury would be salvaged. The others ...

Clifford drifted in and out of delirium for the next two hours. Fortunately, the Hiveborn had not removed Welkin's medkit which he kept in a pocket of his tunic. He administered a painkiller and general antibiotic and did his best to bandage the chest wound.

At one point he found Clifford grinning at him, perfectly lucid. "Who would have thought?" he said. "Nurse Welkin. I think you missed your calling."

"Just don't tell the other guys, okay?"

"Your secret's safe with me," said Clifford. "I promise to take it to my grave."

Welkin winced. He gave Clifford some water then watched as his friend lapsed back into delirium. An hour later he died, murmuring a name Welkin didn't know. "Susie? Don't tell anyone, okay?"

Those were the last words he uttered.

For a long time Welkin sat, his head bowed. Outside, shadows closed in and it grew dark. When he finally roused he said goodbye to his friend, covered him with his own jacket, and left, moving disconsolately through the shadows inside the building.

Whether by luck or by some spirit that felt he had now paid his dues, he managed to get back to the building where he had left the others, unmolested.

He ran into Roddy first. He had just stepped out of a cross corridor on the rooftop when a laserlite was shoved in his face.

"Welkin?"

Welkin nodded wearily. "Yeah, it's me. Where are the others?"

"Back there." He inclined his head behind him. "You go first." Welkin complied, aware that Roddy's laserlite never left him for a second. One part of his mind noted this: The kid's got good discipline. Probably that's how he stayed alive.

When he reappeared in the midst of the others there was a collective gasp of relief. Gillian threw herself at Welkin but he held her at arm's length. She stared at him a moment then nodded curtly. "Okay, damn you, you're right. As usual. Get on your knees, hands behind your back."

Daniel exclaimed in surprise. "What are you doing, Gillian?"

"What I should have done straight off, as Welkin was kind enough to remind me. Keep him covered, Roddy."

Roddy nodded as Gillian quickly inspected both of Welkin's ears. When she was satisfied that he was not carrying a parasite she leaned close and blew sharply into one ear. He flinched away, rubbing his ear as she burst out laughing. Then they were hugging.

After he had told them everything that had happened, their jubilant mood lapsed into a kind of dull despair. Gillian's eyes glistened as Welkin recounted Clifford's last moments.

"Well, that's that, then. We're cut off."

Hatch said, "Don't know about that. Arton isn't going to just sit there forever."

"You think he'll come looking for us?"

"Maybe."

Welkin expelled a deep sigh. "His orders are clear. If he doesn't hear from us by noon tomorrow he's to head back to Martha."

"People don't always follow orders," said Gillian, giving him a look.

He ruffled her hair. "No. They don't always." He looked around at them. "I guess this mission has been pretty much a failure."

"Not yet," said Gillian.

Welkin looked at her. 'What do you mean?"

Daniel stepped forward. "What she means is, we have started our examination of the parasites."

Welkin was startled. "Here? In the field?"

"Why not? At least, if we can learn something, we may be able to get that information back to Martha even if none of us ever get there. Besides, I have most of the equipment I need. I brought a basic field lab with me, just in case. Actually, it was Sarah's idea."

Welkin relaxed, feeling better already. "Sarah thinks of everything. So. Have you learnt anything yet?"

"Yes. And no," said the doctor enigmatically. "It is too soon to tell but I intend to work through the night."

"I'll let you get on with it then." The doctor went to the far side of the "blind spot" Roddy had directed them to earlier. Welkin turned to the others. "While I was sitting with Clifford, I decided we had to take the risk and warn Martha. So I need a volunteer to take a spare radio, find a location some distance from here, and send off a compressed data burst."

Hatch stepped forward. "I'll do it."

Gillian shook her head. "This is a job for me. I'm small, I'm fast, and I've been escaping predators—especially the two footed kind—since I was a kid. No offence, but you Skyborn are a bunch of softies when it comes right down to it."

Everybody chuckled, except Hatch who glared at her for a second. "You saying I'm fat?"

Gillian gave him an appraising look. "Noooo. You're just kind of big-boned." He looked slightly mollified. "And getting bigger."

Soft laughter now. Hatch harrumphed. "I enjoy my food, okay?"

Gillian put a hand on his arm. "And so you should," she said soothingly.

Hatch suddenly grinned at her. "Ah, don't play your tricks on me, girl. I say we toss for it."

Welkin shook his head. "Gillian's right. This won't be about brute force and shooting your way out. But Roddy here could go. He's small and fast."

Roddy nodded eagerly. "Any time," he said.

"No," said Gillian. "Roddy's only just joined us. That's not fair, asking him to risk his life for people he's never met. It has to be me, Welkin. You're too tired and in any case I still do a better sneak than you do."

"Don't I know it," he said ruefully, thinking back to a time when she had sneaked up on him during a training exercise and caused him no end of embarrassment.

In the end, Gillian got her way. Welkin didn't have the energy to argue and vetoing her going would smack of favoritism. In the pre-dawn hours, after a few hours of sleep, Gillian packed the radio transmitter, some supplies, and came over and kissed Welkin.

"I wish you weren't doing this," he said.

"Now you know how I felt when you and Clifford went off."

They talked briefly and intimately then Gillian left and the shadows swallowed her up. Welkin lay back, staring at the stars. A knot of ice, the size of his fist, had formed in his stomach, and he grimly fought it.

Gillian moved with absolute caution.

She had made her way across several rooftops while it was still dark, putting as much distance between herself and the others as possible, yet making sure she had a clear route of return as well. She didn't mind taking risks, but that didn't mean she was willing to throw her life away.

She had decided to remain on the rooftops. It would give her better reception, though it would also allow the Hiveborn to pinpoint her visually with greater ease. All they'd need was to launch some low flying cruisers or spybirds and crisscross the area of the radio burst. She'd hoped to get to her designated sending spot before dawn broke, giving her the cover of darkness for her retreat. But shortly after leaving Welkin, she ran foul of a Hiveborn search squad.

She was crab-crawling along a parapet overlooking a laneway, keeping below the topmost edge so no silhouette would show, when she heard them. At least half a dozen pairs of booted feet crossing the membrane stretching across the laneway. As far as she could tell, they were coming directly for her position where she crouched in the deeper shadow under the balcony.

She cast wildly about. It was too late to scramble back the way she'd come, even if she could do so without making some tiny giveaway noise. The nearest cover was a good 30 feet away and ahead of her was the corner—a trap. Except for one thing. There was a ventilator shaft poking from the rooftop, its grating hanging off to one side.

Without thinking about the consequences of what she intended, she swiftly reached the shaft, performing a complicated maneuver which involved planting her hands on the ground then sliding fluidly feet first into the open shaft.

As soon as she was inside she started to drop. At the same time she heard one of the Hiveborn speak, but the words were lost as she plummeted down the narrow shaft. She rammed her boots and shoulders into the sides of the shaft. And, as soon as her fall was slowed by this, she added her bare arms, increasing the friction.

Her fall slowed. She managed to bring her knees up to her chest, jamming herself inside the tube. Her descent had dropped to a crawl and she breathed out, only then realizing she'd been holding her breath.

Then she hit. The impact was still hard enough to jar her tailbone and expel the breath from her lungs in a *whoomph*.

She sat there letting the splintery pain in her coccyx ebb. Then she took stock. She was stuck pretty solidly, her knees to her chest and her backpack with the radio at her back. Easing this up and over her head gave her more room to play with and she managed to get to her feet and rummage through her pack, fishing out her trusty flashlight.

She flicked this on.

She'd been lucky. The ventilator shaft was a new one, obviously built by the newcomers. An old one could have been so weak it would have collapsed under her weight. The only problem was, she couldn't at first see any way out of the shaft. She was standing on a thick heavy grille that let air through but which didn't seem to have any means of being opened from this side, which made sense if you were a million-year-old paranoid alien organism that had grown cautious and canny over the millennia.

Stay calm, Gillian told herself, as she felt the first icy pricks of claustrophobia. There was a way out of every situation.

Not true, said another part of her brain, but she decided to ignore that part for now. There *was* a way out. The way she'd gotten in. Scaling the 50-foot-long shaft, as mountain climbers scaled a chimney, using their body as a kind of vertically creeping wedge. It was obviously an option. Just a slow laborious and no doubt exhausting one. But one she had no doubt she could achieve.

She breathed out again, feeling a whole lot better. That's when she noticed something. Ten feet above her was the open mouth of another—horizontal—

shaft. On the way down she'd luckily been applying pressure to the sides of the shaft that didn't include the opening, otherwise she would probably have broken something.

Tying a rope to her backpack and the other end to her ankle, she stuck the flashlight between her teeth, sucked in a lungful of air, and starting climbing.

The sun was high when Welkin awoke, amazed not only by the fact that he had gone back to sleep but that he had slept for so long. Hatch shrugged, explaining that there was nothing to do for now, and what was the point of waking him when he'd been so tired?

Welkin sat up, sniffing the air, then wrinkling up his nose. "What *is* that stink?" he asked.

"Come see," said Hatch, then blocked him with an outstretched arm. "On second thought, maybe you should have breakfast first."

"Are you kidding?" said Welkin. "You want me to puke it all up again?"

Hatch grimaced. "You may not want breakfast after you see this."

He led Welkin to a small semi-enclosed area where Daniel was working and which was still within Roddy's scanner blind spot. Here the doctor had organized a makeshift field lab, spreading his instruments on a horizontal ventilation shaft. His lab, such as it was, was blocked from aerial view by an overhanging section of the strange chimney which almost met a retaining wall.

Here the Hiveborn squad they had captured lay on makeshift beds. They were all asleep, or comatose—Welkin couldn't tell which—but looked somehow healthier than they had the day before. He commented on this.

Daniel turned from his bench and greeted Welkin. "You're right about them," he said, indicating his patients. "I'm not sure exactly what the Hiveborn use, but they flood the bodies of their hosts with a cocktail of chemicals and hormones that I haven't seen before. At the very least, I'd say they enhance the body's function by at least a factor of two or three. But that comes at a cost. One seems to be a dulling of the complexion and hair, which suggests that certain nutrients—minerals and vitamins—normally needed for the proper health of the epidermis and hair, are being hijacked for other purposes, presumably the metabolic needs of the parasite. A number of other bodily functions seem to be hijacked as well, though at this time I can't even hazard a guess as to why."

"How are they doing?" Welkin asked.

"Oh, they'll all be okay. Physically, anyway. I can't yet say what the long-term psychological and emotional effects of possession will be. Only time will tell us that."

Welkin was relieved that the prisoners were technically no longer prisoners but new recruits, though he didn't kid himself that all the recruits would be willing ones. Old animosities die hard and some of these people had, in their previous lives, been ardent and unforgiving enemies. They would need watching.

"So what stinks so much?"

"That." Daniel pointed at a congealed mess inside a jar. It took a powerful leap of the imagination to realize that what he was looking at was a parasite. Or more than one. "I'm afraid I bungled the extraction process."

Welkin felt a pang of concern. "They're not all like that, are they?"

"No, no. I may be clumsy but I learn from my mistakes. No. We have four fine healthy parasites, though I believe we will need some of the red jelly to keep them alive or else alternative hosts."

Welkin frowned. "What do you mean?"

"Dogs, cats, large rabbits, horses. Well, maybe not horses. They could be dangerous."

Welkin ignored the doctor's attempt at humor. "Have you found out anything yet?"

"Several things. But let me get back to my work. I will have more to tell you by lunchtime."

Despite the stink, mention of lunch made Welkin realize he was hungry. As he sat munching rations a few minutes later, he wondered where Gillian was and if she was all right.

Sweating heavily, and not without a few cuts and scrapes, Gillian made it to the cross shaft. Dragging herself inside she collapsed, breathing hard. When she'd recovered, she hauled up her backpack and started crawling cautiously along the new shaft, careful to make as little noise as possible.

Some 20 yards along she came to a grille and peered down into what looked like some kind of workshop. Several men and women were busy building small electronic devices by command with boxy circuitry 3-D printers and fabricators. They did not chat and seemed utterly absorbed in what they were doing.

Gillian didn't linger. She needed to get out of there, send off the radio burst, and get back to Welkin. Spying could wait for another day.

Moving even more quietly than before, she slid along inside the shaft to the next grille. This one showed what looked like an empty room. Feeling that it wasn't far enough from the busy workers she crawled to the next one. This room too was empty.

After listening carefully for several minutes, Gillian carefully prized up the grille and let herself down into the room, handgun between her teeth.

But she met no opposition.

The room she found herself in was filled with containers of what she quickly discovered was the red jelly Welkin had mentioned. On impulse, she grabbed several small containers of the stuff and placed them in the bottom of her backpack. They weighed her down a little, but they might turn out to be useful to Daniel.

Gillian padded across to the door, eased it open, and peered out into a deserted corridor. Opposite her was a door marked "Staircase." She was across the corridor and through the door in seconds. From there she found her way, unchallenged, to the roof. An hour later she was holed up in a tangle of pipes near one of the blind spots, crouching beneath an overhang much like the one Daniel was using.

The sun was high in the eastern sky by the time she had the transmitter set up, had encoded and compressed the data package for high speed burst, and was ready to send. Welkin had told her she shouldn't expect to have more than six minutes from the time of sending to the arrival of the Hiveborn. That meant she had to be gone in five, tops. She'd already scouted out three different escape routes, augmenting one of them with a rope and a gravity braking grip. All she had to do was grab the grip and jump off the building. Seconds later she would be down in the street, dropping into a cul-de-sac's manhole which she had already prized open.

Gillian took a deep breath, set her stopwatch, and hit the "send" button. The transmitter hissed for a second then pinged. The message was away. Now she had to play the waiting game. If Martha didn't answer within five minutes she was gone. If necessary, she would abandon the transmitter (after frying it of course; she didn't want the enemy to have Martha's frequency).

The first minute ticked by. And the second.

The third had just gone and she was definitely starting to get antsy when the receiver crackled. She tuned it. "Hello? Hello? Martha? This is Gillian. Confirm you received message."

"Gillian. Is everybody okay?" Gillian started. The voice was Ferrik's.

"Ferrik? Yes, we're all okay. We—" She bit her lip. She had to assume that the Hiveborn would be monitoring their exchange. "The sardines got into the fish factory, but they're about to get canned, if they're not careful. But they located some of the funny fish."

Ferrik chuckled. "Stardust to Sardine. Got you." There was a pause. "Martha is sleeping at the moment. She isn't taking any messages or giving any. She might've taken some poison pills."

Gillian groaned. "Understood," she said. "Must fly. Lot of big fish in the vicinity. The kind that eat little fish."

"Tell Welkin to tune into the frequency he and I discussed. Talk soon. Over and out."

Gillian shut down the transmission and checked her stopwatch. Five-and-a-half minutes had elapsed. Not good. She stepped back and gave the transmitter a burst from her laserlite.

Then she heard a noise and turned in that direction.

The last of the dispossessed Earthborn was waking up. Daniel's assistant gave him water from a canteen and he drank thirstily, then sat up gingerly, looking around, blinking.

"Welcome back," said Welkin.

The man shuddered and started to cry. It was like this with all of them. The enormity of what had happened to him hit and hit hard. The man started frenziedly wiping his arms clean, then his chest and legs, as if something disgusting was crawling all over his body. He began babbling, but Welkin leaned forward and slapped him.

The man stopped, his hysteria abated almost instantly, and he gazed back at Welkin. "Who are you?" he asked.

"No time for that. We're not out of danger yet. Your parasite—the bug that was controlling you—is in a jar over there." The man stared across at the bench holding the jars. The expression on his face was one of disgust mingled with fury. "Take a deep breath. It's over. What's your name?"

"Wignell. Friends call me Wiggy."

"Okay, Wiggy, we have to move. Now. Can you handle a gun?"

"Damn right I can."

Welkin gave him one. "That's for the enemy out there. You don't touch the parasites in the jars, got that?"

"Why not?" Wiggy's tone was sulky.

"Because we need them."

"You need them?"

"To find a way to kill them. All of them."

"To kill them? You swear that's what you're doing?"

"I swear."

"Okay." Wiggy got unsteadily to his feet. Welkin helped him and introduced him to everyone including the other awakened ex-zombies. It turned out that Wiggy knew one of them. They had been in the same tribe before being captured by the Hiveborn. One of the others was a Skyborn, a former sub-Elder. Welkin regarded him with suspicion, but the man seemed completely cowed by his recent experience and only too happy to follow orders. In any case, Welkin detailed Hatch to keep an eye—and, if necessary, a gun—on him. Welkin didn't want any unpleasant surprises.

He looked around. They were packed and ready to go. Gillian was late. He'd left a message stuck to the wall of the "chimney" which—in family slang—told her where they were heading. No one else would be able to decipher it.

"Okay. Let's get moving." He shouldered his own pack and picked up his laserlite, his heart heavy, and a part of him shouting at him to stop. To wait just a little bit longer. But he couldn't endanger everyone just because the woman he loved hadn't come back from a dangerous mission.

But if she'd been taken, then he swore that he'd come back soon, alone, and find her. He would not leave her in this place.

He had just turned to give the order to move out, when he heard running feet. Gillian burst into view, panting hard. She threw herself at him and started kissing him. He kissed her back. She broke off. "Hiveborn. They're tracking me. I think I've thrown them off but we should get the hell out of here."

Welkin pretended to turn to give that order then whipped around, backhanding her. She dropped, but he caught her, easing her to the ground. Everyone stared at Welkin in shock.

"Doctor, get the parasite out of her. Now!"

Daniel bustled forward. He and his assistant carried Gillian to the side and he produced his bag of tricks, then stopped. He looked up at Welkin. "There's no parasite here," he said. "She's not possessed."

"What?"

"She's not possessed."

Hatch frowned. "What made you think she had been?"

Welkin was thinking hard. "She wasn't sweating."

"Well, that's a fine reason to pop somebody in the snoot!" His joke lessened the tension in the group, especially amongst the new recruits who knew nothing about Welkin.

"Doctor, check again. Look for signs that she was recently possessed."

Daniel sighed, started checking, clearly not convinced. But a moment later his sharp intake of breath made them all turn. He looked up at Welkin. "You're right. There's inflammation and swelling in the ear passage identical to our friends here." He gestured at the recently reawakened men and women. "I'd say an extraction was made just in the last few minutes."

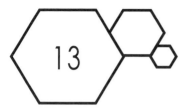

13

Ferrik thought fast and furiously.

The information of the newly revived zombie—Thompson—cast a whole new light on the problem. If they detonated the charges, they would do miniscule damage. And if, as Thompson said, this was an enormous nursery, then the security—especially the security designed to stop that information leaking out—must be enormous too.

Of much greater importance was the need to get this knowledge Earthside. And fast. If necessary, they could come back and do their damnedest to raze the place to the ground.

He came to a decision.

"We're leaving," he said. "Deactivate your remote detonators."

"What?" demanded Veeda. Her eyes went directly to Ferrik's ears.

"I don't have time to explain now," said Ferrik. "We have to get out of here." He explained to Thompson where their ship was. "Can you lead us back there, avoiding any checkpoints?"

"There's no way to avoid the main checkpoint, but you shouldn't be challenged."

"What about the 'directive' you mentioned?"

"That was just to question the people I had come across. There's no general alert or anything like that, if that's what you're worried about."

"I was. Good. Okay, everybody. Move into smaller groups and let's get going," said Ferrik. "No detours, no confrontations, I don't care what you see. If you screw up, I'll leave you here."

Thompson led the way back to the security checkpoint. As he had suggested, they passed this without incident. Ferrik supposed that leaving any top secret area was in any case easier than entering it. On *Colony*, of course, they wouldn't have gained entry in the first place. It was certainly a weakness of the Hiveborn. Perhaps in the whole history of its existence the single entity that was the newcomer had never experienced disloyalty or internal division of any kind. Perhaps it had no concept of it. The thought suddenly startled him. Did the Hiveborn assume that all other races were similar? Did it think the humans were a single intelligence with myriad bodies? And if so, could that be used against it?

They were within sight of their docked ship, when the unexpected occurred. They had just turned a corner and were passing between high walls composed entirely of long horizontal pipes that were frosted over. Ferrik felt the chill from the pipes on his skin as he passed.

Then something brushed his ankle. He looked down, saw nothing, started on his way again when the same thing happened.

He signaled to the others to keep going and hunkered down to peer beneath the bottommost pipe where there was an 18 inch gap. "Space!" he exclaimed, flinching backwards. A pair of eyes was staring back at him. As his own accustomed themselves to the gloom under the bank of piping he could just make out the figure of a small girl. She looked to be about ten years old.

Instinctively, he started to smile, to let her know there was no danger, then stopped himself. The Hiveborn possessed children, even toddlers; they had no regard for age or physical condition. If it was living, it was possessed.

Ferrik let his voice sound stern. "What are you doing here?"

The girl tilted her head. Ferrik blinked. "You're not one of them," she said in a light voice. "I've been watching you." She leaned down into the light and exposed her left ear then twisted round and did the same for the right. There was no parasite in either.

Ferrik laughed, mostly from relief. He stuck out his hand. She took it and he helped her crawl out from under the pipes. When she stood up he saw that she was somewhat emaciated. She noticed his look and shrugged. "They don't make it easy to steal food."

Ferrik eyed her. "How did you get here?"

"Like the others. But the thing died and no one noticed. So I started hiding."

"How long have you been here?"

The girl shrugged again. "A long time. I think. Are you leaving? Can I go with you?"

"Sure. But we've got to hurry."

He took her hand but she shook it off. "They don't hold hands," she explained and walked stiffly beside him after that paying him no attention. Ferrik had to suppress a smile but he took her advice and followed suit.

When he arrived at the ship shortly after the others he was greeted by those left behind, and those who had just arrived, with odd looks. There was also something wrong but before Ferrik could ask Harry demanded, almost indignantly, "Where did you get her?"

"She found me. Her parasite died some time ago. Hetti? Veeda? Look after her." He noticed the odd looks again. "What's wrong?"

Veeda looked down at her feet. Hetti sighed. "Elab's gone."

"What? Gone where?"

"The Hiveborn got him."

Ferrik stared at her. "What are you talking about?"

"They got him, Ferrik. We got back and he wasn't here. We found a— pool of blood outside the ship … " Hetti said, her voice trailing off.

"So we replayed the external vid recorders," said Veeda. "It seems some kind of Hiveborn official demanded Elab accompany them. He tried to bluff his way out. And they shot him." She took a deep breath. "He's dead, Ferrik. They dragged him away."

Ferrik took a full minute to digest this then got a grip on himself. There was nothing he could do for Elab. Finding him in this ant's maze would be near to impossible and right now he had what was probably the most important piece of Intel the family was ever going to get.

He couldn't risk that no matter what. So he made the toughest decision of his life.

"Prepare to lift off. Thompson, you're with me." He turned and headed for the cockpit, followed by Thompson. At the door he suddenly stopped and looked back at the girl. "What's your name?"

"Mig."

"Well, Mig, it's nice to have you aboard. I'm Ferrik." To the others: "Get ready for lift off. Sit down and activate straps."

Getting out of the alien moon base was nowhere near as easy as getting in.

In the cockpit, Ferrik had Thompson strap in behind him and Goose. He had already explained to the man that he wanted him to feed him any information he felt was relevant. The curious thing about possession was that the host remembered everything that went on around him or her but couldn't, afterwards, automatically retrieve it. It was a bit like childhood memories: different stimuli sparked them into existence, whether that stimuli was a smell, a song, a sound, or even some odd color. It was the same, it seemed, for the newly awakened. They had information inside their brains that they didn't know they had. It just needed the right stimulus to pull it out and make it useful.

And if there was any time Ferrik needed some useful information, it was now.

High overhead, the portal that gave access to the huge elevator shaft was closed. Ferrik was just starting to ask Goose how they could get it open when a crack appeared on one side, growing steadily, like an eclipse of the sun.

"You were saying?" asked Goose with a grin.

Ferrik powered up then hesitated. He badly wanted to fly them out of there but he knew in his heart that he wasn't the most experienced man for the job. He sighed. "She's all yours," he said to Goose. Goose gave him a startled look then murmured something that sounded like "thanks."

Goose continued warming up the engines. He released the docking clamps, making sure all hatches were airtight, then waited.

Ferrik frowned. "What are you waiting for?" he asked.

"Them." Goose nodded in the direction of three ships which had just lifted off from the docking bay and were hovering. "I'm going to fall in behind them."

"And they're just going to let us go?"

"That's what I'm counting on."

"Surely they'll demand a check?"

Goose shrugged. "It doesn't understand the concept of treason—or even of spies. It just doesn't get it. That doesn't mean it's not aware of the idea. Don't forget, it's been around a long time. But it thinks differently to us."

Ferrik swallowed. He wasn't used to someone talking about the Hiveborn as a sole entity. Goose's use of the singular pronoun was unsettling.

The other three ships suddenly shot up from the docking bay. Above them, the portal had opened halfway. Goose raised the ship and shot after them, intending to fall in behind them. *Safety in numbers*, thought Ferrik, nodding.

They were halfway to the portal when the great hatch stopped. "Uh oh," said Ferrik.

"Read you loud and clear on that," said Goose. He nailed the throttle and the shuttle, big as it was, poured on an impressive display of speed. The other three ships had stopped just as suddenly as they had lifted off. They now fanned out, blocking the shuttle's path.

"We've been compromised," said Ferrik.

"You have control," said Goose, indicating the board.

Ferrik nodded. "What are you going to do?"

"Arm the weapon banks," said Goose. He pulled a kind of drawer out from under the main board which acted like a mini console. Quickly, he flipped switches and made some adjustments to the settings indicated by several readouts. He heard a humming noise and saw a progress bar on one of the readout screens expand from zero towards what he presumed was full capacity.

"Weapons are charging," said Goose.

"Will they be able to pick that up?"

"Yep. Only they probably won't. Those are simple messenger and courier ships. Neither tactical nor defensive. So they're not used to fighting."

"The portal!" cried Thompson. Goose and Ferrik peered up. It had started to close.

"I figure we've got about two minutes to get inside that thing, then we're history," said Goose.

Ferrik nodded, then glanced over at him. "I'll fly and you shoot. Ready?"

"Nope, but let's do it anyway."

Ferrik banked hard, drawing a cry of consternation from Thompson, but Goose just whooped. Ferrik's maneuver was designed as a feint, making it look like he was going to try and dart around the outside of the formation the three ships had settled into.

But he had no such intention. For one thing, it would make him a sitting duck to all three ships. For another, it would take too long, wasting precious seconds.

The feint worked. Goose's estimation of the kind of ships—and therefore the kind of pilots—facing them must have been pretty spot on. No well trained battle pilot would have fallen for such a flimsy deceit. As Ferrik feinted, two of the ships broke formation and swooped down to intercept him. At the last second, when collision seemed inevitable, Ferrik flipped the entire shuttle over in a spectacular banking maneuver, and crammed on every bit of acceleration he could find. At the same time, Goose opened up on the main weapon banks, spraying the two attacking ships with sharp short pulses of raw energy. They scuttled away. The shuttle bellowed up and away from the ships, shot past the third—still in formation—with barely two yards to spare, and hurled itself towards the rapidly narrowing gap in the portal.

Behind them, Thompson clutched his seat, white-knuckled. Goose's eyes went wide. "Gonna be close," he murmured, almost to himself.

With an audible whoosh and a terrifying clang the shuttle sped through the gap and into the elevator shaft. Goose expelled his breath in a deep sigh. "When I said close, I wasn't talking millimeters!" He shot Ferrik an accusing look.

Ferrik cleared his throat. "We're not out of the woods yet. Keep your eyes peeled and your fingers on those buttons! Heck, put the defenses on automatic for back-up."

"Aye, aye, Captain," said Goose, peering up at the dark shaft.

"I don't get it," said Hatch, scratching his head. "Something Sarah thought of. Post hypnotic suggestion. Or something similar."

Daniel nodded, stroking his chin. "Of course. They take possession. Plant some deep-seated command of which the host knows nothing then extract themselves, leaving almost no evidence. They probably even wipe out the memory of being possessed in the first place."

"My thoughts exactly," Welkin said. "Okay. We need a stretcher for Gillian." He paused. "Handcuff her as well." The others looked at him. "Look, we don't have a choice. Just do it, okay? Come on, let's get out of here. If I'm guessing right, they won't be crashing in on us any time soon, not till Gillian does whatever she's supposed to do—or till she fails to do it."

A moment later Hatch hissed, "Three cruisers. North-east."

Welkin squinted but couldn't see them. Hatch had better eyesight than anybody else in the squad. "Moving this way?"

"Nope. Now they're circling."

"Probably the spot where Gillian made radio contact," Welkin guessed. "They want to keep up appearances. Okay, we've got to get off the rooftops, people. Let's go."

They jogged across the roof to the nearest stairwell and piled inside. Roddy led the way as he knew the area like the back of his hand, having patrolled it dozens of times during his masquerade as a zombie.

They found a deserted warehouse and holed up there for a couple of hours. During this time, Gillian woke.

"What the—? The hell are these handcuffs doing on me?" She struggled into a sitting position, her face wrathful. Welkin hurried over, expecting an explosion.

"Calm down," he said. Gillian had opened her mouth to let off a blast but something in Welkin's tone shut her up. She closed her mouth and stared at him.

Welkin sat down beside her and lifted a canteen to her lips. She drank thirstily, never taking her eyes off him. "Okay," she said, wiping her mouth with her sleeve. "I'm calmed down. So what gives?"

He indicated the handcuffs. "They got to you."

Gillian stared back at him. Then started shaking her head. "No way. No way! I made the call, then I got out of there."

"You don't remember anything out of the ordinary?"

Gillian thought back. "Usual adventures. A close shave. That's it. Nobody got to me."

Welkin beckoned Daniel over. He brought Wiggy with him, showing Gillian Wiggy's left ear. "See the rawness, the swelling? We just removed a parasite from Wiggy here." Wiggy beamed at her. Gillian gave him a curt nod which seemed to hurt his feelings.

"So?" she said, defiantly.

"So you have exactly the same signs of recent possession," Daniel said. "Plus Welkin noticed that when you came pounding into camp you weren't sweating."

Gillian glared at them. "And that's your evidence?" She snorted. "Well, if I was possessed, where's the goddamned bug?"

Welkin sighed, told her Sarah's theory of post-hypnotic suggestion. Gillian's mouth dropped open and for the first time she looked uneasy.

"So I could be this walking time bomb?" she asked in a small voice. Welkin put his arm around her. "We don't know," he said.

"Well, that's great. That's just frigging great. So what happens now?"

"First off, what happened? Did you talk to Sarah?"

Gillian looked dumbstruck. "Tch, I completely forgot." She looked suddenly anxious. "Hey, you don't think they made me forget, do you? No, don't answer that. I don't want to know. I didn't manage to make contact with Sarah. Ferrik said everything's jammed over that way, which I guess isn't good news."

"Ferrik? You spoke to Ferrik? When? Where is he? What did he say?"

"If you stop interrupting me, I'll tell you." Welkin mimed throttling her then sat back and grinned. He made a gesture that said, Please continue.

Gillian did. "His mission was successful, but I got the impression that there was more to it than that. He didn't want to say too much on an open channel. He did say he'd been trying to raise Martha but wasn't having any luck. He thought they might have been infiltrated, maybe the radio had been sabotaged." Grim looks greeted that news. "I let him know our situation. He said he'd be in touch on some frequency you arranged with him."

Welkin nodded. "But you definitely told him we'd recovered some parasites?"

"Yep."

"Good. In that case, we're out of here. Now."

Gillian frowned. "Why? What's going on?"

"Nothing," Welkin said mysteriously. "We've just got to go."

He ordered everybody up and moving and, after a whispered conversation with Roddy, they moved out. Once again, Roddy took point, guiding them through a maze of corridors, workshops, storage rooms, and even some underground passages that provided access to various kinds of machinery.

They kept on the move for the better part of three hours, though much of that was spent in cautious scurrying, and endless waits to make sure the coast was clear. At the end of that time Roddy came back to where Welkin was helping Gillian—still handcuffed—negotiate some obstacles.

Roddy had just opened his mouth to speak when Gillian crashed into him. At first Welkin thought it was an accident but then Gillian rolled to her feet holding Roddy's handgun. She got off a shot at Roddy who was just getting up. He dropped like a sack of bricks. Then she brought the gun around, aiming for Welkin. But he dived aside as the blast ripped through the air. Then she turned the gun on the containers holding the parasites and pulled the trigger. The pulse hit them but was too low to do any damage. She changed the setting and vaporized them then turned to flee.

A fist connected with the point of her chin and she made a soft "*Ugh*" sound and went down.

Welkin clambered over to her, prized the gun from her fingers, and checked she was okay. Then he checked on Roddy, but the lad was just stunned.

Daniel stared at the remains of the specimens, making a clucking noise with his tongue. "Oh, that's too bad, that's too bad," he kept saying to himself.

Hatch, whose fist had dropped Gillian, carried Roddy to the wall and leaned him against it, forcing some water between his lips and splashing more in his face. He stirred. Gillian came to 20 minutes later.

She sat up with a groan. "Oh," she said when she saw the damage. "I did that, didn't I?" Welkin nodded. Gillian suddenly burst into tears and buried her face in her arms. Welkin hugged her briefly.

He then held her at arm's length. "Hey Doc, is that hypnotic probe a one-off thing, or is it embedded?"

Gillian's eyes went wide. "This can't be forever," she began.

Daniel came over. He placed his thumb and forefinger above and below Gillian's left eye and pulled the flesh wide. He peered into her eye. "I'd say whatever triggered her response was a one trick pony." He sat back, staring at Gillian. "We'll just need to keep an eye on you for a while, that's all."

Gillian breathed a sigh of relief.

"Thank Pleiades for that," Welkin said. "Now Doc, do we need more parasites?"

Daniel shrugged. "I've made a preliminary examination and I still have my notes, but I won't pretend this isn't a setback."

From over near the wall Roddy groaned. "It's my fault," said the youth. "If I hadn't let her get my gun … "

"If the fault is anybody's, it's mine," said Welkin. "I suspected this and all I did was handcuff Gillian's hands in front of her."

"Yeah, should have hogtied her," said Hatch. Gillian looked up. Hatch was grinning at her. She smiled back weakly.

"Well, what's done is done. I guess we have to go fishing again."

A crackle and hiss came from Hatch's backpack. He dug out the other radio set, tuning it to a frequency Welkin quickly gave him.

Ferrik's voice came through loud and clear. "Welkin, I hope you're where you're supposed to be. ETA—fifteen minutes. Oh, and it's going to get pretty damn hot so don't mess around. And by the way, we swapped *Capella* for a later model. Out."

Everybody looked at Welkin, frowning.

"What's he mean?" Hatch asked.

"He's coming to get us in a new ship. I think. We made an arrangement, just in case."

"And you didn't tell anyone?" Gillian asked.

Welkin shrugged. "Seemed safer that way."

Gillian looked like she wanted to argue then got a sudden rueful look. "Okay, it's just as well you didn't tell me."

Welkin grinned. "Guess so."

"What about the parasites?" Roddy asked.

Welkin shook his head. "We've taken enough risks," he said. "We're getting out of here. We're going home."

No one argued with that.

The shuttle rose up the shaft like an express elevator. The walls of the shaft blurred past. Overhead, Ferrik could see a swathe of stars. He expelled a sigh of relief. "God's praise," he said. "I thought the topside portal might be shut."

"You might yet wish it had been," Goose muttered.

Ferrik looked at him. "What are you talking about?"

"It's gotta be open for a reason."

"They opened it for those three ships to exit. No mystery there."

"Aye, but why's it *still* open?"

Ferrik thought for a moment then scowled at him. But they didn't have long to find out. The surface portal rushed towards them and a second later they burst out of the shaft into clear clean starshine.

And into the midst of about a dozen scout ships.

"I hate it when I'm right," said Goose.

"*I* hate it when you're right."

"What are you going to do?" asked Thompson, still gripping his chair.

"I thought we'd panic first," said Ferrik, "then do *this*!"

The shuttle had grabbed considerable height in its rush from the shaft, but the bulk of the scout ships sat above and around them like a huge mushroom. Instead of racing for deep space, Ferrik slammed the shuttle over and put it into a steep dive. For a moment it looked like he was heading back into the shaft. Thompson cried out. Goose muttered something. But at the last second, Ferrik banked hard, and flattened out barely 50 yards above the moon's surface. The terrific dive had given him a massive burst of speed. With this he caromed across the surface towards a canyon in the wall of some lofty mountains. The electrostatic disruption caused by his wake kicked up a plumed road of moon dust that quickly enveloped their rear. Only one shot was fired at them during this time.

Seconds later, they hurtled into the canyon. Meanwhile, Goose had called up a topographical schematic of this section of the moon's surface and started calling out rapid fire directions to Ferrik as he slalomed through the canyons. The dust roiling in his rear effectively stopped any direct pursuit from that direction and it seemed that the scout ships, not anticipating this electrostatic effect, had opted for the time-honored technique of dogging their tail.

Big mistake.

"Ohmistars! There goes one of 'em. *Ka-boom*!" Mig called out gleefully. "And another! Double *ka-boom*!"

"Hope you're strapped in," Goose said without looking at the girl.

"You betcha," she said. The smile dropped from her face the moment no one was watching.

Unable to match Ferrik's precision flying, their vision obscured by the dust and their instruments undoubtedly glitchy due to the electrostatic discharge, two of the pursuing ships then crashed headlong into the canyon walls, causing more debris to be ejected.

In quick succession three more obliterated themselves in the occluded and lethal canyon.

"Okay, I want to make a dash for space. I need a high peak to put between me and them," Ferrik said briskly.

Goose squinted at the schematic in front of him.

"Got just what you need. Okay. Fork coming up. Take the left hand canyon. Bearing oh three two two. Turn in five—four—three—two—one—now!"

Ferrik banked left, following the bearing precisely, only glimpsing the canyon wall at the last second. He didn't know it, but he was using a method of maneuvering developed by rally drivers long ago on Earth.

"Three klicks then you can take her up," said Goose. He continued to call blow by blow directions but it was only moments later that he suddenly stopped and after a somewhat theatrical pause, bellowed, "NOW!"

Ferrik brought the nose up and drove the ship into a screaming climb. The canyon walls fell on either side. A sharp jagged series of peaks dropped away to his left and ahead lay clear space, arched over by the brilliant snaking glow of the Milky Way.

Goose checked the screen. "Only two ships in pursuit and they're starting to drop back. They don't have the legs of this little beauty!"

As the surface of the moon fell behind, Ferrik set a course for Earth. Half an hour later he parked the ship in a high orbit over the Tasman Sea that separated mainland Australia from New Zealand. He tried contacting Martha, but some sort of jamming process was in operation and he could only pick up garbled bits of voices. Some of it sounded worrisome: shouts, explosions, cries cut off midway.

He didn't know what to do. Before setting out, he and Welkin had devised a fallback plan if Welkin's mission was in any way compromised, but it very much depended on Welkin contacting him.

He had Hetti scan all available frequencies including those they knew were used by the Hiveborn, but they picked up little. He was just on the point of deciding to head back to Martha when Gillian made contact.

The exchange was brief. Gillian sounded as if she might be in peril. They had secured parasites but the mission itself was in danger.

After he signed off, he decided to move the ship closer to New Zealand, surmising that a line of sight link, unobstructed by mountains, might give them a better chance of making contact with Sarah. At first, this didn't seem to be the case. Then they got a momentary break-through, a "window" amidst whatever was jamming all the ingoing and outgoing signals.

He sent a data burst of everything they had learnt about the situation on the moon, then apprised Sarah of Welkin's situation and that he wanted to try to rescue them. Sarah, after some hesitation, agreed, though her final words were ominous: "Proceed with rescue. But Ferrik, if you fail, it's imperative that Welkin and Gillian do not fall into enemy hands. Do you copy?"

Ferrik signed off and passed the word along that they were heading to Melbourne. Goose raised an eyebrow, but Ferrik just shrugged. "Give me the fastest vector in and out," he said. Turning to Hetti, who was manning her post at communications, he said, "I need you to send an encrypted data burst to Arton. He'll be in the vicinity of Melbourne. Zero in on Welkin's receiver. I need a tight beam burst that'll reach him only."

Hetti nodded, though she looked slightly doubtful. "No guarantees. Paired quantum devices need to be set with one unique individual match before separation. For a particle device, there's always some spread, even in the tightest of beams—"

"Just do it, Hetti," Ferrik said tiredly, turning back to the control board.

The risks never seemed to stop, the danger never seemed to end. Ferrik actually longed for the days back on board *Colony* before they reached Earth when the most dangerous thing he'd ever done was talk back to a sub-Elder, for which he had been reprimanded, nothing more. Now life was just an endless adrenaline rush, and not the nice kind, like flying a *sim* shuttle through the Dragon Nebula or shooting the rapids of Tau Ceti III.

In his next life, he decided, he wanted to be a farmer. How dangerous could that be?

Sighing quietly to himself, he set a general course for Melbourne. When Hetti was ready, he encoded a message for Arton who was on strict orders to observe radio silence. Hence, he would not be able to answer or confirm that he had received the data burst.

Ferrik would just have to trust fate. And luck.

As usual.

"Ready to send data burst," said Hetti, looking up from her console.

"Do it," Ferrik told her. He saw her punch a button. "Now get me Welkin. And when you do, give me a link on his location and throw it up on the main screen. Overlay an aerial shot of Melbourne. Superimpose as we get within range."

It took some time to identify Welkin's receiver from amongst the wash of electromagnetic signals emanating from Melbourne, but after tense moments Hetti finally nodded.

"Got him."

Ferrik grabbed the mike, thumbing it on. "Welkin, I hope you're where you're supposed to be. ETA—fifteen minutes. Oh, and it's going to get pretty damn hot so don't mess around. Out."

"So what's the plan here?" asked Goose.

"I'm going to go tearing in, guns blasting, making as much noise and mess as possible, slam to a stop at Welkin's position, pick him up, then get the hell out of there."

Goose nodded. "I like it. Nice and subtle."

"I thought you'd approve."

Thompson was staring at them with wide eyes. "Shouldn't we try sneaking in?"

Ferrik and Goose both turned and looked at him. In perfect unison they said, "No," then turned back to their respective consoles.

"A nice day to visit Hell," Goose murmured.

Ferrik winked. "I hear the weather leaves a lot to be desired."

Goose shrugged. "Dunno. Me, I hate the cold."

Ferrik put the shuttle into a long shallow dive, heading straight for Melbourne. "Strap in, folks," he said. Thompson's chair fumbled towards declination, looking for a liquid-filled seat belt but there was none. A formfoam nozzle turned towards him instead, promising to engulf him if the slightest danger threatened.

Welkin checked his watch for the fifth time in two minutes, then peered out from the tangle of pipes and cables under which they were all crouched. Immediately in front of him was a large flat area which he and Ferrik had chosen as a rendezvous point from aerial photographs of the city. He glanced to his right and saw that Hatch was positioned, sighting his laserlite to provide covering fire in case they were disturbed while boarding. To his left, Roddy was similarly stationed. On the other side of the landing area, the rest of the group lay hidden. He, Welkin, would cover things from this quadrant.

If all went according to plan, they'd be on board and the ship lifting off before anybody had fired a shot. Of course, things seldom went according to plan.

A minute before Ferrik's ETA, he heard it.

A dull roaring explosion followed, in quick succession, by several more explosions. Then, like some odd echo, another series, but this time further away across the city. Welkin frowned. He didn't think Ferrik could be hitting both sets of targets, they were too far apart. And then he realized.

Arton. Of course.

He'd be laying down a diversionary fire, splitting any retaliatory force. Welkin whistled softly. Good old Ferrik. The guy had natural tactical instincts.

He brought his laserlite up to his shoulder just as he heard the unmistakable whistle of a spacecraft decelerating rapidly.

Then, everything happened at once.

From the corner of one eye he saw the unfamiliar shuttle coming down fast. But from the other side, swooping out of the sun like they had been waiting for this moment—and maybe they had—were a dozen cruisers. Even as he saw them, they opened up on the shuttle.

"Unfriendlies, eleven o'clock!" he barked into his headset mike. He dimly heard affirmatives from Roddy and Hatch, but he paid them no heed. He was already firing, sending a shower of lethal pulses into the midst of the cruisers which were too tightly packed to avoid taking heavy damage. Even as he became vaguely aware that Hatch, Harry and Roddy had also joined in, six of the cruisers were spiraling down or dropping like bricks. Three others had been hit.

Then something exploded nearby. Welkin felt a huge thump on his back, as if a giant had stepped on him, then he was flying through the air, the breath sucked out of his lungs. He landed about 20 feet away, sprawling in a heap, but miraculously unhurt save for some grazes. He twisted over, bringing his laserlite up, and it was this instinctive action that saved his life. The cruiser that had fired on him—and which was diving in from behind his position—was re-targeting him. Another second and they'd have had him.

Instead, he squeezed the trigger and the cruiser burst into flame. The rider was catapulted through the air, landing somewhere nearby out of sight. Welkin heard the meaty thump as the body hit the rooftop.

He squirmed beneath some cover just as Ferrik touched the shuttle down. He heard the frantic call, "All aboard and make it fast! That means everybody!"

Welkin jumped to his feet and broke into a run, firing as he moved. He winged another cruiser but missed two others. Hatch downed one of them and the third, in trying to dodge the fire, collided with the one Welkin had winged. Both lost control and plummeted to the streets below.

Welkin had the farthest to go. The ramp would be on the other side where Gillian and the others had been waiting. He saw Hatch charging for the ship, moving surprisingly fast for a man so large and bulky.

Meanwhile, Welkin skidded around the outside of the shuttle, panting hard. He could hear, from the sounds coming over the headset, that the others were already aboard. He was still 15 yards from the ramp.

And then he knew he wasn't going to make it.

Four cruisers rose up suddenly from below the roof-scape, pointed straight at him. They were so close he could see the expressions—or lack of them—on the riders' faces. With a sinking feeling he knew he was a sitting duck. All they had to do was open fire.

He swallowed, putting on a burst of speed, even as he saw them reach for their firing buttons.

"Gillian," he cried out then all four cruisers disintegrated in a whirling blast of sound and fire. For the second time Welkin was flung off his feet, this time banging his head on a flange of the shuttle. He sat up dizzily, blinking. What had happened?

He heard a whoop on the radio. It was Arton. "Get your carcass on board, Welkin!" yelled the other pilot. "I can't keep saving your butt all day, you know."

Welkin regained his footing and ran for the ramp. A second later, he was pounding up it. Hands reaching for him, the ramp already closing as he climbed.

Then the shuttle lifted off with a bone-crushing acceleration that squashed him to the deck. With a thump the ramp shut and locked and he was enveloped in a cool darkness, all the outside sounds suddenly reduced to muffled distant noises that somehow felt less dangerous.

Before he could get back to his feet for the third time in three minutes, Gillian was in his arms, kissing him, crying. For a second, he thought she had been hurt. He started patting her body down, checking for injuries.

"Are you hurt? Are you wounded?" he asked, a horrible fear making his stomach do flip-flops.

Gillian laughed. "Me? I'm fine. What about you? What's all that blood?"

"Blood? What blood?" He suddenly caught sight of himself in the mirrored surface of a hydraulics housing. His hair was awry and one side of his face was awash with blood.

"Guess I must have cut myself."

By now Gillian was also smeared with blood. The shuttle juddered. "Hey, what's happening?" He started to get up. "I've got to go help Ferrik."

Gillian pulled him back down. "There's nothing you can do," she said. "Besides, we're already in space."

He blinked at her. "We are?"

"Yeah. This thing moves like the clappers. Look."

He followed her pointing finger and gazed out a porthole at the deep darkness of space. As he stared a brownish green arc of the earth's rim swam into view then slid out again.

He sat back. "Yeah, I guess we are," he said. With nothing better to do, he leaned forward and kissed Gillian and kept kissing until he had nearly asphyxiated her.

After Welkin had been cleaned up and bandaged, he met with Harry and the others stationed aft, then made his way to the cockpit. Ferrik handed the flying over to Goose and the two former Skyborn embraced and pummeled each other's backs.

"Nice rescue," said Welkin. Ferrik grinned back as Welkin stared at the cockpit. "Where did you *get* this thing?" he asked.

"Oh, we ran into some Hiveborn and we ... ah ... borrowed it."

"Hope you're not intending to give it back. Seriously, though, what kind of specs does it have?"

Gillian came in behind Welkin. Ferrik said, "Off the chart. First off, it'll—"

"Puh-leease!" said Gillian, wincing. "We all just nearly died, could we have a conversation on something a little more meaningful than 'how big is my spaceship'?"

Welkin and Ferrik looked at her then eyed each other. "Yeah, sure," said Ferrik, then to Welkin, "As I was saying, she'll do triple the speed of our other ships. She's got more shielding, more armaments, better internal gravity calibration ... better everything."

Gillian was shaking her head behind them but smiling. Boys and their toys!

"Where's Lucida?" Welkin said.

Ferrik's beaming face flat-lined.

Welkin looked about. Suddenly no one was speaking. "She didn't make it, did she?"

Ferrik reached out for Welkin, but he pulled back, just out of reach. "I just ... " Welkin started, but didn't finish.

"Elab's gone, too," Ferrik said. He winced with acrimony. "Space! Here I am chortling about a lousy Hiveborn vehicle we stole and we've lost two of our friends. I'm such an idiot!"

Welkin put up his hand for silence. "It's all right." He fell silent for a moment, gathering his thoughts. "It's all right. We'll grieve later. Call a general meeting. Right now."

By the time Ferrik had managed to patch through to Arton, they were approaching a high orbital position directly above New Zealand. Arton was flying formation some 500 yards off their port. He joined the meeting by video link-up.

Ferrik, as captain of the lead ship, was nominally in charge. "Okay," he said. "We've already picked up laser fire at Martha. It looks like they're under attack. Our other shuttle is still grounded there providing power, and a separate mission is on its way to Melbourne. So, we have to decide what to do."

"There's a choice?" said Harry. "We go in blasting. Flatten their ships and decimate their ground forces!"

"Thanks Harry," said Ferrik. "Any other suggestions? Welkin?"

"Well, I guess we all feel the same as Harry, but we don't know the situation down there. We don't know what Sarah has planned. Any luck breaking through the jamming signal?"

Hetti shook her head. "I think they strengthened it after our last breach. I don't think it ever occurred to them that we might be using one of their own ships to try to contact home."

There was a moment's silence. Hetti's use of the word "home" stirred odd emotions in all of them. Welkin summed it up. "Guess that's what we're fighting for here, isn't it?" he said. "Home. We can't take any chances."

"I've got a suggestion, but I'd like to hear yours first, Welkin," said Ferrik quietly.

Welkin sighed. "Okay. I figure we've got two available ships of size, one of them of Hiveborn origin and on a par with anything else they have. I've got a feeling the backdoor is going to be heavily defended. If that's the case, we're going to need our best ship to get us in there—and it's vital that we achieve this. I reckon we position *Procyon*, with Arton piloting, high and free to act. The rest of us—with Ferrik piloting—will take the Hiveborn ship and sneak back into Martha, along with the newly awakened folks. We'll also agree to a number of special frequencies and try to communicate. Maybe some outdated ones as well, even if it comes down to using simple codes."

Ferrik nodded. "That's pretty much what I was going to suggest," he said as he brought *Procyon* up on the forward holoscreen. "No point in bottling up both ships where they'd do no good at all. Besides, I think that when Sarah learns what we found on the moon, we might just have another mission to carry out. And for that we're going to need this baby." He patted the console. All the faces were sober. "Any dissenters?"

Hatch raised his hand. "I want in on Arton's crew." Hatch made it plain he was raring for a fight.

"I want to as well," said Mig.

Before anyone could note the odd, mechanical inflexion in Mig's voice, Ferrik held up his hands for silence. "Welkin and I will post the crew in the next fifteen minutes. We'll take into consideration any special pleading."

Twenty minutes later, Hatch, Roddy, Mig, and three of the former zombies boarded the *Procyon* under Arton's command, as did some of the techs and engineers who had been part of Ferrik's original complement.

Welkin shook hands with Hatch at the docking tunnel.

"You take care," he said. Gillian was waiting behind him. "We're counting on you babysitting our kids."

Hatch grinned. "Hey, I like the sound of that. Uncle Hatch!"

Gillian snorted.

"Pardon?" said Hatch. "You got something to say?"

"Me? Nah. Just clearing my nasal passages."

They parted. The hatches were dogged, the docking tunnel retracted. Moments later both ships started dropping to lower their orbits before nosing over and diving for the mountain they now called home.

From high orbit, it had become apparent that there was little air cover for the Hiveborn operation; and, what there was, was congregated around the mountain itself. With this in mind, Arton aimed to disperse the enemy by laying down covering—and distracting—fire while Ferrik's ship scurried into the rear valley and found the backdoor.

For once, it all went according to plan. Except for the bit about the backdoor.

Coming down fast, both shuttles took the defending ships completely by surprise. A withering fire dispersed them as planned and Ferrik darted away, looking as if he was intending to loop up and over and come back for another strafing run. Instead, at the last second, he broke away, pretending to go out of control, exactly as if he had been hit and was now experiencing difficulties. Watching from a distance, Arton whistled. It was a very convincing show.

"Taught him everything he knows," said Arton.

"Yeah, right," said Hatch. "I just hope he *is* pretending."

"One can only pray."

But Ferrik's troubles had only just begun. As he yawed off course, disappearing into the dark, he cut his lights and main torch engine, then flipped over the mountain top in a kind of upward free fall and literally dropped into the valley on the other side. It was an impressive maneuver. Unfortunately, just as he re-lit his torch and arced down towards the supposedly concealed backdoor, all hell broke loose.

The enemy was waiting for them.

"Talk about being outnumbered!" yelled Ferrik, as blindingly bright pulse fire raced up towards them in deceptively slow motion, burning tracks across their optic nerves. "You want to risk it, Welkin?"

Ferrik was shouting, though the noise inside the ship wasn't high. But Welkin shouted back as well. "Go for it. Go in at top speed. We won't get a second chance."

"Top speed?" Ferrik looked at him then shook his head, doubtful. "Are you crazy or what?"

Welkin would have smiled if he hadn't been so busy directing the ship's return fire at the blockade of Hiveborn vessels. He knew that if they did not make the backdoor on this first attempt, there would be no second chance; the Hiveborn would stop them at all costs, even if it meant ramming them at high speed.

The shuttle streaked down into the midst of the melee. Pulses were coming at them from every direction. Then Welkin got lucky. He scored a direct hit on the drive assembly of a Hiveborn scout and the ship erupted in a great blossom of fire. Ferrik didn't even try to veer off. He shot through the cloud of debris and flame. Both men blinked as they burst out the other side, no worse for wear than for a few clanging impacts as pieces of scout ship collided with them.

Suddenly the shuttle bucked badly and there was a muffled roar. "We're hit," said Ferrik matter-of-factly. The ship started to destabilize.

"Can you hold her together?" Welkin demanded.

"I'm trying." They were hurtling towards the side of the mountain. Welkin activated the coded signal that opened the outer portal of the backdoor. There were still three fighters crowding them but the good thing was that they were so close it was difficult for the Hiveborn to get in good shots.

The ship shuddered again, but Ferrik shook his head at Welkin's look. "That's not a hit. We just lost our starboard engine." There was a pause. "And just as well. It'll slow us down a piece."

Something loomed ahead of them, swerving towards a position that would block them. "Keep going," said Welkin. He took careful aim at the scout ship that was now almost dead ahead. When the ship came into the crosshairs, he depressed the firing stud. A stream of pulses leapt out at the ship, stitched along its hull, then hit the torch assembly. Like the one before it, it exploded in spectacular fashion. Ferrik plunged through the outer edge of the fireball then into the backdoor tunnel. The shuttle slammed off the side of the tunnel, hit the opposite side. Ferrik struggled to control it, to damp its speed. "We're too fast." He kept muttering under his breath. "We're too fast ... "

Welkin quickly activated the portal behind to close it, but not before one scout ship, smaller than the shuttle, gave chase through the narrowing gap.

The scout ship, like their own shuttle, had trouble stabilizing in the narrow tunnel at such speed; but their problems were compounded by the fact that they were riding in the first ship's slipstream. The tunnel walls also played havoc with their position sensors.

As a concentrated burst of pulse fire from the scout ship scorched past their port side, Welkin had an idea. "What'll happen if you enrich the feed to the emergency maneuvering jets?" he asked Ferrik.

The pilot frowned without taking his eyes off the forward screen and position sensors. "Not sure. Maybe nothing. We'd just produce a lot of burn off."

"As in lots of thick black smoke?"

Ferrik frowned again. "Yeah." Then his face cleared and he suddenly smiled. "Yeaaaah!"

He flipped a switch. "Engineering? Enrich the fuel injection to the rear jiggers."

"What?" came the tinny reply.

"Just do it. Now!"

Thick clouds of smoke erupted from the flaming jets that helped keep the shuttle craft from slamming the walls. Behind them, the scout ship was quickly enveloped in black smoke. Moments later there was a very loud and satisfying explosion and for a brief instant the inside of the smoke became livid with the light of a fireball.

After that it was just a matter of slowing down. That, however, was easier said than done. Their momentum was fierce; the ship's mass meant that nothing short of a small mountain was going to stop them any time soon. And they were running out of space.

"Two klicks to go," said Welkin, trying to keep his voice steady. "Do something."

"Do something? Do what?"

"I don't know. Prang the thing in!"

Ferrik stared at him a moment then grunted. "Fine." He dropped the ship onto its belly, still controlling its altitude through the various jigger jets. A furious cascade of sparks kicked up where metal met rock and concrete. A dull bone-jarring screech made Welkin's head ache and his teeth feel like they were about to come out of his jaw.

Harry's voice came over the intercom. He had to shout to be heard. "What in blazes are you doing up there?"

Welkin hollered back, "You don't want to know." To Ferrik he said, "Is it working? What's our speed?"

"It's working. I think."

"You think?"

"How far now?"

Welkin checked his schematic for the ship's position in the tunnel. "Half a klick."

"Speed has halved. Still dropping. I think we're going to make it."

"Can the ship take it?"

"Don't know," said Ferrik. "It's made of a much denser alloy than our shuttles. Wouldn't surprise me if it just came away with a few scratches."

The ship started to lose stability as its speed dropped below a controllable level. It yawed and slithered, banged into the walls, bounced back, banged again. It was like riding a wild buffalo, though none of them had seen a buffalo outside of holophotos.

The end of the tunnel loomed ahead. "Brace for impact!" Welkin shouted over the intercom. But no impact came. Instead, the ship scraped and slid to a stop just inches from the reinforced end wall, giving one final shudder before it settled.

The silence that followed was deafening.

Ten minutes later they were racing through the tunnels and corridors of Martha, heading for the War Room. They were all pretty banged up and bruised from the final moments of the "landing." Welkin's wounds were bleeding again and his bandages were soaked bright red. He paid them no heed as he hurried along with Gillian, Harry and Ferrik. Most of the engineers had stayed behind to start repairs on the ship, while Daniel, his assistant Karl, and the remaining reawakened zombies went to the infirmary.

"My God, it looks like a war zone!" exclaimed Gillian when they burst into one of the main tunnels. The place was full of debris. The walls and some parts of the ceiling were blackened from laserlite fire. There were also bodies, though it was hard to tell if they were attackers or defenders. They did not stop to find out. Welkin had a horrible feeling that he might find someone he knew.

They found Sarah and Angela in the War Room. When Sarah looked up and saw them, her face split into a huge grin. She leapt up and threw herself at them, hugging and kissing them. She kept saying, over and over, "Glad you made it. That's such a relief."

"But we lost some good people," Welkin said. He looked to Gillian, as if asking her to continue. Gillian shook her head.

"I know about Patrick and Mira," Sarah said slowly. "Who else?" Her face drained, leaving it spectral in the wan light.

"Lucida," Welkin said, after taking a deep breath. "We lost Lucida. And Elab."

Sarah winced as each name left Welkin's mouth. "I'm so sorry, Welkin," she said. Many had come and gone, but the passing of these two brought with it a grief as fresh and deep as Sarah's first comprehension of death.

It was some time before anyone could talk coherently; although they were all used to sudden death, these latest casualties hit each of them hard. Welkin forced himself to give Sarah a quick summary of everything that had happened to them. The loss of the parasites reinforced her sense of bitterness and futility. But that mishap was nothing compared with the other losses.

In her turn, Sarah brought them up to date on the Hiveborn attack, adding, "The situation right now isn't good. The Hiveborn control the two upper levels and we know they have saboteurs scattered amongst us. We're constantly having to drain resources for bomb-searching squads. We still have power from the shuttle we had linked up down here, but geothermal sources are barely there. The mazes slowed them down and we certainly decimated their number, but they've got the high ground at the moment. Excuse the pun."

"Excused," Welkin said above Gillian and Angel's combined groan. "Any counteroffensive against those ships?"

Sarah's eyes lit up. "You're reading my mind. I've got a team out there now, ready to strike, but the situation is still too dicey for them to make an attempt."

"Use Arton."

"Arton? Where is he?" asked Angela.

Welkin quickly explained that Arton was waiting "upstairs" in the Martha shuttle, ready to join any sorties. Then he frowned. "Didn't you get Ferrik's data burst?"

Sarah shook her head.

Welkin looked at the others. "You'd better sit down."

Ferrik told her what had happened on the mission and what they had found on the moon.

Sarah stared at him. "The whole place is a *nursery*?" She was trying to digest this information.

Ferrik nodded. "It's vast. And the guy we awakened, Thompson, says there are over six hundred of these gigantic vats. He also says that's where they manufacture the red jelly as well."

"Let's get Daniel up here." The call went out and 20 minutes later the good doctor poked his head inside the War Room and cleared his throat. "Can I come in?" he asked hesitantly. He had never been inside the room before.

"Doc, take a seat. Glad you made it back okay," said Sarah, indicating a chair. Daniel sat down, looking around at all the faces.

"Welkin tells me you managed to perform some analysis of the parasites in the field?"

"'Managed' is the correct word. What we did was crude but we learnt a few useful things. It's a shame we lost the parasites." Gillian went a little pink at this but no one noticed.

"Well, the good news is," said Sarah, "that we have plenty of them. On ice. I'll have them delivered to the infirmary." She nodded at Angela who activated a patch and started quietly issuing orders. Daniel looked confused, as did Welkin and the others. "I told you," Sarah explained, "we've had infiltrators. They were breeding the bugs here, probably for weeks. Then they set about building a little band of saboteurs. Very clever."

Daniel was looking excited. Sarah frowned. "What is it, Doc?"

"You said breeding. That must mean they had a supply of red jelly here or some way to manufacture it."

"Why? I thought the red jelly was an enriched nutrient solution."

"It is. Complex and highly efficient. But one thing we did determine in our analyses is that the bugs can't reproduce on their own."

"Well, they did a pretty good job of it here in Martha, Doc."

"I'm sure they did. But if I'm right, it's the red jelly itself that facilitates their fissioning form of reproduction. Without it, I'd hazard a guess that they can't reproduce. I don't suppose you have any, do you?"

Sarah was thinking hard but managed to shake her head at the doctor's question. "I'm afraid we destroyed it all."

"That's a pity. I would have liked to confirm my supposition."

Sarah stared at him. "How theoretical is this, Doc?"

"The signs were all there, Sarah. I just need some experimental confirmation."

"So we need to get you some red jelly?"

"If you can."

Sarah sighed. "It won't be easy."

"The faster you can get me some, the faster I can confirm it."

At the back of the small crowd, the expression on Gillian's face suddenly changed. She reached into her backpack and brought out some sealed containers. Pushing her way forward, she deposited the containers on the table next to the doctor. Daniel blinked and looked up at her.

"What's this?"

"Red jelly. Is that fast enough for you?"

Welkin turned. "How on Earth did you—?"

"Don't ask. Long story."

"One that will have to keep," said Sarah. "Doc, get on this right away. I want confirmation as soon as you can. If you're right … " Sarah suddenly got a horror-struck look. "Ohmigod. Theo!"

"What about Theo?" Welkin asked.

Sarah explained about Theo and the bomb then looked at her watch. "It's due to detonate in thirty-two minutes."

"Call it off!" said Gillian, aghast.

"I can't. The Hiveborn are jamming us."

Welkin slapped his forehead. "That's not all," he said. They all looked at him. "If the red jelly is needed for the bugs to reproduce, then the one place we've got to destroy is their moon base. And for that we need a bomb. An antimatter bomb. Even an atom bomb."

Sarah looked stricken. Hoarsely, she said, "And the only one we've got is about to be blown up. Along with a lot of innocent people."

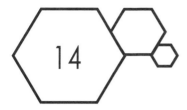

14

They ran.

Welkin called ahead, telling the repair crew to get the shuttle in order and get it turned about. They were heading back out. Pronto.

The chief engineer tried to tell him they needed at least another hour. Welkin shut him down. "In another hour two hundred thousand people will be dead and the war against the Hiveborn may be lost. Forever. So just work your usual miracles, Chief, and get it done."

There was a startled pause on the other end of the patch. "You got it."

Welkin acknowledged Harry who was running alongside him. Both were puffed. "Engineers! The only species that hasn't changed since siege warfare and the Middle Ages."

Harry nodded, but saved his breath for running.

Behind them, Gillian and Ferrik sprinted along. All were armed, but they weren't ready when the attack came. They raced into a narrow corridor, hit a T-junction, spun into the left-hand passageway, then burst into another large tunnel.

Immediately, they seemed to be surrounded by armed men and women who all turned with an eerie synchronism, weapons coming up. "It's them!" Welkin yelled. "Fire!"

He opened up, blasting three of the Hiveborn before they could get off shots. Then it turned into a free-for-all as laser pulses exploded through the gloomy air of the tunnel, leaving faintly ionized trails behind them. In the thick of the melee, it was hard to tell friend from foe. The laser bursts blasted Welkin's night vision, so that half the time he was shooting at shadows.

Meanwhile, Ferrik, Harry and Gillian—who had been slightly behind Welkin because of the narrowness of the passageway—started to get separated from him. Gillian, who could still see Welkin through the press of bodies, firing steadily, yelled out to him. She thought she saw his head half turn her way as if he had heard, but then a Hiveborn blundered between them, blocking her view.

Then a hand snapped onto her wrist and dragged her backwards. She twisted ferociously, bringing up her gun. Her finger was already starting to squeeze the trigger when she heard a voice. "It's me, Harry! Come on."

She let herself be carried along as she and Harry and Ferrik retreated from the engagement. "What about Welkin?"

"Nothing we can do right now," said Harry. Gillian could tell by his voice that he was just as torn as she was.

Moments later they had shaken off the half-hearted attempt to follow them. Indeed, the attempt had been so dispirited that Gillian figured the group they had stumbled into had some other more pressing mission. That was good news for Welkin. Chances were they would rather let him escape than compromise their immediate mission.

As soon as they could, they made radio contact with Sarah and explained what had happened. Moments later she came back on the line. "We've spotted Welkin. He's making for the shuttle."

Gillian breathed out in relief, feeling her legs go weak. She clutched at Harry to keep herself upright. Then she stiffened at Sarah's next words. "He's not responding," she said. "We know he can hear us, but he's not responding … "

Harry snatched the patch from Ferrik. "What's that supposed to mean?" he demanded.

"You know what that means, Harry. Now stop wasting time and get to that shuttle. Before Welkin does. Go!"

They looked at each other briefly, then, without speaking, Harry started up the corridor they had been crouching in. A moment later he broke into a run, the others right behind him.

There was a vast feeling of peace, like nothing else Welkin had ever known. And there was urgency too. Urgency because he had a very important mission. He must carry it out at all cost. His own life meant nothing. He was just one of many, one tiny spark amongst billions, all striving together in the great orchestra of life everlasting, a part of the immortal Hive. Fragmented feelings and memories of a thousand worlds and species floated through him. All lived within him and the others around and within.

He felt no hatred of the humans or his erstwhile friends. Dimly, he understood that they were motivated in all they did by a gut-wrenching fear of mortality and pain and isolation—things he, Welkin, no longer had to concern himself with. Indeed, a part of him yearned to bring this precious gift of solace, of community, to his former comrades.

He sighed. Sadly, his old comrades wanted to destroy the Hive, to thwart their plans. They did this out of ignorance, but nevertheless he would have to stop them. He knew what he had to do. He even felt a miniscule sense of glory, a feeling that he was enabling the Hive to continue its grand Galactic destiny: unification. Oneness.

Welkin knew a way to blow up the ship. All Hiveborn ships had a bomb built into their core, though clearly the detonation device on this had malfunctioned. He would remedy that manually. The precaution of placing bombs on their ships had resulted from an incident that took place some two million years ago on a world on the other side of the Galaxy. But the Hivemind never forgot …

Harry, Gillian and Ferrik burst into the tunnel end where the Hiveborn shuttle sat positioned for take-off, humming with readiness. They raced inside.

In the cockpit, Goose looked up as Ferrik dropped into the pilot's seat. "Where's Welkin?" Ferrik asked as the alien computer raced through the checklist, prepping the ship for take-off.

Goose eyed him. "Isn't he with you?"

Harry explained what had happened. Goose's eyes widened. "He could be on board. The ramp's been down the whole time."

"Didn't you post a lookout?" demanded Gillian.

"Of course I did." He thumbed an audio tab. "Westwood, you there? Westwood, come in?" No answer. He tried again but failed to raise the man.

"Guess that's your answer," said Gillian. "He's on board."

"Well, we don't have time to look for him now," said Ferrik. "Everybody take your acceleration pills. This could get bumpy." He hit the button that started the automatic lift-off siren. All over the ship, people would be buckling into their stations. All except one.

As the ship lifted off and started gliding down the tunnel, Harry said, "I don't like this. He didn't get on board just to see the sights."

Gillian squirmed in her seat. "We have to assume he's going to destroy the ship. He'll also try to communicate what he knows … "

"Good thought. Harry, take the comm. board. Jam all outgoing signals. I don't want anybody to know we're coming. Especially our little lunar friends."

"What about Arton? Maybe—"

Ferrik shook his head. "This baby's faster than Arton's heap—besides, we can't risk a patch; plus, Sarah will need him here."

Harry managed a sour grin but complied. "You got it."

The ship was picking up speed. "What about our friends outside?" Gillian asked.

Ferrik shrugged. "You haven't seen Goose's shooting. For their sake, I hope they're not within firing range."

Goose grinned, tooling up the weapons board and checking his reserves.

Ferrik continued, "As soon as we're airborne and away, I want search parties to tear this ship apart. Last thing I need is an enemy agent on board my ship."

Harry said quietly, "The problem is, it's also his ship."

Gillian gasped slightly. "Harry's right. He probably knows this ship better than any of us now."

"Better than any of you," said Goose, pretending to be slightly affronted. "I used to fly this baby and even if I was bug-brained at the time, I know it like the back of my hand."

Ferrik caught Gillian's anxious look and smiled. "Listen, we're not going to shoot him, okay? All weapons will be on stun." Gillian's tight face relaxed.

Goose said suddenly, "Outer portal, half a klick and closing."

"Okay, people. Time to rock 'n' roll."

Gillian looked at him. "What do you mean, rock and roll?"

Ferrik's face went blank. "Oh, you poor ignorant Earthborn."

Gillian bristled. "If we live through this, I'll give you 'poor ignorant Earthborn'!"

"Portal's coming up!" Goose barked. And sure enough the outer portal swung into view as Ferrik nudged the shuttle around a long curving bend in the tunnel. He activated the opening sequence and the portal started to slide up into the mountainside.

Outside, all looked dark and peaceful.

With an unnerving *whoosh*, the shuttle shot out of the portal into the dark valley. The circular gate rushed past in a sickening blur that made them painfully aware of just how fast they were going. Certainly fast enough to turn instantly into a cloud of free floating molecules were they to accidentally run headlong into an enemy ship.

Luckily, except for a cloud of unfortunate night-feeding fruit bats, they encountered no blockade. Ominously, Arton's craft was nowhere to be seen either.

They all exchanged looks. "Somehow," said Harry, " I don't think that's a good sign."

"You think they know Welkin's on board?" asked Gillian.

"I don't see how," said Ferrik, frowning ahead into the darkness. Running this valley was reminding him of the moon run he and Goose had used to escape the Hiveborn's lunar base.

"They'd at least know he was intending to get on board the ship," said Goose, speaking from experience. "And they'd probably want him to find out what our plans are and then find a way to communicate them. That's just a guess."

"Okay," said Ferrik. "I'm climbing for orbit, then I'm going to put her into a very steep dive to reach Theo's position. We're going to pick up a lot of heat from the re-entry. I'm pretty sure this baby will take it but it's going to get hot in here." He adjusted a control and the ship started to climb, pressing them all back in their seats. "Artificial gravity will come on in a second. Goose, get those search parties organized. Now."

Goose jumped up. "I'm on it. Harry, you're with me."

Together, they scrambled aft.

"What do you want me to do?" asked Gillian.

"I want you to run internal scans of the ship, compartment by compartment. Look for anything out of the ordinary in the EM spectrum, any fluctuations. Get the ship to activate a continuous self-diagnostic, in case anything comes up on that. And look for signs of biologicals … "

Gillian went cross-eyed.

Ferrik clucked his tongue good-naturedly. "People. Bodies. You can program the ship to check for breathing, heartbeat, human body temperature, non-random noises, like footsteps or scuffling. Also tell the computer to alert us if any access panels are opened, whether by authorized or non-authorized personnel."

Gillian whistled but jumped to it.

A few minutes later, still unopposed, the shuttle reached low orbit. Almost immediately, Ferrik nosed the ship over and dived for the vicinity of Melbourne and Theo's last known position. As he did so, he started sending encrypted data bursts, hoping Theo would pick up and answer. Problem was, Theo was on a "war footing." This meant that (a) he would be observing radio silence and (b) he would be forced to assume, by the ancient protocols of war, that any attempt to persuade him to abort his mission was probably a ploy on the part of the enemy and, hence, would have to be ignored. Hearing Ferrik's voice, even getting the correct recall signal, wouldn't necessarily convince him to abort either since Ferrik—like any of the others—could easily have been possessed. There was no way for Theo to tell otherwise.

And that meant, Ferrik thought quietly to himself, that they might have to attack his spaceplane, somehow disabling it without damaging or detonating the bomb—if it was still on board.

Ferrik suspected he was probably the only person on the ship who realized this. It made him feel very much alone.

Theo held his position even as the squadron of cruisers flew low overhead. He had brought the ship down low over the north east of Melbourne and found a forest clearing heavily overhung by trees. A semi ruined tower block, the lower wall of which had crashed outwards, left a kind of artificial cave behind. Theo had nudged the HOTOL into this cave, then reduced the ship's energy signature to a minimum.

He'd sat here like this for the last 30 minutes. There were still 12 minutes until detonation. The bomb had already been armed, the detonation sequence begun. Even if his ship were taken now, it would be too late. Without the disarming codes, no one could stop the bomb. It couldn't even be vaporized, since the magnetic bottle inside the exterior casing was all that kept the anti-hydrogen safe from contact with "ordinary" matter.

In another nine minutes, Theo would take the ship out of hiding, ram on every inch of throttle, and streak up and over Melbourne. The bomb would be dropped from the rear bay to explode exactly one kilometer above the city. "And may God have mercy on all our souls," Theo murmured to himself.

The left side of his face bandaged, Renko stood nearby. He watched the cruisers pass out of sight. They had failed to spot the hiding shuttle.

"Everything ready?" asked Theo mechanically.

Renko nodded. "Everybody's okay. They know this has to be done."

"I didn't ask you that."

"Yes, you did."

Theo smiled briefly. "I guess I did." He hesitated. "Any word from Martha?"

"Nothing. Johnson thinks the jamming signal has been strengthened for some reason. Nothing's getting in or out." He paused. "You were hoping for a recall signal?"

Theo nodded, his mouth suddenly dry.

"Would you obey it if you got it?"

Theo didn't answer at first, then he said, "I don't know. If Martha's been taken … "

Renko understood. If Martha had been taken then Sarah, possessed by a bug, could easily issue the correct recall signal. How would Theo know the difference? Maybe he thought he would know, them being lovers and all. Renko swallowed. He was just glad he didn't have to make that kind of decision.

Theo looked at his watch again. Ten minutes to go.

Welkin moved carefully. He knew they were looking for him. Another 20 yards and he would be at the console where he could manually set the bomb. Originally, he had planned to simply detonate it, blow them all out of the sky, but on the way he had passed the cruiser bay and had conceived an even better plan. He would code a timing sequence into the bomb then escape. There was information in his head that was vital to the Hive. If he timed it just right, he might be able to use the blast of this bomb to destroy the other more terrible weapon the human forces were planning to use.

Either way, he needed to get off this ship. Losing Melbourne would be a set back, certainly. It would slow down the schedule of assimilation—although many more Hiveborn could be brought from the moon. Other centers of industry could be revitalized. The Hivemind always took the long view. The very long view …

Ferrik started scanning as soon as he was within range of the metropolis. He kept sending out the data bursts containing the recall signal. He still didn't have a plan if Theo refused to disarm the bomb, other than the crude and painful necessity of disabling the other shuttle, with the possible loss of life.

They were coming in low from the east when Gillian suddenly exclaimed, "Got him!"

"Theo?"

"No, Welkin." Ferrik felt intense disappointment, much as he wanted to find Welkin. "Where is he?" he asked.

"Aft compartment E-8. He's in the maintenance corridor that runs above it. Wait a sec. He's moving off." Gillian studied the screen in front of her. "Seems to be heading for the cruiser bay."

"Get there first. Stop him!"

Gillian patched through to the searchers, then dashed out herself, leaving Ferrik and Goose alone on the bridge.

A moment later Goose peered closely at his own screen. Ferrik noted it. "Got something?"

"Maybe. Might just be an artifact in the search program, but—"

"Where?"

Goose transferred the coordinates to Ferrik's console. Ferrik nodded. "Lying low. Just what I would have done. What's the countdown?"

"Four minutes."

"Pray to Pleiades."

"Amen to that," said Goose.

Ferrik banked the craft and brought it into a low trajectory that would pass over the clearing where the ghost signal lurked.

"It's him!" Goose shouted excitedly. "Engines coming up to full power. Weapons online. It's definitely him. He's gonna make a break for it."

"Get the tight beam on him!" Ferrik cried. "Quickly."

Goose manipulated several controls. "We're locked on."

Ferrik thumbed the audio. "Theo, if you can hear this, we're on a tight beam. Nobody else can listen in. It's Ferrik. Sarah sent us. Everybody's here. Gillian, Welkin, Harry, the whole bunch. We need you to stop the detonation, Theo."

Silence greeted this.

"Theo, are you listening?"

Goose said, "He's lifting off … orienting the ship … he's gonna make a dash over the city, sure as my name's Archibald."

Ferrik flicked him a look, mouthed, "Archibald?" Goose shrugged. Ferrik patched through to the other shuttle again. "Theo, you have to listen. I know what you're thinking. Maybe we're zombies. We'd have the recall signal, right? We'd have all the memories of who we are, could answer any question you put to us. But you have to trust your gut, Theo."

He had done it. The bomb, hard-wired into the ship, was set to blow itself and everything within a radius of 50 feet to molecular smithereens in exactly three minutes, some 25 seconds before the antimatter bomb was due to explode. As Welkin headed to the cruiser bay he thought, *Maybe we'll get lucky. Maybe we'll get two birds with one stone, as the humans say.*

That was the last thought he had—as a zombie.

The stun ray hit him as he stepped into the bay. There wasn't even time to register disappointment, just the tiniest flicker of surprise, then he folded up like a manikin and hit the deck.

"Quick, get that thing out of him," said Gillian, eyeing the tiny trace of cilia poking from Welkin's left ear. She had a revolted look on her face as the medic shouldered past her and bent over his new patient.

Moments later the parasite had been removed and bottled. The medic eyed it, grinning. A fine specimen.

"Revive him," said Gillian.

"I wouldn't recommend that," said the medic. "Better he sleeps off the extraction trauma."

Gillian would have loved nothing better than to spare Welkin any unnecessary pain but it wasn't possible. She shook her head. "No can do," she said, grimly. "We need to find out what he was up to."

The medic made a face and unstoppered a vial of ammonia beneath Welkin's nose. Welkin reacted violently, knocking the vial out of the medic's hand. He sat up, spluttering and coughing. "The hell was that—?"

He looked around. Gillian and Harry and three others were staring down at him.

"Welcome back," said Gillian in a shaky voice.

Then he remembered. He felt a deep revulsion, as if his whole body had been filled with some kind of disgusting slime. He started to try to wipe it away, but realized it was just in his mind. Then he remembered.

"Pleiades! There's a bomb!"

He tried to get to his feet but Gillian and the medic held him down. "We know there's a bomb. Ferrik's talking to Theo right now."

"No, not that bomb. It's on board. On board *this* ship."

Gillian and the others stared at him. "That's not possible. How could you have gotten a bomb on board?"

"I didn't. The Hiveborn build their ships that way. To stop them falling into enemy hands. Help me up."

Welkin staggered to his feet then broke away, rushing back the way he had recently come. Gillian and Harry followed.

He found the bomb. One minute to go. While Gillian and Harry anxiously looked on, he set about disarming it.

" … your gut, Theo."

Theo stared bleakly at the transmitter, licked dry lips.

"You gonna answer?" asked Renko.

"You think I should?"

"What if they're legit? What if the situation has changed?" Renko looked scared. Theo totally understood that. He was terrified. Terrified of making a mistake.

"The recall signal—?"

"Is the correct one."

Theo sighed. He had half hoped … "Take the ship up. Quarter speed. Watch out for enemy activity." He opened a patch. "Ferrik?"

There was an explosive sigh of relief. "Theo? Pleiades, it's great to hear your voice." The relief sounded genuine. Could the Hiveborn zombies have faked such real raw emotion? Theo didn't know—and there was the rub.

He just didn't know.

"We've got a problem, Ferrik."

"I know. How do we do this?"

"Beats me. Any suggestions?"

"Yeah, how about I don't shoot you down. That has to mean something."

Theo thought about it. "Not bad. Problem is, we'd have to take things to the very edge, the last second. And I want you to know that I'm willing to detonate the bomb while it's still on board."

Beside him, Renko paled but said nothing.

On the radio, Ferrik said, "I figured that. I'd do the same."

"I know you would. So where does that leave us?"

"Running out of time." There was hesitation in Ferrik's voice, then, "Listen, Theo. We're on a tight beam so I'm going to tell you what we found out and why it's absolutely imperative that you don't destroy that bomb. Yet."

"Yet?"

Ferrik quickly told Theo about the moon base, the red jelly, and how—if they could destroy the lunar nursery with all its red jelly manufacturing capacity— they might just be able to wipe out the Hiveborn, stop them from reproducing.

"So once the current crop of parasites dies, there'd be no more to replace them? Is that it?" Theo asked.

"That's it. Space, Theo. One minute and forty seconds left."

Theo looked at Renko, who shrugged weakly. Theo thought hard. Ferrik's story was so wild, so unexpected, that part of him was convinced. He couldn't see the Hiveborn making up such an outlandish story. It had the ring of truth. If the parasites needed the red jelly to reproduce then it stood to reason they'd place their nursery as far from the field of hostilities as possible. It was their one great vulnerability. A moon base made perfect sense.

If the rest were true.

If.

"Fifty-five seconds until detonation, Theo," Renko said, his voice soft and unearthly, as if he were already a ghost.

Choose, Theo thought to himself. *But for Pleiades' sake, choose rightly ...*

Welkin worked feverishly.

There was less than half a minute to go. His hands were slick with sweat and kept slipping as he tried to grasp tiny wires, rearrange settings. Behind him he could feel Gillian and Harry standing in frozen fascination as the readout screen counted down.

I've sentenced my friends to death.

Welkin felt a terrible guilt but had to push it aside, forcing himself to concentrate.

When it got to ten seconds he heard Gillian gasp and felt her hand grip his shoulder, the fingers digging in painfully.

But he knew what he was doing.

He remembered all the settings, knew that if he made the alterations in the wrong order the bomb would detonate. There were just so many of them!

His fingers flew frantically from one adjustment to the next and all the while the countdown screamed in his head: *six, five, four ...*

Four more adjustments. Just four more.

Three seconds.

Three to go.

Two seconds.

One left. He made the adjustment. There was a loud click. They all flinched, thinking the bomb was about to explode. Instead, the screen shrank to a point of light and winked out.

Welkin, still crouching in front of the readout screen, sat down suddenly. He was drenched in perspiration. "Never again," he muttered.

Gillian dropped beside him. "Never what again?"

"I'm never leaving home again. Ever. After this, it's strictly desk jobs for me."

"I'll sit right next to you," said Gillian with feeling.

"I'll be on the other side," said Harry in a very strained voice.

Ferrik told Goose, without looking at him, to get a weapons lock on Theo's ship. Goose nodded and said nothing. He knew Theo was a friend of Ferrik's.

Ferrik patched through to the other shuttle. He was now out of time. "I'm sorry, Theo—" He started to give Goose the go-ahead nod when Theo's voice cut in on the speakers. "Bomb is disarmed. Repeat. Bomb is disarmed."

Relief flooded Ferrik and he heard himself whooping for joy. Goose joined in, slapping his back. Other hoots and whistles echoed up from the aft compartments.

If Theo needed any proof that he had made the right decision, it was the sudden outburst of hollering and delight that he heard over the radio. He couldn't quite imagine Hiveborn zombies whooping it up, no matter how perfect their impersonations were. He sat back and relaxed for the first time since leaving Martha. He even managed a weak grin when Renko gave him a beaming thumbs up.

But the feeling of goodwill spreading through him was short-lived.

Theo heard the distinctive muffled explosion as a laser pulse struck his ship somewhere aft. The ship bucked like a stung bronco and instinctively he banked and broke left, losing height rapidly. His first thought was a bleak one. He had been wrong. Ferrik and his ship were a plant. A very successful plant.

He cursed his own stupidity then the speakers burst to life. "Theo!" It was Ferrik's voice. Before Theo could retort angrily, Ferrik shouted, "Three bogies, ten o'clock. I'll take the higher ones upstairs. You get the third."

Theo chopped off what he was going to say and actually smiled. "Copy that, Ferrik. Good hunting."

"Same to you, mate. Over and out."

Theo rolled the ship over. This gave him a quick glimpse "upstairs." "There he is!" he yelled as Renko took over weapons control. The attacking ship was bigger than Theo's, probably more heavily armed too. And it had the high ground.

Not good.

Either Theo would need to do some fancy flying to get out of this one, or Renko would need to do some fancy shooting.

Theo came out of the roll barely 300 feet above ground. Immediately he dropped even lower, hugging the contours of the land, hurtling across wooded hillsides, between derelict buildings, and across natural pasture. If there was one thing the family was good at, it was hedgehopping.

Theo hoped that the Hiveborn's countless millennia of experience didn't include barnstorming.

"Can't get a lock on the bugger," said Renko, cursing softly. "Won't stay still long enough."

Theo made his moves as unpredictable as possible. A hail of laser pulses rained down on the landscape below or slashed past the forward screen, making him squint. But try as he might, he couldn't shake him.

Theo suddenly pulled a loop-de-loop, soaring up and curving over backwards in an attempt to drop down behind the enemy's tail. The other pilot saw it coming however and broke left, coming round in a sharp high-G turn that put him deftly back in Theo's rear. Theo groaned in frustration. The other pilot was better than he was.

Of course, he was outgunned. These Hiveborn shuttles and scout ships were faster, tougher, more heavily armed and more maneuverable. Put a competent pilot into one of those and they would have the upper hand every time.

But I wonder if they've ever played chicken, Theo mused silently. *Guess there's only one way to find out …*

He slammed the shuttle around, braked using the main ionjet scramtorch engine—not a technique recommended by the flight engineers—and for a second they seemed to be standing perfectly still in midair. Then the massive thrust grabbed hold of the ship and hurled it back the way it had just come moments before—and straight at the enemy ship.

The distance between the two craft closed rapidly. Beside him, Theo heard Renko gasp quietly to himself. "Get a lock," he told his weapons officer.

Renko recovered from his shock, worked his board, then looked up, almost smiling. "Got it."

As the other ship rocketed towards them, growing larger and larger by the second, Theo clenched his jaw, determined he wouldn't falter.

"Wait for him to break," he warned Renko. "We don't want to run into a fireball full of debris."

"Copy that."

The ships closed terrifyingly fast. Theo kept muttering under his breath, "Come on, break. Break, dammit!" But it didn't appear that the other pilot intended to. Then, just as Theo thought he would have to veer off, the other ship suddenly gave a telltale wobble—

"He's going for it."

"I see it, but don't believe it."

—and broke to the right. At the same instant a massive pulse leapt out from Theo's spaceplane and scored a direct hit on the other, larger, ship's engine. As the explosion came to their ears Theo's ship was already 400 yards away and climbing for height. Above him, he caught sight of the end of a dogfight as the remaining enemy vessel, badly damaged by pulse fire from Ferrik's ship, dipped away, leaving the field of battle.

Ferrik's voice, jubilant, came over the speakers. "Where the hell did you learn to fly?"

Theo laughed. "The school of desperation."

"Well, sign me up."

"Copy that. Now what?"

"Let's rendezvous in orbit. After this lot, things are probably going to get seriously hot."

"What was that just now?" Renko asked via the patch.

"That?" said Ferrik. "That was just a warm up."

They matched orbits some 20,000 miles above the Earth. Here, they transferred the bomb to Ferrik's larger ship where it was decided that Theo would head back with his crew to Martha and aid Arton in harassing the Hiveborn as much as possible.

Theo hugged them all goodbye then boarded his own ship. They unlocked the docking clamps. After a few exchanges, the Hiveborn shuttle under Ferrik's command initiated its drive and within moments it was hurtling towards the moon.

Theo dropped into a lower orbit, hanging there for about half an hour. Then he cut a new trajectory and within moments the onboard plasma computer had them chasing after Ferrik's craft.

Renko gave Theo an odd look. "I thought we were heading home."

"That's what they think too," Theo said, nodding at the viewscreen. On it was a distant moon in half phase.

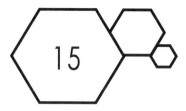

15

Sarah hadn't heard anything from C Level for over an hour now. She had to assume that, like A and B Levels, it was in the hands of the enemy.

"Anything?" she asked. Angela, at the comm. board, shook her head.

Sarah turned back to her own console just as Angela said, "Wait a sec." Sarah looked back at the harassed woman. She was very glad she had brought Angela into the War Cabinet. Apart from her instincts, the woman had marvelous stamina. Sarah herself felt exhausted and drained and would have given anything just to lie down and sleep for a week.

Angela's eyes went wide as she looked up from her board.

"Now what?" said Sarah tiredly.

"Parasites have just been found in the water supply and the sewage pipes."

Sarah frowned. She flipped some switches on her console, transferring various video feeds to the main screen. On one of these they saw a large number of men and women systematically emptying bin-sized vats into a stream that ran through a narrow gorge.

"That's Myateh Gorge." Angela raised an eyebrow. Sarah explained, "That's where we get most of our water. They're dumping parasites in it. Jesus." Sarah thought for a moment. "Get Daniel on the line, quick."

Moments later she was talking to the doctor. Sarah cut to the chase. "Doc, I need some way to detect who's been possessed and who hasn't."

Daniel's face contorted in thought. "Well, it's not that easy. A DNA test would prove it since we've just learnt that the parasites exchange genetic material with the host. Nothing permanent but it enhances the host organism, makes it easier to control."

"Fascinating. But I need something my scanners can pick up inside Martha. Anything. Body temperature … "

Daniel shook his head. "Body temperature is unchanged except that it doesn't register exertion. That could be a risky. No, let me think." Sarah tapped her fingers impatiently as the doctor considered the problem. After several long moments Sarah said, "Doc—?"

"There is something. It could be a bit tricky."

"What is it?"

"When the parasites mate with the human brain they seem to emit a low EM signal. It's continuous and only occurs when the two brains are hooked together. If you could find a way to boost this signal and calibrate your sensors for it, you should be able to scan for zombies. Probably wouldn't work well over long distances but inside these tunnels … " He shrugged, which eloquently said it all.

"Thanks, Doc. Send up all the relevant information and the frequency at which the signal operates. I'll let you know what happens." She cut the line then called for Hetti and found her helping out in the infirmary. She told her to get up to the War Room on the bounce.

The data from Daniel had popped up on Angela's screen as Hetti arrived. Sarah told her exactly what she wanted and when.

Hetti blinked several times then looked at Sarah to see if she was joking. She wasn't. "You want this inside of an hour?"

"Preferably less."

"Have you thought this through?" Hetti tapped Angela's screen. Her fingernail clicked on the glass. "This is a very low emission signal. Enhancing that … I dunno … "

Angela said something hesitantly. Hetti looked up at her, distracted. "What's that?"

"The tunnels. Most of the walls are granite. Won't they reflect and bottle up the signal?"

Hetti stared at her then her eyes widened. She gave Sarah a look. "You don't need me when you've got her here," she said. To Angela she went on: "You're right. I should have thought of that. I was thinking of it as an outdoor general problem. But inside Martha with our existing scanners … it might work at that."

"Get on it," said Sarah.

Hetti sat down at Angela's console. Sarah frowned. "What are you doing?"

Hetti smiled. "I can do it from here right now. Calibrating the scanners will only take a few minutes, then we should start to get results. I'll have to cancel out false positives and echoes but the computer should be able to handle that. I'm not great with programming but ancient software is very sophisticated. And, the help function usually works, if nothing else … "

While Hetti worked Sarah made encrypted contact with her surface team. Strictly speaking, they weren't on the surface yet. They were still making their way through old mine workings to get as close to the Hiveborn vessels still sitting on the surface. With the taking of the upper levels, it was a moot point whether this counterattack would be anything more than an empty gesture.

Still, there was such a thing as serendipity. Good fortune sometimes came to those who were open to it.

The woman in charge of the operation was one Lieutenant Mawson, a tough no-nonsense disciplinarian who had run her own tribe of misfits before either Skyborn or the Hiveborn had arrived. She was, in many ways, a counterpart to Sarah herself.

Sarah made contact with her, confirmed that the link was secure, then brought her up to date on the situation inside Martha. "You may soon be the only free agents we have left, other than the crews on the ships. And for various reasons we can't count on them, other than Arton's lot. You've been in contact with him?"

"We have," said Mawson, her words clipped and fast, as if she was impatient to get on with her mission. Sarah thanked her silently for that.

"I'm automating the sit-reports. They'll be downloaded onto your e-board at regular intervals. If you get the Omega signal, you'll know what to do."

"I understand," drawled Mawson laconically.

"Okay. Good luck," said Sarah and cut the connection. She stared at the patch pad for a moment, wondering if Mawson was up to the task set before her. Of course, it was too late if she wasn't.

"Got it!" cried Hetti behind her. Sarah spun around. Hetti was grinning; so was Angela who was standing behind her, leaning over her shoulder staring at the computer readouts.

"Put it on the main screen," said Sarah.

A schematic of the Martha tunnels appeared on the big wall screen. Then another layer was superimposed over this.

Sarah frowned. "What am I looking at?"

"Okay," said Hetti. "This first super shows all warm bodies inside Martha. That's a fairly simple scan, picking up human body heat, eliminating rats, pets and so forth." Sarah noted that there were several clusters scattered throughout the tunnels but by far the largest, and most expansive, was the border region around C and D levels. Damn. She should have thought of this before. It was much better Intel than even the video feeds.

Another layer unfolded onto the screen. "This," said Hetti, "shows the parasites' signature EM signal. The computer is doing its best to assign a signal to a specific body but it can only do that where it has fairly accurate triangulation from at least three pickups. Usually not a problem but there are some blind spots, such as here and here and here." A series of red dots appeared on the screen as Hetti spoke. "But the good news is, once the computer has tagged someone, they stay tagged. So effectively those blind spots will disappear."

Suddenly, a large number of the "bodies" changed color.

"I'm coding by color. Green for our troops, red for theirs, blue where we're not sure. Over time, the blues should vanish."

Angela stared at the big screen. "Wow," she said.

Wow is right, thought Sarah. The analysis gave them a big picture that they could not have imagined earlier; nor was it a reassuring picture. Almost without exception the upper two levels—A and B—were completely red. C level was about 90 per cent red and the rest green with a smattering of blue.

With a sigh Sarah saw that D level was fatally penetrated, almost 40 per cent already. Even as she watched, greens turned suddenly to red as they—presumably—began emitting the telltale EM signal that meant a parasite had engaged its neural links with a human brain.

"How come there are a handful of greens up on levels A and B?"

Hetti shrugged. "My guess is, we got some free thinkers pretending to be zombies. Don't know how long they can last though."

"I don't know," Sarah said thoughtfully. "Welkin said that man Roddy had been with his squad for at least six weeks after losing his bug. Obviously it can be done."

"Rather them than me," said Angela, shuddering.

"I'm with you there," agreed Hetti.

"Monitor their activities," said Sarah. "My bet is, those that can't escape and rejoin our forces will attempt some kind of sabotage."

"No problem," said Hetti, tapping commands into her computer keyboard. "The computer can keep a record of that kind of thing."

But all that was the good news. Overall, the screen showed a preponderance of red—and it was spreading. Fast. The tunnels were divided into cells—areas that were boarded off, forming chambers or a series of them. This was how the family had constructed living quarters, workshops, dormitories, storage compartments, and so forth. As Sarah watched, more and more cells turned red.

It was like looking at a huge chess board where, as the enemy took new territory, the color of the squares changed to the color of the victor.

The good news was, now she could see where to send reinforcements and where not to waste her time. She gave Angela a series of orders. Angela jumped on another computer and started relaying battle instructions to the various field commanders. She also hooked up the main screen schematic to the commanders' e-boards. This way they could make immediate responses as local conditions changed.

But there was another problem. A number of red "knots" existed inside the green zone of Martha. Infiltrators, saboteurs—the newly possessed.

"Angela, hand-pick some people for eradication squads. They'll need access to this screen. Tell them to get knockout gear from Daniel. I want people stunned or tranquilized, understand? No killing unless it's absolutely necessary."

"I'm on it," said Angela.

For some time, Sarah sat and watched the screen. She was pleased to note that some of the red knots turned green, easing her fear of sabotage, but the outcome was, she reckoned, still pretty inevitable. They could not check the overwhelming numbers. Hiveborn reinforcements seemed in unlimited supply.

It was just a matter of time.

Catherine Mawson consulted her e-board.

The new schematic from the War Room was painfully clear: Martha was being overrun and there didn't seem to be anything anybody could do about it. Worse, Mawson's little op—the taking of the Hiveborn surface vessels—wasn't necessarily going to change anything. Indeed, as Sarah had explained to her, it was more in the nature of a long-term investment. Somebody had to survive this day—and arrangements had been made for that—and those somebodies would need transportation and aerial defense. The Hiveborn ships could do all that.

It might not be able to withstand the full brunt of a Hiveborn attack but it might give a new colony time. Time to come up with a solution—or else just take off and find some quiet part of the solar system that didn't interest the Hiveborn. Mars maybe. Of course, even if the greenhouse machines were still operating, which she doubted, the city bubbles would need to be intact. Then again, beggars couldn't be choosers. The infrastructure was there—if only the Hiveborn would leave them alone long enough to get it all up and running.

Mawson shivered despite herself, managing to turn it into a general movement of climbing to her feet and shaking off fatigue—she didn't want her squad getting the idea she was jumpy. Her sergeant, a sparsely-bearded youth by the name of Chalker, looked up. "It's time?"

"Yeah," said Mawson. "Round everybody up. Run buddy checks."

Mawson didn't know if it was time or not. What she did know was that if her people sat around any longer they'd start getting the waiting jitters. They'd start gnawing at their own confidence—and hers. Better to be doing than sitting. In fact, Chalker had already been acting strange—a real case of cabin fever.

She contacted Arton on their secure encrypted line, nevertheless using code whenever she could. "Hornet to Hawk, you there?"

"Hawk here," came Arton's voice. "You coming out to play?"

"Roger that. Bringing some toys with me."

"Oh goody."

Mawson groaned inwardly. Some of these Skyborn and their archaic language! Most of them seemed to have grown up watching centuries-old vids. What was that about? "ETA twenty minutes," she said.

"Acknowledged," said Arton. "Guess I'll go see if there are any bullies on the playing field."

"You do that."

"Don't you go stirring up any nests now! Over and out."

Mawson killed the connection and took a deep breath. How come she got the it-might-all-depend-on-you job? Why couldn't it just be a simple hit-and-run?

Destiny. Future of the human race. Blah. She hated words like that.

"Okay you lay-abouts, lock and load!" she barked.

Everyone moved but Chalker.

Neck hair prickling, Mawson's hand went to her utility belt but Chalker's hand already held a pistol. He fired without flinching and Mawson fell across her command seat. Before the rest of the crew could react, Chalker sprayed the cabin on wide beam. It didn't matter he had only stunned the personnel. With what he had in mind they would all be dead soon anyway.

By late that afternoon it was all but over. As Sarah stared at the wall screen—now 92 per cent red—she finally had to admit that they had lost. No, she corrected herself. They had lost the battle—not the war. The jury was still out on that one.

Fighting had been fierce for a time around the border between D and E levels but the further into the tunnel complex the Hiveborn penetrated the easier it became for them, the more options they had. Martha was shaped vertically, much like a pyramid. The main bottlenecks—and the best chance of blocking the attack—were near the apex. As the attackers came lower and lower the mine workings opened out, providing many more tunnels, corridors and cell complexes.

"We did well to hold them this long," Angela reminded her.

Sarah nodded. "I know that."

"Now what?" Angela asked softly. "We go quietly or we try and kick the stuffing out of them?"

Sarah smiled. "We go quietly," she said.

Angela stared at her, as if she hadn't heard right.

"No, we don't give up." Sarah went to her console and tapped in a special code then held her finger poised over the execute button. "Way down in the bowels of this complex near the converted shuttle power source, there's a secret room. No one knows about it except me and Daniel. When I hit this button a gas will be released into every tunnel … "

Angela looked suddenly horrified. "No—!"

Sarah shook her head. "Don't be so melodramatic. It's not a lethal gas, just a knockout. It'll put everybody to sleep for twenty-four hours. It's one of Daniel's theories. He thinks that the parasites derive a kind of psychic sustenance from their hosts. If the hosts completely shut down for such a period of time, there's some chance the parasites might die. There's also a chance that Welkin and Ferrik will be successful—at least in the long term."

"What would have happened if you'd been killed?"

Sarah showed Angela the watch on her wrist. "This. It's a dedicated one-parent-only transceiver. It also monitors my life signs. If they're terminated, the gas is released."

Angela was nodding. She looked at the wall screen, now almost 95 per cent red. "Do it," she said.

Sarah swallowed then hit the button.

A moment later a red warning signal flashed on the screen. "NETWORK DAMAGED. UNABLE TO COMPLY. NETWORK DAMAGED. UNABLE TO COMPLY ... "

The screen filled with the words. Sarah's head fluttered. Having this trump card up her sleeve had been one of the few things that had kept her going through the darkest hours of the last couple of days. And now it too had been stolen from her.

Or had it? She sat up with a jolt, getting a cold, sick feeling in her stomach.

"What's wrong?" asked Angela. "Why didn't it work?"

"The physical comm. system is down somewhere, no doubt thanks to our zombie friends."

"There's no way to get the signal through?"

"No." Sarah stared straight ahead. "Not by landline."

Angela frowned. "What's that supposed to mean?" But she had already guessed. She stared fixedly at Sarah's doomsday watch.

Sarah removed a blaster from the drawer beneath her console, calmly placing it on her lap. Angela stared at it in horror.

"No, you can't do that!"

"I'm not letting them take my family," Sarah said. Her voice shook slightly. "They'll be possessed, scattered. This is our last chance to stay together. To be free."

"Just take the watch off," Angela said desperately. "It'll think you're dead."

"It's a little bit more sophisticated than that, but I appreciate the thought."

Angela grabbed Sarah by the shoulders, shook them. "You can't do this."

Sarah stared imperturbably back. "*Noblesse oblige*," she said.

"I don't know what that means and I don't care. You can't do it! The family needs you."

"The family needs this," Sarah said, gently removing Angela's hands. "They need this chance. I can't see any other way, Angela."

"I won't let you do it." There were tears in Angela's eyes.

Sarah set the blaster to kill then raised it and placed it against her chest, directly above her heart. She hooked her finger around the trigger. It was somewhat awkward as she would have to fire in reverse.

"No, Sarah. *Please* ... "

"Lie down on the floor, Angela," said Sarah. "That way you won't hurt yourself when the gas is released." Her finger tightened on the trigger.

Angela shut her eyes tight then suddenly opened them. "Wait!"

"What is it?"

"I'll go."

Sarah frowned. "Go where?"

"To the secret room. I'll release the gas manually."

"If anyone was to go, it'd be me," Sarah said bluntly.

"But if they get you, the family really is lost, Sarah. I'm expendable."

Sarah thought a moment. "Maybe that's true. But you don't stand a chance. The odds are way stacked against you."

"Then—then you can do what you were going to do anyway. You shut this place up. Lock everybody out … "

Sarah glanced at the wall screen. There was a lot of red between here and the secret room. But why not try it? What did they have to lose?

She put the blaster down and Angela sat heavily in her chair. Sarah realized she had been holding her breath. "Okay," she said after a brief silence. "But I figure they'll be in here in thirty minutes."

"Thirty minutes," Angela repeated.

"And when they come through that door," Sarah told her, "I'm pulling the trigger. You understand?"

Angela nodded, not trusting herself to speak.

"Okay, listen close. This is how you get there and what to do when you arrive … "

Angela didn't dare breathe or move a muscle. The Hiveborn search squad was no more than a few feet from her cover.

She had made it out of the War Room okay, despite the big screen showing a concentration of Hiveborn in the vicinity. Then matters went from bad to worse, the takeover rate escalating exponentially, as such things do. Sarah's plan involved what she called the snowball effect. Very soon the snowball would crash into the bottom of the mountain, having obliterated every trace of free humanity inside Martha.

Before Angela had left, Sarah had handed her a small e-board which duplicated the big screen and the changes occurring there. With this, she had managed to avoid Hiveborn in the immediate area, but as she moved deeper she found her way blocked. It seemed that the Hiveborn had found it easier to penetrate down the sides of the Martha complex than push through the center of the opposition. Or maybe the main thrust in the center had been designed as a decoy, a way to drain off vital reinforcements while smaller squads had taken out the stairs and elevator shafts and ramps at the extremities of the workings.

It made sense, like everything the Hiveborn did.

But in practical terms, it meant that there was a great deal of red between Angela and her target, a small hidden chamber down on J Level—indeed, Angela hadn't even known there was a J Level. It didn't show up on normal schematics of the complex. Sarah had explained this was because it was a marginally unrenovated section of the tunnel, largely also unused by the family. Being in its original state, it was also dangerous: no safety reinforcements had been used down there. But all this served an additional purpose: it added to the concealment of the hidden room. Hopefully, the Hiveborn—like Angela—didn't know there was a tenth level either.

After dodging another Hiveborn unit, Angela made her way to an access shaft that had been closed off some time ago, making it an ideal way to move between levels secretly. There were a number of these but unfortunately they were not all connected. This meant she would have to traverse dangerous territory as she moved from one vertical access shaft to another.

It was while she was doing this on G level that she was nearly caught. The only thing that saved her was that she had paused to get her breath and happened to look at the e-board which she had strapped to her left wrist. She almost gasped.

A Hiveborn squad was just round the next bend, headed her way. And there was nowhere to hide. Well, not quite nowhere—just nowhere she would want to hide.

Drainage in these old mines was a continual problem. The walls seeped moisture and some of the tunnels had small streams running down their centers. This runoff had to be taken care of and the original builders had constructed a series of drains and cisterns and pumping stations. The problem was, the drains collected all the sludge and refuse left in the tunnels, not to mention the fact that they provided a simple sewage system.

There was a drain at Angela's feet. She could see the water inside it glistening between the gaps in the metal grille that covered the pit.

There was no time to think. No time to get squeamish. She knelt quickly, lifted the grille, and slid into the murky slimy liquid beneath, closing the grille just as someone came round the corner. The grille snicked quietly into place just as the bearer's weight came down on it.

As the dozen or so Hiveborn passed overhead, Angela crouched in the darkness of the pit, staring up through the grille, unable to avert her gaze. The footsteps overhead echoed eerily, like a solemn drum roll.

The smell—and the *feel*—was shocking. She nearly dry-heaved, only stopping herself by slapping a hand across her mouth. Once she made a slight retching noise, and above, one of the Hiveborn paused, looking back the way she had come. Angela froze, willing the Hiveborn to keep going, and to dismiss the sound.

After what seemed an eternity, Angela exhaled mightily. She checked her e-board. All clear.

Climbing out of the pit was harder than climbing in but she eventually managed it, having wasted too much time with the whole thing. Drenched from the knees down, she swore softly to herself. She needed to keep a constant monitor on the e-board. No more surprises, thank you very much. Luckily, her boots didn't squelch as she walked.

The next access shaft was 200 yards from Angela's current position. As she made her way there—detouring around the red tentacles of Hiveborn patrols—she wondered if she was the only free human left. Except for Sarah that is. *Please God, don't let them have found the War Room yet ...*

Sarah watched the red dots circle closer and closer, like buzzards sensing easy prey. The location of the War Room had been a closely guarded secret, but with most—if not all—of the family now in Hiveborn possession, she had to believe that its location was now known by the enemy.

It was just a matter of time before they brought up heavy lasers and gravity cannon and started tunneling through the reinforced door.

She glanced at the screen. There was a handful of green holdouts. Most, like her, appeared to be barricaded into difficult to access spots, forcing the Hiveborn to smoke them out one way or another. As she watched, one such holdout quickly turned red. She winced, then forced herself to search for that other lone blip.

And found it.

Angela was still on the case, still "green." There was some chance yet, Sarah reflected, that she wouldn't have to use the blaster sitting on her lap.

She heard a dull noise through the bunker door, then a double thump. Her eyes flicked across to her own green signal. Nearby, just outside the door, there was a concentration of red.

The Hiveborn, left to themselves, didn't waste a lot of effort on words and when they did speak it was direct and to the point. Ego no longer entered into matters; this was the one trait the Hiveborn possessed least of all, unless there was now a kind of superego in force, though hardly the one envisaged by Freud and psychoanalysts.

Each component of the Hive worked to its utmost efficiency. The components were also the ultimate team players, perhaps because there was now only one mind.

Curiously, they continued the human tradition and conceit of individual names. It was a deliberate policy of the Hivemind, something learned from thousands of encounters with individualistic species. In the beginning, the Mind had thought that by possessing the separate units of their socially, but not mentally collective creatures, it would be integrating them fully into its own nature. But this hadn't worked and it had taken a few thousand years for it to accept that there was something fundamentally different in the wiring of some species like these humans. It wasn't all that common. Most species were far more communal than humans, far more emotionally and mentally integrated, even when they existed to all intents and purposes as individuals. But every now and then the Hivemind encountered a difficult species. If the Mind had ever thought to have a rating system, it would certainly have placed humans at the top for most resistant species they had met.

For creatures like these, the Mind had learnt it must allow for small expressions of that fundamental need for individuality. Hence the keeping of the names, the maintenance of dress habits belonging to that individual prior to possession, and a dozen other tiny inconsequential things.

Over time, of course, the Mind would experiment with the species, making small genetic changes, or attempts to expunge the last vestiges of separateness. But it would take time and, the Mind conceded, might never be achieved at all.

So now as this small group of possessed humans worked together, they addressed themselves by name and maintained individualistic ways of speaking—accents, idioms, sometimes even jocular references—that had belonged to the pre-possessed humans. In some way, these small concessions soothed the human spirit imprisoned deep within. And the units lasted longer and worked better. Really, it was just a matter of cost-benefit economics.

"Taylor, get that thing over here," said a burly man with thick eyebrows and heavy jowls. His name before he had been possessed was Lucas. He was studying the reinforced door before him. He didn't know what was behind it, just that he had to break in there and do so as quickly as possible. A lot of the "orders" were like that. Need-to-know basis only. But that was okay with him. He didn't need to know. He had absolute and unwavering confidence in the Hivemind, of which he was now an inextricable part, and could not even conceive of doubting or questioning its requests.

Taylor, along with three others, manhandled a heavy portable laser unit out of a flatbed trolley they had used to transport the device, then dragged it across to the door.

"Get it ready and calibrated," Lucas ordered. It was another feature of Hiveborn organization—and indeed biology—that not every unit was equal, though command positions often changed willy-nilly. Partly it was because hosts had to physically update themselves, that is they had to connect to the Hivemind to receive orders. It was easier to manage this by using a hierarchical command structure whereby only a small number of "commanders" downloaded the latest orders then passed them on verbally. Also, some hosts had better minds than others—the wiring was more efficient. That meant they provided a better quality *processor* for the parasite connector planted in their ear and could therefore process information more efficiently. Like many species before them, the humans mistakenly believed that the parasites were intelligent semi-autonomous creatures in their own right; individualistic species could not help but think this way. In reality, while the parasites had a minimal consciousness and information processing capacity, they were more analogous to adaptors; they allowed two different systems to connect, the Hivemind and the human, and to download commands and other data. The parasites had the added benefit of suppressing the human personality and co-opting the brain and its wiring for their own purposes. It was like attaching a small external hard drive to a computer which then took over the computer, used its computing powers, and also acted as a link to the mainframe.

The laser suddenly sprang to life as a coherent beam of light drilled into the reinforced door. Lucas nodded in satisfaction. "Don't stare at the beam," he warned the others. He didn't need units with damaged optic nerves.

"How long is this going to take?" Taylor asked.

"Fifteen minutes, estimated."

"Why estimated?"

"We're not sure how thick the door is or if it's the only obstacle."

Taylor nodded and lapsed, like the others, into silence.

Sarah gripped the blaster, eyeing the screen. Because the War Room was semi soundproofed, and because the video feed that could have shown that part of the tunnel system was down, she couldn't tell what was happening outside. The main screen still showed a knot of red-coded Hiveborn. It couldn't be a coincidence that they were congregated right outside the family's War Room. That would be too much to expect. Maybe they were having a coffee break. Did they drink coffee? Did they take breaks?

The answer to each of these was that she did not know.

For the hundredth time, her eyes went to the lone green spark making its way deeper and deeper into the tunnel complex.

"You can do it, Angela," Sarah whispered to herself. It sounded like a prayer.

"Nearly through," said Taylor, squinting briefly into the hole the laser had drilled in the door. The portable unit was swung back into position and reignited, blasting sparks from the hole.

"Good," said Lucas.

Angela stank. The smell of effluence and mineral sludge filled her nostrils as she cat-footed down corridors and along passageways. It was lucky for her that the Hiveborn hadn't been told to sniff out lone Earthborn by their smell alone, otherwise she would have been easily discovered.

She paused at an intersection to listen. Sarah had warned her not to rely totally on the e-board. There were blind spots, she had said, and it was always possible that if they got to Sarah, if they possessed her, they might re-configure the feed to the e-board in order to deceive and entrap Angela. As if there wasn't enough going on already to make a girl paranoid ...

Angela darted across the intersection, moved into a main passageway, then veered off into a smaller corridor that dead-ended in a rough cut section of the mine. In the floor here there was what appeared to be a normal drain, complete with grille. There was even a few inches of oily water in the bottom. But there was also a hatch in the side of the pit which gave entry to the next access shaft. This one would take her all the way down to I Level. One above J.

She closed the hatch behind her, locked it, and started climbing down. She was almost there. For the first time since she had proposed the hare-brained scheme to Sarah, she allowed herself to start thinking she might actually pull it off.

Sarah was standing, blaster gripped in a steady two-handed fist, the muzzle aimed squarely at the door. She figured she would give Angela a few more seconds; get off one or two shots, then turn the gun on herself.

Don't kid yourself, said a voice in her head. *If they're making all the effort of breaking into this room, then they're going to be ready for anything. There won't be any second shot.*

Sarah lowered the blaster. She went back to her chair and sat down, keeping the bulk of the console between herself and the main door. She still couldn't tell what the Hiveborn were up to, but in her bones she knew.

They would be coming through that door any moment now and Angela still hadn't reached the chamber. Such a pity. She had started to hope this moment would never arrive.

There was a thump outside, though it came to her more as a vibration than a sound. She quickly placed the muzzle of the blaster under her chin. The action pushed her head back slightly and made her feel even more vulnerable.

The seconds ticked away and Sarah found herself counting them, like that somehow made them more meaningful, the last seconds of her life …

The laser was switched off. "That's it," said Taylor, squinting into the hole again. "We're through. Far as I can tell there's just a normal metal door inside. Can blow it no sweat."

"Come on, let's crack this one wide open," said Lucas. He and the others attached magnetic clamps to the outer door and, now that the locking mechanism was completely vaporized, hauled it open easily. As Taylor had said, what greeted them now was a fairly standard metal door and bulkhead. Nothing a little plastic explosive wouldn't take care of.

Lucas attached the shaped charge to the door himself, pressed in a radio detonator, and ushered everyone back.

When the area was clear, he punched the button on the remote control. There was a flash of light followed by a dull booming sound, the echoes of which reverberated through the nearby tunnels.

Sarah felt rather than saw the explosion. Her trigger finger jerked in reflex.

Lucas and the others charged forward through the billowing smoke, blasters drawn. Within moments they were inside the concealed room. Somewhere amidst the smoke, a blaster discharged and he heard a woman cry out.

Angela couldn't see how she was going to get through. It was an impossible situation. Both according to the e-board and her own visual checks, the way ahead—the *only* way to gain access to J Level—was packed with Hiveborn. As far as she could see, there were no alternative routes, no detours. There was only the one shaft leading down to J Level and no doubt that was how Sarah and the others had wanted it.

Angela bit her lip, unsure what to do. She couldn't wait much longer. For some time now she had been aware that Hiveborn were massed outside the War Room. If they were trying to break in, then it was only a matter of time before they succeeded and that meant any minute now Sarah would kill herself.

Dammit. She's only doing it so I can get through—but what if I don't? The thought burned her. She felt anger rise up inside her like a dark liquid, though she wasn't sure at whom she was angry.

She peered out again. She was hiding in one of the many hidey-holes established in the weeks before the attack. This one was barely more than a broom cupboard with a "door" that perfectly matched the surrounding rock, except that it was punctured by spy-holes and various sensors. The room also contained food, water and medicines.

Angela was grateful for the water. She was thirsty, maybe dehydrated, though that might have been a stress reaction. She had been in dangerous situations before, but something about the Hiveborn made her skin crawl and awakened deep-seated fears she would rather not face.

She eyed the distribution of red on the e-board screen and scowled silently to herself. She was completely encircled now. No way forward, no way back. The encirclement didn't alarm her. There was nothing purposeful about it— at least she didn't think so. Realization came to her that was so sudden she wondered why she hadn't thought of it before. The Hiveborn probably had an e-board or similar gadget to pinpoint unprocessed humans.

Level I—the floor she was on—contained most of the food processing and ventilating systems and would be of prime interest to the Hiveborn. From snippets of things she had heard, she suspected the Hiveborn might be intending to take over Martha and keep it as some kind of secret base. Why, she couldn't imagine. Did the Hiveborn have enemies? Non-Earth types?

Angela shuddered to think. Every time someone new turned up from space it became a bigger headache for the humans. And to think they used to run scared of the Skyborn!

Angela sighed. She knew she was putting off a decision, letting her mind wander. Despite everything she had said to convince herself otherwise, there *was* a way through to J Level.

It just wasn't very pleasant.

The fact was, she could just walk right through, minding her own business. Roddy—that lad Welkin had picked up in Melbourne—had done it. Their own wall screen had shown that members of the family, even up on A and B Levels, were doing it. Masquerading as Hiveborn. All you had to do, it seemed, was not lose your nerve. If you didn't run, the Hiveborn didn't chase you. If you didn't cower, they didn't suspect. Of course, that was all before she had considered the possibility that the Hiveborn had their own detection device.

Great. All I have to do is hobnob with alien bugs!

"Okay," she whispered to herself. "Take the punt. All I've got to do is bluff a pack of alien bugs. If I get detected, I take as many of them with me as possible." Angela stuffed some of the food concentrates into her pockets, checked that the passageway was clear, then quickly swung open the door, stepped out, and closed it behind her. The soft click made her stomach lurch. Her mouth suddenly went dry.

She was about to step around the corner into a chamber full of Hiveborn when she realized she still had the e-board strapped to her wrist. Probably not a risk factor, but who knew? She quickly stowed it in a spare pocket.

Taking a deep breath she went round the corner. And faltered.

Fortunately, no eyes were on her. Some two dozen Hiveborn were industriously at work examining a hydroponics bay, looking for hidden chambers and corridors. Angela quickly got herself under control and walked through the room as purposefully as she could manage. She looked neither right nor left nor did she look down. She kept telling herself, *I have a job to do, I have a job to do …*

It was as close as she could come to thinking like a zombie.

Miraculously, she made it across the room and into the short corridor that joined the hydroponics bay to a series of workshops. It was lucky no one had accosted her in the first chamber. She suspected that if they had, she would have freaked and started blasting—and that would have been that.

Making it this far boosted her confidence. The access shaft was gained from inside the toilets just off the third workshop. She hoped Hiveborn peed otherwise she might have some explaining to do.

She made it through the first two workshops without incident and each success emboldened her a little. The Hiveborn were single-minded and one-tracked. Whatever they were assigned to do, they carried out methodically and assiduously, never turning aside, never getting distracted. Like a nice little nest of ants.

She was halfway across the third room when a woman stepped in front of her. "I need your assistance," said the woman.

Angela stifled her reaction, came to a stop. "I am needed elsewhere," she said, feeling her stomach do a flip-flop. She had heard one of the Hiveborn say this back in the first workshop. She tried to copy the slightly flat tone.

"This won't take long," said the woman.

The woman didn't budge. Angela didn't know what was protocol. She had to make a decision, fast. In another moment she would start sweating. "Okay," she said.

As the woman led her to a wall panel that she was in the process of dismantling, Angela desperately checked for escape routes. She felt a terrible sense of doom. Everything was going wrong. What would the woman want her to do? What if she couldn't do it?

Fighting back panic she realized the woman had said something to her. She rewound the conversation in her head. "Hold this wrench," the woman had said, "while I loosen the nut inside."

Angela could have laughed. That was it? She felt a wave of relief sweep through her and took hold of the wrench while the woman lay down on the floor and reached up inside the panel to loosen the nut.

It's now or never, Angela thought. She set her blaster on stun and gave the zombie a flash burn across her left earlobe. With luck she had killed the parasite, but she didn't have time to check that out. Two minutes later Angela was inside the toilets, breathing hard, though not from exertion.

As the smoke cleared, Lucas and Taylor peered about, guns swiveling. There was complete silence now and they realized they were in some kind of security office, maybe even a command center. They had already unearthed two such centers, both unused and disconnected from the command net.

"Over there," said Taylor.

Covering one another they moved closer and saw a woman sprawled on the floor.

Angela climbed down the shaft, launching faint echoes as her hands and boots slapped the rungs. Below, she could hear running water.

She reached J Level fairly easily though she had to ford a small creek that had gouged a channel in the lowest tunnel before she could get to the hidden control chamber. She managed this without mishap. Her e-board assured her there were no Hiveborn on this level, which wasn't surprising since, according to Sarah, she had just used the only access that existed. Of course, Sarah didn't tell her everything.

All that remained now was getting inside the concealed room and inputting the code. She just hoped she wasn't too late.

"She alive?" Lucas asked.

"Doubt it," said Taylor. There was a serious flash burn on her temple. He felt for a pulse. "Belay that. I have life signs."

"We'd better get her to the infirmary," said Lucas. They picked up the unconscious woman. Efi's hair fell aside, revealing her flash-burnt face.

Sarah was still holding the blaster tightly beneath her own chin when she noticed that the knot of red outside the War Room's door had dispersed. Obviously, they had been taking a break after all—or whatever Hiveborn did for recreation.

She lowered the blaster once more and took a deep breath. The lone green dot on the screen had made it to L level. Maybe everything was going to be okay.

A moment later the rear wall blew in.

The blast sent her flying across the room. On the way, her head connected with something hard and she lost her grip on the blaster. As the smoke settled, she sat up groggily. A tall bull-necked man loomed over her, grinning.

"Hello, Sarah. My name is Lucas. And I have something for you."

Sarah's eyes traveled down his chest and along the arm that was thrusting towards her, holding the slimy mucous-covered form of an alien bug.

A wave of nausea seized her and she thought she was going to puke over the bug itself—not that it would have made much difference to it, one part of her brain dimly observed.

Then in the background, faint at first, she heard a soft hissing sound. She started taking shallow breaths.

Still standing over her, Lucas was starting to blink. He seemed to have forgotten why he was there. One of his men sagged slowly to the floor followed by another. "Rock a bye baby, on the tree top … " Sarah began.

Lucas began to frown, staring back at her. Then he keeled over.

Sarah let herself slump as she felt the narcotic gas take hold. She mentally cursed that she hadn't taken someone's suggestion and prepared an oxygen filter for herself. But at the time, she had been too concerned that she might have been taken over herself when and if the gas was released. If that had happened, then the gas trick would have been wasted.

Sarah's last thought was of Welkin and the others. If their mission failed then everyone in the family would probably wake up as a card-carrying member of the Hive.

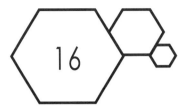

16

Welkin watched the moon loom large on the forward screen. It was hard to fit the idea of the relentless Hiveborn with this, the serene image in front of him. He said as much to Ferrik, who nodded.

"Serene. Right. One hundred and seventy below at night and two hundred and sixty-five in the daytime. Hard vacuum. Silicon and a little water. Killer cosmic rays. And now Hiveborn demons. Yeah, I see what you mean. Serene. Face it, Welkin, you're a romantic."

"Just what the world needs," said Gillian. "A bit of romance."

Ferrik sniggered. "Well, in that case, we better liberate this symbol of dreamy romanticism from the alien devils who are occupying it."

"Couldn't have put it better myself," said Harry, just coming up from aft. "So what are we talking about?"

"How to destroy their moon base," said Welkin.

"Easy," said Harry. "We fly in, blast the outer portal, drop the bomb into the shaft with a timer, and get out of there." He looked around at the others who appeared quite skeptical at this plan. "What? It's not brain surgery, you know."

"Won't work," said Ferrik. He threw a schematic on the forward screen. "I had Thompson whip this up. It shows the layout and structure of their base. Notice there are at least a dozen levels, maybe more—he didn't get to all of them and the Hiveborn seem to operate on a need-to-know basis. The vats containing the jelly and their little cuties are arranged in concentric circles around the elevator shaft on all but the top two levels. Thompson estimates there are at least six hundred of these. The outermost vats are more than two miles from the shaft."

"So they could be outside the blast radius?" said Gillian, frowning at the schematic.

"They could be," Welkin agreed. "Explosions are tricky things to predict. They can be deflected, channeled, absorbed, canceled by a whole lot of different things, including reinforced bulkheads, blast doors, access corridors, angle of the original blast, whether the shock waves have to travel horizontally or obliquely to take out a target, which would be the case here. In other words, we can't guarantee the bomb—as powerful as it is—would take out the entire installation."

"What about explosive decompression when we blow the inner portal?" Harry asked.

"No go," said Ferrik. "The place is designed like a submarine or a shuttle. Airlocks, bulkheads, emergency hatches, the works. We can pretty much assume they've done their darnedest to anticipate any emergency. Maybe even an antimatter bomb emergency."

"So what's the point then?" asked Gillian, looking around at each of them in turn.

"The point," said Ferrik, "is that explosions, as Welkin pointed out, are unpredictable."

"So how do we do this?" insisted Gillian, peering at the schematic.

"I figure there's only one way to guarantee success," said Ferrik. "We have to go in at top speed. Straight in, no stopping, no slowing."

"Yeah. We blast the outer and inner hatches from at least a mile up," said Harry. "The decompression is going to send a lot of junk shooting out like shrapnel so we'll have to watch ourselves."

"Why can't we just lob the bomb in, like Harry said?" Gillian said hopefully. "Then get the hell out of there."

Welkin shook his head. "Like Ferrik's explained, it's not that simple. Judging by the schematic we've got to get the bomb positioned as deeply as possible. If it's not placed at the very base then a lot of those vats could survive. In fact, whole sections here … " he tapped the image, " … are so self-contained they might easily be unaffected. And our mission isn't just to slow the Hiveborn down. It's to deliver a knockout blow."

"If we can," said Gillian pensively.

"Yeah. If we can."

"Okay," said Harry, brightly. "So the plan is, we go in dive-bombing, blast the outer and inner portals to smithereens, fly into the central shaft at top speed, rocket down that for a mile or so, position the bomb, then get out of there, blasting all the scout ships that'll be hot on our tails and trying to kill us or at least block our way?"

Ferrik looked up. "Sounds about right."

"Nice plan," said Gillian. "Which part kills us first?"

"Gillian's just given me an idea," said Welkin. "We need to rig the bomb with a dead man's switch."

"Dead man's switch?" said Harry. "Why don't I like the sound of that?"

"Could it be the word 'dead'? Anyway, it's simple enough. The bomb is armed then somebody holds the trigger. If they let go—or die—it triggers the bomb. That way nobody can take us unawares; and, if we crash or get blasted, the bomb goes off and we hope it takes out as much of the installation as possible."

"Sounds like a plan to me," said Harry, looking slightly pale.

"Sounds like suicide to me," said Gillian.

"You want to live forever?" said Welkin.

Gillian snorted. "I'm not against the idea."

Ferrik ordered everyone to battle stations as the moon magnified on the forward screen. Goose reappeared from the aft weapons bay where he had been re-calibrating their offensive armory. He allowed that he was reasonably satisfied with the state of the weaponry, but Welkin could tell he was a little awed by the Hiveborn's level of technology. Indeed, he dropped one enigmatic remark when Welkin pushed him. "We haven't seen anything yet," he said, shaking his head.

"We know they're more advanced than us."

Goose sighed. "More advanced? If I'm right, they make us look like ants. You should see the torpedoes this thing has."

Welkin stared. "Then why haven't we seen anything more powerful?"

Goose snorted. "Ever try to domesticate ants using a sledgehammer?" He sat in the co-pilot's chair and went to work. Welkin stared at the back of his head for some time, wondering. Beside him, Gillian and Harry—on sensors and tactical—exchanged looks.

Meanwhile, they had entered the orbit of the moon. Almost immediately, Ferrik started dropping lower, till he was skimming a range of jagged mountain peaks which looked alarmingly closer than they actually were.

"Bug Base Alpha coming up in three minutes and forty-two seconds," said Goose. "We should be coming at 'em out of the sun. I like that. The old ways are true and tried."

Ferrik made a harrumph sound. "Ignoring the fact that they'll pick us up on their sensors the moment we no longer have some nice thick mountains between us and them … "

Goose gave him a pained look. "There you go again, spoiling the fun."

"Brace yourselves," said Ferrik. He dropped the ship even lower, hoping to give the Hiveborn as little time to react as possible. But as it turned out, he was wasting his time.

A full minute before they broke over the crest of the last mountain range, a flight of scout ships and fighters soared overhead. Ferrik banked, veered into the mountain valleys as he had before. Above and behind him, the squadron of ships wheeled about and came back fast, hammering the entire valley with blinding pulses of laser fire and electromagnetically accelerated pellets.

As before, Goose read the upcoming topography of the valley, feeding Ferrik data only seconds before he needed it. Ferrik could probably have used the computer, but doing it this way had one major advantage: it made their maneuvers unpredictable. That was the human element, he thought. The wild card in this war.

Harry, on tactical, returned fire from the rear weapons' battery. Firing into a packed group of pursuers, he could hardly miss. He took out three ships before they broke from the cover of the mountain passes and streaked across the plain of *Mare Ibrium* towards the great portal. As they neared it, it opened up, spewing forth at least 50 ships.

Harry frowned at them. "Tell me what the plan is again."

Harry never found out. Ferrik threw the ship into a banking spiral, twisting left and right as a wall of laser pulses flashed towards him like a thousand knives. Goose and Harry sent a deadly hail of return fire, blasting five ships into clouds of expanding fireballs.

Meanwhile, Gillian used the sensor array to try jamming the other ships. Hopefully, this would stop them coordinating their attack, reducing their effectiveness and, just possibly, causing them to be as much of a problem to their brethren as to the Earthborn-controlled ship.

But the odds were heavily against them. Ferrik didn't like to admit it, but he couldn't see how they could survive this kind of onslaught for long. It was just a matter of time before they caught a bolt of lightning. So far, all that was keeping them intact was some dazzling flying skill and the fact that the attackers were getting in each other's way. Any minute now they would realize they would do better to form a wall of lethal fire and keep to one side, so as not to fire into their own ranks.

Then, as the Hiveborn started to do just that, Welkin had an idea. He leant over and explained it to Ferrik. With all the noise and maneuvering no one else could hear what they said.

Ferrik nodded.

He suddenly banked hard and arrowed towards the clump of attackers. At the last second he veered straight up. As he did so, Welkin—who had slid across to the weapons console beside Goose—released a spread of torpedoes straight down at the outer portal which was still open.

As Ferrik clawed for height, the attackers below him altered their attitude so as to get a good shot. The torpedoes tore through the ranks of the Hiveborn. Six ships were obliterated as the torpedoes passed amongst them. The rest, nearly a dozen, dropped into the open shaft. Seconds later a huge fireball erupted from the shaft. It caught the cluster of Hiveborn unawares but did little damage other than to knock out two of the closest ships.

But what came next did considerably more harm.

A great raging tornado of debris blasted up from the shaft as if it were a high speed cannon aimed straight at the Hiveborn ships. It tore through their assembled ranks, ripping them to shreds. Over 20 of them exploded on contact as very hard objects moving at fantastic speed slammed into vital power systems. The rest were riddled with holes and impact damage.

By the time the barrage was over, only two ships were still airborne and they weren't in any condition to fight. Four fighters that were outside the blast radius made a half-hearted attack on Ferrik's ship; but when Goose cooked one of them and sent another rocketing straight at the lunar surface, the other two backed off.

"What the hell was that?" asked Gillian, mouth open. It had all happened so fast that most of them were still taking it in.

"Explosive decompression," said Ferrik. "It was Welkin's idea."

"We blew the inner hatch. A vast volume of air had to go somewhere very fast. So it went straight up."

"Damn," said Goose softly. "That was something."

"And now for the encore." He flipped the ship over and dived nose-first straight towards the shaft. Everyone gripped their chairs, white-knuckled and staring, as they hurtled toward the lunar surface.

"I knew I should have gone with Theo," said Harry as they soared into the shaft entrance. They were moving so fast everything was a blur. Harry couldn't even tell how far they were from the sides of the tube. Looking out at the rushing wall made him feel ill.

Within moments they had roared out of the base of the tube and into the large chamber. But instead of docking, Ferrik piloted them through a wall of energy near the base. As they approached it Ferrik was about to veer off but Goose urged him to keep going.

"We'll crash," Ferrik said nervously.

"No, we won't. It's a kind of force field—acts like an airlock. Hiveborn ships can pass right through it."

Ferrik stared straight ahead. "You'd better be right."

He kept the ship on its heading. His hands tightened around the armrests. A moment later they slid through the field. It was like passing through a waterfall. They emerged on the other side and immediately Ferrik could tell by how the ship handled that they were now moving through air.

"Damn," he said softly. He had to forcibly unclench his hands.

Now they were in new territory—for Ferrik. But here Goose took over and guided them down another mile. There was, oddly, no resistance. Perhaps all the scout ships and fighters possessed by the lunar base had been used up in the base's initial defense.

Welkin hoped it was that.

They passed more than a dozen levels, most of them enclosed by transparent plasteel which would have left them unaffected by the sudden decompression even without the force-field. Inside, Welkin saw many Hiveborn staring out at them, most of them expressionless, even incurious if that were possible.

Moments later Goose settled the ship down beneath a large overhanging bulkhead that seemed part of some power core. If it was, then this was the perfect place to set off the bomb.

But it wasn't going to be that easy. The others kept watch as Harry, Gillian and Thompson readied the bomb on a tractorized pallet. When they were ready they lowered the ramp and wheeled the bomb down it, still suspicious of the lull in the attack.

The ground troops struck.

With a series of clanging impacts, several large metal baffles dropped suddenly, revealing at least sixty armed Hiveborn. Welkin and the others returned fire though they were hugely outnumbered. Fortunately, Goose was still at the weapons board and quickly turned the ship's guns on the attacking troops, decimating them and driving the rest back.

But things weren't to go completely their way.

First, Thompson took a direct hit to the chest from some kind of antique projectile weapon, the non self-cauterizing type. Blood gushed down his chest, turning to pink foam where it emerged from what was obviously a punctured lung.

Gillian quickly slapped a square of plastic over it, taped up the sides and top and left the bottom open so that the blood could run free and not back up into the lung itself. Whenever Thompson breathed in the plastic was sucked into the wound, sealing it tight and preserving what lung function he had. She sat him at a 45 degree angle and made him as comfortable as possible.

While she was doing this she stumbled over one of the Hiveborn. The man moaned and blinked up at her. Gillian whipped out her blaster, aiming it point-blank, but something about the man's expression made her stop.

She knelt down beside him, peering into his ears. The left side of his face was swollen and red from a third degree laser burn but both ears were clear. There was no parasite. Presumably, it had been damaged in the exchange of fire.

She helped the man sit up, then gave him some water from her canteen. He was dressed differently than the others; he even seemed to have some kind of ceremonial haircut.

"Are you okay?" said Gillian.

"I think so. How are you, Gillian?"

Her head whipped back in surprise. "How do you know my—Ohmigod. Elab! Is it really you?"

The man grinned at her and it was indeed the old Elab grin. She threw her arms around his neck and hugged him. "Everybody thought you were dead."

"That's okay," he said, grimacing. "I thought I was dead too."

She called Harry over and he did a double take, then seemed to have a heart attack. He and Gillian helped Elab onto the shuttle and into the sickbay. When Gillian reappeared her face was covered in happy tears but it also held an apprehensive expression; she saw Welkin and Ferrik arguing as they huddled over the bomb which had been moved into a protected area.

She hurried over.

"It's screwed," said Ferrik. "And so are we."

"Let me think," said Welkin.

"There a problem?" asked Gillian, though she seemed distracted and not that interested in her own question.

Ferrik shrugged. "The arming mechanism on the bomb took a direct hit."

"Which means," said Welkin, "that it'll have to be detonated by hand."

Gillian almost forgot what she had come to tell them. "But that means—"

"Yeah, it does," Ferrik said sourly. "Somebody's going to have to play hero."

"Unless we can rig something," said Welkin.

"We don't have time. We need to get out of here, now," said Ferrik fiercely. The others looked at him. "Sorry. I just don't want to lose anybody."

"War is hell," said Welkin, poker-faced.

Ferrik suddenly grinned. "Screw you," he said, thumping Welkin on the shoulder. He stood up. "I guess we ask for volunteers."

"Nope," said Welkin. "I'll do it."

Gillian stared at him, aghast. "No you will not!" she snapped.

"Gillian … "

"No, just you shut up and listen to me for once." She was breathing hard and looked, for a moment, as lethal as a tigress defending its family. "If you stay then I'm staying with you, so when you volunteer you're volunteering me too. Just remember that, okay? If you want to do this macho hero act, then we draw straws. But that's not what I came to tell you anyway, because we've got a bigger problem."

"Bigger than not being able to detonate the bomb that could save the entire human race?" asked Ferrik.

"Maybe."

"This I have to hear."

"There's something more important that I have to tell you first." She told them about finding Elab. Ferrik's face was a study in amazement.

"He's asleep now," added Gillian. She then quickly explained what she had learnt from Elab. It seemed that he had been part of a special unit that was part defensive, part medical, and part religious, though Gillian was hesitant to mention the latter information since it wasn't clear that the Hiveborn had any religion. Welkin, however, who had been connected to the Hivemind several times now, confirmed that at once.

"Of course they have a religion. That's why they're here. They're missionaries. Didn't you know that?" He seemed puzzled that no one had understood this.

"Missionaries," said Ferrik. "Got it. They're saving my soul."

Welkin looked at him soberly. "That's right. They're saving it by joining it to the Great Soul—the Godhead … Whatever you want to call it."

"Personally, I want to call it all mumbo jumbo; but hey, that's just me."

Welkin ignored him and turned back to Gillian. "There's more, isn't there?"

She nodded. "There's a queen."

Ferrik stared. "What?"

"Of course," said Welkin, smacking his fist in his palm. "*That's* what I always sensed. A single mind at the center of the lattice."

"In part. According to Elab this queen *is* the Hivemind. He seems to think she's the most closely guarded secret amongst the Hiveborn. She's the original progenitor of the parasites and she's incredibly ancient. Her body is now part organic, part nanomechanical. Most of her brain is formed of chemical memories that have drifted through the Hive for eons. Net linkage is useful but her memory is, mainly, like a mist that sits around her head. The neural vapor can latch onto a zombie and interchange memories and thoughts with it."

"Are there other queens?"

"Not in our solar system. Just one queen per hive but Elab thinks there are other hives out there—maybe thousands of them. Just not anywhere near here."

Welkin said, "But this doesn't change anything, Gillian. In fact, it's made setting off the bomb even more important."

"The bomb won't touch the queen."

"What?"

"She's in a specially protected bunker. The blast doors on it are only an inch thick—but solid neutronium. With a gravity control inside."

Ferrik muttered, "Space! You'd need a nova to crack open an egg like that."

Welkin had been staring at the floor, thinking. Now he looked up. "Unless the blast doors happened to be open when the bomb went off."

Ferrik grinned suddenly. "That'd sure scramble her Highness's egg."

Welkin and Harry moved cautiously. They were inside an access tube and time was running out. The map Elab had drawn for them indicated that the blast doors to the queen's chamber were about 700 yards from where the ship was situated, but two levels down and buried inside a great slab of diamondoid. From studying the map it had become quickly clear that there was no way they could reach the blast doors.

So they were heading for a control nub, which was not only a lot closer, it was also likely to be less protected. From there they hoped they could electronically open the doors and lock them in that position, long enough at least for the bomb to do its work.

There was just one snag.

Everybody was looking for them. Well, that wasn't strictly true. Nobody was looking *for* them but everybody knew that an enemy ship had grounded in the lower dock and shot a bunch of their brethren to smithereens.

That had to be a snag, Harry maintained. "Pretty shortly we'll have every last one of the bugs after us."

"Please, Harry," said Welkin, then suddenly held a finger to his lips. They had reached a junction inside the tube. To their left was a grille. Welkin was peering through this. A squad of Hiveborn passed underneath, moving on the double. They were heavily armed.

"This is crazy," Harry whispered. "We should have just blown the place."

"Too late now," said Welkin.

They took the left branch of the tube. A short time later they came to another grille which looked down into some kind of dormitory. It was, as Elab had told them, empty at this time of the "day." They removed the grille and quickly scrambled down into the room, replacing the grille behind them.

"So they do sleep," said Harry, gazing about. Each of the beds had a raised platform at the head with a depressed section out of which they knew a kind of connector probe emerged. This in turn linked the ship's comm. system and the Hivemind as well to the individual "unit."

"Wonder what they dream?" mused Welkin as they crossed to the door and peered out. The control nub was on the other side of the chamber they were looking at. Unfortunately, right now, there were three Hiveborn in the room.

They hung back, waiting to see if the zombies would leave. Several minutes later Welkin muttered that they would just have to go out blasting. They couldn't wait any longer.

Harry put a hand on Welkin's arm. "That'll attract a whole lot of unwelcome attention."

Welkin shrugged. "You have a better plan?"

"Yeah," said Harry. "Meet you back at the ship."

Before Welkin could stop Harry he had stepped through the door. "Hey, zombies, what's up?" The Hiveborn looked over at him, then stiffened. They grabbed their weapons just as Harry took flight down a corridor. The Hiveborn gave chase, leaving the chamber empty.

Welkin cursed softly at Harry's crazy scheme but took advantage of it nonetheless. He went over to the nub and examined it. Elab had drawn the controls he needed to manipulate on the back of the map.

He followed the step-by-step instructions. When a light blinked green he knew the queen's blast neutronium doors were opening; though thin, these kilotons of weight were made moveable only by gravitronics. It would take a few minutes for the doors to open completely and just as long for them to close—even supposing any Hiveborn could reverse the damage he was about to inflict on the control nub.

As he stepped back to blast the nub, a laser pulse grazed his shoulder. He ducked instantly, firing back blindly. The pain of the burn hit him suddenly and he felt the urge to vomit. But he had bigger things to worry about. Another weapon had just joined the fray and he was pinned down with no way out.

Well, whatever happened, he had to destroy the nub before someone computed a countermand.

Keeping the nub between him and his attackers, he pushed himself slowly backwards, sliding on his back. When he was at a safe distance he switched the laserlite to fan mode and nudged it up to its top setting: vaporize.

Welkin pressed the stud. There was an intense hissing noise, like a thousand hornets had just been released nearby. At once the nub started to collapse in on itself, flaring brightly as its temperature soared. Then there was a brilliant flash and when Welkin could see again all that remained of the nub was a tangled melted foundation.

Unfortunately, the foundation wasn't high enough to give him any protection.

As the smoke cleared, two Hiveborn leapt up and ran at him letting loose a withering flow of pulses. Welkin opened up with his own laserlite. The leading Hiveborn took a hit in the chest and dropped like a brick. Welkin felt a searing pain in his leg. He rolled aside, firing blindly. The remaining Hiveborn went down without a sound.

Welkin groaned, clutching his leg. Space! The pain was excruciating. First degree, easily. The trouser leg had gone and underneath was blackened ruptured skin, already seeping with blood and fluids from some of the non-cauterized blood vessels.

Looking at it, he realized his chances of getting back to the ship before they had to detonate the bomb and get out of there were pretty remote.

But he was going to try anyway.

He levered himself up, using his laserlite as a crutch. If anybody came on him right now, he was as good as colonized. Or dead.

Limping across the chamber, Welkin headed back into the dormitory, then stood looking at the tiers of bunks and the grille above. He felt weak and dizzy. In this state the three-storied bunks looked like Mt. Everest.

But he couldn't not try. That wouldn't be fair to Gillian.

He clambered onto the first bunk and had made it to the second before a wave of intense nausea swept over him, leaving him even more disoriented. He was sweating now; maybe a fever was setting in. If he didn't get into the access tube shortly, he knew he would never make it.

Grabbing hold of the bar at the base of the topmost bunk, he tried to haul himself up by sheer force. The moon's lighter gravity made this a lot easier and indeed he wouldn't have succeeded if this had been Earth.

Even so, it took every ounce of strength and determination he had. And it hurt like hell. He lay on the top bunk gasping like a stranded fish. He was soaked in sweat and his vision was blurry. Above him, within reach and yet seemingly miles away, swam the grille.

Welkin reached up, felt it with his fingertips. He managed to unhook the clip. The grille swung down. Somehow—and it seemed to take hours—he rolled onto his stomach then slowly slid back onto his knees, his chest and face still pressing against the bunk.

He would have been quite happy to stay like this but Gillian was talking to him. "Get in that tube, Welkin. I'm not kidding! I'm going to kick your butt if you don't get in that tube now!"

"All right," he muttered. "Lay off me, will you?"

Swaying from side to side he pushed himself up. The action raised his head up through the open grille and into the tube. But how was he to get inside it? It seemed too much and anyway, it wasn't fair. All he wanted to do was rest. Just rest. If he could only close his eyes and take five, he would be okay.

"No way," snarled Gillian. "Get in there now or there'll be big trouble."

He moaned, flopped an arm inside the tube, then another. Somehow, he didn't know how, he got his legs under him and pushed. Once again the low gravity came to his aid. He slid up into the tube, even hitting his head on the top.

"Ouch."

Now he was inside it. A cool breeze washed over him. It felt wonderful. "Head towards the breeze," said Gillian. He frowned then. He had forgotten something. Oh, the grille. He had to close the grille.

He looked at it and knew it wasn't going to happen. Instead, he started crawling towards the breeze, sucking in a great lungful of the reconstituted cool air.

Harry ran like he had never run before. Unfortunately, running on the moon was something of an art form and he didn't think he was going to get a chance to serve an apprenticeship in it. Within the first 200 yards he pushed off so hard he bashed his skull on the ceiling. The Hiveborn behind him were only marginally better and certainly their aim, while dealing with the new locomotion, wasn't great. Harry thought briefly that it was odd they were weren't better adapted to moving on the moon; but perhaps, like him, they were new to it. Too, if his pursuers were newly colonized, the bugs would still be learning how their surrogates functioned.

In any case, the trick seemed to be in finding a sliding gait, like skiing cross-country—something Harry had only ever seen in vids.

Being shot at and chased was a wonderful teacher though. Harry picked up the new technique in record time and even started outdistancing his pursuers.

Then he turned a corner and found himself charging towards a squad of Hiveborn. When they saw him they hefted their weapons, taking aim.

Harry swerved into a side corridor and lobbed a laser pulse into the ceiling at full blast. As he had hoped, part of the ceiling came down in a shower of plasteel and moon rock.

He checked his watch. They had been away less than 20 minutes.

That meant they had ten to go before Ferrik would leave. Harry put on a spurt of speed, bashing his head on the ceiling again.

Welkin couldn't go any farther. His arms and legs had been getting wobblier and wobblier and finally he had collapsed on his face, feeling the cool metal of the access tube pressing against his cheek, forcing his jaw open at an odd angle.

Directly in his line of vision was a metal seam where two sections of the tube had been fitted together. In the corner was an ant.

Welkin blinked, eyeing the ant in puzzlement.

An ant on the moon?

Must be a stowaway, Welkin thought. He half-coughed, half-laughed at that. It seemed the funniest thing he had ever heard. Ants taking over the moon. Hive against hive! Okay, ants didn't have hives but they were pretty close.

With enormous effort he managed to slide his hand out towards the insect then watched with satisfaction as it clambered onto his hand, motoring back and forth and all around as ants do. He had forgotten where he was or why he was there. Then the ant crawled onto the sleeve of his tunic.

"Can't stowaway on me back to Earth, ant!" he murmured. "Picked the wrong transport … "

"No he didn't," said a voice, and suddenly he was being dragged. The sides of the tube blurred past, not because he was moving fast but because he couldn't adjust his field of vision.

Some indefinable time later he emerged into brighter light and hands were grabbing at him, lifting him. Then there was cool darkness again. And he felt better.

He looked up. Gillian was bathing his face and Harry was leaning over him.

"I'm on the ship?" said Welkin, frowning.

"Nearby," said Gillian. "We gave you some shots. Harry's patching up your leg."

"We still on the moon?"

Gillian nodded but said nothing. "We're not going anywhere," said Harry.

"Why?"

"Hiveborn attacked while you and I were away. They brought up some kind of heavy blaster, managed to burn a hole right into the ship's engines. They're just so much junk now so we're stuck here."

"What about the bomb?"

Ferrik suddenly joined them. "We're taking a vote on what to do," he said.

"Detonate it," Welkin said. "Blow the whole hive sky-high."

"I figured you'd say that," said Harry, "so I already voted for you."

Welkin managed a weak grin. "Remind me to thump you later."

"You got it," Harry said, finishing the bandaging.

"So why are you fixing me up if you're just going to blow me up?"

"Well, we're not in a huge hurry. The Queen's blast doors are completely jammed and nobody can get in at us," said Ferrik, "so we're letting people do whatever they feel they need to do before the end. Goose is sending off a data burst. Not much hope it'll get through but you never know. Anything you want, Welkin?"

"Yeah, I always wanted to try a hamburger."

Gillian said, "What's a hamburger?"

"Just something the ancients used to eat. You got them in a hamburger *joint*."

Harry said, "I wouldn't mind one of those chocolate malts."

"What's chocolate," Gillian asked.

"Don't you know anything?" said Welkin, ruffling her hair. She leant down and kissed him and he suddenly blinked. "Was it you who got me out of the tube?"

Gillian looked down, her eyes filling with tears. He could see she had been scared when she found him. Ferrik said, "Yeah. She got a funny feeling, said you needed her. We couldn't stop her."

Welkin squeezed her hand. "Thanks."

Goose appeared, said, "Well, it's time. Everyone's ready—or as ready as they're ever going to be."

A few minutes later they gathered around the bomb, still on its pallet. Thompson was sitting on his haunches nearby, looking deathly pale. If his blue eyes hadn't been moving Welkin would have been convinced he was dead.

Gillian led them in a short prayer, the kind of soft chant the Earthborn sometimes spoke before going into battle: "Lord of earth and moon, sun and stars, good and evil, past, present and future: you have given to our hearts the will to serve our brothers and sisters even unto death. Grant us boldness to pursue our quest and courage to follow it to the end. We have been faithful unto the end, and go to our death knowing that our kind and our kindred will be free from the scourge that now destroys them. May our spirits live in the freedom that our people now inherit. We have lived well and now we die at peace with ourselves and all the world."

Gillian gripped Welkin's hand fiercely when she finished the prayer, looking around at each of them with tears in her eyes.

"I'm glad I've known you all," she said and the others nodded mutely.

Ferrik took a deep breath. "We're here to carry out our mission, to see that it's done. That was the job we were given by our family ... "

He picked up the new detonator switch, connected to the bomb by a cable. He removed the safety panel, revealing a red button, and lightly placed his finger on it.

"Anybody got anything more to say?"

Welkin shook his head, hugging Gillian to him. No one else spoke.

"I guess this is it then." He cleared his throat. "May this thing that we do here today serve our family well."

"Amen," said Welkin.

Ferrik raised the remote, went to press it … but at that exact moment something exploded nearby. They all jumped. Welkin scanned the area and discovered a group of Hiveborn sprawled on the ground. They had been sneaking up on them but someone had ambushed them in turn.

A whistling sound from above made them look up. One of the family's shuttles was dropping fast towards them. At the last second it braked and came to a thumping stop. An exterior patch crackled and they heard Theo's voice.

"So are you guys just going to stand around, or you want a lift out of there?"

For a long moment nobody moved, then grins of disbelief broke out on every face. Goose gave a whooping cheer. Ferrik directed several people to check any of the new Hiveborn casualties to see if any were still alive and if so to take them on board.

Welkin said, "Wait a minute. The bomb. It won't detonate by itself."

Everybody froze, staring in horror at the antimatter device.

"Space! I forgot," said Ferrik.

"Give it to me," said Welkin. "I'll stay. You others get going, fast. He took the remote detonator from Ferrik.

Gillian sat down suddenly beside him. He stared at her but before he could say anything she said, quite simply, "I'm not leaving without you."

"Gillian, please."

She said nothing, just settled herself more firmly.

Then a cold damp hand landed on Welkin's wrist. He turned to see Thompson staring at him with a ghastly expression, a mixture of pain and something else—hate maybe.

Before Welkin could stop him he took the detonator from him. "I got a debt to settle. You guys get out of here."

"Thompson … " said Ferrik.

"Either way, I'm not going back," he said. "We all know that. This is my chance to do something … " His eyes seemed to be pleading with them.

Ferrik nodded. "Okay."

On impulse, Gillian leaned over and kissed him. He shook his head, coughing up blood. "You better go—quickly. I don't know how long I can … "

He didn't finish the sentence. He didn't need to. They said their farewells to him, clapping him on the shoulder, whispering words that were only meant for him, then they hurried aboard Theo's ship.

Thompson watched it go. A wave of great sadness and loneliness swept over him, then his eyes fell on one of the dead Hiveborn scattered about. In its ear, still twitching slightly, was one of the parasites.

A great loathing filled Thompson. He pressed the red button.

The moon's surface lay calm, untouched. The wreckage of many Hiveborn ships was scattered about the outer portal, but nothing moved. The whole scene might have been a still photograph.

Suddenly, something blasted from the gaping, ragged hole of the portal and streaked for orbit. Behind it came a blinding silent shaft of hell, a raging inferno that spewed upwards from the surface for several miles, licking behind the retreating craft, and casting lurid shadows across the lunar landscape below.

The entire surface of the moon for a radius of more than a mile around the portal lifted slowly into the air before dropping back into a huge and fiery crater. Many lesser explosions now plumed outwards like geysers of magma.

Inside the ship, everybody was crowded into the cockpit, gazing at the devastation in the forward screen. Welkin said quietly that, judging by the size and depth of the crater and the conflagration raging in its depths, it was highly unlikely that any part of the installation survived.

A huge cheer echoed throughout the ship.

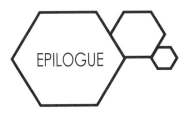

EPILOGUE

Sarah woke. She tried to sit up but someone pushed her back down. She was alive. How strange was that? She'd expected to be dead.

As her vision came back into focus she looked into the faces of Welkin, Gillian, Harry and Ferrik. Then Theo stepped into view holding some flowers. Behind him were Efi, Daniel and Elab, his face heavily bandaged but the grin clearly visible.

Sarah burst into tears.

Harry exhaled loudly. "Phew. You don't see that every day." Gillian cuffed him.

Theo leant down to kiss Sarah and gave her his square of cloth that doubled as a handkerchief. She sniffled and mopped at her eyes. "What happened? The parasites—?"

"All dead."

"Dead?"

"It's a long story," said Welkin. "Suffice it to say that we found something on the moon that was crucial to their survival and we … er … took it out."

"And all the parasites suddenly died," said Daniel.

"The family?" asked Sarah anxiously. "Did everyone make it?"

Daniel shook his head sadly. "I'm afraid that the parasites went into some kind of spasm when they died. We don't know for sure what this was, but it proved fatal to about five per cent of all those who were possessed at the time. I'm sorry. We also had a few casualties from the knockout gas, it can cause a bad reaction."

"And Arton's crew. I lost contact with him after you left. And Mawson."

Welkin held back his own despair. They had lost not only Arton, but Hatch, and others. "We found the wreckage of both ships." He shrugged. "I guess they died so we could escape."

Ferrik's brow furrowed. "It was odd. Looked as though they'd collided in midair, suicidal almost."

Sarah shut her eyes for a moment and more tears leaked out. Then she let out a long sigh and shuddered. "But we won."

Gillian gripped her hand. "Yeah, sis, we won."

"So now we can just rebuild ... it's a new start—"

Welkin nodded. "We can rebuild the whole world if you want to."

Sarah's smile widened. "I want to. And we'll never forget those who gave us this opportunity."

Later that day, Welkin felt something crawling across the back of his wrist. When he looked down he saw an ant. *The* ant. He went outside and placed it carefully on a bush. "Guess you made the right choice after all," he said.

A commemoration service for those who had died was held a week later. The centerpiece of this was a small monument bearing the names of all those in the family who had not survived. At the top, and most prominent, was the name of Jeremiah Thompson—the man who had made the ultimate sacrifice and saved humanity.

Welkin and the others had insisted on the words. They knew the quiet modest man they had barely gotten to know would have been pleased.

A month later there was another ceremony, a marriage this time. Welkin and Gillian wed before the eyes of the entire family. Fifteen minutes later, Sarah and Theo followed suit. And 15 minutes after that, Harry and Veeda wed.

In the years that followed there were many changes, including children. First among the newborn were twins, Jeremiah and Hatch, for Welkin and Gillian, and Arton, for Theo and Sarah.

Melbourne itself was reoccupied and turned into what Sarah liked to call a beacon of hope. Using the technology and supplies of both the Skyborn and the Hiveborn she began an audacious program to drag the world into a new era of modernity and peace, the first step of which was distributing radios and satellite internet to communities all around the world— communities which could now talk to each other because of access to the orbital highway. New engineers began to study the Hiveborn ships. There were even monthly flights between continents, using the shuttles, a great store of which were found on *Crusader* still tied with its umbilical tube to *Colony*, and also on another Hiveborn craft in a holding pattern above Earth.

The secrets of the Earth ancients and the Hiveborn began to unfold, as humanity looked once again to the stars …

Three mercenaries

Poison coursing through their veins

And only six weeks to find a stolen dragon relic . . .

Dragonsight

The long-awaited sequel to *Dragonfang*.

"The action never stops in *Dragonsight*, Book 3 of The Jelindel Chronicles. Countess Jelindel dek Mediesar, Daretor and Zimak are sent on a desperate quest to recover a stolen red jade talisman, the dragonsight and, with a slow acting poison ticking through their veins, they have only six weeks to find the talisman and take the antidote. There's magic and mayhem aplenty as they're hunted through the paraworlds for the enigmatic dragonsight, before the final violent confrontation at the Tower Inviolate. And then, in sight of their goal, the ultimate treachery. A terrific page-turner, crammed full of action, intrigue and lashings of magic." **Ian Irvine**